ALL IN

BY WESLEY HARPER

Book one in the Three Rocks series

This is a work of fiction. Names, characters, places, and incidents are products of the author's imagination or used fictitiously. Any resemblance to actual events, locales, or persons, living or dead, is entirely coincidental.

ISBN- 979-8-9943033-0-6 (paperback)

ISBN- 979-8-9943033-1-3 (e-book)

2026 Second Edition.

Cover design by: Juniper Hartmann of The Red Fox Creative
Photographer: A. McKay
Editor: Pace A.

To my own Team Merc. Decades of friendship, support, and shenanigans. Breakers always.

Hello.

I can't believe you're here, holding my book in your hands. I wrote it nearly on accident, a hobby of sorts combined with a fortieth birthday challenge. When finished, I sat on the couch, exactly where I am sitting now, and announced to my family that I had written a book. I also announced my intention to delete it. That did not go over quite as well as the original announcement. Looking at my teenagers, I realized this was A Thing. A Parenting Thing. Which meant, as terrifying as it was, I needed to follow through. Now here we are, the second edition. The story remains the same, just a few minor edits, a little bit of finding my voice I suppose, and a new cover. My daughters still have a hand in both of those, and because of that, this will forever be my favorite book.

Content Warning

The content and trigger warnings for this book contain spoilers. Please skip ahead if this isn't for you.

This book has a main character that struggles with anxiety and panic attacks stemming from a past (on page) attempted sexual assault. Alcohol addiction and the poor parenting choices that go with it are also included as well as a surprise pregnancy.

Prologue
Harper
ten years ago

I swing my bare feet from my perch on the truck tailgate and lean my head onto Avery's shoulder. "I'm going to miss you so much," I tell her as the sky slowly darkens above us.

Avery leans her head onto mine, steals my almost-empty solo cup, and laughs. "Okay Tex, just how many of these have you had?"

"Tex?!" I snort, taking my cup back and chugging the last of the lukewarm beer. "Really, you finally come up with my nickname now? It's been a decade since we met and two days before I leave the state!" I shake my empty cup and hop down, grabbing Avery's hand, leading her back over to the keg at the edge of the trees.

"Harper, don't look now but Sam totally just checked you out," she whispers in my ear. "He's across the fire with Jordan."

I refill my cup and motion for Avery to hand hers over, sneaking a glance behind her as I fill hers all the way to the brim. I make eye contact with Sam, who is indeed talking to Avery's boyfriend Jordan, our designated driver for the night. He's also the guy with the older brother that got us a keg. If this is my last night hanging out with the friends I've known forever, I might as well make it memorable, right? I shoot Sam a wink and toss my hair, then turn back to Avery, who rolls her eyes at me and drags me over to a camp chair, pulling me into her lap.

"You're impossible, Harp. Do you even like him?" she whispers.

"Who cares about like? I just want to make out with a hot guy," I whisper back, making her laugh and shake her head.

1

Ever since the day we met in elementary school P.E. class, Avery and I have been inseparable. We spent our childhood years catching salamanders at the pond, climbing trees, and running through orchards. Those days morphed into lounging by the pool, floating the river, and awkwardly turning from tomboys into, well, still tomboys.

I don't think we've spent more than a week apart since that fateful P.E. class so long ago. I've tagged along to her family's beach house too many times to count and if Avery isn't at my house on the weekends, my parents ask where she is. Although we claim we will see each other again at college in a couple of years, I know Avery is going to be wading through offers from the best schools in the country while I stay for in-state tuition in what is soon to be my home state: Texas.

I lean into her, soaking up one last bonfire snuggle fest, sipping my beer, and every once in a while glancing back over my shoulder to make sure Sam is still watching me. Wink. Hair toss.

***

I'm leaning against a tree, looking over the dark river below, wondering if this will be my last time to see the Willamette River, when I sense Sam approaching me. I don't acknowledge him, wanting to see what his first move is. Suddenly my left arm is twisted behind me and something sharp is against my right side, poking between my ribs.

"Sam, what the fu-" I yelp, words cut off by a voice I don't recognize.

"Shut the fuck up," the deep voice demands.

I hear my solo cup hit the ground, muffled by the layer of leaves, and feel the warm beer splash onto my bare feet, but I don't recall dropping it. My heart hammers in my chest. I can't move. I am pinned between the tree and whoever thinks they're really funny right now. Please be a joke. The pain in my wrist tells me it's not a joke.

I open my mouth to scream but nothing comes out. My left wrist is twisted harder, fire shoots up my arm. Something sharp pinches close to the palm of my hand.

"I've watched you all night, flirting with Sam, never even noticing me. Notice me now?" he growls into my ear, pushing his leg between mine.

2

I try to place his voice, his smell, anything. I must know him.

The stabbing in my side moves away, only for a rough hand holding something cold to slide under my shirt, skirting my stomach, trying to slip under the waistband of my shorts. Fuck. I bite my cheek so hard I taste blood as a blade slides against my skin. Fucking country boys and their fucking pocket knives. My mind races, my breath stalls. His hand fumbles with the knife, trying to undo the button on my cut offs.

I demand my legs to run. I can't move.

I tell my mouth to form words. I can't yell.

Breathe.

Harper.

Think.

Harper.

Run.

Harper.

I am frozen.

His breath on my neck, the knife on my skin. Metallic adrenaline. Blood.

The button on my shorts pops, a grunt sounds. Rustling clothes. A ripping sound. My vision blurs. His hand. I am shaking. Everything is cold.

"Harper? Harrrrper! Tex! Let's go!" I hear Avery's voice somewhere far behind me.

My lips are tingling. I can't feel my hands. I can only feel my heart trying to escape through my chest, pain shooting through my wrist, and his hand once again pushing the knife against my skin.

I demand my legs to run. I can't move.

I tell my mouth to form words. I can't yell.

Run.

Harper.

Scream.

Harper.

Fight.

Harper.

I am frozen.

"Make her go away," the rough voice demands.

A tiny trickle of liquid drips down my side as the knife breaks skin.

"Harper!" Avery's voice is closer. Not close enough.

Black. Darkness. Cold.

I'm on the ground. How did I get here?

There are no sounds. There is no oxygen.

"Harper!" Avery crashes down next to me. "What happened? You're shaking. Harper. Look at me. Harper!" I can hear the panic in her voice and I look at her blankly. Why am I on the ground? Why is my hand sticky? Where is my shirt?

"Jordan!" Avery screams.

"No, Avery, no. I don't want him, I only want you," I whisper. My body finally listens to my commands to move and I climb right into her lap.

"Harp, what happened?" Her voice is high, unsteady, unsure.

"No, just you," I gulp in the chilled night air. "Thank you, thank you, thank you."

"Anything and everything, always," she whispers our words for each other. Her hands frantically check my body, rub my back, wipe my tears. She stills, "Harp, your hand. What happened to your hand?" She gently holds my left hand in hers, wiping bright red blood with her bare hands. She's wrapping it in her shirt.

I don't feel a thing.

I am numb.

Chapter One
Harper

"Tex!" my childhood best friend exclaims as she rushes around the counter of the coffee bar.

I smile quickly at the decidedly *not* smiling, bear-sized, bearded man holding the door for me and gleefully jump into her arms, wrapping my legs around her waist like we are still nine years old or perhaps long lost lovers. Avery laughs and spins me around, the smell of coffee, salty sea, and rain in her wavy hair.

"I'm so glad I'm here, thank you, thank you, thank you," I whisper.

"Anything and everything, always," she whispers back, setting me down.

My heart clenches at her words. It's been too long since I've hugged my very best friend. I hold her at arm's length and take her in; she's tall and lean, muscular runner legs that go on for days, wavy beach hair under a beanie, her trademark flat smirk with an eyebrow raised in my direction.

"What? Do I have dog hair everywhere? Slobber? Zero's still in the Jeep, I just couldn't wait to hug you," I say, quickly blinking away the tears that suddenly blur my vision. Pull it together, Harper.

"Well, probably, but I was more looking at your very Texas clothing choices. You have turquoise sunglasses on top of your neon hat and it's as gray as can be out there, possibly even raining, and you're also basically barefoot," she laughs with an eye roll, nodding toward the window at the drizzly Oregon Coast weather.

I glance down at my torn cut offs, flip-flops, and off-the-shoulder tee shirt, then take in her very Pacific Northwest outfit that includes hiking boots and a Patagonia fleece. She does have a valid point.

"Well, it was sunny a couple hundred miles ago and I forgot that I needed to be hike-ready at all times, Aves. I've lived in Texas for a decade! Ya'll don't realize how hot it's been and it's only May!" I put a Texas twang into my words to emphasize my point. Reality is that I am going to freeze, absolutely, one hundred percent, fucking *freeze* living here. My blood thinned *very* quickly after moving to Texas.

She gives me another eye roll with a smile and then walks back behind the counter to pour me a coffee. The last time I was here, it was a convenience store of sorts, not very different from all of the gas stations I've stopped at over the last two-and-a-half days. Since purchasing the store, Avery has transformed it into The Town Mercantile and it is so much more than any and all of the pictures and videos I have seen.

The coffee counter is a deep, dark wood that contrasts with the sleek glass case holding drool-worthy pastries and fudge. A long driftwood table runs the center of the space with everything from small souvenir trinkets to local artists' jewelry, organic sunscreen to postcards. There's a selection of Mercantile-branded clothing with a display of hats and beanies in the corner that I can't wait to browse. A cooler along the back wall has a wide selection of local beer and wine, pre-made sandwiches and salads, and, even though I can no longer eat it, I'm quite giddy to see that she has Tillamook vanilla bean ice cream stocked in the freezer, our favorite growing up.

I feel a lump forming in my throat and swallow it down. "I can't believe all you've done with the place, I'm so proud of you! It's incredible!"

Vegetarian at age ten, marathoner and ultramarathoner by thirteen, author before we even graduated high school, and now business owner, lawyer, and landlord/boss to yours truly. My friend is a badass. A pulled-together, doesn't-take-shit badass with more willpower in her pinky finger than I will ever have in my entire body.

6

Reading my roller coaster of emotions, Avery hands me the steaming coffee which, based on the amount of caffeine I have consumed since I left Austin a few days ago, I absolutely do not need. She takes my shaking hand, tells the cute teenage girl working behind the counter thank you, and leads me outside. The same man holds the door for us, startling blue eyes watchful as I pass, a smiling boy now at his side holding what appears to be the exact hot chocolate Avery and I would make as kids: more whipped cream and sprinkles than actual liquid.

I hear Avery exchange quiet words with the two but I focus on pulling my shit together. Special hot chocolate will not be the reason my tears finally fall.

I attempt to reset my emotions as we walk to my car.

breathe in two three four, hold two three four, out two three four

An excited bark greets us at the Jeep and I turn to Avery, a question in my eyes.

"I can already tell what you're going to ask. And yes, beach now. Last one to the rock makes dinner!" Avery takes off with no warning, her hiking boots and long legs eating up the nearly empty parking lot as she sprints for the beach trail without even giving me a chance to leash Zero.

"Cheater!" I yell as I open the back door of the Jeep to let Zero chase after her.

I kick off my impractical flip flops, grab Z's leash and my hoodie from the floorboard, and attempt to run barefoot without spilling my emotional support coffee or dropping anything from my hands. Unfortunately that proves impossible and I slow down, laughing as Zero easily catches Avery.

I balance my coffee cup and the leash in my left hand, use my right hand to shove my keys down my bra and stuff my phone in my back pocket. Wait. Did I shut Zero's door?

"Shit," I mutter under my breath and turn around, only to see the unsmiling door holder walking toward my Jeep, his adorable son running ahead of him. The little boy shoves Zero's door shut with a bang and eagerly waves to me.

"Thank you, kind sir!" I holler to the dark-haired boy, who giggles at my over-exaggerated mock curtsy and waves back to me enthusiastically. I hold my coffee cup high in thanks to his dad, who just watches me, not acknowledging me in the slightest.

With a shrug, I turn back to the beach trail, following the sounds of my best friend and best dog, sipping my coffee, knowing that as soon as my toes hit the sand, the anxiety that's been following me for two thousand miles will slowly start to fade away.

***

"Well, it hasn't fallen down yet, so it has that going for it," I tell Avery as we pull in front of the tiny cottage I'll be staying in. "Have you thought of a name yet?"

I remember thinking it was so cool when I first came to this town as a little kid and saw that every house had a little sign out front with a name. The Windbreak. Big Blue. Sarge's Surf Shack. The Beacon.

Avery laughs at my dig toward the state of the cottage, jumps down from the Jeep, grabs my backpack, and walks to the front porch, carefully navigating the steps, making me wonder if the wood is rotted. I find Zero's water bowl under a blanket and follow after my friend, making sure to place my feet on the same steps she did.

"It's not much, but it's furnished and I know you'll work your magic, then we can name her together," Aves says as she pushes open the squeaky door.

Zero barrels into the cottage after sniffing around the deck where it appears a small critter has made a home, crashing into my knees as she slides on the floor, my least favorite habit of hers. I fill her water bowl and she enthusiastically sloshes water all over the tiny kitchen before sprawling on the living room floor, tired from her beach hijinks. I grab the old towel sitting on the counter next to the kitchen sink and mop up her mess, shaking my head. Perhaps someday my dog will learn to drink water like a normal dog, but today is not that day.

After telling Zero to stay, I walk back outside to start unloading the pieces of my life I deemed necessary to bring with me. Avery and I fall into an easy silence as we sort through my meager belongings. I've always been on the minimalist side when it comes to possessions and this mad dash north has confirmed that. Clothes, Zero's belongings, my favorite cowboy boots, enough hats to make my mother sigh, bright pink rain boots, a handful of books, the blanket Avery gave me when we were teenagers, and the one plant I've kept alive for more than three weeks. I'm pretty sure there's a coffee mug or two under a seat, not because I packed them, but because I have a bad habit of taking my coffee with me and then forgetting the mug.

I felt bad when I moved in with Ethan, not having any furniture or real belongings to contribute toward our house that never became our home, but that has paid off now. I fled the state within hours with just my dog, a few boxes and bags, and no regrets.

I wait for the lump in my throat to return or the tears that have threatened since hugging Avery to finally spill over, but I only feel relief. Relief to not be driving, relief to be in the same state, no, the same town as my best friend, relief to be starting over.

Avery finishes helping me unload the Jeep and then heads for Rock Beach, the next town over, one with an actual grocery store, to get groceries for our dinner, giving me a chance to settle in.

As I unpack, I start making a mental list of cottage fixes and upgrades. Kitchen faucet, living room paint, bathroom shelving, bedroom bookshelf. My mind starts to get too busy, so I pull on running clothes, lace up my shoes, put Zero's e-collar on, grab the remote, and head outside to the rickety front porch.

The first thing on my renovation list is to make this the perfect morning coffee porch. Or an afternoon wine deck. Yoga space? My mind wanders to the possibilities as I attempt to stretch away two thousand miles of driving combined with a diet of peanut butter M&Ms, cold brew coffee, and Lifesavers mints. It's a losing battle.

I run to the end of the beach trail nearest The Town Mercantile that Avery and I used earlier, just over the bridge, and stop to take in the view once more. The creek runs into the base of Rejection Rock, the biggest of the three rocks the town is named for, and spills into the ocean on the south side. It still amazes me that towering trees can grow on a rock. Waves crash into the smaller two rocks, both just out of reach, even at low tide. Unfortunately it's high tide now, which means that I can either slog through dry sand or take my run back to firmer ground.

As Zero and I jog the streets, I take in the aging town that I visited so many times in my youth. Much of it is just as I remember: a wide assortment of tiny cottages and larger family homes line the narrow streets, the nine-hole golf course that is still flooded from the winter rains, and a single restaurant that's barely bigger than my cottage still overlooks the creek. The fire station across the way from The Town Mercantile could use a new coat of paint and the Post Office has a "PERMANENTLY CLOSED" sign out front. It's probably a bad sign when the Post Office moves out.

In another couple weeks the town will start to fill with summer residents and tourists, but in mid-May, it's nearly empty. I smile and say hello to the few people I pass, most of them giving me a small nod in return.

I run past Avery's family's beachfront house and laugh to myself about some of the shenanigans we got up to as kids. I wonder if the three-wheel bike is still in the garage. Just across the beach path that runs between the two houses, a man sits on the stoop of the neighboring house.

"G'afternoon!" I huff as I run past. I wonder if he's a relative of the family that used to spend summers here, letting us use their swings anytime we asked.

The man's eyes flick to mine and I do a double take. Unsmiling Door Holder, dad of Jeep Door Slammer, looking just as surly as earlier. But also, the endorphins from my run must have finally kicked in because I feel a jolt of energy as we make eye contact. His clear blue eyes hold mine for a beat before he nods and looks away.

Okay, well, not the warmest welcome to town, but one day at a time.

***

"You're really holding me to cooking after your blatant cheating in that race? This is bullshit. You realize what a terrible idea this is, right?" I ask Avery as we walk into her family's beach house.

I'm eager to see her newly built cabin at the top of what used to be a narrow tsunami path but we decided to relive our youth and have dinner at the house we frequented as wild kids and wilder teenagers. I put

10

the heavy bag of groceries on the kitchen counter and immediately walk through the house, letting memories wash over me as I make a beeline for the ocean view.

The puzzle table in the corner of the living room looks lonely without a half-finished puzzle spread out or mugs of special hot chocolate on the faded whale coasters and there's still board games peeking out from their spot under the worn coffee table. The bowl filled with sand dollars rests on top of the table and I wonder how many of those Avery and I found. Her grandmother's chair sits in the corner, a sewing basket within reach. Grandma Minnie taught both of us to cross-stitch one rainy winter night when we visited during the record-setting king tides. It's a hobby that I still sometimes go back to, an oddly calming activity if I'm feeling stressed or anxious.

Grandma Minnie's house in Salem as well as this house had always been filled with framed cross-stitches and a quick glance around the room confirms this is still the case. I once asked her which was her favorite, as she had so many.

"Happiness is being married to your best friend," she had replied, nodding to the simplest cross-stitch in the room, hung just above a small bookshelf that housed wedding pictures. The small, framed stitching still hangs there, a thin layer of dust along the top.

"You've worked every job out there from waitress to private bartender, personal assistant to farm labor. You're telling me you never honed your cooking skills at any point over the last ten years?" Avery startles me back to the present as she joins me in the living room. She bumps her hip against mine and throws a blanket over the couch for Zero, who climbs up and immediately tucks her nose under her paws, curling into her dober-ball pretzel position.

I'm not the only one that needs to adjust to the chilly temps. I make a mental note to dig Z's hoodie out from under the back seat of the Jeep and order her a waterproof jacket. I'm not always that great at taking care of myself, but I'm a damn good dog mom.

"Cooking is the worst. But the salmon you got for me looks amazing, I probably can't mess that up too bad," I tell her with false confidence, glad I'm not in charge of Avery's vegetarian dinner. I give

Zero's nose a rub and tuck the blanket around her a little tighter. So much for a vicious Doberman, she's just a fuzzy ball of blanket now.

We head back into the kitchen and work in companionable silence, a small speaker playing Zach Bryan softly in the background. There's a chance that cooking could indeed be relaxing as Avery claims or I'm just beyond the point of exhaustion, this is the calmest I've felt in weeks.

***

After a surprisingly delicious meal, we grab s'mores ingredients and head out to the small fire pit at the edge of the yard. We continue to share stories from the last few months of our lives, catching each other up on our families, as we wait for the fire to have perfect coals for our marshmallows.

Avery laughs at my story about the time I ended up at a BYOB rodeo with a group of strangers. I hadn't known BYOB rodeos were a real thing until we walked in carrying gas station cases of cheap beer and the cop at the gate saluted us. Aves pauses and gives me a look. Shit. I know what's coming. Lifelong friends are the WORST.

"Harper, why are you really here? I know you liked Ethan a lot, but you straight up fled the state when you guys broke up." She pulls out the big guns, using my real name and tilting her head like Zero does.

I knew the question was coming, but even after two thousand miles of overthinking it, I'm still working through this in my head. I don't see it as fleeing per se, but more of an overanalyzed-but-too-chickenshit-to-pull-the-trigger, long-time-coming move that just happened to be decided at the last minute, right after breaking up with my live-in boyfriend. Seeing as how she's offered me a kickass job, gave me a free place to live, and has also put up with my bullshit for nearly twenty years, I suppose I owe her a little more of an explanation.

I pop a homemade vanilla marshmallow in my mouth (who knew homemade marshmallows existed?!) and put another on a roasting stick, contemplating how to answer. She waits patiently, getting the graham crackers and chocolate set out for me as I stare at the coals, slowly

12

turning both my answer in my mind and the marshmallow on the stick. I take a gulp of wine from the glass in my left hand and sigh.

"It was well past time, Aves. I almost came the last time you offered me the job a few months ago, but Ethan convinced me to stay, that it was 'almost the turning point in his career.'" I attempt to use one-handed finger quotes, nearly spilling my wine and causing Zero to look up from where she's buried herself under a pile of blankets in the chair next to me. "That turning point came, but nothing changed for the two of us, just his paycheck. His hours, his stress, he was always checked out from everything but work. I knew we were well past over, he knew it, too. The last few weeks, maybe even months, we were just dragging it out, going through the motions. He didn't want to be the bad guy and kick me and Z out of his house, he's really *not* a bad guy, he's just not the guy for me. I felt like it was just one more thing I was failing." I pause, unsure where I'm going with this train of thought. "I don't know. I don't know what I'm doing."

I set my wine on the armrest of my chair and pull my marshmallow from the fire to inspect. Happy with the results, I swing the roasting stick toward the graham crackers and chocolate on Avery's armrest.

"When you called, you were so upset. Did he do something or say something to make you take off so quickly?" Avery asks. She expertly pulls the marshmallow from the roasting stick and hands me the perfect s'more. Little known fact: s'mores make the world go 'round.

"Yes and no," I avoid eye contact. I take a big bite of my s'more as Avery puts a new marshmallow on for herself. My next bite is smaller and I talk through the crumbs. "We were supposed to meet for drinks with friends after he finally left the office. He was late, as usual. As I sat there drinking my beer at a bar in a restaurant I didn't really even like, surrounded by people that were more his friends than mine, I just kinda realized it was time. I was done with the bartender temp job, nothing was holding me there, my closer friends had mostly moved away after college...I was just done." I shrug and take the last couple bites of my sticky s'more.

When I had gotten up from my seat and told everyone I was taking off early, I had planned to go home and talk to Ethan, figure out my next move. I don't want to tell Avery this next part, I hate the weakness inside me that still rules my reactions at times. I can feel my heart beating harder, echoing through my ribcage. Avery's eyes move to my hand and I realize I'm rubbing my scar.

breathe in two three four, hold two three four, out two three four

"When I went to leave, some asshole that had been sitting a couple barstools down from me caught my wrist to get my attention. I went from ready to change my life and take on the world to a freaking terrified sixteen-year-old girl. I mean, we're in our mid-twenties Aves, how many times has some random guy grabbed my hand in a bar or even at the fucking grocery store? I can usually handle it but I just lost it, is that like PTSD? What is wrong with me?" I rub my scar harder, fighting tears. That stupid lump in my throat returns and I swallow hard. The tears fall anyway.

"Harper..." Avery trails off and takes a shaky breath of her own.

"I'm fine now." I hurriedly use my sleeve to wipe my cheeks. "I just really hate that part of me, that scared girl that still lives inside me, and I hate admitting she's still there." I can feel that scared little girl's fear and adrenaline right now. Fuck, I need to pull it together. "But anyway, I called Ethan when I got to my car and he asked why I wanted to meet at the house. I told him about the guy, and he laughed and said it was a compliment that I was getting hit on."

I'm definitely throwing Ethan under the bus, the poor guy never knew when I'd laugh something off or when my anxiety would grab hold. He really is a good guy, he had just tried to joke when I was in no state of mind to laugh. He didn't know all the other shit that I had just decided before getting up and being grabbed.

Great, now I feel guilty. Am I the asshole? Probably.

Avery winces. "Well, fuck Ethan and every other guy that thinks grabbing someone is a fucking compliment." She pulls her marshmallow from the fire and I make her s'more, handing it to her before licking the dripping marshmallow goo from my fingers.

14

"Yeah, so I started throwing my shit in bags, stopped by Emmy's to give her and Patrick a hug, called you on my way out of town, and now here we are, you saving me like always."

Again, that's not completely true. Ethan and I had a lengthy conversation back at our house and he apologized profusely for his comment. He told me he knew I was right, it was past time to call our relationship off, then he helped me load the Jeep, telling me to make sure to get Zero treats on my way out of town. Which she then barfed up onto my belongings an hour later. Because, dogs.

"Harper, I'm not saving you. You do realize I'm about to have you working your ass off, right?" Avery laughs softly, helping me out by making things light again. "It might look like I have my shit together, but I need you here to actually pull it together for me."

I wipe the last remaining tears that cling to my lashes. "Well, as soon as you stop hogging the marshmallows and let me make another s'more, I'll be ready for my list of duties, boss," I say, reaching for the bag of marshmallows.

There's already been too many tears, luckily there's no such thing as too many s'mores.

Chapter Two
West

I slide the glass door open, step outside, and set my Buffalo Trace on the table next to my favorite adirondack chair. I'm not a big drinker, in fact I very rarely drink these days, but tonight calls for a bourbon. Voices float across the path and the flicker of a fire glows next door. Just as I settle in to relax, the door opens behind me.

"Uncle West?" Colt slips out the door and climbs onto the chair with me. "Why didn't my mom come tonight? She was supposed to be here after dinner." His voice is timid and his lower lip quivers slightly so I wrap my arm around him, tucking him into my chest.

He's right. She was supposed to be here; she had called earlier in the week and promised to spend the weekend with us. When they first showed up on my doorstep, I had thought it was a fun weekend visit, a few days for my sister to relax while Colt and I had uncle-nephew time, but that was well over a week ago.

Is it bad to lie? Yes. Is it bad to lie to children? Also yes. How am I supposed to handle this? I can't tell the kid that he might live here now, can I? I keep my expression neutral and pull him into my lap, mulling over how to answer. I don't know everything going on in my sister's life, but I do know I am the reason for most of her struggles. Maybe this is my chance to make it up to her and Colt, redeem myself, help them find a new path.

"Is Miss Avery making s'mores?" Colt spies the fire pit next door.

"Looks like it, bud," I reply, fairly confused by this quick change in topic.

"Hi, Miss Avery! It's me, Colt! I like s'mores, too!" Colt hollers, scrambling down off my lap. He stands and waves from the edge of the deck.

"Hi, Colt! It's me, Tex! Come have a s'more!" yells Avery's friend.

"S'mores, Uncle West! Let's go! Maybe the lady's dog is there!" Colt jumps off the deck excitedly and takes off across the beach path without looking to see if I follow.

So much for a regular bedtime. Isn't that a kid thing? Stories and bedtime? Fuck, I really need to figure this pretend-parenting thing out.

All I wanted was a quiet night to organize my mind, figure out how the fuck to take care of a kid for an undetermined amount of time and still run my shop, do some carpentry work on the side, but here I am, trudging through the dar-

My mind goes blank as I look up and see Avery's friend, who is laughing at Colt's attempt to pet her dog without the beast licking his face. I forget to say hello, or even breathe, as she looks up at me, her eyes red-rimmed like she's been crying. We stare at each other and this time, unlike earlier, I don't look away. Something shifts inside me. I stand frozen, unable to tear my gaze away from hers.

"Hi, West, this is my childhood friend, Tex, she's moving here to be my savior. Tex, this is my friend West, and my ever better friend, Colt." Avery interrupts my staring contest with her friend with the introduction, looking at me with a slight smirk when I glance at her.

Avery notices everything. I may have only known her for a couple of years, but she quickly became one of my favorite people nearly immediately after we met. In the time she's known me, she sure as shit hasn't seen me act like this. Have I ever acted like this in my life?

I now know what someone means when they say "visceral reaction" because that has to be what this is. Or maybe it's a heart attack.

"Savior now? No pressure there. I thought I was just your personal assistant!" Tex laughs as Colt climbs into her lap. "Nice to meet you," she adds, giving me a half-hearted smile that doesn't reach her eyes as Avery hands her a roasting stick with a marshmallow on the end.

I can't really blame her, I probably came off like an asshole both times we ran into each other earlier today. No, I know I did.

Tex puts her chin on Colt's shoulder and they lean forward together to roast the marshmallow over the coals.

I nod stupidly at the introduction, apparently unable to speak. Avery gives me a raised eyebrow and I shrug before sinking into the chair the dog just climbed out of. I've seen Tex multiple times today, each time felt potent, but not like this.

This morning at The Mercantile, she was a blur of energy, making my pulse race as she blew in like a fucking hurricane. Her laughter as she jumped on Avery was like a punch to the gut. Her lean legs had wrapped around Avery as the two of them happily spun around, and I had a momentary vision of them wrapping around me. I hadn't thought of a woman like that since leaving Portland so I just stared.

When she made Colt giggle from across the parking lot with her goofy curtsy, I think I was frozen with shock; he hasn't laughed so easily all week. Colt and I had both stared at her retreating figure until long after she rounded the corner and disappeared onto the beach.

Then catching her on her run, her sunny smile made me forget why I had stormed out of the house moments before.

But now? Something in her guarded hazel eyes has me unable to take a full breath.

"Keep turning, yep, just like that," Tex is telling Colt, both of them staring into the fire at the marshmallow that hasn't yet caught on fire, but with Colt's track record will at any moment. "You're really good at this, did your dad teach you?" she asks Colt as she looks over at me, her eyes slightly less red.

"Uncle West isn't my dad!" he squeals, giggling again.

Colt's a pretty happy-go-lucky kid, but I've never seen him take quite so quickly to a new person. Avery had to bribe him with pastries for a week when they first met last summer and Kelsey, the teenage employee at The Mercantile, is still working on winning him over with extra sprinkles on his special hot chocolate. I don't think it's the s'mores and the dog, it's just something about *her*.

"That's Zero, she's a one-year-old Doberman/Tasmanian devil mix," Tex says as her dog sniffs my boots, having given up on stealing a marshmallow.

I chuckle at that, remembering how enthusiastically the dog sprinted to the beach from The Mercantile parking lot, as well as how she ran circles around Tex when I saw them on their run earlier. No wonder why Tex and Colt are getting along so well, the dog and Colt might be twins. They definitely seem to have similar energy levels.

I settle back in my chair, content to listen to the two women as they tell Colt stories of their childhood visits to this house. They tell him about hiking to a suspension bridge with Avery's grandpa, winning sandcastle contests over the Fourth of July, the time their kite got away from them and flew halfway across town before getting stuck on a roof, and how they used to race up the old tsunami trail, which is now the road that leads to Avery's new house.

Colt refuses to give up his spot on Tex's lap so I have an excuse to steal glances her way. Her left hand fidgets often, her thumb rubbing the inside of a finger as she smiles down at Colt, who continues to snuggle deeper into the pile of blankets on her lap. Her eyes light up when she teases Avery, soften when she ruffles Colt's hair or checks on her dog that has curled up under her feet, and every once in a while, when they flicker my way, there's a heat to her guarded gaze that has nothing to do with the fire.

When Colt seems to be drifting off to sleep in the nest of blankets, I lean down to gather him in my arms. As he sleepily reaches for me, I find myself close enough to breathe in Tex's light peach scent. I subtly inhale one more time and see her shiver, goosebumps erupting along her neck. Her surprised hazel eyes find mine and she gives me a ghost of a smile. My heart hammers in my chest as I bid the women a quiet goodnight.

***

I'm back in my favorite chair, this time with coffee, checking my email, but mainly watching the fog rolling along the beach, enjoying a few minutes of quiet before Colt wakes up. I hear a couple of excited barks and in a break in the fog I see Avery, Tex, and Zero. For once, Avery isn't running her morning miles, but the dog sure is. The giant Doberman splashes through the receding waves and happily chases the small sandpipers at the water's edge, always circling back to the girls, nosing Tex's hand on her way by. Then, with Colt-like energy, she races off to chase the sea foam blowing along the beach.

I turn back to my iPad, knowing I don't have long before Colt will be up. He's been with me for over a week and I'm guessing that soon I will need to feed him something better than Cheerios followed by The Mercantile's special hot chocolate for breakfast every morning.

This time of year my shop, Rock Beach Tattoo, is only open for appointments, not walk-ins, so it should be easy enough to schedule those and my carpentry jobs around Colt and a babysitter. A babysitter I still need to find. Kelsey's mom, Mrs. G, asked if she could help out and Kelsey gave me the info for one of her friends that lives in Rock Beach, so I'll give her a call later today. At this point I'm just assuming my sister isn't coming back any time soon. I clench my jaw and blow out a breath before taking another sip of coffee. My eyes follow the trio on the beach as my mind drifts to Colt.

Guilt settles in as I think of my nephew sleeping soundly inside. Without my mistakes, he wouldn't be here, in more ways than one. I introduced my younger sister to Liam, Colt's dad, nearly a decade ago. Liam and I were instant best friends when we met, me right out of high school and him a couple years older. We bonded over our love of tattoos and art. When Jessie and I's parents died, Liam was the one who pulled me through the grief. He, too, had lost his parents in a car accident and knew the lonely road Jessie and I were traveling. Without his steady support, I'm not sure how I would have survived that loss.

We opened our tattoo parlor a year after they died. I felt like I was using the money my parents had left me to build something they'd be proud of, something lasting, in more than one way. I poured my grief into our shop one day, one hour, one tattoo at a time.

In reality, I was a young, over-eager moron slowly shoveling my parents' money into a failing business with an addict as my business partner. I just didn't realize it until much, much later. I knew Liam had an untamed streak but I was happy to overlook it because, turns out, partying is really fucking fun.

When Jessie got pregnant, I figured Liam would settle down, focus on the business a little more. In all fairness, I do think he tried. Just not very hard. They got married and had a hell of a party to celebrate, but then he continued on the same path of partying and irresponsible decisions. I wasn't the best help. After all, I wasn't the one about to become a father, I could still stay out until all hours, fuck around, and sleep on couches as long as I kept up my end of the business, which I did. That all changed the second I met my nephew.

I knew from the first time I held him, the moment I looked into his barely-open eyes, that it was time to become the man this strange little alien-looking baby in a tiny blue beanie needed me to be. I tried to pull Liam up with me. After all, he was my best friend, my nephew's dad, my business partner, and my sister's husband.

Breaking even wasn't good enough anymore, I wanted our business to make money so Colt could have a college fund. I started remodeling the shop, learning carpentry skills as I went along. I fought hard to make our business a success, constantly fixing Liam's "mistakes" that were really just bad fucking decisions. I tried for three fucking years. Liam didn't change. It killed me, knowing my hand in where he ended up. Where Jessie and Colt ended up.

When I finally found a buyer for my half of the business, I was out. Done. Finished. Jessie refused to come with me so I gave her a hug, slid a prepaid cell phone with my number programmed in it, and a spare key to my new house in her hand, and left.

I walked away from both my sister and my nephew. Looking back, it's obvious our parents' deaths made Jessie desperate to keep her own little family together and it was his parents' deaths that set Liam down his dark path. I should have seen it sooner. Stepped up sooner. Instead, I enabled him over and over again.

Zero suddenly appears on my deck, jolting me back to the brisk morning. She gives my wool sock a lick then races back to the path that leads down to the beach.

"Sorry!" Tex calls from the bottom of the path, giving me a wave.

I lift my coffee cup in return, much like she did yesterday in the parking lot, and watch as Tex, Avery, and Zero walk up the path. I tell myself not to notice Tex's legs in her black leggings, or that her eyes are back to happy and bright, instead of red-rimmed and teary. Of course I notice both.

Tex leans toward Avery and says something quietly, her eyes on me, and Avery smirks as she swings her gaze my way. My mind races with the possibilities of what she just whispered. Probably that I'm a grumpy bastard, which is a fair assessment. Avery nudges her friend with her shoulder and veers my way while Tex and Zero continue on their way.

"Good morning," Avery says as she steps onto my deck. "Got a minute?"

I nod and push the other chair out with my foot, giving her space to sit. She settles in and we watch Tex and Zero disappear down the street. Scratch that, I watch them. I realize with a start that Avery is merely watching me while I watch her friend. Shit.

"So, I need a favor," Avery says, laughter in her usually serious eyes. I glare at her suspiciously. "What? You're a carpenter and I need a carpenter." I continue glaring, waiting for the catch. "The deck at Tex's cottage needs fixed."

There it is. Less than twelve hours after she caught me staring at her friend in the light of the fire, she's trying to push me toward her. Avery knows my past and why I've accepted and embraced my solitude, something I thought she understood as she lives alone on top of a goddamn hill with no neighbors to be seen. I refuse to bring anyone down with me again. Especially someone like her friend, who smiles despite red-rimmed eyes, wins my nephew over in a matter of seconds, and could easily make me consider moving beyond my life of solitude.

"Okay, so actually I have a few jobs for you, probably enough to keep you busy until your shop is ready to have walk-in hours, and I'm sure when the weather cooperates you can just let Colt tag along with you." Avery sweetens the deal for me. It's hard to live here year round with a business that is very dependent upon tourists. I could use the extra work; I have a lot of Cheerios to buy.

"Your cabin already needs work?" I ask in surprise, knowing she'd had it built within the last handful of years. It's a beautiful minimalist cabin nestled among the trees with uninterrupted ocean views from the expansive deck I built. It reminds me of an actual treehouse.

"No, but remember back when the Scott family sold their two cottages here in the village and then Eldon's son inherited and sold the house up on North Road?"

There were a few rough years for our community with many families selling their homes and others leaving theirs to get beaten down by the rough winters and then finding them unusable in the spring, only to put them on the market. It's how I was able to afford my house. I nod slowly, thinking how upset Eldon would have been to know how quickly his son sold the house. I wish I would have known it was for sale, it's my favorite house in this little town.

"Well, I bought them. Plus two more besides the little cottage Tex is in. I hired Tex to manage the repairs and return them to their former glory. Or more accurately, to whatever glory she sees fit, which is both a terrifying gamble and a sure thing."

"I'm sorry, what?" I haven't had enough coffee this morning to be sure, but I'm fairly certain that Avery had just told me she's a multimillionaire. I'm not surprised in the least, she's fucking crazy smart, but I *am* surprised she just told me. Avery's a very private person and she values anonymity, she wouldn't want anyone to know she owns that many houses as well as The Town Mercantile.

"I have work that needs done, you need to work. Tex is in charge, she has your number." She sums it up in a few short words while I'm still trying to process the bomb she'd just dropped. Five houses? Six? Damn, it's seven with hers.

Avrey smirks at my dumbfounded expression and then checks her watch. She bolts up, mutters something about The Merc, and jogs off before I can put together any follow up questions.

24

I shake my head and return to my coffee, once again lost in thought. This time it's the memory of guarded hazel eyes and Colt's happy giggle that distract me from my emails though.

Chapter Three
Harper

"Whoa, whoa, whoa. Hey, my man, what's going on this morning?" I ask Colt as he stomps past my cottage alone. Zero starts inching off her dog bed, trying to sneak over to him.

Colt stops in front of the semi-stable but also semi-rotted porch where I've been enjoying my steaming cup of coffee but won't look up at me, he just eyes Zero and fidgets.

"Want to give Zero her morning treat?" I ask him, unsure what to do about this wandering and obviously upset five year old. West's house is only a block up the street but there isn't another adult in sight.

"Okay," he whispers. He sniffles and reaches his hand out as I dig a treat out of my jacket pocket.

"Gentle, Z," I say, giving her a stern look that she ignores. Gentleness is not exactly her strong suit. In fact, there's no chance she's going to be gentle or sweet at any point in her life. She's more honey badger than honey.

Giggles erupt from Colt as Zero ignores the treat in his hand and instead licks his tears. She gently takes the treat and retreats to her bed, flopping down dramatically. Colt follows and sits down next to her. She wiggles forward until her head rests in his lap. My eyes widen as I watch the entire thing. What the fuck just happened? I would have bet my first paycheck I'd never see the day she was this gentle.

"So, what's going on this morning?" I ask Colt, watching him absentmindedly pet Zero. She rolls onto her back, long legs waving in the air.

27

"I don't want to live here! My friend Charlie doesn't live here, Uncle West isn't even my dad, there's no kids, and it's not fun," he blurts out, his eyes still on Zero, refusing to look at me. Tears once again run down his cheeks and he furiously rubs them away with his sleeve.

My heart breaks for him. "Well, I'm probably not as fun as your friend Charlie and I'm not a kid, but I just moved here, too, and I only know you and Avery and your Uncle West. Maybe we can be friends?" I ask him, still unsure of the family dynamic. Where is his dad? And mom? Which one is related to West? I rub the scar on my finger nervously, unsure I'm doing anything right in this interaction as Colt still angrily swipes at his tears.

"Friends?" he repeats cautiously, finally glancing up at me.

I nod. "But only if you like building sandcastles, stomping in mud puddles, and climbing the rock at low tide, because those are my favorite things."

"Grown ups don't do that stuff, Tex, only kids," Colt tells me, and can a five year old roll their eyes because I'm pretty sure he just did.

"I guess I better get my rain boots on so we can jump in every puddle between here and Uncle West's house then," I say, getting up to grab my boots. "See if you can put Zero's leash on and I'll show you how we Texans jump in mud puddles."

"Colt!" I hear West's voice as I shove my feet in my pink rain boots.

"I've got him!" I holler back, holding my hand out to Colt, Zero's leash in his other hand.

West jogs down the street toward us, a panicked look in his eyes. He barely looks at me before dropping to his knees and opening his arms for a hug from Colt. "You had me worried, bud, I didn't know where you had gone. Remember how we talked about not going to the beach alone? I guess I should have said that you can't go around town alone, either."

"I'm sorry Uncle West," Colt says with sad puppy dog eyes. "I didn't know where you were and I just wanted hot chocolate to make me feel better but then I saw Tex and Zero and they made me feel better instead."

Way to crush my heart, kid.

"Oh, bud, I was having my coffee out on the porch, waiting for you to wake up! I would never leave you home all alone, I will *always* be at the house or on the deck or in the yard when you're with me," West reassures him.

"My dad does sometimes," Colt says with a child's indifference.

My eyes fly to West, and I see anger flash across his face, turning his blue eyes cold. He takes a deep breath and gives Colt another squeeze.

"Let's go get that special hot chocolate and maybe see if we can get your new friend a thank you treat as well?" West asks, looking at me with raised eyebrows.

"We have mud puddles to jump in on the way!" I say brightly and immediately stomp in a puddle in the small driveway, making Colt giggle. It's the best sound I've heard all morning, which includes my coffee brewing and Z's happy barks on the beach.

One side of West's mouth turns up as he looks at me and my heart beats a little faster. How did I not realize yesterday how goddamn good looking this man is? Oh, because I felt like my life was in shambles, much like his nephew does now. What a pair we are. We're going to need *a lot* of puddles.

Colt and I happily jump in every puddle between my cottage and The Mercantile and then dry our boots carefully on the welcome mat. West waits patiently before holding the door for us, his hand briefly touching my back as he ushers both of us inside before stepping in behind us.

Ethan would have sighed impatiently at me, always serious with no time for fun. Was he always that way or did his job suck everything good out of him?

After introducing myself to the middle-aged woman behind the counter, I let West treat me to an extra hot vanilla latte with almond milk, grab a free dog treat for Zero who is waiting outside, and smile at Colt's adorable whipped cream mustache.

I thoroughly enjoy Colt's endless chatter on the way back to the cottage, walking in companionable silence with West, who seems lost in thought. I sneak glances at him out of the corner of my eye, hoping to get a better glimpse of the swirls of ink that are peeking out of his rolled-up flannel sleeves. Instead I just see his eyes following his puddle-stomping nephew with a bit of a defeated expression.

***

"Honey, I'm home!" I call out as I let myself into Avery's hilltop cabin.

Despite the gray sky and light drizzle, the view from the top of the tsunami evacuation route is breathtaking. The living room has an entire wall of windows overlooking the entire town of Three Rocks below. It's like living in a treehouse, but a treehouse with a fireplace. I instinctively move toward the warm fire, hearing Avery moving around in the back hall. I don't think I've been really, truly warm since leaving Texas.

"G'morning for the second time. Sorry, I had a few emails to answer and got sidetracked," Avery says as she comes into the room, laptop in one hand and coffee in the other. "But now it's business owner time. Ready to be bossed around?"

"By you? Anytime. But please use a deep voice and tell me I'm a good girl," I wink, wiggle my eyebrows, and bite my lip suggestively. Or, more likely, ridiculously.

Avery snorts at my book boyfriend joke attempt and sits down beside me, putting her laptop on the coffee table in front of us. She sips her coffee, looks out the window, takes *another* sip, and looks out the window *again*. I realize she's stalling.

"Ummm….out with it. What is this? What are you hiding? Why am I really here?" I question her, using her words from last night. Bingo. She looks guilty as hell.

"Well, you know how I said I wanted you to renovate the cottage, do some light personal assistant stuff, and manage The Merc? So, that was two months ago." She shifts uncomfortably even though this is the most comfortable couch I've ever sat on.

"Oh shit, do you not need me here? Is this a pity job? I'm a pity job, aren't I? Avery, this isn't okay! You can't hire me for a job that doesn't exist!" I panic, hating the thought of taking advantage of my friend. Fuuuck. She told me months ago about the job, of course she hired someone else. Let me just add this to the list of "shit Harper fucked up" that's probably a mile long by now.

"Tex, calm down! It's not that. I need you here but the job is a little different. Okay. So. The quick version is this: I bought half a dozen cottages in Three Rocks and they all need flipped into rentals, starting with the one you're in, but that one is actually for you to live in. I want you to manage The Mercantile as well as manage the rentals. Live-in manager, but living in your own space," Avery says in a rush. There's a beat of silence as she nervously takes another sip of coffee.

"I'm sorry, you bought a *dozen* houses? What the hell, Avery? Did you rob a bank?" I exclaim after I've recovered from the shock of her announcement. I know her teenage novels did well, but she also put herself through college and law school. What kind of non-evil genius is she? Is this witchcraft? Can she teach me?

"Close enough, I invested well and then my books resurfaced on BookTok and a whole new generation of teenagers are going crazy for them. My publisher's media team deals with that, so don't worry about that in your job description, but this is my new investment. Plus, I bought them over the last few years as the town seemed to be dying a slow and painful death. And it's only *half* a dozen, not a dozen. They're mostly small cottages that all need some TLC so they were a good investment."

"What. The. Hell." This is for sure witchcraft. My best friend is a non-evil genius. And a ninja secret-keeper. How was she hiding all of this from me? Oh, wait, I was five states away and she also kept her books a total secret until they were published.

"If you could also continue my mission to save this town, that'd be great. Okay, that's all!" Avery says, standing up.

"No you don't!" I tackle her back onto the couch. "Avery, you're amazing. And crazy. Mainly amazing. I'm so proud of you. I'm going to need to reheat this latte and then fuck it, let's do this. Boss Bitches and all that. Email me everything you have that I need, I know you already have it drafted. I'll grab my laptop out of the Jeep because of course I forgot to bring it in and then let's get started."

I return with my laptop and reheat my latte to perfect burn-my-mouth temperature. We go through the property list, Avery overwhelms me with graphs and nerd stuff, and I reheat my coffee twice more. I read through every email and document she sends, printing the ones I want hard copies of. Soon there are papers scattered across the coffee table, only one of which I spill coffee on, and Avery has answered all of my questions. She retreats to her office to do lawyer shit while I mark a map of the town with the properties I now manage.

The houses are spread throughout the village area of Three Rocks with only one out on North Road. I stand and pace in front of the windows for about thirty seconds before I realize that indoor pacing isn't going to cut it. I grab the ring of keys on the coffee table, my new notebook, my favorite pen that might or might not say "fuck off" on the side, and head down the hill.

***

The first rental on my list is my own little cottage which needs deck repair but then will be put last on the remodel list. I can live anywhere as long as I have Zero and she doesn't seem to mind the peeling paint or dated fixtures.

The second house is only a few doors down along the creek and I have a sudden flashback of the Scott family matriarch, Grandma Georgie, tending flowers all summer long. She used to give Avery and I candy when we'd walk by after dinner. I make a note that this should once again be a garden paradise, assuming I can find someone to help me keep the plants alive.

I'm still making notes on interior repairs as I walk to the third rental, which is aptly named "The Glass House." It's tucked into a cove, hidden from both the road and the beach. The space is small, minimalist, and bright. Skylights and multiple walls of windows similar to Avery's bring tons of natural light into every room as well as give the house its name. I already love it. As soon as I step onto the small back deck, my brain kicks into overdrive and I love it even more.

An outdoor shower will go around the corner, but a soaking tub for two would be perfect right here on the deck. I can picture a floating deck with two chairs and a small fire pit, just far enough toward the beach to catch the sunset without being seen by beach-goers. How the previous owners let this house go is beyond me. It's absolutely incredible.

The fourth house on my list, situated along the golf course, is nearly the opposite of the house I just left. It has boisterous family fun written all over it. The yard is a mess but the house appears to be in great shape. The lowest level is a garage that has a stack of firewood and some old beach cruisers on one side but the rest of the space is wide open. I have a vague idea of skim board storage and a ping pong table, but I can't quite pull it together. Pinterest will help. The main floor has an open kitchen, large living area, a master bedroom with its own bathroom, plus a half bath tucked under the stairs. Upstairs has a huge loft area that will be perfect for movies and board games, along with three more bedrooms and a full bath.

About half a mile out of the main village along North Road is the fifth rental. The information from Avery says it was owned by a man named Eldon, who passed away, and then his son quickly sold the house. It's a midsize beach house with an open kitchen, butcher block counters, and big windows that show off the amazing views of the rolling dunes. The ocean is barely visible past the beach grass. I can't get a real read on it, though. It just doesn't *feel* like a rental. It feels like it wants to be lived in. Worn, but in a homey way. All I can picture is sitting in the leather chairs that face the huge back windows, morning coffee during a rainy week, book in hand. I wander outside looking for inspiration. I listen to the wind through the trees, watch the beach grass ripple. I feel calm, peaceful. I let myself take a few breaths, then just write a giant question mark in my notebook on the page meant for this house.

As I walk back from North Road to the last rental that's just a couple houses away from West's, I pass the beach access path that was always used for the Fourth of July 5k Fun Run. I suddenly remember the ridiculous outfits we wore the last year we ran, how Avery, unsurprisingly, left the rest of the field in the dust. I remember the parade that followed, with the volunteer fire department leading the way, lights and sirens announcing the start. The sand castle contest in the afternoon and the fireworks display at night. Weren't there also community bonfires throughout the summer? With what Avery has told me about the state of the town, I'm guessing this isn't true anymore. What a bummer.

Wait.

That's it. That's the answer.

I fumble my phone out of my pocket with cold hands to find the correct email from Avery. Thank God she's so freaking organized and detail-oriented. According to her nerdy spreadsheet, the village area of Three Rocks only has three dozen year-round residents (which now includes Zero and I), about two hundred total in the surrounding area, and only half of the summer residents came back last year for the full season. There were only two village events in the last two years, both put on by the volunteer fire department, but I don't see any pie charts, graphs, or summaries on those. The town isn't only lacking people, it's lacking community.

34

Chapter Four
West

I try to read the Post-it note stuck to the front door of Tex's cottage. She should have been a doctor for all I can decipher. Her handwriting is terrible. I think the note says the door's unlocked and to help myself to coffee. Since Colt spilled half of mine earlier, that's an offer I can't refuse. Mrs. G has Colt until 2 p.m. and I need to get as much done as possible before then.

I cautiously let myself in the front door. No dog greets me and I pour the last cup of coffee from the beat-up, old coffee pot on the counter into the beat-up, old Yeti in my hand. I only have a small section of deck to repair here then I'll work on the planter boxes and raised beds down the street.

I glance around the room, taking in Tex's small space. There's a pile of books stacked haphazardly on the floor next to the fireplace, a hanging plant that might be some sort of fuzzy cactus with a pink Santa hat on it even though it's nowhere near Christmas, and three coffee mugs hanging under the cupboard that don't look like anything Avery would have. I look closer and realize they aren't decorated with flowers, but with bright curse words written in cursive.

The front door bangs open and Zero careens in, beelining for the water bowl. Tex is right on Zero's heels, three different drinks precariously balanced in her hands. Her phone is shoved down her shirt, she has her keys hanging off her pinky finger, and she looks a little like a hot mess. Emphasis on the hot, which hits me like a ton of bricks. And the mess, if I want to be fair. How she and always-put-together Avery are best friends is beyond me, they seem like polar opposites.

"Oh, shit, I didn't even notice your truck!" Tex jumps sideways when she looks up and notices me standing in her kitchen. "Oh good, you found the coffee. I'm headed to the hardware store, do you need me to grab anything for you?"

She's a whirlwind of motion which seems to be her normal state, unless she's crying by a fire. Her eyes look slightly more green today, her tangled hair is tucked under a neon yellow snapback, and her feet are bare even though it's only fifty degrees. She gives me a bright smile as she sets two of her drinks on the counter and grabs a notebook from the couch. She digs a pen from between the cushions and tucks it under her hat. I'm definitely staring, awkward as fuck, but my eyes don't want to move away.

"No, I'm good," I say, after I convince my brain to form words. "I'll replace those rotten boards, fix that middle step, then head to work on the planters down the street. Thanks for the liquid energy." I hold my Yeti up and edge my way backwards toward the door.

Tex gives me an uncertain smile as I escape the suddenly claustrophobic cottage. What the actual fuck is happening? I have a younger sister, I grew up with her friends always invading my space. I have my own female friends, including this woman's best friend, yet none have made me feel or act as awkward as this. I'm fairly certain I just came off like an asshole, again.

As I grab my tools from the back of my truck, I tell myself yet again to shut this shit down, immediately. Tex is endless energy, neon trucker hats and bare feet. I'm quiet isolation, flannels and work boots. She's young and carefree and sure as shit doesn't need someone like me dragging her down before she can get her life here started.

I angrily yank my flannel off, throw it in a heap on the grass, and get started pulling up the rotten boards around the front steps. I immediately lose myself in the work; there's no feeling a crowbar can't fix.

Of course that only works until flip-flops and dog feet appear in my peripheral vision. I tell myself not to act like an awkward teenager

36

and force myself to look up. Her eyes widen as she stares at my left forearm where my favorite tattoo, the one I designed the day Colt was born, wraps around my forearm. Her lips part slightly before she seems to catch herself.

"I'm headed out, text me if you need anything in town," she says, quickly looking away.

Without waiting for me to answer, she hops over the stairs I've torn apart. She gets in her Jeep, Zero jumping in the backseat, and has country music blaring out the open windows before I can react. I shake my head, confused as shit, and get back to work.

***

Tex:
hey, do you have time to meet me at the glass house to go over the deck additions so i can start getting prices together for avery?

West:
Does 1pm work?

Tex:
i'll meet you there.

I check my watch, hoping I'll have enough time to finish the planters and grab a quick shower before I meet Tex. I've been distracted all morning, working slower than usual, too busy arguing with myself about this undeniable pull I feel toward the sunny-in-the-gray, flip-flops-in-the-rain, bright burst of energy known as Tex. She's been here all of four days and if the local rumor mill is to be believed, which, oddly enough they're usually right, she's running away from something, or someone. Definitely not what I need in my life. I shake the image of her red-rimmed eyes from my head and grab my tape measure.

After stopping at home for a quick shower, I walk down to The Glass House. I arrive right at 1 p.m. and see Tex's Jeep in the driveway but no sign of her neon hat or wild dog. I give the front door a couple knocks then try the handle when I don't see or hear anyone. It's unlocked.

"Hey, it's West!" I call, opening the door slowly. Still nothing. "Tex?"

I pause for a minute to take in my surroundings. I've known this house was here but I've never been down the driveway, let alone inside. There's a simple stone fireplace in the living room that catches my attention but then all I can see is glass. It's not just a line of windows like so many of the beachfront houses here, it's walls of glass, just pure glass on two sides of me. I can't see the road or the ocean, just trees and beach grass, so it still feels private.

Also, the house is definitely empty. No Tex and no Zero. An uneasy feeling comes over me and I feel the hairs on my arms stand up. Something is off. I stand still, silent. I can barely make out a quiet whine.

My eyes move around the room and I see what I thought was a seam in the glass on the far side of the kitchen is actually a door, a door that's barely cracked open. I stalk over as silently as anyone wearing boots can and the soft whine gets louder.

As soon as I step outside, I see her. She's sitting on the edge of the deck, just out of sight from where I had been standing in the living room. Her feet are on the ground below and she's leaning forward with her arms wrapped around her knees, forehead resting on her arms, neon hat on backwards.

Zero stands guard over her, still and unmoving. The dog looks at me as I approach and her whining increases but she doesn't growl.

My heart beats faster as my adrenaline surges.

"Tex?" I ask softly, trying not to startle her. Her shoulders shake and Zero's whining gets even more urgent. "It's just me, are you okay?"

Tex looks at me over her shoulder, eyes wide and red, and then buries her face again. Zero nudges her and when she doesn't respond, the dog rests her chin on Tex's shoulder. She's visibly shaking and I can hear her breathing erratically. I take in our surroundings but don't see anyone else; there's no way Zero would have let someone hurt Tex and get away.

"I'm just going to sit down next to you," I say quietly, acutely aware that my deep voice and large stature can be intimidating, as I slowly lower myself to the deck. She flinches and curls tighter around herself, but nods.

38

"O-kay," she whispers.

"Are you hurt?" I ask, trying to fish my phone out of my pocket, thinking that Avery is much better equipped to handle whatever is going on right now.

"Don't-call-her," Tex whispers brokenly between shuddering breaths, then takes a larger hiccuping breath, gulping the air. She turns her head and her red eyes find mine. "Just-wait."

With her eyes locked on mine, all of a sudden I can't breathe either. I feel like I got sucker punched. Zero noses my hand, so I give her ears a quick rub.

"Okay, I won't. I'm here," I say, keeping my voice low, eyes steady on hers.

She lowers her eyes as she sits up and cautiously scoots toward me. I stay still, letting her decide the distance, surprised when her thigh presses against mine. We sit quietly, unspeaking, as I fight to keep my adrenaline from spiking again.

I don't know what to do, but I'm so focused on her, on every shudder of her small body, that I realize her unsteady breaths match mine. With each inhale, her shoulder presses against my arm. I slow my breaths and hers follow. Finally, she stops shaking. She's still rubbing the inside of her finger so hard I'm worried she's going to take off a layer of skin though.

Zero jumps down from the deck and faces us, nosing Tex until her hand uncurls and starts stroking the dog's ears. I want so badly to pull Tex into my arms, tuck her under my chin, breathe in her peach scent, and hold her until I can reassure myself that she's okay. But I know as soon as I touch her, hold her, this pull I already feel toward her will become even more overwhelming. Or she might punch me. So we sit, breathing steadily, with Zero watching over us.

"Okay, I'm okay now. Can we pretend you didn't see me crying the other night or witness my panic attack just now? Please?" Tex whispers after a few minutes of silence.

Well, fuck. Now what am I supposed to do? She obviously isn't okay, but it isn't my place to say anything.

"Hey Tex, you said you wanted to talk about deck additions?" I say, nudging her shoulder and standing up.

I reach my hand down and after a small pause, she puts her hand in mine and I pull her to standing. Her hand feels small in mine and her fingers are ice cold. The contact is fleeting, she pulls away quickly and tucks her hand in her jacket pocket. She gives me her little half smile, then looks down at her feet. I see her take a deep breath then she looks back up with a smile that I know is forced.

I hate that smile.

"I love talking about big decks," she says, her voice just barely higher than usual.

She pulls her hand back out of her pocket and reaches toward me. My heart races, loudly thumping against my ribs. I don't move a muscle.

And then she pulls the measuring tape off my belt. With a grin and a wink, she heads for the house, slipping inside the door with Zero at her side.

What the fuck just happened? Five hours ago she had me feeling like a fumbling boy, five minutes ago I was helpless to help her, and five seconds ago all I could think about was that hand reaching for me and how it would feel against my skin.

Fucking measuring tape.

***

I can see her vision for this house so clearly as she walks me through the changes she wants to make. I measure the space for the floating deck with Tex's help, take notes and pictures on my phone, and then turn back to see her looking out toward the beach as she patiently waits for me to finish up. She had splashed water on her face as soon as we walked back inside but is obviously still recovering from her panic attack. Her bright neon hat is the complete opposite of her mood right now although she's doing everything she can to hide it with her half-hearted banter.

"Do you trust me?" I ask her suddenly.

"What? I mean, no. I only trust like two people and my dog," she replies with a wry grin. That's fair, that's about how many I trust as well.

"Let me rephrase: can you give me five to seven minutes? Maybe ten. Twelve? And also your notebook and pen, please," I say, nodding to the notebook she has been randomly writing in during the walk-through.

"You can only use the back pages," she says, still eyeing me with suspicion. She hesitantly hands it to me, along with a pen that has "fuck off" printed on the side in block letters instead of a company logo. Maybe we do have more in common than I thought; I need one of these pens for myself.

I glance at my watch to make sure I have enough time before I'm due to pick up my nephew then flip to an empty page near the back and quickly start sketching the house. Tex tries to peek at what I'm doing so I raise the notebook a couple inches and turn my body slightly. I get an overexaggerated sigh and an eye roll in response. I smile and sketch faster, moving around the space to make sure I'm somewhat accurate despite my speed. I get lost in my drawing, putting more attention to the details and changes Tex seems most excited about.

"Shut the fuck up, you're an artist?" she breathes, having snuck up behind me and peered around my elbow. "This is amazing, West. Is that Zero?!"

I grin and finish the last few details. "Is this what you're picturing?" I ask, handing her the notebook.

"Yessssss," she whispers, walking backward until she's at the spot where the floating deck will go.

She holds the notebook up as she closely examines the details I've added. The deck that will go where she is standing will be an octagon, which will be more work for me but will absolutely be worth it. I know Kelly down at the hardware store has a friend that makes amazing custom fire pits, so the one I drew has tall pine trees within an outline of the state border. A wine bottle with two glasses sits on a simple driftwood table with two chairs on either side.

Tex's eyes dart between the notebook and the house as she walks slowly toward the existing deck where I've drawn the soaking tub she described with Zero laying next to it. I've added a privacy wall that's actually a narrow raised planter along the edge of the deck by the tub with seagrass extending the height. I also added an outdoor shower around the corner with stone steps that lead from the deck, a simple swinging door with a towel rack on the inside.

"West, this is it, you see what's in my brain, holy shit," Tex looks at me, her eyes bright and happy once again. "Can I keep this?"

I breathe a sigh of relief. She scared me earlier, and although I told her I'd pretend I didn't witness her panic attack, that look in her eyes is still with me, much like her red-rimmed eyes from the first night I met her. She might be all sunshine on the outside, but there's something softer, more vulnerable, that she keeps hidden. I curse myself for wanting to know that softer side. Needing to know.

Walk away, keep your distance. You've brought enough people down.

She's not for me. No one is for me.

Excuse yourself and walk away, asshole.

But what comes out of my mouth is not that at all.

"If you don't mind Colt tagging along, I have time to walk the rest of the properties with you," I offer. "Make sure we're on the same page for my part of the work. I'll need to take some pictures and measurements anyway. I can get a few more sketches for you, too."

Her eyes light up and I'm done. Fucking done.

***

Colt is, of course, ecstatic to go on a walk with Tex and Zero. He is completely obsessed with both of them. He hilariously slowed his pace yesterday, going so far as to drag his feet, when we walked past her house on the way to The Mercantile, hoping she or the dog would magically appear outside so he'd have an excuse to stop. He's also taken to randomly peering across the path to Avery's grandmother's house in case they show up over there again. Apparently I am not the only Conrad man that can't act normal around Tex.

We pass by Tex's cottage and head straight for Grandma Georgie's old house so Tex can see the raised beds and planters I finished just a couple hours ago. She makes a list in her notebook of planter dimensions to take to the nursery, claiming she will need all the help she can get to keep plants alive. Colt informs her that gardens are green and

42

have greenhouses, so that means that the actual house should be green; they compromise with Tex promising to paint the front door green.

"The Green Door Garden!" Tex says suddenly. "Colt, you just inspired the name of the house, how about that? I hope y'all help me find inspiration at the next couple of houses, too."

He grins widely at her, dimples showing, and they happily hop, skip, and jump down the road together. They play "I spy" on the short walk and Colt is constantly touching her hand or leaning into her side. She takes it in stride, ruffling his hair and playing tag. I sketch a quick flower garden as we walk, remembering some of the details from when Grandma Georgie spent the summer here my first year in town.

We pass by The Glass House and Tex gives it a side-eyed glare; apparently she hasn't forgiven the house for her panic attack. Although it might have helped me gain a tiny sliver of her trust, I don't think I've forgiven it either.

There isn't much work to be done at the house on the golf course, a few steps need to be replaced but the rest will be up to Tex. I take a few pictures of the garage, honing in on a dusty corner that could fairly easily be turned into a surfboard rack with wetsuit storage as well.

Tex is quieter on the way up North Road. Colt races ahead with Zero as she walks silently beside me. I'm still fighting the urge to comfort her in any way I can. I want to reach for her hand or tuck her into my side. The memory of her curled around herself makes my breaths come more quickly and I clench my fists. She senses the change in my demeanor and gives me an uncertain look. Before I can break the silence and find a way to reassure her, she breaks into a jog.

"Last one there is a rotten egg!" she shouts, taking off up the road.

She catches up to Colt within seconds and swings him onto her back. They bounce their way to Eldon's old house and disappear up the driveway.

I find them around back, Tex and Zero standing together, staring out at the dunes that lead to the beach. Colt runs my way to ask if he can go to the beach with Tex. Zero watches me with what feels like judgment but Tex is still staring toward the ocean, lost in thought. I can see her left hand fidgeting. I give Colt my permission and he takes off as fast as his little legs can carry him, Zero racing along with him. Tex jogs over to give me a key and asks me to look around for repairs, then she chases the tireless duo down the path.

If I could have any house in this village, Eldon's is it. To most, it's just another beach house. The massive fireplace is the best part of the house and I could see myself having my morning coffee in those chairs by the windows on a cold winter morning, just enjoying the quiet solitude. Tall, healthy trees surround the yard and now that Colt is living with me, I picture a treehouse hidden amongst them. Eldon had taken up woodworking after retiring and had drawn up plans for a shop beyond the garage. We talked about building furniture during the winter months. He died a week later.

I'm not thrilled with the house being turned into a rental but I do think that Eldon would appreciate families getting to enjoy time together at his coastal retreat. He had been half hermit, half family man. Gruff, slow to open up to strangers, but strong in his morals and loyal to his family. The only time I heard him laugh was when he was with his granddaughter, who's a couple of years older than Colt.

I don't see anything that needs repaired on my quick tour, Eldon kept the house in immaculate shape. Instead, I sketch what caught my eye when I walked up the driveway: Tex standing in profile, loyal dog at her side, wind in her hair, looking toward the ocean waves, hand fidgeting. I don't know why I draw her, or why I leave it for her to find. I use a page in the middle of the notebook, knowing it will take her longer to find.

"Those are the perfect trees for a treehouse," Tex says from behind me and I quickly turn the page, suddenly feeling guilty. "Running down to the beach with Colt and Zero made me realize this would be the perfect summer house or full-time home for a family. But also, I want to drink my coffee in the chairs by the windows and make s'mores in the fireplace during the winter. Enjoy the quiet, you know? It just doesn't feel like a rental, it feels like a home and I can't even put my finger on why. I barely have any changes, but can you draw it anyway? I like your sketches more than pictures."

44

I'm not all that surprised she mentions a treehouse, she seems like the treehouse kind. But her comment on the quiet, that does surprise me. She has once again thrown me off. I don't mention the sketch I just finished, instead I just give her a smile and nod.

"Uncle West, I'm hungry," Colt interrupts.

"Let's stop by the last house on the way home, bud, then we'll have a snack. I'll finish the drawings back home." I raise my eyebrows at Tex, silently asking if that's alright with her.

"Only one house left, my man, we can do it!" She takes Colt's hand and they play 'Simon Says' on the walk back toward my house. 'Simon' demands more ridiculous actions by the minute and Tex is doubled over laughing as she tries to comply with "Simon Says to tiptoe on one foot and whistle at the same time." Colt never has this much fun with me.

The final house is just a few doors down from my own and Tex stands in the living room spinning in a slow circle. I can see her brain turning the space over.

"I see a girls' weekend, wine on the front porch swing, a small fire pit out back. A bookshelf with romance novels, puzzles, and board games. Houseplants, a whole shelf of them in that corner that gets the most light. A basket of journals where you can write something for the next guest. Slippers, robes, and face masks," she writes quickly in the notebook. "Pink everywhere. Barbie, but less. Or more?"

"That sounds boring," Colt grumbles. I'm not going to say it out loud but I agree. I can admit that it would be an amazing way to draw in renters though.

"You're right, pal, super boring, we should get out of here," Tex says with a smile, not a bit bothered by his comment.

We part ways at the corner, Colt giving Tex a quick hug before nearly strangling Zero with a chokehold hug. I stand awkwardly, unsure what to say. I promised I wouldn't mention the panic attack, but I also want to make sure she's really okay.

"Hey, West," Tex breaks the silence. She reaches her hand out timidly, lays it on my forearm, and looks me in the eyes. "Thank you. For all of today. Thank you."

I can see she doesn't want me to say anything else, so I give her a smile and a small nod, then follow Colt up the stone path to my house. I turn back at the door to watch as Tex walks down the street, her dog glued to her side. Her posture is tired and when she turns back and catches me watching, she just gives me a shrug.

Chapter Five
Harper

Sitting on the floor in front of the fireplace with Zero stretched out next to me, I force myself to put my notebook and "don't be a dick" pen aside. I've been focused on work all day, which I love, but on my road trip up here I had perhaps too much time to ponder the direction my life was headed. I decided that I would spend at least fifteen minutes in the morning and fifteen minutes every night for self-reflection. It's good to have goals, right?

No, I don't know what self-reflection really means or why I thought it was a good idea. Well, I do know why. I'm great at a few things: helping other people, getting shit done, and avoiding feelings. Unfortunately my expertise in avoiding feelings hasn't helped my anxiety (exhibit A: panic attack a few days ago) and also left me in a relationship for approximately four months past its expiration date (exhibit B: Ethan). It's time to face the facts. And feelings.

My beach walks the last few mornings have been like therapy, only cheaper, colder, and sandier. The ocean waves, my happy dog, the cold fucking fog. Morning reflection, check.

It's been harder at night to shut my brain off after I've been working all day. Instead of quiet self-reflection, I find myself comparing kitchenware prices, researching new vendors for The Mercantile, looking up rentals all over the coast, emailing local farmsteads, and writing lists upon lists while I pace my small cottage. I'm so excited about my job, more excited than I've been about any job before, but it's time to rein it in and refocus a bit.

I look down at Zero's head resting on my thigh and realize I've been rubbing my scar. It's on the inside of my ring finger, not too noticeable to others but it's all I can see when I look at my hand. That fucking scar.

Avery thinks it's from a ring. She spent the two years after I moved checking every male high school student's hand for any sort of ring. She had wanted me to go to the police, my parents, school staff, really anyone. I refused. There was no way for me to identify who had hurt me. I just wanted to forget.

That didn't happen.

It's about time I did something I told myself I'd do years ago: turn it into something I want, not something that happened to me. I use a fresh page to write a list, yes I freaking love lists, of the things that calm my mind, hoping an idea magically comes to me.

*morning beach walks
*coffee on the deck
*ocean waves
*time with friends
*reading
*Zero snuggles
*knitting
*lists
*puzzles
*cross-stitch

According to this list, I'm actually seventy-six years old, not twenty-six years old.

I rub my thumb over the jagged, uneven line again. It's definitely past time for me to take the scar back for myself but, unfortunately, the list didn't help. It also didn't count as self-reflection. Or did it?

No. It didn't. So I choose meditation. Or at least an attempt at meditation. Zero nudges my hand and I stroke her soft ears as I breathe slowly.

breathe in two three four, hold two three four, out two three four

I close my eyes and see the ocean at low tide, gentle waves, the wind moving through beach grass.

breathe in two three four, hold two three four, out two three four

It might be two minutes, it might be twenty minutes. Evening reflection, check.

It must work, at least a little, because I dream of ocean waves washing ashore in a steady rhythm.

***

I've decided that working for your best friend can actually be more terrifying than working for anyone else. Kelsey, the amazing college-bound employee, Marabelle, the current-but-unhappily-so manager, and I worked all day yesterday at The Mercantile, preparing for this meeting. We passed my laptop back and forth, drank an alarming amount of caffeine, and consumed too much sugar in the form of new recipes Marabelle was testing. I soaked up all the information they could give me. This presentation isn't just for me, if it goes well then Kelsey and Marabelle will have new job titles by this afternoon. I also can't let Avery down after all she's done for me, especially at our very first Friday morning meeting.

"Okay, so I know you asked for a rental remodel plan with a budget, and I'll get to that in a minute." I shove papers around Avery's coffee table, once again wishing I was slightly more organized. I grab what I'm looking for and hold it up triumphantly. "But first, we are bringing back the summer events of our childhood! We'll kick it off in…oh shit, in a week, with a Memorial Day weekend community bonfire. The Town Mercantile will be the official host to kick off the season. I've talked to Sarah at the cafe and John down at the golf course, I'm waiting to hear back from Brian over at the fire station. If we have different hosts for the bonfire each week, it makes them super easy to manage. Hosting just means providing the firewood and s'mores, a few activities if you're up for it. Super easy. Dealer's choice.

"Also, we have three major events to put together. First is the Fourth of July celebration, which I know we can bring back full force. Parade, sandcastles, fireworks, the whole shebang," I say, unable to read the expression on Avery's face. Was she always this intimidating and I just didn't realize? This must be her lawyer face. I continue my spiel. "I'm thinking of a Block Party Bash at the beginning of August, I just need to talk John into hosting it down at the golf course. We'll pull something together for Labor Day, maybe a Farewell Summer party, combined with major beach clean up, and we're done for the season."

Giant. Silent. Pause.

My thumb moves to my scar.

"I freaking love it," Avery breaks her silence, taking the poster from my hand. "You really took my whole 'save the town' thing and went for it."

"Kelsey is creative, so she made the mock poster and she's helping me with social media, because I hate all that bullshit and I know you do, too," I say, feeling encouraged. "Kels also showed me this viral TikTok about some girl building a tiny home and it gave me the idea to document the remodels as we get them going. I sent you a demo video that we made last night at my cottage, just with the deck work and a few changes inside. But that way you can watch us transform The Glass House from a glass shoe box to a romantic getaway, The Green Door Garden from piles of dirt into a bright, beautiful garden. I mean, assuming the local nursery can help me keep plants alive."

Avery laughs, having seen my black thumb at work over the years.

"I was thinking we'd also do different options for welcome baskets or experiences once the rentals are open. In general, we'd have a s'mores welcome basket no matter what. Those homemade marshmallows we had the other night were ah-freaking-mazing, I'd sell my soul for those. But if someone is coming into town with family, they can do the Family Experience, which adds in a round of golf, SUP rentals in Rock Beach, hiking maps, and popcorn and selection of candy for a movie night. Maybe I can come up with a few scavenger hunts around the village for preteens, just all the fun stuff we used to do as kids, but for our guests! Give them the real Three Rocks experience. The Romantic Getaway would include a Seascapes Spa couples massage, dinner reservations at River House, it'd be like a combo gift-slash-welcome basket and also concierge service. You can just rent our awesome houses *or* you can have a whole experience without trying to organize it from afar. It'd help guests that are coming from out of state, who want the real

50

coast experience but don't know where to start...." I trail off, realizing I've been talking super fast.

"No, keep going, I'll save questions for the end," Avery encourages, shuffling through my disorganized stack of papers. She finds West's drawing of The Glass House and studies it with a smile.

"Okay, well, I printed out a plan for each rental with remodel costs, our target renter, estimated timelines, etcetera. I'm still pricing out some of the add-ons we can do, talking to other businesses about package deals to offer, but the actual remodel details are already there," I tell her. I'm so nervous, I just need to shut up. I can't remember the last time I was this excited about anything in my life, let alone a job. "West and I walked the properties and they're in better shape than you'd think; the ones that are furnished won't take much work at all. Like this one, the golf course house, it's basically ready to go after a few steps are replaced, the yard gets wrangled into submission, and I do some shopping for kitchen essentials, bunks, and bedding. In the timeline, I put the ones that need the least amount of work first, that way we can get a couple rentals going as soon as June 10th, assuming I paint fast enough. That gets us, well, you, some income to offset all your money I'm spending." I hand Avery the tentative timeline and budget and she nods as her eyes scan the page.

"Tex, stop with the nervous bullshit. This is amazing. This is exactly what I needed, you to come in and rock the heck out of this so I can sit in my cabin and work, emerging only to run, test your cooking skills, and make s'mores with you," Avery says, flipping through the pages on The Green Door Garden. "It sounds like you're going to be spending a lot of time over the next month on the rentals and community events though. How's The Merc holding up?"

"Okay, I've only been here a week, so I'm still getting a handle on that. Kelsey has really been running the store for you, even though Marabelle is supposed to be managing while I get my feet under me. The design ideas that Kels sent me for the next round of apparel are amazing. I'm unsure how she finished school early, basically runs the store, and helps West with Colt. She's only eighteen years old and she's really got her shit together. She took my social media idea and ran with it. The reel for the cottage is great, she made me look like both a badass and hilariously helpless." I'm not sure how Avery is going to react to what I'm about to suggest, she's loved all my ideas so far this morning, so here goes nothing. "I think we need to reorganize your empire."

"Empire?" Avery snorts, finally looking up at me and setting the stack of papers back on the table.

"So we have The Mercantile as a store, the coffee shop within, the rentals not only as remodels but then managing them, community outreach events, and social media for all. Marabelle's strength is the coffee shop. She's an amazing baker and she was showing me ideas for new pastries, seasonal offerings, even new sandwiches and more premade items. Also, I'd die happy if she made my latte every morning. If we set her loose with only that on her plate, not the rest of the store manager duties, I think it'd take off even more and she'd be much happier."

Avery hums, nodding her head slowly. Her long fingers tap the side of her coffee mug and I can see the wheels turning in her head.

"Kelsey loves her hours at the Mercantile because she's a people person, so I'm not going to take that away from her, but she is more of an asset when it comes to apparel and social media," I continue. "So that leaves me with the rentals, which, with this 'experience' plan, will hopefully be a big fucking job at least during summer months, as well as overseeing the community events, and working side-by-side with Kelsey on social media contect. Oh, and Mercantile manager."

"Okaaayyy," Avery says, drawing out the word as she contemplates my ideas. "So if we go all in on this and everything goes as planned, you're going to get overwhelmed fast."

"Well, yeah. But really, it would basically just be moving Marabelle to full-time coffee shop duties, one new hire that is at least close to full-time, two new part-timers for rush hours at The Merc, and then Kelsey and I sharing everything else. She wants to work a lot of hours this summer before heading off to college, I really think we can handle it and she's fully on board. She's mature for her age and I'm immature for mine, it'll be like there's two of me." I complete one of the worst sales pitches of my life with a wince.

52

Avery raises her eyebrow at me. "Two of you? I can't even handle one of you most of the time. This could either be the start of your world domination or the end of times."

I laugh, loving this mood Avery is in. Something is up with her, she just hasn't let me in on her secret yet, I just know it. It's more than me taking this off her plate, I can't quite put my finger on it though.

"Avery, I love you, but you want me to remodel half a dozen houses and manage a store, two things I've never done, and also save an entire town. I mean it's a tiny town, but still, save an entire town. And then manage the rentals when they're done. I also think we could expand the gift basket idea to The Merc. I'd love to support other small businesses and local farms. Farm-to-Mercantile baskets with fresh flowers and vegetables that you can pick up when you get to town. Mix and match farmstand goods, leaving the farmers more time to work and the consumer gets one-stop shopping." I hold my breath in anticipation.

"I love it. I love you and I love your ideas and I know you're going to kill it," my very supportive best friend says to me with a big smile. "Free rein, have at it. Your lack of organization will drive me crazy, but I trust you. Your ideas are amazing and I can't wait to see how it goes. Let's do this."

I crush her with a sideways couch hug, then we start to go through each rental, one at a time.

***

I freaking love a good plan. Now, to execute. I continue to start my days with the sun, or at least when the sun should rise as this is the Oregon Coast and most mornings are foggy and overcast. I roll out of my warm bed, grumble at Zero about the weather as I bundle up, then we head for the beach. An hour walking the shoreline, breathing in the salty air, letting the wind and waves drown out the thoughts in my head, catching sight of the bald eagles fishing in the waves, it's only the lure of hot coffee that brings me back to the cottage.

I'm spending my coffee time on Monday morning doing a little yoga on the deck, practicing my breathwork and focusing on my senses. Sitting cross-legged on my mat, I start with my breathing.

breathe in two three four, hold two three four, out two three four

I go through eight cycles before shifting my focus to my senses.

I hear the ocean waves crashing in the distance.

I feel the solid deck beneath me.

I smell what remains of my coffee mixed with salty sea air.

I see cute little bare feet appearing on the edge of my mat.

"Hi, my man, are you joining me for yoga this morning? Where's Uncle West?" I ask Colt.

I can't decide if I want to continue to avoid his uncle who, true to his word, pretended he didn't witness my panic attack, or if I want to suck it up and face him. I mean, we're going to cross paths, this town is tiny and we'll be working together on the rentals, I have to face him. I know I do. I can't avoid him forever.

I don't necessarily have to say "Hey, West, nice to see you. Thanks for helping me calm down after a weird noise sent me back in time to when I was sixteen, but don't worry, I'm a totally trustworthy person and definitely not crazy, your nephew is for sure safe hanging around with me." Maybe step one is to stop actively avoiding him. Time to put my self-reflection to work.

The truth is, I have never recovered from a panic attack that quickly, and while I'm telling myself it's the morning beach walks and perhaps general exhaustion, I'm pretty sure his solid, steady presence helped the most.

I guess I don't really have a choice, I'm about to find out how my anxiety reacts to seeing him again because I'm sure he isn't too far behind his nephew.

breathe in two three four, hold two three four, out two three four

"Whatcha doing? Can I do it, too? Uncle West said I could come over and wait two whole minutes with you until he gets here, but I ran really fast," Colt says, exaggerating his breathing to show just how fast he ran.

"I'm doing some things that help me have a better morning. I start with some special breathing and then I do yoga to stretch my body. Want to try?" I slide sideways on my mat as Colt worms his way in.

54

He immediately settles onto the mat next to me, squirming around until he's as close as possible to me without actually sitting in my lap. I've never met a kid so adorable.

"Okay, so whenever I'm having a hard time, like I'm sad or mad, I do this with my breathing, ready?"

He solemnly nods, putting his hand in mine and inching even closer until his knobby knee presses into my thigh.

"We blow all our air out, then we slowly breathe in as we count to three, then we hold still and count to three again, then we slowly blow air out while we count to three one last time. Like this." I overemphasize my breathing as I show him, choosing three seconds because shouldn't a kid have less lung capacity? "Breathe in two three, hold two three, out two three."

Colt watches me closely then matches my breathing next time through. His seriousness is adorable, I can't help but bite my lip to hide my smile. I give his little hand a squeeze and he squeezes back. We do two more big breaths before he gets wiggly. It's definitely time to move around.

"Am I interrupting something?" West asks from the bottom of the steps, looking pointedly at Colt's hand in mine.

My heart jumps at the sight of him, at that almost smile behind his newly-trimmed beard, and since when do I get butterflies in my stomach? I guess this is how my anxiety is reacting, with fucking butterflies. Better than with another panic attack, but this is definitely not ideal.

"We are doing yoga breathing stretches. I'm really good at it," Colt says excitedly, scrambling off the yoga mat and jumping off the edge of the deck. "And now we can all go get special hot chocolate together!"

West raises his eyebrows at me in silent question. There's a war happening inside me. I want to keep my walls up, retreat to my safe zone, but West's smile combined with Colt's excitement is pulling me away.

"Well, I do need to share some things with Kelsey, so I'll walk over there with you, but Zero has to stay home since this is a work meeting," I say, keeping my eyes on bouncing Colt. He's halfway down the block by the time I have my boots on.

***

"I feel ridiculous, Kelsey," I moan dramatically as I stand barefoot on the kitchen counter of the newly dubbed "Breakers Bliss" house.

Our girls' weekend getaway is getting a fresh coat of paint in the kitchen and Kelsey has decided to document our girls-only crew getting it ready. Avery doesn't want to be on camera so she's the one filming this very bad idea. Kelsey is about to throw a paintbrush, *with* pink paint on it, across the kitchen for me to catch as I balance on the narrow counter. We're painting the inside of a few cabinets with pink chalkboard paint. There will be a mason jar of chalk inside the cabinet so guests can leave messages to the next girl gang staying with us. Our cleaning crew, AKA me, will make sure they aren't too offensive before new guests arrive.

Kelsey and I have bright pink snapback hats that say "BREAKERS" on the front, thanks to a rush order from Rock Beach Custom Apparel, which will be included in each welcome basket and not for sale anywhere else. Kelsey also drew a heart on my cheek with the paint and left a pink chalk handprint on my camera-side back pocket. She painted my toenails pink during our lunch break meeting to prepare for these shenanigans. At this point, I'm lucky my hair isn't pink. The girl is all-in on her social media manager duties and I am here for it.

Kelsey nimbly climbs onto the counter across from me and Avery gives us a nod. Kels dips her paintbrush in the can and tosses it my way. Miraculously I catch the handle and make a swipe on the inside of the cabinet before winking at the camera.

"Got it!" Avery exclaims, obvious surprise in her voice. "I don't know how you pulled that off, but here it is." She's shaking her head in disbelief, a very Avery move.

Kelsey and I hop down from our respective counters and stand on either side of Aves, watching the video. Kels shimmies her shoulders, unable to contain her excitement. She is going to grow up to be unstoppable, I can just tell.

"Yes! I can work with that!" Kelsey squeals, smiling ear to ear. "Okay, Team Merc, next is Tex jumping on the bed, then I'll grab a few pics and get the reel ready for you guys to approve."

I happily jump on the bed, do a flip, and end up sprawled in the middle of the comforter. Kelsey approves, has me do another for slow motion, then kicks Avery and I out so she can take some pictures and finish the pink paint.

"I love that girl already," I tell Avery as we walk toward The Mercantile, shoulder to shoulder. "She's like the little sister I never knew I wanted. We went for a run on Saturday and I saw her last night with Colt down on the beach. Are we sure she's only eighteen? She seems older."

"She's lived here her whole life, it's just her and her mom, I don't know a thing about her dad or if he was ever in the picture. Kelsey never mentions him. You know how many people live here in the winter, it's not many, and most are older adults. She grew up in an adult world so she's not your average teenager. She's headed to Oregon State in the fall so don't get too attached. Good afternoon, Betty!" Avery calls to an elderly woman sitting on her porch between my cottage and The Merc.

"Hello, Avery, so lovely to see you. Who is your friend?" Betty calls back, sounding very proper.

"Hi, I'm Tex, I grew up in the valley with Avery, we've been best friends since we were six," I say, heading up the walkway to introduce myself. "Oh my gosh, you knit, too?!"

After Avery introduced me around town as Tex, I just went with it. She used to be the only one to call me that, but now I guess fresh start, fresh name? Also, Kels claims our followers will love it especially combined with my accent, which isn't really an accent, seeing as how I grew up here in Oregon. I just learned when to add a twang, usually to tease Emmy, my Texas best friend, and her husband Patrick.

"Well, I'll be, you know how to knit?" Betty asks, squeezing my hand.

"I didn't bring my needles with me but if you have spare, I'd love to stop by one evening this week and we can knit together," I tell her, excited at the prospect. Because, again, apparently I'm seventy-six years old. "I don't know how to follow patterns but I love to knit hats; I used to donate them to Dell Children's Hospital back in Austin."

"I would just love that, Miss Tex. You come by any time and I'll be out here with extra yarn and needles," Betty tells me, smiling and giving my hand another squeeze.

"I can't believe you knit," Avery mutters as we walk back to the street. "What are you, seventy?"

"It's calming," I say in retort. "You're just mad because you never figured out how to do it even though I tried teaching you a dozen times. Also, it was *your* grandma that taught us to cross stitch. That's a seventy-year-old hobby for sure."

"Key word there, Tex, is grandma," Avery says, laughter in her voice. She has a point.

We make it back to The Mercantile and check in with Marabelle, making sure she's ready for what we are hoping will be a busy Memorial Day weekend. She gives me an updated list of bakery items she'll have ready and we spend a few minutes in the cooler making sure we have all the ingredients she will need. Based on her list, I will gain a minimum of five pounds by next week. Taking away most of her store duties and leaving her with just the coffee shop has already elevated her baking (and happiness) to a new level.

The week flies by in a blur of work and fun: interior painting at a different rental each day, sticky note lists left all over town, early Mercantile shifts, making a goofy gardening video with Zero's assistance, kitchenware and linen orders, chasing Colt up Rejection Rock at low tide when Kelsey is babysitting, hiring two new employees, and meeting more of the town's summer residents as they trickle in before the holiday weekend.

As promised, I stop to knit with Betty, who introduces me to every single person that walks by. Her house is on the corner near the bridge which means that most of the town's residents walk past her house at some point during their stay, so she knows nearly everyone. I had taken her for a sweet old lady, a grandmotherly sort, but that was absolutely a false first impression.

58

"Tex moved to town after leaving her rodeo clown fiance back in Austin. If you find a big ol' engagement ring near the creek, it's probably because she flung it in during the first high tide she was here," she tells the first passerby, an older man named Tom who's carrying a metal detector. "He's a real piece of work," she tells me after he walks away. I bite the inside of my cheek to stop from laughing.

"If you see any paparazzi in town, it's just because Tex's ex-boyfriend is a famous actor, he's trying to win her back," she informs a middle-aged couple whose names I immediately forget. Their eyes fly to me and I give a modest shrug, hoping to play into Betty's game. She seems to be having a grand time with this. Who am I to dampen an old lady's fun?

"She's hiding from her ex-husband, he's in the mafia." The mafia, great.

"Her great-grandfather invented salt water taffy." Apparently great-gramps was alive and making candy in the 1800s.

"Her ex-fiance mysteriously disappeared, never to be heard from again." Wait, did she just insinuate that I killed a guy?

"She sold her sex toy business, made millions!" I about lose it at that one, as does the mom carrying an infant that's blessed with that scoop.

A family with three blonde kids is told that I'm a descendant of One-Eyed Willy, the pirate from The Goonies.

I can't wait until these stories catch up to me over the next few weeks as I'm sure they will. Despite Betty's wild stories, everyone I meet is welcoming and happy to meet Zero and I. They're all excited about the upcoming community bonfire and eager to hear about our other summer events. I almost feel like I have a handle on things. It's a good feeling.

Chapter Six
West

I chase Colt toward the rock, splashing in the low tide waves as we race, knowing I only have an hour left until I have to get to the shop. Mrs. G offered to watch Colt while I have back-to-back clients. Both already have their designs and are repeat customers so it should be an easy day before the Community Bonfire that's been advertised all around town. You can't walk a block without seeing a poster advertising the event stapled to a power pole or someone's gate.

I'm curious to see what Tex and Avery have pulled together on such short notice. Usually I'm content to sit on my deck and avoid any gatherings, not that there have been any recently, but chatter around town has piqued my interest. I also want to support Avery, who has been a good friend to me over the last couple of years. It has nothing to do with seeing her best friend.

Although I'm pretty sure she's been trying her hardest to avoid me since her panic attack, I've seen Tex around town beyond the "yoga breathing stretches" with Colt. She's been busy putting up fliers, knitting with the eccentric elderly lady who always tries to sneak Colt candy, running with Avery and Kelsey, and carrying paint cans and ladders into the rentals. Everywhere I look, she's there. She also continues to be the one person Colt wants to see every day. Same, bud. Same.

I've also happened to stumble upon a few of the social media accounts they've put together for the new rentals and upcoming town events. The video with Zero digging in the planters at The Green Door Garden is Colt's favorite, especially when the dog carries flowers to Tex who claps her hands and the garden magically transforms into the finished state.

The accounts seem to have grown at a rapid rate, I should ask her if she'd like to do some marketing for my shop. I have to be smarter with my time since I have Colt to consider, appointments over walk-ins, and I bet social media would help get my name out to the tourists.

A sand volleyball game is happening between the creek and the dunes, the net moving slightly in the wind. Shouts and cheers can be heard above the crashing of the waves against the rocks. The ball bounces our way and Colt gives chase but is overtaken by a blur in a gray flannel. Colt is suddenly airborne, lifted up and swung around, eliciting a shriek followed by a giggle.

"Tex!" he hollers, delighted. She gives him an extra hug and ruffles his hair as she sets him down gently, holding out her hand for a fist bump before she grabs the ball.

I glimpse a flash of neon bikini under the flannel but then she's gone, running back to the game. I look down and realize both Colt and I are staring after her.

"Oh, have you met Avery's friend, Tex?" Tom somehow managed to sneak up on me with his metal detector in hand, headphones draped around his neck. A part-time resident with wild bushy eyebrows, I cannot recall ever seeing him without either a beat-up paperback book or his metal detector. At least he seems to have kicked the smoking habit.

"Tom, nice to see you." I shake the hand that he offers and give him a nod.

"She's going to do great things for this town if she doesn't run off too quickly. I heard she left her fiance back in Texas, up and left without telling him. Threw the ring in the creek as soon as she got here. What kind of man lets a woman like that go?" he asks, shaking his head. A fucking moron, if you ask me. Which I guess technically Tom just did.

"Tom!" Tex hollers from the makeshift volleyball court. "Are you telling lies about me again? He wasn't a rodeo clown and I'm still holding out for you!"

Tom and I both laugh but then I'm left wondering if there really was a non-rodeo-clown fiance. For some reason that irks me, not that she

62

would have left him, but that he existed in the first place. Tom claps me on the back and continues along the waterline on the hunt for lost trinkets, or perhaps engagement rings.

The alarm on my phone blares, cutting those thoughts short and telling me it's time to head back.

"Let's go, bud, Mrs. G said you guys were going to make cookies this afternoon while I go to work. I'll be home in time for the bonfire, I triple promise," I tell Colt to convince him to leave the beach. He's learned that regular promises aren't always kept and now demands double and triple promises when things are important. He looks longingly toward Tex and the volleyball game and then trudges back toward me. I feel ya, bud, I really do.

***

The bell above the door jingles just as I'm cashing out my last appointment of the afternoon.

"One sec!" I call, handing Kelly her receipt. She owns the hardware store so we know each other fairly well. "See you in a couple hours then?" I ask. Tex invited her to the bonfire earlier in the week.

"Since when are you so enthusiastic about hanging out with people?" she asks suspiciously. "There *will* be people there, right?"

"Just trying to help Avery out," I answer, trying to sound nonchalant. She gives me a hard look but doesn't comment further.

I check my watch, eager to pick Colt up and take him to the bonfire, and perhaps also a little eager to catch another few minutes with Tex. That goddamn neon bikini has haunted me all afternoon.

I walk around the corner to the front of the shop with Kelly, ready to tell whomever walked in that we'll have to schedule them for another time.

"Surprise!" Jessie exclaims and grabs me in a hug before I can react. I give her a solid squeeze, despite being confused as fuck. This *is* a fucking surprise, considering I haven't seen my sister in over three weeks, when, you know, she left her child with me and promised to be back by week's end.

Kelly sees my expression and gives me a wide-eyed look as she skirts around us and out the front door, closing it gently behind her.

"Hi, sis, what are you doing here?" I ask, trying and failing to put some warmth into my voice. I'm confused, frustrated, and also worried about how Colt will react when he sees her. If he sees her? Again, what the fuck is she doing here?

"Well, I wanted to surprise you with a visit and Derek doesn't work this weekend so here we are," she says hurriedly, like she's trying to get the words out before she loses courage.

Wait. Derek?

"Hey man, I'm Derek." A skinny, dark-haired guy holds his hand out to me. I didn't even realize he was there. I shake his hand, an automatic response, as he barely looks at me, turning to Jessie instead. "Babe, you ready? I thought we were getting dinner and going to the hotel."

"Hotel? You're not here to see Colt and stay with me?" I ask darkly, glaring at both of them.

"Of course we're coming to see Colt! I just told Derek we'd grab dinner at Mo's first, then we were driving past your shop so I thought we should stop in to, you know, let you know we'd see you for a bit tonight," Jessie says, avoiding eye contact.

A bit? See us for a bit? Really? What I see is rage. Can you see rage? I can right fucking now. This is why I moved out here, I can't handle this again. But after spending three weeks being the only parental figure Colt has, I also can't *not* handle this.

"Okay, well, I'm closing shop for the day. Colt is really excited for the community bonfire tonight, so that's where we will be," I tell her flatly. I grab my keys and head for the door. I'm going to need to calm the fuck down before I pick Colt up and try to figure out what to tell him about this visit with his mom.

"Maybe we'll see you later," Douchebag Derek says, walking out without waiting for Jessie.

Maybe?

"West, wait," my sister says, grabbing my arm as I move to follow him out. I wait, gritting my teeth. "I'm sorry. I can tell you're mad. I should have called. I just figured you'd think it was an empty promise. We'll be there, at the bonfire. I swear."

64

I give her a sad smile, put my arm around her shoulder and walk her outside. I lock the door slowly, giving myself a few seconds to calm down. It almost works. I give Jessie a real hug and she leans into me, burying her face in my chest and taking a deep, steadying breath. I'm almost expecting tears when she pulls away, but she just gives me a quick look that I can't decipher and follows Derek around to the back lot.

It's only a twenty minute drive home but I spend every second of it debating how to handle Jessie's possible visit. Should I tell Colt that we might see her? What about that douchebag? How would I explain that his mom isn't staying with us? Is she actually going to show up in the first place? Fuck. I'm not cut out for this. It was much easier an hour ago when I was wrestling with my feelings about Tex, my coworker and acquaintance. Coworker, that's what I'll call her. I can't handle anything other than Colt at the moment.

***

Colt can barely sit still to eat dinner and his excitement about the community bonfire is contagious. I haven't told him that his mom stopped by, a decision I might regret, but he's so happy at the moment that I just want to let it ride. He gestures wildly, nearly falling off his chair, as he tells me about the cookies he made with Mrs. G. He asks if I think Zero will be at the bonfire, how many s'mores he's allowed to have, and if jellyfish would be able to fly if they didn't live in the ocean. His questions get wilder and wilder until he catches the giggles and can't ask any more. I'm laughing to myself as I clean up the pasta dishes, happy that Colt is happy. Whatever may come tonight, we've done well together the last few weeks.

I finally give in and we head down to the beach early to run off some of his energy. Kelsey is helping Tex get the bonfire going but I steer clear. I see some of the summer locals that live on my street and walk over to say hello, keeping Colt in my sights. He's already found a couple kids to play with and they have a bucket that they're filling with beach treasures. Every once in a while one of them holds up a shell or rock and they all exclaim over it.

As I talk with Carl about helping him get his dory boat back on the water, I see Colt freeze. I follow his gaze and see Jessie and

Douchebag Derek walking down the beach. I quickly excuse myself and jog in Colt's direction.

"Hi, honey, you look like you're having so much fun," I hear Jessie say. She has tears in her eyes as she kneels down and opens her arms for a hug.

Colt bolts. Flat out, straight up, *bolts*. Fuck. I should have told him.

"Stay here," I order Jessie, using my big brother, no-nonsense voice.

I take off after Colt. I catch him just as he flops down on the sand by the creek. I sit next to him, grabbing a few rocks and sticks that the waves washed up. I hand him a rock and then throw another in the creek. He copies me. I hand him another. And another.

"I don't want to leave," Colt says after throwing a dozen or so rocks into the water.

"She's just here to visit, bud. We are still trying to figure out some grown up things, but you're going to stay with me longer," I promise him.

Even though I have no legal rights, there is no fucking way I'm letting Jessie take him home, wherever that is these days, with Douchebag Derek involved. Something about that guy pisses me off. I don't trust him with my sister and definitely not with my nephew.

We sit and continue to throw rocks. I see someone approaching out of the corner of my eye and take a deep, calming breath. I remember the breathing that Tex taught Colt and wish I would have thought of it a few minutes ago. The rocks seem to have helped though.

"Hey, can I throw rocks, too?" Kelsey asks Colt, sitting down on his other side.

He silently hands her a rock and she skips it across the creek. She gives me a nod toward the bonfire, letting me know I can head back and deal with my sister. I bet Avery sent her, although Avery probably would have just come over herself. Huh.

"Hey, Colt, I'm going to talk to your mom, okay? See if Kelsey will teach you how to skip rocks," I say, smiling and mouthing "thank you" to Kelsey after Colt nods.

66

I ruffle Colt's hair as I stand, then try Tex's breathing trick as I make my way back toward the bonfire. I see Jessie and Douchebag Derek in the midst of the crowd, drinks in hand, chatting like Colt's heart wasn't just shattered. I don't think this breathing trick is going to cut it.

"I'm assuming you finished?" the douchebag snaps at my sister as I approach, looking at her drink. Her eyes widen at his tone and she freezes.

I can hear my blood pumping through my veins as adrenaline and rage take over my body. Why does she look so scared? Where the fuck did she find this dirtbag and why is he going to be spending any part of Memorial Day weekend with my nephew? My hands clench into fists as I take a step in his direction.

"Well *that's* not something you should assume." Tex's voice comes from behind me. "And if it *is* something you have to assume, you're absolutely doing it wrong."

I stop short as she steps up beside me, wild beach hair under a backwards Mercantile snapback, flannel and cut offs over her neon bikini. For all the time I spent considering that bikini today, it's the enraged look in her eyes that takes my breath away. The steely glint in her expression, the way she straightens to her full height, shoulders back, chin up. She lays a hand on my arm, stilling my anger. She has that don't-fuck-around energy about her.

It takes him a second to get her meaning, then his eyes narrow. Not only does he pause and take more than a second to peruse her body from head to toe, but he also takes a step toward her. I want to put my large body between them but Tex squeezes my arm. Her eyes flash in response to his attention and she takes a step forward, putting herself between me and the douchebag, releasing her death grip on my arm. I suck in a breath, unsure how this will play out. I hope Kelsey still has Colt down by the creek. Tex must have heard my inhale because she glances over her shoulder at me and gives me a wink.

"Don't. Just don't. I can already hear the names you're going to call me before grabbing her wrist, or, hell, maybe mine, and I am *done* with that bullshit. I suggest you take your small dick energy far, far away," Tex says to the irate-looking douchebag. She turns and offers her hand to my wide-eyed, silent sister. "Hi, I'm Tex, want to make s'mores and become new best friends and have a sleepover with my giant Doberman?"

"Jessie," my sister says quietly. She clears her throat. "I'm Jessie, nice to meet you."

She shakes Tex's hand, giving me a "wtf just happened" look. I grin. Jessie needs some of that don't-fuck-around energy.

"Welcome to my favorite place in the world, Jessie! Let's go get sticky," Tex says, looping her arm through Jessie's. Douchebag's snake-like eyes follow the two women and I clear my throat. He barely spares me a glance before he stalks off, pulling his keys out of his pocket.

Apparently I'm adding "drive Jessie home" to my list of things to do this weekend, which is a hell of a lot better than her spending another minute with that fucking asshole.

After making sure Colt is still with Kelsey, I drop into an empty chair in front of the bonfire. I scrub my hand down my face, still working through how to handle this whole weekend with my sister. Tex has obviously taken her in, maybe I should just grab Colt and head back to the house.

"Uncle West! Is it s'mores time?" Colt barrels into me with no warning. I pull him into my lap for a hug. Kelsey gives me a thumbs up and veers toward her mom, who sends a smile my way when she sees Colt gripping me tight.

"Sure, bud, let me get us the supplies, I'll be right back," I say, standing up and then setting him back in my chair. S'mores solve almost everything when it comes to him and he definitely needs one or two right now.

"Mom! Did Tex teach you how to make a s'more?" Colt spies Jessie and Tex across the fire.

He scrambles back off the chair and around the fire toward them. I guess throwing rocks worked. Tex's eyes widen and she looks at me before standing up and hurrying over, giving Colt a smile and a fist bump as she passes him. She waits until we are far enough away from everyone to not be overheard then turns and faces me head-on, nervous eyes locked on mine.

"Why didn't you tell me she was your sister? Is that why Colt looked upset? I sent Kelsey to check on y'all. Was that okay? Did I just make things worse? Was that Colt's dad? This is bad. Oh my God. Colt. Did he know his mom and dad were coming today? I'm so sorry. How do I ruin everything?" Tex bites her lip and if I could drag my eyes from hers, I know I'd see her left thumb rubbing her finger.

She's the one that sent Kesley to help with Colt. She's the one that stepped in and defended Jessie. She's the one who calmed my rage with a simple touch. Of fucking course. Seeing her this worried about my nephew after watching her defend my sister, my "acquaintance and coworker" feelings are struggling to hold their place.

"Hey, no, it's ok, you were amazing. That asshole wasn't Colt's dad. I promise it's okay. He was really just some douchebag that probably latched onto my sister and gave her like one compliment so she fell for his bullshit. You saved me from having to break his nose, but honestly, your comment about his assumptions on finishing might have been worse than any damage I could have done." I shake my head as I remember his expression. "Tex, I promise, you handled that perfectly. I hope Jessie remembers you standing up for her, and for yourself, too, because she needs that. It's complicated, but what you've given her in the last few minutes, just... thank you."

"Well, Colt is my favorite person in this town besides Aves, he's like my mini soulmate or maybe my dog's soulmate? I don't know, but what I'm trying to say is that he's the best, and so whatever is going on with his mom, I want what's best for her, too. Also, I might have a thing against assholes like that. He's lucky he didn't actually try to grab my wrist, he seems like the type." Her expression changes, just for a second. A flicker of darkness. "I'll stand up for Colt and Jessie any time, and you're welcome for saving your knuckles," she says with a wry grin. She smiles and then sticks her tongue out at Colt across the fire before heading in Avery's direction.

I shake my head as I watch her walk away, unsure I'll ever learn to keep up with her. I grab marshmallows, a roasting stick, graham crackers, and chocolate before heading back to Colt and Jessie.

Colt's in the chair Tex left open when she got up, not quite ready to sit with Jessie. He stands up when I hand him the roasting stick and expertly turns his marshmallow over the coals, furrowing his brow in concentration. I steal his chair and scoot closer to the fire in case he needs a hand. His marshmallow doesn't even come close to catching on fire.

"Just like Tex!" he exclaims proudly, pulling the marshmallow from the fire and turning to me, beaming. Hearing her name, Tex looks over at us, smiling. I feel my heart miss a beat.

"Good job, Colt!" she calls, giving him a thumbs up. He grins even wider.

Kids are resilient, that's for sure. I watch him lick his sticky fingers then suggest he help his mom make a s'more. My sister has tears in her eyes the whole time they share the roasting stick. She quickly wipes them away before Colt turns to hand her the s'more. There's a lump in my throat watching them together. Maybe the evening isn't a total loss.

After Colt has helped both of us make our s'mores, I tell him it's time to head home. He looks to the other side of the fire where Kelsey, Avery, and Tex are wrapped in a blanket together, laughing with Brian and his wife.

"Can I tell Tex goodbye first?" he asks.

"Go for it, bud," is barely out of my mouth before he's skipping over to the trio.

Tex winks at me as she scoops Colt up and flips him upside down. Kelsey tickles his sides, making him giggle and squirm in Tex's arms. When Tex finally sets him down, rightside up, Avery walks Colt back over to me.

"You okay?" Avery asks quietly, looking at Jessie behind me.

They met briefly last summer when Jessie brought Colt for a visit and it might have taken months, but Avery pulled the whole story from me, bit by bit. She was the first person I texted when Jessie left Colt with me and she showed up with special hot chocolate within fifteen minutes. She's a good friend, through and through.

"Yeah, we're good," I reply, giving her a tired smile.

70

"You know where I live; I'm here for all three of you," Avery tells me. "Anything you need, including midnight special hot chocolate, let me know."

A good friend indeed.

***

I wake up the next morning with a crick in my neck from sleeping on my couch. I insisted that Jessie take my bedroom, both because I'm a nice brother and also because I wanted to make sure that if Douchebag Derek made a surprise appearance, I'd be the first to know. I quietly make myself a cup of coffee and step onto the deck. The sun is shining this morning and there are a few people already on the beach, a telltale sign of a holiday weekend. I had planned on doing some walk-in hours at the shop this afternoon and am torn on if that's still a good idea. I know my sister is Colt's mom, but she left him with me for weeks. I want to make sure he's happy and feels safe and comfortable.

"G'morning," a quiet voice says, then a cold nose nudges me.

"Good morning, Tex. Hi, Zero," I say, leaning down to give Zero the scratches she demands. I give Tex a smile, drinking in her bright eyes, hair tangled from the wind. She always looks the happiest when she passes by my house after her morning beach walk. Her cheeks flush slightly under my gaze.

"I just saw you sitting out here and thought I'd ask if your sister was still here and if she wanted to hang out later? I got the feeling she had a bad experience with that asshole, sometimes it helps to have a friend that understands. Can you give her my number?" Tex asks, left hand fidgeting.

I feel immediate relief that Jessie, and therefore Colt, might get to hang out with Tex later, but there's a heaviness, too. That comment on understanding. I want to rewind and break Douchebag Derek's nose. And then find whoever hurt Tex and do the same.

"She said last night that you were pretty badass for standing up to a strange man like that. I'm sure she'd love to hang out," I reply.

There's a beat of awkward silence as we silently stare at each other. She seems to be sizing me up just as I am her.

"Great! I'm off to a morning shift at The Merc, maybe I'll see you around," she says abruptly, hopping off the deck.

I smile as I watch her and Zero walk away. I still can't figure her out. She presents herself to the world, or at least this town, as young, wild, and carefree. She charms everyone she meets from Colt to Betty, Kelsey to Tom. She's breathing life back into this town without breaking a sweat. She'll hand you a cinnamon roll and coffee with a smile, but if she winks, there's no telling what she's about to do. She stood up for my sister, a total stranger, without thinking twice. But there's more to her, pieces of her true self that she hides from everyone. I'm beginning to realize that some of those pieces come from a darker place. Her eyes tell me she's more resilient than she lets on. I think if I get more than a glimpse of the real Tex, she just might breathe life back into me, too.

"What are you smiling about, big brother, sitting out here all alone?" Jessie asks, stepping through the slider and following my gaze. "Ah, perhaps because you're watching SpitFire walk away? Dang, she wasn't kidding about giant Doberman, that's a badass dog!"

"SpitFire? Really?" I chuckle.

This is the side of my sister I miss the most. The side that I helped to extinguish when I introduced her to Liam and all the stress and heartbreak that followed. She had already been broken from losing our parents, I just put the final nail in the coffin with Liam.

"I call 'em as I see 'em," Jessie says, giving me a cheeky grin. "Now, how about some coffee?"

She's so much lighter this morning than she was yesterday. I didn't see it through my anger, but now, looking back, she was tentative, cautious last night. I thought it was just her guilt, her nerves to see Colt again, but what if it was more? The hug she gave me outside my shop, that look she gave me when she pulled away, was there more to it? What did Liam and Douchebag do to her? I know this isn't the time to interrogate her, as much as I want to.

"Colt and I usually walk down to the store in the morning, he gets special hot chocolate and I refill my mug." I hold up my plain white coffee mug then check my watch. "Tex is working this morning, she asked me to give you her number but if we walk down, you can talk in

72

person. If you want to wait approximately seven minutes until Colt bursts through the door, wanting to go, we can do that. Or I left the pot on, mugs in the cupboard above."

"I'll wait. And West, thank you. I'm sorry," Jessie says as she sinks into the chair beside me. "I can't believe I not only left my son with you for weeks, but then I showed up with that asshole." She reaches her hands up and covers her face. "What is wrong with me?" she moans, rubbing her face before bringing her hands back to her lap. I can see tears threatening to spill over.

"Hey, you're here now, we've got this, we can figure it out," I say, putting my hand on hers. I should have done more to get her out here sooner. A lot sooner. What an asshole brother I've been.

"God, I finally left Liam, only to leave my kid with you and instead of sorting my shit out, I got in deeper shit. I'm sorry, West, I really am. I'm also so fucking thankful that you're here, and that you've obviously helped Colt so much. Some guy in a weird fisherman vest told me that my brother is amazing, and another guy said that you were 'one of the best men around' and that just made me really fucking proud to be your sister. I know Mom and Dad would be proud of you, too."

Hearing that is a punch to the stomach. I don't think they'd be proud of me. In fact, they'd have every right to *not* be proud of me.

"Mom, that's a bad word," Colt exclaims from the doorway. Neither of us had realized he was there.

I reach over and wipe the tears from my sister's cheeks and then snag Colt and pull him in for a hug. My chest is tight and I have a lump in my throat. Jessie and I have been through a hell of a lot together; losing our parents fundamentally changed both of us, and we leaned on each other for many years. Maybe we can get back to that. Back to being a family.

"That was a bad word, I'm sorry, Colt, I just really wanted Uncle West to know how much he means to me. I should have chosen a better word though," Jessie admits, trying to hide a smile at Colt's expression.

"How about special hot chocolates for all of us?" I ask. Distraction is my go-to with Colt. "It feels like a special hot chocolate kind of morning. We can show your mom around town a bit, go for a little walk, and Tex asked if you guys wanted to hang out with her this afternoon."

"Yay!" cheers Colt, running back inside to get dressed.

"Thanks, West. You're the best big brother I've ever had," Jessie says, smiling at me as she wipes more tears.

"Hey, we got this, we'll figure it out. But first, coffee," I say, pulling her to standing. "Actually, first, go brush your teeth."

"Jerk," she mutters and throws an elbow into my ribs as she walks past me into the house.

That's more like the sister I remember.

Chapter Seven
Harper

"Fuck," I whisper as I watch Zero race down the beach in the wrong direction, oblivious to the beeping of the e-collar as I frantically hit the button. Between the wind and the constant roar of the ocean, there's no chance she hears my yells. So much for off-leash training.

With a sigh, I resign myself to the fact that my morning beach walk will now be a morning beach run. At least I put a sports bra on this morning. As Zero gets smaller in the distance, I calculate how far until the river that will halt her northward progress. Thank god she hates swimming. The asshole crow that got us into this situation mocks me from atop a pile of driftwood as I start to jog.

Just as I start to string together every curse word I've ever heard in my twenty-six years of life, the small dot that is my dog starts getting bigger. Apparently she finally figured out that I'm behind her, not ahead.

"You big dummy, you scared me," I tell her as she leaps around me, ecstatic to have raced nearly out of my sight and back. "Just leave the crow alone, he's obviously smarter than you."

She's been chasing him for days and each day he's led her a little further away from me. This morning Zero followed him into the beach grass and out of my sight. I'm assuming when she realized her mistake, she went looking for me, just in the wrong direction. The real question is how their game will play out tomorrow. I'm guessing not in my dog's favor.

Zero looks at me with hurt eyes. Damn dog. I turn and we start back toward our tiny cottage. It's definitely a curse word mug sort of day.

Well, it would be a curse word mug day, except the kitchen faucet floods the counter (and the floor) when I go to fill the coffee pot. I throw in the towel, as in, I mop up a small flood and then throw the towels into the washing machine, and head for The Mercantile instead. It will be multitasking: caffeine fix and checking in on the store, making sure Marabelle and Lucas, one of our new hires, have things running smoothly after the first busy weekend of the season.

After pulling my damp layers back on, I step outside into the drizzle. I pull my hood up and quickly walk the short distance to the store, shaking out my rain jacket before stepping inside. The Merc is nearly empty, everyone seems to be moving slowly this week after the holiday weekend. I haven't even seen Colt or West this morning even though I've walked past their house twice and Colt has a habit of showing up unannounced. Jessie tracked him down the other morning, laughing when she found us on the porch debating if a roly-poly bug is the same thing as a potato bug. I thought they were but he very seriously informed me they were not. Google confirmed he was correct.

It was fun spending time with the two of them over the weekend. Colt had been more tactile than usual, holding my hand, hugging me, and climbing on me even more than he normally does, which I hadn't thought possible. As the day went on, I realized that he was merely seeking out stimulation to help his emotions. I understood.

While I don't like most people touching me, I do seek out physical affection from my friends when I'm upset. Emmy running her long nails through my hair is basically heaven and Avery has been my snugglefest friend for decades. So I did the same for Colt that Ems and Aves do for me: nonverbal reassurances throughout the day. I carried him piggyback, flipped him upside down like a sack of potatoes over my shoulder, and pulled him into my lap when we built sandcastles.

I also got a little insight into the man that is West when Jessie opened up about her past with Colt's dad, Liam. I don't understand how both Jessie and West blame themselves for Liam's alcoholism, but I also accept that it's a complicated issue. I'd like a few minutes alone with Liam, just to tell him what a fucking idiot he is, addiction disease or not, for missing out on the coolest, funniest, sweetest kid in the world.

76

"Good morning, boss," Lucas greets me, pulling me away from my thoughts and back into the present. "The usual?"

"Yes, please, I'll be in the back checking in with Marabelle," I tell him, slipping behind the counter and through the kitchen door.

After a quick inventory check, Marabelle pushes me back out the door, telling me to recover from the busy weekend. She seems so much happier now than the first couple times I met her. The reorganization of Avery's empire is working. Having Kelsey and I officially take over Mercantile manager duties has worked out well for all of us. Hiring Lucas didn't hurt either.

Lucas is easygoing and works hard, although he did tell me that he might have to leave with no notice if his grandfather calls. Avery and I reassured him that he could shut the entire store down in case of emergency and we would understand. Marabelle watches over him like a mother hen and he treats Kelsey like a little sister. He fits in well and is a female customer favorite. Bonus: he just offered to fix my kitchen faucet after his shift. I do still need to hire another part-time employee, but that's for another day.

Back home I decide to take Marabelle's orders to heart. Although I did take Saturday afternoon off to hang out with Jessie and Colt, I spent the majority of the weekend working.

The community bonfire was a huge hit. I got to meet most of the year-round residents and plenty of the summer residents were there as well. Many have headed back into the valley for their kids to finish out the school year, but they'll return in a couple weeks and the town will be bursting at the seams. Or at least that's my hope.

With no sign of the drizzle letting up, I build a fire in the fireplace and grab my notebook. Zero settles in beside me and I flip through the pages of to-do lists and random journal entries to find a blank page. A drawing of Zero and I in the middle of my notebook stops me.

I'm drawn in profile with Z standing on my far side but looking head on. My hair's flying in the wind, barely contained by a backwards hat. I have my fleece zipped tight, right hand on Zero's head, left hand clenched.

When did West manage to pull this off? I thought he was just drawing houses the day we walked the rentals together. AKA panic attack day. AKA the day that must not be named. Were Colt and I really at the beach that long? We probably were.

I look closer at the details. Zero's ears are slightly crooked, just like they are in real life, and... I wasn't clenching my hand that day. I don't think West knows the scar exists, but thanks to him seeing me upset multiple times, he definitely knows this habit well enough to make it part of this drawing.

I flip to the back of my notebook and find my list from the other day. The things that make me happy. I close my eyes and again see the ocean waves. My thumb automatically moves to my scar.

breathe in two three four, hold two three four, out two three four
I've got it. I know what I'm doing today.

***

"Oh. Hi," I say as I walk in and realize that the only tattoo artist in the admittedly tiny, most likely one-person sort of shop, is West. "It's you."

"Hi," he replies, glancing up at me then immediately back down. I think he sighs. "It is me."

"How did I not know it was you?" I ask, suddenly flustered. This is awkward.

I stand, undecided, barely inside the door. I've been banking on a stranger, not the man that witnessed, and calmed, my darkest moment since moving here. Especially not the man that has warm blue eyes, broad shoulders, and a heart-twinging smile. When he actually smiles, unlike right now.

No, I'm doing this.

I step into the small building that's somehow both dark and welcoming. A small reception area is just inside the door and a few dark leather chairs fill the rest of the entry. A binder with an intricate design on the front sits on a coffee table, I'm sure full of tattoo designs. There are large canvas prints of different Oregon beaches on the walls and I smile at Rejection Rock. There's also a stunning photo of Haystack Rock of Cannon Beach and another of lesser-known Haystack Rock of Pacific City further down the hall.

78

"I thought you would know it was me since I'm the only tattoo artist within twenty miles," he replies evenly. "And since you booked the appointment." Fucking online booking. Why didn't I look more closely?

I don't know what to say so I stay silent. This is not how I pictured this going. Now it feels even more awkward.

I sign the waivers, let him scan my ID (he is now one of two people in town who know my real name, thanks to Avery consistently introducing me as Tex), and quietly follow him to the back. He gestures to the table and I hop up, sitting cross-legged and trying to hide my anxiety.

My eyes are drawn to a picture of a younger West, looking even more masculine than usual as he stares at a tiny dark-haired baby wrapped in a blue blanket that he's gently holding in his giant arms. My ovaries twitch. Not helping my nerves.

I can see West watching me from the corner of my eye but I keep my focus on the picture. West sits on his rolling stool and patiently waits for me to make eye contact. I can't do it. Instead I rub my scar and move my eyes to my hands in my lap.

"Tex, nervous? Didn't think I'd see the day," he says, still watching me. "Didn't you chase Colt up the rock barefoot the other day? That's more painful than this will be."

"No," I snap, making him freeze.

Whoa. Calm down. Focus.

I hear West's slow, steady breathing.

Stop thinking about him. Focus.

I feel my hammering heart. No. The table beneath me.

I smell West's cedar and citrus cologne.

Stop.

I see West's tattoos wrapping around his muscular forearms.

Stop.

I taste my anxiety. No.

Breathing.

breathe in two three four, hold two three four, out two three fuuuuck

79

"I'm not nervous, not about the tattoo. I know exactly what I want. I want a small wave, just a single line, right? Like right here." I rub my thumb along the inside of my ring finger. I awkwardly hold it up, because apparently awkwardness is the theme of this experience. "I know you've seen me do this. It's just that water has always helped calm my anxiety. I close my eyes and see the ocean waves, it's my happy place. And I want it here, because…"

I trail off. What am I even saying? God, I wish I could start this whole thing over. Would it be weird if I walked out and then back in? Yes. Yes, it would. Okay, I can salvage this.

"Nevermind, I just want it here. But I also sometimes panic if someone grabs my hand or wrist or touches me or I don't know, I just can't. I don't want to cry or have another panic attack in front of you. Or ever, I guess? And I have a scar, can you tattoo around a scar? Maybe this isn't a good idea. Fuck. I thought this would be different."

Instead of salvaging this, I'm making it worse. I'm nervously babbling, unable to shut myself up. Maybe I should try the walk out and back in idea. At least this time I would know it's his business I was walking into.

"And I'm sorry I didn't realize this was your shop. Of course it's your shop. I just spent the afternoon with your sister while you were working. Here. Because you work here. She told me about your shop in Portland with Liam."

Stop talking. Seriously. Stop. You're making this worse. Stop. Talking.

"I just thought you were doing carpentry in town or something. I don't know. But I'm sorry. I loved your sketch."

STOP. TALKING.

"Okay, I'm going to stop talking now. No. I'm also sorry in advance if I panic. Or cry. Okay, *now* I'm stopping."

Wow, Harper. That was awkward as fuck. Yep, I should just go.

"Harper, obviously this tattoo means something big, how can I make this okay?" West asks quietly, using the name he just learned as he looks up at me from his chair.

80

Hearing my name from his lips draws my eyes to his. I think I like how he says my name a little too much. And how his clear blue eyes hold mine, just like they did when he found me panicking. A small sense of calm starts seeping in, my anxiety slowly losing its hold.

"Can you tattoo me from over there without touching me?" I nod at the corner, trying to make a joke.

"Harper, it's okay, we'll work through this," he says, rotating toward his desk.

I can see his tee shirt stretch tight over his back as he takes a deep breath. He turns on a desk light and his hand moves quickly over a small sheet of paper. He hands me the paper, and it's just what I pictured, a small ocean wave. Simple. A small reminder that turns something ugly into something that is mine. My choice. Now when I rub my finger, I'll be touching an ocean wave, not an ugly scar.

"Yes," I say, lowering my eyes. "I want that, right here." I tap my thumb to my scar but keep my hand in my lap, not ready yet.

breathe in two three four, hold two three four, out two three four

He calmly waits, watching as I absentmindedly rub the scar.

breathe in two three four, hold two three four, out two three four

"Are we okay? Can I look at the spot to get the size right?" he asks without moving closer or reaching toward me. "I'll go slow, I promise."

"Okay, no, I'm okay," I say, moving my left hand toward the edge of the table.

He gently takes my hand and instead of flinching or pulling back, I'm fine. Nothing. Just the warmth of his hand. I look up; his ocean-blue eyes are steady on mine. I wait for the panic but it doesn't come. I'm completely still, my eyes locked on his.

Is it his blue shirt that's making his eyes look extra blue today? Can he see my anxiety? Are his shoulders always this wide? How long until I start hyperventilating?

"I really do love that sketch," I blurt out suddenly. Are his eyes some weird truth serum? "The one you did at North House. Of Zero and I. It's why I'm here, in a way."

"It was the only thing I wanted to sketch at that house," West says quietly.

"I can't believe you saw me like that," I add, remembering the state I was in when he first showed up at The Glass House earlier that day. "I was a total mess."

"I saw you just as you were, as you are," he replies easily, truthfully, giving me a small shrug.

"Oh." I don't know what to say to that.

"The way you were standing there that day, wind whipping all around, staring out toward the beach like the ocean was calling to you, your thumb rubbing this spot," West continues softly, gently moving his finger along mine. "Your tattoo makes sense."

I realize with a jolt that he's not only still holding my left hand in his, but he's touching my scar, and instead of panicking, I like it. Fuck. I can't like it. Where is a goddamn panic attack when I need one? This can't happen. I can't feel this. Now I really am going to panic. I feel my breathing start to pick up and I glance toward the door.

"Harper, breathe with me. In two three, hold two three, out two three," he says softly, breathing slowly in time with his words.

"How do you know that?" I ask in surprise after following his breath count.

"Tex, you taught it to Colt, he probably taught the whole town by now," West laughs, returning to the nickname I've hidden behind since moving. "He adores you." He looks down at my hand and lightly traces the scar. A slight frown mars his annoyingly handsome face.

"I don't want it right on the scar, just above, that will still work, right?" I ask hurriedly, feeling the familiar lump in my throat that comes any time anyone has ever asked about the jagged line.

I don't want him to ask. He's already seen me in a weak, dark moment, he doesn't need another. Don't ask. Don't ask. Don't ask.

82

Chapter Eight
West

I run my rough finger along her smooth skin, the thin scar making my heart beat in anger. Her visible tension, the slight shake of her hand, and her shallow breaths tell me there's a story behind this jagged line, one she doesn't want to tell and one that I'm not sure I'm ready to hear. The placement of this delicate tattoo feels heavy. I feel the scar again, eye the drawing of her wave, and pause.

"Harper, what if I use this," I lightly trace the part of her scar that runs along her middle knuckle, her eyes following my finger, "as the beginning of the wave, then the wave crests over this raised scar tissue, and finishes beyond the end, so the wave overtakes the scar?" I hold my breath, willing her not to bolt right out of here.

"Show me," she says quietly, using her thumb to rub the scar as I place her hand back in her lap and turn to my drawing table.

The tentative trust she's giving me feels hard-fought, like she waged an internal battle and somehow I came out the victor. As I draw a few different versions of her wave, I can see her out of the corner of my eye watching me, breathing steadily, hands still. To have somehow earned her trust makes my chest tighten.

The very first wave I draw after running my finger over her scar is the one she chooses. I apply the stencil carefully, smiling to myself as the line of the wave both mimics her scar and minimizes it. I see her small smile out of the corner of my eye as I reach for the ink.

Harper doesn't flinch once as I get to work, not at the touch of my hand as I position her finger or at the sting of the needle. I focus on my work but I can still feel the heaviness of her thoughts.

I wipe her skin one last time and smile at the wave that outruns her jagged scar. I can't help but run my glove-clad finger over it one more time. I look up for her reaction and see a single tear running down her cheek. She swipes at it with her right hand and looks away. I let us sit in silence, keeping her hand in mine, until she looks back at her finger. A small smile, another tear. Fuck.

"It's perfect," she whispers, letting the tears fall as she looks me directly in the eye, hazel eyes brimming with emotion.

It's at this exact moment that I know I am truly fucked when it comes to Harper Sage.

***

I lean back onto the rocks with a smile, watching Colt chase Zero down the empty beach with the sun sinking into the ocean behind them. If Zero is here, Harper can't be far, but I don't see her anywhere. I remember her tentative trust from just a few short hours ago, how she quietly watched as I marked her body with my ink, and wonder if she's going to return to avoiding me.

I sat in the back of the shop for an hour after Harper left, with the door locked and the "be back soon" sign hung. I couldn't think. I couldn't *not* think. I've had emotional clients before, tattoos can have an overwhelming meaning behind them, but this one hit me hard. It was like a punch in the gut that I didn't see coming when her hand stopped shaking, a vice around my heart when her tears fell.

A petite body settles down next to me as my eyes continue to track the racing duo as they run toward Rejection Rock. Colt is pumping his little arms hard, running with all his might, and Zero easily lopes along beside him. I think I owe the dog babysitting money; Colt is going to crash hard tonight.

"Hi. Is this seat taken?" Harper asks hesitantly, shifting to make sure there's still a sliver of space between us. Her eyes briefly meet mine and I see something in them that I can't quite decipher.

I've watched her banter with customers at The Mercantile, join beach volleyball games and laugh away the day with strangers, drink beer and flirt with the Friday bonfire group, and gently let down a ballsy teenage boy that asked her out. She easily took down Douchebag Derek and rescued my sister in the process. I've come to the conclusion that she can fit in anywhere, anytime, with anyone. Yet I would wager my shop that no one here besides Avery really knows her and it scared her to let me in.

"I'm glad you're here," I tell her honestly, turning my head to take her in. Bare feet, black leggings, oversized, off-white Longhorns hoodie, shy smile. Her cheeks redden slightly at my comment.

I lean and nudge her shoulder, nodding toward the water where Zero slowly herds Colt our way. "Did you ever think you'd see that? They're tired."

Harper bites her lip and somehow ends up slightly closer to me, watching as her dog and my nephew walk our way. She stays silent, watchful, and pulls her hoodie a little tighter as the breeze picks up.

"Tex! I raced Zero all the way to the rock! She's so fast!" Colt plops down right in Harper's lap and she pulls him close. Obviously her issues with touch don't include Colt; she's happily let him into her space since the first night at the fire.

"You're so fast, Colt! Zero loves playing with you. You're so good with her and it helps me so much when you help get her tired," Harper says, flipping on her happy switch as she tickles Colt. His giggling draws Zero back to us from the dunes and she shoves her nose in his face, making him giggle even harder.

"Race you again, Z!" Colt yells as he bolts up from Harper's lap and pushes his little legs through the soft sand, stumbling when he reaches the packed wet sand. The dog bounds after him, always up for a race.

"West," Harper says softly from beside me, waiting for me to look at her before she continues. "Thank you."

"Harper, I didn't do anything, it was just a tattoo," I reply quietly, fighting the urge to reach for her.

"No, not that. Well, I do mean that, but.." she trails off, licking her lips nervously, pulling her gaze from mine to look out over the ocean. I can see her actively trying not to rub her scar, her nervous habit that I told her to avoid while the tattoo heals. "Thank you for being understanding and taking your time. I was a fucking mess."

"Thank you for trusting me, Harper. I would never rush you, or anyone. I'm a patient man," I tell her, keeping my eyes on her, even as she watches Colt and Zero racing on the sand.

I wonder if she catches my double meaning. I didn't mean to say it like that, but that's how it came out. I'm still confused as fuck about my complicated feelings toward her but after this afternoon, in that hour after she left my shop, I accepted my fate. I accepted that I can no longer resist this unexplained, deep pull I feel toward her. There have been moments I could swear she feels it, too. When I've seen it in her eyes. If we go slow, maybe we can both heal our darkness. Maybe I can be a better man, one deserving of more. Of her.

"Just thank you for it all. You've seen me at some real lows. I swear I'm not usually like this. I didn't realize this move would make me such an emotional wreck. I guess restarting my life is kicking my ass," she says with a self deprecating huff of laughter, shifting against the rock.

Her shoulder leans against mine and I freeze, wanting to move closer and wrap my arm around her, bury my nose in her wind-whipped hair to breathe her in. I stay still. Patient. I feel her sigh, and we sit in comfortable silence, watching the sun sink beneath the horizon, boy and dog chasing waves in the fading light.

***

I try Harper's breathing trick as I stomp down the street in the rain, already knowing where I'll find the little runaway.

Breathe in two three, hold two three, out two three.

Nope, still annoyed. I needed a three-minute shower to hide and have a few minutes to calm down after the conversation with my sister before we walked to The Mercantile for hot chocolate but he took off by himself once again. I'm always glad to live in this tiny town but even moreso now that I have a wandering five-year-old under my watch.

Laughter floats down the street. The small giggle and a joyful "again!" is most definitely Colt. I round the corner of the cottage and pause. Well, this isn't what I was expecting. His rain boots are kicked off on the deck, his bare feet on top of Harper's, his hands in hers, as she dances them around the deck to some sort of symphony music while Zero watches from her dog bed.

"Uncle West! Did you see my note? We are waltzing!" Colt exclaims as soon as he spots me.

I guess the sticky note on the floor outside my bathroom was a note. Is that another thing he picked up from Harper? She leaves sticky notes all over this town. You'd think for someone her age, she'd prefer reminders in her phone, but there are sticky notes all over the rental properties.

"Sorry, I had a visitor again this morning and I figured you would know where to find him, then he asked about my music, then we decided to waltz?" Harper's voice trails off in a question as she takes in my stormy demeanor.

"Of course you're waltzing," I reply, trying to soften my expression and my tone. It isn't her fault Jessie pissed me off. "Because most twenty-two year olds know how to waltz."

"First of all, I'm twenty-six. Second of all, do you *not* know how to waltz?" Harper challenges with a smirk.

She's avoided me since that night on the beach despite the fact that I've spent hours working on the deck at The Glass House this week. She hightailed it off the property when I showed up with a truck full of lumber, claiming she was needed at The Mercantile even though Avery had told me that Harper would be working at the house all day. I had almost convinced myself it was for the best, that I needed to go back to my original plan of being her coworker. If her challenging tone is any indication, she's past the avoidance stage. And I suddenly love challenges.

"Just like that, Uncle West, hold her hands, but don't actually step on her feet like I did, that's just 'cause I'm little," Colt coaches, circling around us like a herding dog, pushing us closer, Zero on his heels as usual.

I hold my hands up but let Harper decide if she's willing to take them in hers, unable to read her body language. She's still smiling but I promised her patience and I refuse to push it. I'm still unsure just how I ended up getting a waltz lesson on a tiny cottage porch barely out of the rain before 8 .a.m but here we are.

She takes my left hand in her right and then after a pause she moves my right hand slowly down to her waist with her other hand. Her hand moves up to my shoulder, lightly grazing bare skin at the collar of my tee shirt. I try to hide my sharp intake of air when her shifting brings my pinky finger to soft, warm skin as her shirt rides up. Her eyes move to mine and I get a slight smile; we are close enough that I can feel her slow exhale on my neck. I match my breath to hers, slow and steady. I don't sense any discomfort, if anything she's pulling me closer. Her eyes stayed locked on mine and her thumb brushes across my knuckle.

"Hi," she whispers, biting her lip as she looks up at me. Her eyes are happy, with little gold flecks that I've never noticed reflecting in the morning light.

"Hi," I whisper back, smiling down at her. I shift my hand slightly on her waist and am rewarded with a quick inhale. She feels it, too.

"Ok, dance!" Colt startles us out of our staring contest and starts counting steps for us.

88

Chapter Nine
Harper

"Have coffee with us?" West asks softly as he pulls me back in after a turn.

Before I can answer, he dips me low, making Colt gasp then clap. West gently pulls me back up and continues to hold me an extra beat. I tell myself to step out of his space but my feet don't move. My heart is beating wildly. My thumb automatically moves to my finger and I feel the wrap on my tattoo, reminding me not to rub. I bite my lip nervously instead. I look up at his dark blue eyes and lick my lips. His eyes drop to my mouth, tracking the movement. I'm somehow even closer to him than before.

"Again!" cries Colt.

I barely remembered we have an audience, too lost in whatever is happening between the two of us. I blink and mentally scold myself, stepping away from West, hands dropping to my sides. There's a kid here. A freaking awesome kid with an already complicated life.

"You two wore me out and it's time for me to get to work. Are you gentlemen going to escort me to The Mercantile?" I direct my question at Colt, unsure I can handle looking at West.

I can still feel him touching my skin even though we're now standing with a bouncing boy and sandy dog between us.

"Hot chocolate!" is Colt's enthusiastic response.

Right. Not the time to daydream.

When we walk together to The Mercantile, Colt between us, West smiling at me over his head, still not the time to daydream.

When West holds the door for us, putting his hand on my low back as I walk inside behind Colt, also not the time to daydream.

When I settle in at my desk in the crowded office in the back, definitely not the time to daydream.

An hour later, I'm getting very little done. There's no way around it. I have sticky notes stuck to the wall in front of me, color-coded lists on my paper calendar, and multiple tabs open on my laptop, but I keep sinking into daydreams about West. His calloused hands sliding up my ribs, his gentle fingers tracing the scar on my finger, his strong arms pulling me up from a dip.

A shadow appears half a second before a hand lands on my desk and I jerk sideways, knocking my calendar to the floor.

"Jesus, Avery, what was that for?" I scramble to clean up my mess as she stands there smirking at me.

"I said your name three times! You seem a little bit distracted," she replies, raising her eyebrow and giving me a very Avery smirk. "I also happened to run by The Glass House where West was finishing the deck railing and I chatted with Colt who says you give out dance lessons, hmmm?"

"Oh! Your long run today, how was it? Twenty miles is easy peasy, right?" I go for an obvious subject change and get a steady glare in return.

"Right. Well, change of plans, my day has exploded. Can you meet me at my cabin in fifteen minutes for our meeting, or are you too distracted?" Avery winks over her shoulder as she strides out the door to jog back up the steep incline to her cabin.

I roll my eyes at her retreating back like the mature adult I am and shove my things in my bag. I walk home, wrangle my dog into my Jeep, and drive up the hill to Avery's cabin. I'm sure as shit not hiking up that hill. She's still in the shower but I let myself in and make a fresh pot of coffee while Zero curls up in the dog bed that has mysteriously appeared in the corner of the living room. I have my rental property updates ready, along with a hot cup of coffee for her as she walks in, drying her hair with a towel.

We quickly work through the rentals, Avery approving all of my shopping lists and budget requests. Easiest boss ever. We shift to marketing, which is a combination of social media and local advertising.

"I hate the social media side of everything, but you guys are killing it. Every time I'm in town someone tells me they love your content. Ugh, I can't believe I just used the word 'content' in reference to social media," Avery says, wrinkling her nose.

"That's all Kelsey, she plans it and then I just do whatever she tells me. I think it's her goal to make me look as ridiculous as possible," I reply, gladly giving credit to our teenage genius.

Avery's phone buzzes for the millionth time and she quickly flips it over to check the notification and tries to hide a grin. Her cheeks look slightly flushed and since when has she ever put her phone facedown when it's just the two of us? Is this what she's been hiding? I knew her recent moods meant something.

"So, who's the guy?" I ask, wiggling my eyebrows at her.

She quickly flips her phone back facedown on the table. She clamps her lips together and looks out the window. Guilty. She's never been able to tell me an outright lie. Her silence is damning her.

"Okay, okay, I'll go easy. But you were giving me a hard time about being distracted and now you obviously have your attention elsewhere, so I'm going to go home and place some orders, spend your money, then slack off this afternoon. I need some beach time as soon as the sun comes out," I tell her. "The gray weather this week got to me. Can we do dinner this weekend? You've been so busy this week! I miss you!"

She's looking at her phone again. This is one hundred percent not work related.

"Did I tell you that I found a wolf at North House the other day? Pretty sure there's an entire den," I say, not changing my tone.

"Oh, yeah, for sure, I gotta go, can you lock up?" she replies distractedly, not even looking at me. She grabs her keys and flat out bails on me.

What the hell, Aves? Damn. I really am going to spend her money now. A lot of it.

Okay, not really. But I am going to stick my tongue out and roll my eyes at the door she's slamming behind her. Maybe I've spent too much time with Colt lately.

***

I hear a familiar shriek and turn to see a blonde blur barreling toward me.

"Surprise!"

My Texas best friend tackles me to the sand. Holy shit, she just knocked the wind out of me. I cough, gasp, and sputter. When I have oxygen again, I roll over to look at Emmy who is sprawled beside me, grinning like a fool. Zero is wiggling around on her back next to Em, ecstatic to see her as well.

"What the hell, Em!?" I have so many questions and so little oxygen. "How are you here? Can you stay forever? Welcome to my favorite place in the whole world, by the way."

"Girls' weekend, Harp! Avery and I wanted to surprise you!" Emmy alligator death rolls until she's on top of me, not caring a single bit about getting sand all over both of us.

"Oh my god, Em, you're going to smother me!" I laugh and push her off me.

"Harperrrrr, this place is ah-may-ZING! Best place to run away to, hands down," Em says as she looks up and down the beach. "Fucking picturesque."

Avery walks up, shit-eating grin on her face. She pulls Em and I to our feet only for Em to hug-tackle me again.

"I just can't help it, I've missed you so much," she says into my neck, wrapping an arm and leg around me like a sandy spider monkey clinging to my side.

"So, I take it there's no guy?" I ask Avery, laughing as I get to my feet once again, pulling Emmy up with me.

"Nah, just had to pick this one up at PDX and I'm a bad liar," Aves answers, still grinning at me.

"She wouldn't let me rent a car," Emmy says.

"I knew as soon as you were in the state, I'd spill the secret. I had to get out of town!" Avery says with a laugh. She really cannot lie to me.

92

"Well, I'm in the same state! Let's get this party started!" Em always brings the energy… and apparently the alcohol. She reaches into the bag slung over Avery's shoulder and pulls out a bottle of champagne. Avery digs out plastic flutes and we all sink down into the dry sand. With a loud pop, the bottle is open and drinks are poured. I cannot believe this day.

"To girls' weekend!" Em starts the toasts.

"To my two best friends being in the same place!" I add, taking another swig. The bubbles are crisp against my tongue and I can already tell this bottle is not going to last long.

"To new friends!" Aves contributes, tapping her flute against Em's.

As I sit in the warm sand on my favorite beach, my two best friends pressed on either side of me, their body heat seeping into my bones, I feel whole. I automatically move my thumb to my finger, smiling down at my wave tattoo.

***

"Oh my godddd, Emmy, I've missed your guacamole!" I moan dramatically. "I miss H-E-B, taco trucks, and barbeque. I miss you dragging me out dancing, I miss walking Town Lake with coffee, I miss you."

We've taken over Avery's family house and Emmy has whipped up the most overboard, completely extra, taco night spread I've ever seen. There's even homemade tortillas. If she wasn't madly in love with her husband, I'd propose to her right here and now.

"You seem different here," Em says, eyeing me over her extra large margarita. "And you got a tattoo. Is this a very early midlife crisis? Do you cook now? Is there a sports car at your cottage? A young lover?"

Avery's cough sounds suspiciously like "older" but luckily Em doesn't catch on. Also, is West really that much older? I don't even know. Nor do I care. Maybe that's the tequila though.

"I feel different here," I reply honestly. "It's been a bit of a roller coaster. I'm not gonna lie, I'm kinda an emotional mess some days. But I think it's a good thing. Feelings are weird. I have a fucking journal, you guys. Who am I?"

"To journals!" Emmy holds up her glass for a toast.

"To feelings!" I laugh. We slosh margaritas in a messy toast.

"It's good, Harp, I'm proud of you," Avery, always the serious one, says as she piles more avocado on her taco and reaches for the salsa. Homemade salsa because Emmy is a real Texan.

"Should I tell you that Patrick ran into Ethan the other day?" Em asks, taking another long pull of her margarita. "Or should I not say anything?"

She has that slightly dreamy look that always shows up when she talks about Patrick, her gawky and sweet high school sweetheart turned smoking hot and still sweet husband.

"Hit me with it, more to write about in my journal," I say, downing the rest of my margarita. Liquid courage.

"He misses you," she says simply. "I think maybe you wrecked him a bit."

"No, I didn't." I snort. "Me fleeing the state might have shocked him a little, but he wasn't wrecked. I've heard from him exactly twice since telling him I made it here safely. He hasn't drunk texted, called in the middle of the night, liked old pictures of us on Insta, or done any desperate man sort of things. He's fine." Is he fine? Do I care if he's not fine?

"Well, Patrick says he looked pretty rough," Emmy says with a shrug.

A creeping guilt is slowly working itself into my stomach. So I do care if he's not fine. Interesting. But I honestly don't think it's me, it can't be. We weren't real. The longer I'm away, the more I realize that.

"That's just stress. And not *me* stress, but work stress. I'm sure our breakup was hard, but I got over it in three days and a couple thousand miles. Maybe he just needs a road trip."

"And maybe we need another round of margaritas?" Avery asks, gathering our glasses.

"Fuck. Yes." Em and I say at the same time, our usual response when Patrick would play personal bartender for us as we floated around their backyard pool.

94

Avery laughs at us and rinses the glasses. She re-salts them before putting them in the freezer to chill while she makes fresh drinks. She slices limes, measures and mixes, all while I lean my head on Emmy's shoulder, digesting what she just told me.

"I'm sorry, I hope that didn't mess you up," Ems says, resting her cheek on the top of my head.

Huh. Am I messed up over Ethan? Honestly, no. I've only thought of him in passing since getting here. He isn't even in my goddamn feelings journal. Not a single page, not a single line.

"No, I've realized that what Ethan and I had wasn't what I thought it was. I'm telling you, this self-reflection shit works, just don't be alarmed if I cry," I tell her honestly. "Maybe later, like when I'm *really* drunk, I'll Amazon Prime Ethan a journal so he can realize I saved us both from a dead end relationship."

"Oh my god, please do," Emmy laughs. "He's a nice guy, but were you really in love with him?"

"I thought I was, but I was wrong," I answer with a shrug, staring out the window to West's house next door.

I'm not ready to share what is happening between him and I just yet, but I do know that whatever is slowly unfurling between us, it feels like so much more than anything Ethan and I ever shared. It didn't take multiple margaritas to have that epiphany, I've felt it in nearly every interaction with him. The drinks didn't hurt though.

"I'm going to go ahead and say that I hope tomorrow morning's plan includes sleeping in, Advil, and caffeine," I say with a wry grin when Avery hands us our new, very large drinks.

"Absolutely, and some self-reflection," Avery deadpans, sitting back down across from Emmy and I.

"You're such an asshole," I tell her, shaking my head. "But I love you."

"To asshole friends!" Em toasts, holding her fresh margarita up.

"To Advil!" Aves adds, raising her glass.

"To self-reflection!" I finish, taking a large gulp.

"Holy shit, Avery," Emmy sputters. "A little strong, don't you think?"

"Doubles," she replies with a shrug.

"To doubles!" I toast, and we all fall into a fit of giggles.

***

The morning comes early, both my internal alarm and my dog waking me as the sun rises. I find Emmy curled up on the living room couch with coffee, the time zone difference making it feel two hours later for her. She gives me a smile and raises her whale mug to tell me good morning, but then returns to staring silently out at the ocean. She's either hungover or having her own self-reflection, perhaps a combination of the two.

I fill my own crab mug with steaming coffee and let Zero out, then burrow my feet under Em's blanket as we sit together on the couch, both of us now staring silently out at the ocean. My silence is definitely a combination of hangover and self-reflection. It did hit me a little hard last night, talking about Ethan. I do carry some guilt over how I ended things, fleeing without either of us really having closure, but I also know deep in my newfound feelings that I'm where I need to be. Definitely where I *want* to be, minus the hangover.

Avery shuffles in, yawning. She lets Zero back in the house for me and then sprawls out over our laps. I half-heartedly smack her ass before setting my coffee on it. Emmy plants a kiss on her cheek and then runs her fingers through her hair. I'm instantly jealous, Em's head massages are the best.

"Want to sneak into The Merc and steal pastries?" Avery asks after a few minutes of silence.

"Yes, please!" Em perks up at the suggestion. "But is it stealing if you own the place? And will there be Advil involved?"

"Let's stop by my cottage so I can feed Zero and find us some Advil. Then coffee and pastries to go. I bet it's close enough to low tide that we can find starfish for Miss Texas," I suggest. "Cold air is good for hangovers. It's science."

"You suck at science," Avery helpfully reminds me. Ouch. But she's not wrong.

The pastries we steal and the lattes we make, combined with Advil, the cold morning air, and splashing in tide pools cures our morning blues. AKA hangovers. We convince Em to climb Rejection

96

Rock and at the top we startle a bald eagle from its nest. All three of us stand in silence, watching it soar away over the ocean.

"Holy shit," Emmy breathes, still staring at the tiny speck in the distance. "That was amazing. Totally worth the hangover."

Chapter Ten
Harper

"So, who's the neighbor that can't keep his eyes off you?" Em asks, hours after our beach walk, looking over my shoulder to West's house as we play ladder ball in the yard. We have beers in hand and burgers ready to be put on the grill. "Tall, broad as fuck, broody expression, has a totally hot lumberjack beard."

I've felt his gaze on me all afternoon. And I like it. A lot.

"Yeah, Tex, just who is West?" Avery chimes in. I shoot her a look. "Is he just your carpenter, tattoo artist, and porch dance partner or is there something you'd like to share with the class?"

"Aves!" Apparently after twenty years she's immune to my glares. Who am I kidding, she's always been immune.

"Dance partner, what?" Emmy bounces her eyebrows up and down and then shoots another look across the beach path to West's house. "I'd make a carpenter nailing joke, but with you, it's more shocking you let him hold your hand long enough to do your tattoo. But I can see why. He can do whatever he wants with my hands." She fans herself in dramatic fashion.

I snort at that ridiculous claim. The only man that has held her hand since she was sixteen is now her doting husband, her one and only love, light of her life, soulmate, etc. You need a lesson in love, you just look at the two of them.

West is sitting on the deck, reading, Colt nowhere in sight. I hope that means he's with Jessie. As if he can sense my stare, West looks up and catches me watching him. He gives me a half-smile and I can't help but smile back. I also can't help the goosebumps that break out over my skin.

Emmy coughs pointedly.

"Okay, fine, shhh!" I roll my eyes at both of my best friends, their eyes wide and innocent.

I lead the girls around the corner to the side deck, out of the wind and out of sight of the beach path and therefore West's house.

"I don't know, you guys, this is not what was supposed to happen," I moan, flopping into an adirondack chair. Em and Aves sit on either side of me in chairs of their own, Zero finds a shady spot along the edge of the deck, and all three of them patiently wait for me to continue. "I was supposed to show up, Boss Bitch the hell out of Avery's job offer, figure all my shit out, and ride off into the sunset with my dog. Instead, Aves pulled a bait and switch on the job, I had a fucking panic attack over fucking nothing and was rescued by a hot, bearded man in flannel. I don't even *like* beards and flannel. But there's this unrelenting pull I feel toward him. I've tried to fight it. I've tried to tell myself I just want to have my way with a hot, older lumberjack, a little rebound action, but it's not that. It's more, you guys, and I can't stop. I mean, I do want to have my way with him, but I also want to snuggle and hold hands and watch the fucking sunset and make breakfast together. I hate this. Feelings are dumb. I'm throwing my feelings journal in the bonfire tonight."

"Oh, dang, you do have it baaaad," Em says, grabbing another beer and handing it to me. "I've known you for a decade and I've never seen you like this. You have heart eyes! Actual heart eyes. Uncharted territory here, people."

"I've known her twice that long and I've never seen her like this," Avery adds for good measure. "We are *definitely* in uncharted territory."

"If it's any consolation, the man couldn't keep his eyes off of you for the last hour. I know I'm loud, but it wasn't my loud ass that he was looking at. It's like there was a magnet drawing his eyes to you. He's got it bad, too. Also, is this where I point out that the woman that just said she doesn't like flannel is wearing a flannel?" Em laughs and nudges my foot.

100

"Shut up and make me a burger, we've got a bonfire to get to," I grumble, rolling my eyes and pulling my flannel tighter around me. I don't mention that I wish it was West's flannel I was wearing.

***

Avery sets her Yeti cooler filled with our favorite Pelican Brewing beers down near the dunes and heads to check in with Sarah, this week's bonfire host, while Emmy and I jump into a sand volleyball game. We played together in high school and on an intramural team together during college so we easily hold our own against three college guys in town to celebrate graduating from Willamette University in Salem. Their fourth friend is soon deep in conversation with Avery near the bonfire.

"Okay, I'm out of shape and those afternoon beers might have caught up with me. The bacon cheeseburger isn't helping either," pants Em, stripping her hoodie off and tossing it in the sand. I throw my flannel on top, giving her ass a loud smack as I jog up to the net. I signal behind my back, telling her where to serve the ball.

"You guys are killing us, we gotta change the teams up," the blonde guy says after Emmy serves three aces in a row. I'm pretty sure his name is Finn but that might be the one with curly hair.

I shrug and duck under the net, giving my new teammates high fives as maybe-Finn switches spots with me. Emmy points at me then makes a slashing motion across her neck, telling me I'm about to go down. Her serve comes fast and dirty, making me dive forward to pop it up for my teammates, who manage to get it back across the net. We fight through the volley and win the point. The guys immediately come up with a goofy cheer that ends with a three-way chest bump where they nearly knock me on my ass. I laugh hard at their antics as I try to dust the sand off, a losing battle.

A prickly feeling comes over me and out of the corner of my eye I see West, his eyes on me, as he holds Colt's hand. Colt gives me an enthusiastic wave so I run over and give him a fist bump. My heart beats loudly as I give West a smile, so loud he must be able to hear it as well. His eyes take in my fitted crop tank and his broad chest rises with a deep inhale that he blows out slowly. I bite my lip to hide my smile as I head back to the line to take my turn serving, glaring at Em across the net as she winks then shimmies her shoulders. I aim my serve directly at her.

Between each point, I find myself trying to catch sight of red flannel as we victory dance or huddle up and regroup. We are fairly evenly matched, despite it being two on three, and the game moves quickly. I'm out of breath, my abs hurt from laughing with my new friends, and both Jack and Hadley swing me around when we get the victory.

"Beer break!" I holler, jogging over to our cooler and grabbing a Sea'n'Red for myself, Kiwanda Ale for Emmy, and a Sunrise Surfer for Avery.

"Grant wants to intern with me, he seems really driven," Avery says, nodding toward the guys who are now gathered around their own cooler.

"I think Finn wants to 'intern' with Emmy," I say, using air quotes. "That boy is smitten!"

"Speaking of smitten," Avery whispers quietly.

I feel West behind me, something that would normally make me uncomfortable. More than uncomfortable. Ever since that night ten years ago, I get jittery when people stand behind me or approach silently. But right now, all I want to do is lean back into his solid chest. Apparently admitting my complicated feelings toward him to my friends has only made my massive crush worse. Much worse.

"You must be West! I'm Emmy. I've heard all about you," Emmy purrs, reaching her hand toward West as he steps to stand beside me.

"All about me, huh?" West says, looking back and forth between Avery and I, then settling his eyes on mine.

I lick my lips, feeling off kilter. Has he always been this tall? This big? I'm also slightly terrified of what is going to come out of Emmy's mouth next. The girl is unpredictable in the best possible way.

"Gotta say, you're living up to the hype already." Emmy gives him a blatant head-to-toe perusal and winks. Jesus Christ, Ems. No chill.

"Please ignore her, she's crazy," I tell him, giving Em a hard elbow to her ribs. "Off work early?" I try a subject change. I sense her

102

intentions, years of being her friend, and quickly move my foot before Em can step on it.

"Oh, well, please tell me more about this hype." West grins, ignoring my attempt at a subject change and focusing all of his attention on Emmy as Avery snickers.

Suddenly the two most serious people I knew, West and Avery, both have a sense of humor. Great. In any other, perhaps less embarrassing situation, I'd be thrilled with their playful sides making a rare appearance. Where did gruff, standoffish West go and why can't he make a sudden reappearance?

"So. Much. Hype," Avery says, looking directly at me. Now I have to murder both of my best friends. I hope Colt will consider taking their place as my BFF.

"Well, I've heard that you're-" Em starts.

"Nope. We gotta go, the guys want to switch the teams up and play another round. Nice to see you!" I put my hand over her mouth and she laughs maniacally before licking my hand, making me pull it away. "Ew! Ems!" I wipe my hand on her back.

"Soooo nice to meet you, West, I hope I get to see a *lot* more of you." Em slowly drags her fingernails down his forearm as she gives me a pointed look. She squeezes his hand and fucking winks at him. I am actually going to murder her. RIP best Texas friend.

"Are we on for tomorrow?" Avery calls over her shoulder as I march my friends back toward the volleyball court.

"Yep, Jessie will be here in the morning so I won't have Colt," he replies, smiling at us before scrubbing a hand through his beard. Why was that hot? I blame Emmy for this whole interaction *and* my reaction to him and his hot beard.

"On for what?" I ask suspiciously.

"Nothing!" sing my two best friends in unison.

Liars.

***

As Emmy swings me around the dance floor, I realize how much I've missed my cowboy boots. Or maybe that's the beer talking. Em plays to the crowds' hoots and spins me faster before we two-step our way back to our table as the song winds down. I slide into the booth next to Avery and steal her beer as Emmy slides in after me. I'm out of breath from dancing and the beer is cold and crisp. I bring the glass to my cheek, eyes wandering around the small bar. Familiar faces smile back at me. I can't believe Avery pulled this together for us.

A couple hours ago I was sitting on the couch with a book when my cowboy boots were unceremoniously tossed in my lap. Avery told me our Uber would arrive in thirty minutes and I needed to get my ass ready. Our Uber turned out to be West, who was back to his quiet, grouchy self. He dropped us at the local dive bar and disappeared to his shop a few doors down the street without a word.

Mysterious secret plans, revealed at last. I bugged the girls multiple times at the bonfire last night but they wouldn't tell me a thing. This is the perfect end to our girls' weekend. We spent the morning showing Emmy the rentals, taking "hashtag girlsweekend" pictures at Breakers Bliss with Kelsey, and then headed for Pacific City to climb Cape Kiwanda and have an early dinner at the Pelican Pub. An hour on the beach with Jessie and Colt and I thought our day was done until my boots landed in my lap.

"Hey! Get your own!" Avery laughs and snatches her beer back. It's rare that Avery really lets loose but she is already more beers in than me.

"I got this round!" I squeeze Em's leg so she will let me out of the booth. She pinches my ass as I pass by and then dives back into the booth next to Aves.

I look back at the table as I walk away and they have their heads bent together, fast friends despite their wildly different personalities. I don't think I realized just how different they really are, but now that they're together it's glaringly obvious. Avery is tall, serious, quiet, nearly standoffish to strangers, and is perfectly content living alone in her cabin on the hill. Em, on the other hand, is pint-sized even in her boots, always laughing, has never met a stranger, only new friends, and will be hopelessly devoted to Patrick until the end of time.

I love them both even though I'm certain they are talking about me and quite possibly plotting something I want no part of. Another glance back confirms it, they're definitely up to something.

"Another pitcher for the table, please, and a second one just for me!"

Steve the bartender, who Emmy charmed into handing over DJ duties as soon as we walked in, chuckles and shakes his head. He has that exasperated head-shake down pat. As he turns back to fill the pitchers and return a card to a couple at the end of the bar, I watch Emmy start a Shania Twain tutorial. She has nearly everyone in the place out on the dance floor. Typical Em.

"All y'all having a real good time at this 'ol honky-tonk?" Steve attempts and butchers a Texas drawl as he sets two pitchers on the bar between us.

"Shucks, darlin', aren't you just as sweet as mama's pecan pie?" I coo, winking at him.

I grab my pitchers with one hand, a stack of new glasses in the other, and turn to head back to the table, walking directly into a wall of chest. A familiar chest. A chest that smells like citrus and cedar and maybe a little like the beer I just spilled on it.

"Hi," West says, steadying me with a hand on my hip.

"Hi," I reply, feeling flustered. "Sorry. Off work already?"

"Slow night, and I wanted to check in and see if you three were getting into trouble," he replies, letting his gaze wander down to my boots and back up before settling on my lips. I can feel myself blush under his heated gaze.

"With Emmy, there's always trouble," I say, tipping my head toward the dance floor.

The pitchers start feeling heavy and West must notice because he reaches his big hand out to take them.

"Dibs on first dance!" Emmy hollers, appearing out of nowhere and pulling West away from me, leaving me with the beer.

He gives me a deer-in-headlights look as all five-foot nothing of her drags him to the dance floor. I laugh as Em shoots me a look and then not-so-discreetly flips me off behind West's back.

"I never thought I'd see the day that West is on a dance floor doing a two-step!" Avery laughs as I set the pitchers on the table and start pouring.

"That girl could get anyone on the dance floor. Can you even imagine trying to tell her no?! She stormed into my life on my second day in Texas when I was having a whole moment about what happened that night and moving and leaving you and general teenage angst, and she merely rolled her eyes at my bitchy attitude. The next thing I knew, we were on a pontoon in the middle of Lake Travis. She's a force." I shake my head, taking a long drink of my beer.

"Oh god, that means I'm next, doesn't it? She's not going to let me just sit here and enjoy drinking beer, is she? Can I hide?" Avery asks, looking around the bar.

"Just drink faster. The drunker you are, the easier dancing will be," I wisely explain. Beer logic. It's science.

"I feel like that's terrible advice, but I'll take it anyway," Avery says, taking a large gulp of her beer.

Sure enough, one-and-a-half hastily drank beers later, I laugh as I watch Em lead two-left-feet Avery in a two-step before I pull shy Parker out of the booth to show him how it's done. I've only ever talked to him in passing at the hardware store, but he's funny and sweet and if his awkwardness is any indication, possibly scared of me. Parker manages not to step on my toes and we start moving faster as the song speeds up.

"Not bad for your first time," I encourage with a smile. He's adorable. If I had a younger brother, I'd want him to be like Parker.

"Thanks, Tex, must be the teacher." He keeps his eyes on his boots to make sure he doesn't step on me. "I'm glad Kelly made me come out tonight."

"You've got it, eyes up here," I tease, squeezing his hands to help him stay in time with the Charley Crockett song that I know Ems put on just for me.

"Hey, cool wave tattoo, I didn't notice it until just now," he says as I reposition our hands. "It looks new, guess you're a real Rock Beach local now if you have a West tattoo."

"You're right about half of that, it is a West tattoo, but I'm actually a Three Rocks local. I don't live here in town," I say, holding my hand up so he can see my tattoo better.

"Dang, gnarly scar, Tex. What happened there?" Cute, sweet, awkward, shy Parker asks the dreaded question. Quickest way to make me feel sober. But oddly enough, I don't feel panicky.

"I don't like talking about it, but the tattoo helps," I say, still wondering why I'm not feeling massive anxiety or starting to hyperventilate.

"Sorry, Tex, I didn't mean to bring up something bad, I just think it's a cool tattoo." Poor Parker looks more than a little horrified. He's eyeing our booth longingly, like he wants to make his escape with his tail tucked.

"No, no, Parker, it's okay. You know what I tell everyone else?" I think he's going to have a panic attack of his own. "Saved a kitten from a grizzly in Alaska. The bear barely got me, only caught my finger, no biggie."

That gets me a grin. It's weird though, I don't feel the world closing in around me. It doesn't feel like all of the oxygen in the room has suddenly disappeared, but I do want to cry. Goddamn feelings journal, I blame my stupid self-reflection bullshit idea. I blink rapidly, ready to excuse myself from our dance, trying to find a reason without letting poor Parker know he's sent me into a tailspin. Before I can, I feel movement behind me and a shadow falls across my dance partner, who stiffens slightly.

Chapter Eleven
West

"Saved a kitten from a grizzly in Alaska. The bear barely got me, only caught my finger, no biggie." Harper's voice carries across the dance floor.

"West, go get her," Avery looks at me with wide eyes from the chair she just dropped into, declaring her dance career over. Her voice is laced with urgency.

Confused, I look to where the skinny guy from the hardware store, Parker, attempts to keep up with Harper's two step tutorial, both of his hands in hers. He's all of twenty-one years old and looks guilty while Harper looks slightly less than relaxed but not necessarily uncomfortable. I start their way, closing the distance quickly, wondering just what I'm supposed to be doing but spurred on by Avery's worried eyes and a strange feeling in the pit of my stomach.

"Mind if I cut in?" I use my height, age, and bulk to my advantage as Parker trips past following Harper's lead. He looks at me, quickly back to Harper, then back at me again. I don't move, just slightly narrow my eyes.

"Of course," he mumbles, giving Harper one last look. She just shrugs at him.

I hold my hand out to Harper, still unsure my role in whatever Avery just set in motion. She wordlessly steps into my space and I quickly move us into the simple step that Emmy taught me a few songs ago. I feel Harper's ribs expand, then hold, and I realize she's doing her breathing.

"Harper, you okay?" I ask, dipping my head toward her and speaking just loud enough for her to hear me over the music but not loud enough that anyone sharing our small dance floor can overhear. "Avery sent me over, but now I think maybe that wasn't the best idea." My heart falls as she looks up at me and I can see tears swimming in her eyes.

"Just keep dancing with me," she says softly, so I continue leading and pretend my heart isn't clenching.

I hear Emmy snicker and look over to the table to see her swiping on the phone connected to the speakers as Avery gives me a small smirk.

A slow, twangy sort of song comes on and Harper gives a sigh.

"Subtle, aren't they?" I ask her, gently pulling her closer but letting her choose the distance between us as we transition to a slow dance.

She glances at the table and then sighs again. "Avery is the only one that would think I needed to be rescued, Em just thinks Avery is trying to set us up. I think you've witnessed every epic meltdown I've had in the last few weeks, so that's just great. I'm not at all mortified by that fact. Or the fact that my very married best friend has been shamelessly hitting on you."

"Well I'm happy to play savior but I don't think I deserve that title, nor do you need saving from Parker, Kelly says he's a good kid," I tell her. "As for Emmy, she spent the whole time she was dragging me around the dance floor talking about her husband. I might be in love with the guy after all her gushing about him."

"He is pretty amazing," Harper says with humor in her voice. "If you tried his smoked ribs, you'd definitely be in love with him."

She tilts her head up and I can see her eyes are once again clear, but a single tear is caught in her lower eyelashes.

"Hi, again," I whisper, bringing our clasped hands up to gently wipe her tear.

"West," she whispers. "I'm sorry." I love hearing my name from her lips, but hate the apology.

110

"No apologies for tears, panic attacks, or overzealous friends," I tell her as I give her a gentle smile. I hope this is a really, really long song.

She buries her face in my shirt and I hear sniffles. This isn't quite the dance I had in mind when I locked up my shop, but I'll take what I can get with this girl. I move us across the floor, thankful that my size can be put to good use as her human shield as we continue to dance slowly and quietly. I can still feel her doing her deep breathing every once in a while but I stay silent and steady, spinning us slowly. The song melts into another. Avery gives me a head tilt from the table, brow furrowed in concern. I give her a subtle nod in return, hoping to reassure her.

"Parker saw my tattoo and asked about my scar. I just told him that it wasn't something I wanted to talk about." Harper finally breaks the silence as she moves even closer to me, her left hand creeping to the collar of my shirt. I slowly move my hand from her waist down to her hip. She tilts her head up and her eyes move to mine. "That's the first time I've ever given an honest answer to that question. Obviously it wasn't really an actual answer and I followed it up with my usual outlandish claim. He was sweet, laughed at my joke and didn't pry. I think he felt horrible. It just felt really fucking good to be direct and not have the panic I thought would come. It was so freeing, and apparently that combined with the four and a half beers I've had, I needed a moment. So thank you, again, West, for just being you."

She moves her hand from barely sneaking her pinky under the collar of my shirt to cupping my jaw, dragging her fingers through my beard. She licks her lips and all I want is her mouth on mine, but I remember the drinks she's had, our audience across the floor, and I even remember that I'm an undeserving asshole. But fuck, I want to taste her lips, pull her against me, trail kisses down her jawline, whisper in her ear…and then throw her over my shoulder and escape this crowded bar. I can see my desire reflected back to me in her gold-flecked eyes. I want to see those eyes first thing tomorrow morning as I kiss her awake, pull her into my lap, and hand her coffee.

Fuck. Pull it together.

"You're welcome, Harper, I'll dance with you any day, unless Colt beats me to it," I say, trying to convince myself to put a little more space between us. Suddenly the music speeds up and Emmy is at my side, hip-checking me out of her way.

"Our song!" Harper and Emmy squeal together, giggling, before Emmy spins Harper and they take over the entire dance floor. Harper catches my eye over Emmy's shoulder and gives me a wink.

"Want to take these two left feet for a spin?" Avery holds her hand out to me, eyebrow raised. If my observations from her quick lesson with Emmy earlier were any indication, my toes are about to be stepped on numerous times.

"Let's see what kind of damage we can do," I say, grabbing her hand and pulling her into step with me. It's not a total disaster, but it sure as shit would be better if I could keep my eyes on my dance partner instead of Harper.

***

"You look deep in thought," my sister says as she walks outside, coffee mug in hand. "I heard you come in pretty late last night. I also heard laughter and wolf whistles. Care to share, big brother?"

"I'm not cut out to be an Uber driver," I chuckle.

I don't add that yes, I am deep in thought, and all thoughts are about Harper. Her red-rimmed eyes that first night as my heart hammered wildly in my chest. Her small body settled in the sand next to mine, a perfect fit. Her smile that lights her face every time she sees Colt. Her ribs expanding under my hands as she matched her breaths to mine.

The drive home was car karaoke combined with Emmy blatantly hitting on me once again from her spot riding shotgun. The giant diamond ring on her finger and her pointed looks at Harper in the backseat told me that she was just doing it just to get a rise out of her friend.

After Emmy had pulled Harper away from me, they had closed the place down, dancing with everyone in there, from nervous Parker who could barely look me in the eye the rest of the night to Lester, the Vietnam vet that's always at the end of the bar, to a group of middle-aged women visiting from Newberg. Steve didn't know what hit him with

112

those three. Emmy even convinced him to come out from behind the bar and take a spin around the dance floor.

Last I saw, the girls were on the deck across the path, Emmy whistling at me as I walked away after making sure they could unlock the door.

"Remember how I called Tex 'SpitFire' after that first bonfire? Well, I spent an hour with the girls on the beach before whatever debauchery happened last night, and I can go ahead and say that Tex has nothing on Emmy," Jessie laughs. "I'm half terrified of her and half in love with her. This must be how those college boys felt."

"The volleyball guys?" I ask, remembering how one guy's eyes had been glued to Harper all night long, following her every move. A little like mine.

"I guess?" Jessie's voice rises into a question as she smirks at my tone. She takes a leisurely sip of coffee and pauses, drawing out my angst like the little sister she is. "Grant hung out with Colt and I while everyone else played a quick game, they even got Avery to play, then Emmy ran the guys off for girl time. Colt was in heaven. Grant was so good with him and of course he adored the attention from the girls."

I give her an even look, waiting for her to add more. Of course she doesn't. She just sips her coffee, looking out at the beach, that amused smirk hidden behind her mug. Why do I even care? Harper ended the night with me. Or, well, her friends.

"Uncle West!" Colt flings the slider open and throws himself at me. "I missed you yesterday when you were working."

"Hey bud, I missed you, too. Your mom was just telling me about your fun afternoon at the beach!" I squeeze him and let him settle into my lap.

"We played frisbees and flied kites and built the biggest sandcastle ever! Tex's friend Grant played with me and mom and told me all about rocks. He knows a lot about rocks. He also has a dog, but his dog isn't here, it's at his home," Colt animatedly tells me. "He said we could have hot chocolate together today!"

"Oh really," I say, looking at Jessie, who is refusing to look at me. "And when are you getting this hot chocolate?"

"Can we go right now?" Colt scrambles off my lap and runs inside without waiting for an answer.

"So, Grant knows a lot about rocks, huh?" I ask Jessie. Oh, how the tables have turned.

She's smiling at her coffee mug in her lap, and it's her real smile, not the strained smile I've been seeing for what feels like years now. I hear her phone buzz and she pulls it out from her waistband, her smile growing bigger.

"Come on, big brother, you're invited, too," she says, cheeks pink, sliding off her chair and running her fingers through her hair.

***

Fine, I'll admit it. Grant is a nice guy. Young, but nice. I don't love that Jessie seems to be latching on to a different guy each week, but at least Grant is polite, funny, and kind. He chats with Colt about rocks and shells and shows him pictures of his rescue dog that was found dumped in a parking lot. He laughs easily, unfortunately doesn't seem intimidated by me or my questions about his future plans now that he's graduated, and keeps his hands to himself.

We run into hungover but happy Harper, Avery, and Emmy on the bridge and Colt and Emmy show me their new secret handshake. Avery looks at Grant, then Jessie, then me, raising her eyebrow. I give her a shrug and she smiles brightly. Apparently she approves. I know she and Grant talked for quite a while at the bonfire, so her approval settles my mind.

Harper smiles at me over Colt's shoulder when she picks him up to swing him around and I have to put my hands in my pockets to stop myself from reaching for her. We aren't there yet.

Emphasis on yet.

"Hi, Harper." I can't help but move closer to her.

"Hi," she replies, biting her lip.

"Good morning, handsome." Emmy comes in for a hug, wrapping her arms around my waist like we've been friends for years.

"Good morning, Emmy. Did you enjoy terrorizing the entire bar last night?" I ask her as she pulls away, trying not to grin. She's impossible not to like.

114

"I think you mean, did I enjoy bringing happiness to the entire bar last night, and the answer is yes. Yes, I did," she retorts. "I also enjoyed *our* dance." She raises her voice for that last comment and touches my forearm, leaving it there until Harper notices. Harper swats her friend and rolls her eyes.

"I'm texting your husband right now," Harper threatens, pulling out her phone.

"Oh good, I already told him they grow these lumberjacks right, you can verify," Emmy says brightly.

"Oh my god, you're impossible!" Harper exclaims. She shakes her head with a smile, obviously amused by her friend's antics. I'm also amused by them, because I'm pretty sure it means that Emmy is pushing for Harper to take a chance with me.

Colt interrupts their banter and asks the trio if they can come over and play but Avery gently tells him that they are getting coffee and then have to take Emmy to the airport. His lip quivers as he looks at Emmy. It's Grant that steps in and asks if they could go look for shells together. Like I said, I'll admit he's a nice guy.

***

I nod for Jessie and Colt to go ahead without me and sink down into the sand. It's the same spot against the rocks where Harper sat with me on tattoo day. I watch Jessie and Colt walk to the water holding hands. It's good to see them together again. I've tried to give them plenty of space the last couple of days, knowing, or at least hoping, that Jessie will find her way back to us as she settles into her new life, whatever that may mean.

I do know that she has spent the last few weeks gathering all of the paperwork she needs to file for divorce. She told me that she had asked Liam to move out after the holidays when he went on a week-long bender. My rage surfaced when she told me he finally came home reeking of cigarettes and perfume, eyes bloodshot and his car dented. I was ready to track the bastard down when she then added that he refused to leave their apartment. She started sharing Colt's room immediately, unwilling to share the bedroom with Liam and also unwilling to let him in Colt's space when he was acting erratically.

The day she left Colt with me was the day she finally left Liam for good. It had been five months of her struggling to find the willpower and money to leave on her own. Liam had somehow gotten into her savings account but yesterday when she arrived, she excitedly showed me pictures of a small, furnished apartment that she wants to look at. She's on the right path, even with the slight detour of Douchebag Derek. I wish she would have shared all of this with me sooner, but I'm working on looking forward, not back.

Colt's happy shrieks pull me from my thoughts and I smile as I see Jessie splashing in the receding waves with him. She is so much lighter than she was last weekend, the transformation is nearly unbelievable.

"Hi," a quiet voice interrupts my thoughts. I look up and see Harper smiling down at me. Zero softly whines as she watches Jessie and Colt at the water's edge.

"Hi," I reply. What the fuck is this sensation in my chest?

"Want company?" she asks, shifting her weight around nervously.

"Zerooooo!" Colt yells, running as fast as he can toward us.

Jessie waves and gives a thumbs up so Harper unclips Zero's leash. The dog takes off toward Colt and I suck in a breath, waiting for a collision. Zero leaps to the side and hurtles past Colt before circling back to nose him in the face. They take off together toward Jessie and the three of them play chase. Happiness radiates from my sister as she runs through the surf.

Harper sinks down in the sand after I nod to the empty space next to me. "So, I think this is when I have to say thank you for last night and maybe apologize for soaking you with both beer and tears. Oh, and for my friend sexually harassing you all night. And this morning. And for our horrific karaoke in the truck on the way home. Is there more? I'm sure there's more," she says with a sheepish smile.

"I'll give you my full list of grievances," I deadpan. I feel her shift so she's pressed against my side. Her cheeks are pink and she's biting the corner of her lip.

116

"Grant and Jessie, huh? How are you feeling about that?" Harper asks. "Avery said he seems really driven, she talked to him a lot on Friday when the rest of us were playing volleyball."

"He seems like a nice kid," I grumble.

"Kid? He's a college graduate with a clear future planned out, that's more than I can say," she says with a light laugh. Her laugh cuts off suddenly. "Wait, how old *are* you?"

"Old enough that Grant and his college boys are closer to your age than I am," I say, glaring out at the ocean.

I knew this age gap would be an issue. It's not only the numbers, it's also the life lived. How many mistakes I've made. How many people I've taken down bad roads. How many people I've lost.

If I could go back, I'd do things a lot differently. If that was the case, would I still end up here, next to her?

"You definitely have a grumpy old man vibe right now," she nudges me with her shoulder.

"Ouch." I rub my chest like she's hurt me.

She looks up at me, her hazel eyes locking on mine. "Luckily I have no time for boys, only men."

My heart hammers against my chest. Could she please say that again but while she does that bite-her-bottom lip thing? Or maybe as she drags her fingers through my beard. Or under my shirt. I stare at her, unable to form words, and she bursts out laughing.

"That's the Emmy influence," she says, winking, and crushing my daydream.

I shake my head, trying to clear the dirty thoughts racing through my mind. "Not a bad influence at all," I say, my suddenly dry mouth making my voice sound gravelly.

There is no chance of resistance, I can't convince myself any longer that this is a bad idea. I'll box up the darkness that follows me and shove it in a corner.

"But I also mean it." Wait, what? She licks her lips and stares right into my eyes.

I angle my body toward her, glancing down at her tempting lips and then back up into her slightly wild hazel eyes.

And then her dog shakes shockingly cold, salty water all over both of us.

Colt wiggles into Harper's lap and innocently asks if we are snuggling. Jessie tries to turn her laughter into a cough.

"No snuggling here," Harper says, lips twitching in amusement. She takes one look at Jessie and they both burst into laughter.

"None at all," I add, not nearly as amused. But as Jessie drops down beside us and Harper pulls Colt into a hug, I'm pretty damn happy.

Chapter Twelve
Harper

I settle into what has become our spot, the little piece of the beach with large rocks as both a backrest and windbreak; it feels secluded yet we can have eyes on Colt and Zero while they play. Zero lays down beside me, resting her chin on her front paws, softly whining, eyes on the path where she knows her small human friend will run down at any second. Sure enough, in a wild blur of motion, Colt trips down the rocky beach path with a solid wall of surly West behind him.

"Zero!" Colt yells and I unclip her leash so she can take off after her playmate. I'm always slightly concerned she will barrel him over but they somehow avoid collision and race toward the gentle low tide waves. They have the beach to themselves, the advantage of midweek romps, no one as far as the eye can see.

West sits down beside me on the sand that's still warm from the sun and I tentatively lean my head on his shoulder. We stay quiet, watching the wild duo chase seagulls, content to just share our space. Whatever is building between us is slow and sweet, which is both exactly what I need and also driving me a little crazy. If the number of daydreams I have about this man are any indication, I'm in deep, and he's barely touched me. That almost-kiss from Sunday night plays on repeat in my mind every day. And night.

"Jessie won't be here until Sunday; she's only coming for the day instead of the whole weekend. I don't want to tell Colt but I know I need to," West breaks his silence, explaining his quiet demeanor.

My heart hurts for all three of them and I press myself closer, leaning into his solid side. There aren't any words I can say that will help, so I stay silent.

"I know she's trying, I do, I just wish things were different," he adds heavily.

"I'm sorry," I say quietly, watching Zero and Colt dig a hole together, sand flying everywhere.

West sighs and wraps his giant arm around me and it's all I can do to not climb right into his lap. I want to wrap myself in his woodsy carpenter smell, burrow into his wide chest, and stay here all night. How can this man make me slow down but also make me want to climb him like a tree?

"Since you're not the bonfire host this week, would you want to come back to my house for movie night after Colt wears himself out with glow tag?" West asks, resting his chin on top of my head.

"You mean after I tire myself out with glow tag?" I ask with a laugh.

Not going to lie, I'm super excited for this Friday's community bonfire. John from the golf course is hosting and his teenage grandson, a summer resident who follows Kelsey around like she hung the moon (also how I follow her around some days), suggested the "Glow" theme. Not only did they order light-up, neon frisbees but John showed me a huge box of glow necklaces for games of glow tag and glow hide-and-seek. Kids and kids-at-heart are going to have a blast.

I love how quickly everyone has embraced the bonfires. We've gotten so many supportive comments from everyone that stops in at The Merc, it's really elevated our summer planning to a new level. Kelsey and I are close to having the Fourth of July celebration planned and social media content is already well under way. She had the brilliant idea to do short interviews with the residents that spent their childhoods here, asking them what they remember most about the annual celebration and what they'd like to see brought back. It only backfired slightly when Betty made hilarious and highly inappropriate comments about the firefighters. We won't use that on the community accounts but it's sure as shit going on the Breakers Bliss Instagram. Betty might need to be the unofficial host of the girls' weekend house.

"Yes, when you're both all tuckered out, can I tuck you guys under blankets on the couch for movie night? Zero can come, too." I can feel West's smile and then his arm around me just barely tightens for a gentle squeeze. "Please?" he whispers.

"You're not going to be sick of me?" I ask hesitantly.

We've seen each other nearly daily for one reason or another since I moved here, even when I was actively trying to avoid him, and this is the fourth night in a row that we've found each other on the beach.

After the near-kiss on Sunday evening, when I was still high on girls' weekend vibes and remembering the feel of West's arms as we danced, I'd tried to pull back, but I couldn't. I have gone from completely guarded to zero self-preservation instincts because of the way this man makes me feel. He already has the ability to crush my newly feeling heart.

I spent Monday running errands for Avery in Rock Beach while replaying and overanalyzing our almost-kiss all freaking day. The beach was empty when I walked down so I'd let Zero run off leash while I sat and wrote in my journal. A few minutes later Zero let out an excited bark and I saw West and Colt headed down the rocky path. Colt and Z took off to dig holes together and West sat down next to me with a small smile. We didn't talk much, instead he did a quick sketch in the back of my notebook of Zero and Colt running along the beach while I leaned against his solid shoulder watching his large hands work quickly. I might have daydreamed about his hands doing other things.

By Tuesday it seemed to be our new normal. We didn't mention it during the day when Colt raced up my front steps on the way to get his special hot chocolate or when we saw each other at The Glass House, me dropping off heavy Pendleton blankets and him working on the floating deck. Yet when I walked down to the beach, West was waiting for me in this spot, saying "I was really hoping you'd be here" quietly as I sat down next to him. He showed me pictures of the progress on the deck, I told him about my short shift working the coffee counter at The Merc. When Colt and Zero finished their sand-flinging, we walked to the creek and back, swinging Colt between us, throwing rocks in the waves, and letting our hands brush together when we walked back, boy and dog finally tired.

My past relationships have included awkward group dates with boys that were fun but, well, immature high school boys; college friends-with-benefits situations that were a carefree way to pass time, zero feelings necessary; and my one attempt at something more serious was Ethan, which was a half-hearted and half-assed attempt at best. Since being here and taking a little deeper look at my life, I've realized that just like my work resume, my relationship history is all part-time or temporary. I haven't been willing to put my time, effort, or heart into anything in my life besides Avery, Emmy, and Zero. With how strongly I feel pulled toward West, I'm well out of my comfort zone.

"If I didn't think you'd bolt after the kid and the dog right now, I'd tell you that I've looked forward to seeing you every single day since you moved here," West replies. He pulls his arm from around me and leans sideways to look down into my eyes. "So I'll settle for telling you that I'd love for you to hang out with us Friday after the bonfire for movie night. I won't be sick of you."

I can see the honesty in the little crinkles at the edges of his blue eyes as he gives me a small smile.

"I'd love to," I say quietly, my heart pounding against my ribs.

I tuck myself closer to him and slowly reach for his hand, leaning my head on his shoulder once again, tangling my fingers with his. His thumb slowly brushes mine as we watch Colt and Zero play, the sun bursting through the clouds behind them making the waves sparkle. I can't remember a time I've felt this content, this settled.

***

Unfortunately the settled feeling does not last long. After spending all day yesterday triple-checking the rentals, I have a color-coded list in my notebook, a large cold brew from Dutch Bros in my cup holder, and I'm sitting in the Ikea parking lot trying to convince myself to go in. It's 11 a.m. on the dot and the doors are open.

Confession: the first and only other time I'd been in an Ikea, I had a panic attack. All I remember was looking up, Emmy no longer

122

being next to me, and instead of an easy exit, it was a fucking maze of fake rooms and arguing couples. I hate not knowing where exits are, it makes me feel trapped. The next thing I knew, I was downstairs in the warehouse area, hyperventilating and sweating while yanking off as many layers as I could as I ran for the parking lot. Not my best moment.

I have since learned slightly better tools for managing my anxiety than stripping, but after my panic attack at The Glass House, I'm feeling a little on edge about this shopping trip. When West asked why I was rubbing my tattoo last night during our beach time, all I said was that I wasn't looking forward to a long day in Portland before the bonfire. Fairly certain he knew I was lying but who wants to admit that Ikea gives them panic attacks?

I recheck my list for the eighteenth time, make sure I have two highlighters in my back pocket, pop my AirPods in and turn on my Chris Stapleton playlist. I'm two steps into the store when a text notification buzzes.

West:
Colt and Zero say hi.

A picture comes through of Colt sitting on my cottage porch, licking his whipped cream mustache and holding his special hot chocolate with Zero next to him, a spot of whipped cream on her nose. A-fucking-dorable.

Those two are pretty good motivation to get this shopping done quickly. The sooner I'm done, the sooner I'm back, the sooner I can get my feet back in the sand with those two. And West.

I'm nearly done with my list, counting out dinnerware sets, when icy dread washes over me. I freeze.

breathe in two three four, hold two three four, out two three four
I hear the voice.
The voice from the party.
It's been ten fucking years.
The voice that will never leave me.
I can feel my hands start to shake.

123

I frantically rub my scar.

No.

I rub my tattoo.

Ocean waves.

breathe in two three four, hold two three four, out two three four

Focus.

Salty sea air.

Zero running on the beach.

Girls' weekend.

Chasing Colt up the rock.

West steady beside me in our spot.

breathe in two three four, hold two three four, out two three four

A man and woman come around the corner and the man laughs and says "anything for you, wifey," in a deep voice and his wife melts into his side. He kisses her temple and they both smile at me.

It's not him. It's definitely not him, he's twice my age. It's an adorable couple. They're even holding hands.

Fuck. I can't believe that just happened. Is this part of the whole self-reflection and feelings bullshit I thought was a good idea? Is Ikea just cursed? Is it because I'm back living in Oregon?

breathe in two three four, hold two three four, out two three four

I want to get past this on my own, but my heart wants to hear West's voice. His calm, steady voice telling me that he's there with me. His breaths matching mine.

breathe in two three four, hold two three four, out two three four

I've already done it on my own. I'm not hyperventilating, I'm not balled up crying, I'm not stripping as I sprint through the store.

That's my bar, my line in the sand: strip-sprinting. Great.

breathe in two three four, hold two three four, out two three four

Fucking anxiety. Fucking Ikea. Fucking feelings.

I pull out my phone, pull up West's text, smile at the pic of Colt with Zero.

Harper:

tell me something good.

124

Instead of a text, my phone buzzes with an incoming call. I answer but don't say anything. I don't trust my voice.

"I've been thinking about you all morning." West's quiet voice is in my AirPods, drowning out the sounds of this stupid, cursed store. "I can't wait for the bonfire tonight, to see the way the flames bring out the little gold flecks in your eyes, like that first night I met you. You looked so fucking beautiful, I couldn't speak."

"Wow," I breathe. "You're good at that."

"Harper?" His voice is low, worried. "You okay?"

"I'm sorry, I heard a voice that sounded like a nightmare." I'm not sure what to say. I can hear shuffling on the other end.

"Tex, you okay?" Avery sounds worried. More than worried. I bet she's looking over her shoulder, her version of the scar rub.

"Yeah, I'm okay. I thought I heard the voice, but I'm okay," I say, looking around to make sure I'm still alone in this section.

"Promise?"

"Promise."

"Can I make fun of West for what he just told you?" Aves is the best at reading me, knowing I need it lighter now.

"Yeah, but I also want to hear him say it again," I tell her. "So don't be too relentless." There's rustling again.

"I'll say it whenever you want to hear it, Harper." West is back, the deep rumble of his voice a delicious contrast to his sweet words.

"I'm good now," I reassure him, and probably Avery who I'm sure is still listening in.

"I meant it, I was speechless when you looked up at me," West says. "And it's alarming how many times you've done that to me since."

This man. The one waiting for me back home, my dog and his nephew by his side.

"West, thank you," I say, hoping he can hear that I mean it in so many ways.

"See you tonight," he says, and my heart beats faster in the best way possible.

I give my tattoo one last rub, take one more deep breath, and command myself to move forward. Or at least get back to the task at hand.

I go back to counting dinnerware sets, still slightly shaky, but I still have my sweater on and I'm not sprinting through the store, so this is still somehow better than my last Ikea experience.

By the time I've run up Avery's credit card balance and Tetris'ed everything to fit in the Jeep, I'm calm. Or as calm as I can be after drinking that much cold brew. I snap a quick pic of the boxes piled in the Jeep and send it to Avery and Kelsey.

Tex:
unpacking is going to take forever, glad we aren't hosting tonight

Aves:
I'll meet you down the hill to help, text me when you're home.

KelseyLove:
putting the team in team merc

Tex:
prob home around 4p

Aves:
I'll be there.

KelseyLove:
me toooooo!

Just before I pull out of my parking spot another notification comes through. I pause to check.

West:
I'm really looking forward to movie night and so are
these two.
126

A new picture of Colt and Zero comes through, they're in the yard at West's house playing in a sprinkler. I can smell the wet dog from here.

Chapter Thirteen
West

I smile as I watch Colt chase Harper across the beach, their multiple glow sticks keeping them in my sights. John went all out for the glow party; locals and tourists alike are gathered around the bonfire to keep warm between the games of frisbee and tag. Harper, Kelsey, and Avery have already had a huge impact on our community and the summer is just getting started.

"She's pretty amazing, isn't she?" Avery asks, once again watching me watch her friend. She has Zero on a leash and the dog is not pleased to be excluded from the games. She whines softly and nudges Avery's hand every few seconds.

"You guys have really pulled this town together, Ave, I'm impressed," I tell her honestly. "I even had Doug from the glassblowing place next door to my shop call me this afternoon. He wanted to know who was running our events. Impressive that Rock Beach business owners have heard about what's going on in Three Rocks."

"Well, thanks, but that's not what I meant by that. What's really going on with you two?" Avery gives me a hard look, one I know well from her.

"I don't really know. I didn't see this coming. You know me, I'm happy with my solitude and haven't looked twice at anyone since I moved here. But I looked twice at her the first time I saw her. She didn't even look once at me, her eyes were only on you," I chuckle, remembering how Harper threw herself at Avery. I hadn't seen Avery smile or laugh like that in all the time I'd known her. "Something about her just drew me in. I like her a lot. A fucking lot. But I have Colt to think about. She's young, is she really staying here? How many times has someone mentioned how she's running away? I'm just a cranky bastard, an asshole who left a trail of destruction behind. She deserves better," I word vomit on my friend, the only one who really knows both of us.

"West, you're right," Avery says, looking me straight in the eye.

"What the fuck, Ave? You're supposed to at least try to tell me I'm not a bad guy," I say, crossing my arms, eyes moving to quickly check on the glow tag game in the distance before coming back to glare at my apparently brutally honest friend.

"You're right," she repeats. "Harper draws everyone in. You're not the first. I know you've witnessed everyone from your nephew to the Willamette guys to Tom be pulled in by her charm. Put her in any situation and she'll hide how overwhelmed she is behind humor, and then she'll thrive. Not only thrive, but she'll pull everyone along with her. She's funny, hardworking, caring, kind, a little scary when she's on a mission, and she's been my best friend since we were six."

Well, fuck.

"But, you're calm, steady, and quite possibly just what she needs. She doesn't let anyone in, West. No one else sees her the way she lets me see her. She let you in though. You're the one she reached out to earlier." Avery gives me hope with those words. "Yeah, you're older than her and you might actually end up with Colt for a lot longer than anyone thought, but when Tex really goes for something, she doesn't fuck around. She jokes constantly about not being much for commitment, running away from her life, but that's all bullshit. That's just her walls. She committed to me when we were barely older than Colt. She committed to Emmy on her second day in Texas. She committed to Colt the first time she met him. Stop making excuses. I saw it that first night at the fire pit. There was something between the two of you. Something big. Something bigger than either of you ever expected. It's different with her. She's different now, she's different with you. Accept the fact that she's awesome and do something about it."

I rub the back of my neck. I don't know what to say to that. Luckily I don't have to say anything, as a breathless Harper appears, Colt riding piggyback. Her eyes are happy and clear as she steps closer to me. Colt manages to scramble from her back to mine and his little arms wrap tightly around my neck.

"Movie night!" he excitedly reminds me, like I've somehow forgotten.

I've been looking forward to movie night all day long. Even more so after the brief phone call with Harper. I need to reassure myself that she's okay, that whatever had happened earlier has passed. I hate thinking of her having a panic attack alone. I'm still haunted by the look in her eyes when I'd found her at The Glass House.

"Miss Avery, are you coming to movie night, too?" Colt asks hopefully.

Avery smiles at him and tickles his feet that stick out along my sides. "Sorry, friend, I'm going to make sure John doesn't need any help with the bonfire, then I'm going to bed early because I have a big run to go on tomorrow morning." She gives me a pointed look and I return it steadily, even as Colt climbs his way to my shoulders.

"Well, this is an awkward standoff that I want no part of," Harper says, looking between her best friend and I with an amused expression. "Y'all are too similar, you're freaking me out."

"I was just thanking West for taking the week off to finish the work at the rentals," Avery flat-out lies.

"Well, I can guarantee that's a lie. Nice try, Aves. But yes, West, thanks for finishing up this week," Harper says, glaring at Avery.

"I still have a few small things to pull together at The Glass House, but I'll be able to get to them this week before heading in to the shop," I reply, rubbing my hand down my face, trying and failing to translate the silent communication happening between them.

"Movie night!" Colt impatiently reminds us from his perch on my shoulders.

"You four have a great time tonight!" Avery says brightly, pinching Colt's toes and giving my shoulder a pat as she hands Zero's leash to Harper.

Colt cheers as we start walking back up the beach toward the house, Zero trotting along with us.

***

"In my defense, I was left unsupervised." Harper grins, pillow in one hand and blanket in the other. I had stepped into my bedroom to change into a clean shirt after making the popcorn and came back out to this.

"You built a fort!" Colt comes flying back into the living room after changing into his dinosaur pajamas, ecstatic to see the elaborate blanket structure Harper had constructed in about two minutes flat. He scrambles under the blankets with Zero right behind him. "Come on Uncle West, come see Tex's fort!"

Harper smiles brightly at me and then ducks into the fort. I try to fold my 6'2" frame small enough to crawl under the blankets. I manage to catch my shoulder on the side and nearly rip the damn thing down but Colt and Harper lunge for it and hold it steady. They both grin widely at me as I hand over the giant bowl of popcorn. I reach back out and grab the remote from the couch cushion. I flip to Disney Plus, my newest streaming service, downloaded the day Jessie didn't show up for the first time, and find Colt's go-to movie: Cars.

When I turn back, Colt has snuggled in between Zero and Harper. Harper smiles at me as she ruffles Colt's messy hair. I lean back onto a pile of pillows, unsure just how I went from my quiet, isolated existence to having a kid, a dog, and a girl that I desperately want to make mine crowded in a blanket fort in my living room, but damn happy this is where I find myself.

An hour later, I'm still damn happy but also damn restless. As Colt drifted toward Zero over the last hour, Harper inched her way toward me. Colt is now using Zero as his pillow and Harper is using me as hers. She's on her side facing Colt but her back is pressed tightly along my side and her foot is hooked over my shin. Her head is nestled on my bicep and all I want to do is roll onto my side and pull her into me. I peek at my nephew but of course he's wide awake. I smile when I see that he has one hand absentmindedly playing with Zero's ears and his other hand tucked into Harper's hand. Avery's right: Harper committed to Colt the day she met him.

Harper feels my movement and turns her head to smile at me. Fuck, every time her eyes are on me, I feel them deep in my chest.

132

"Hi," she whispers, biting her lip. She slowly reaches her hand toward me, keeping her other hand wrapped around Colt's.

"Hi, Harper," I whisper in her ear. I see her shiver. I shift slightly so I can entwine my fingers with hers and then rest our hands on her hip, gently rubbing my thumb over hers.

"Shhh," Colt whispers, making Harper shake with silent laughter.

"Sorry, Colt, I'm just happy and couldn't keep it in," Harper says and squeezes my hand.

"That's okay, I'm happy, too," he smiles at her, then me. "Zero is happy, three, and Uncle West is happy four!"

Harper gives me another smile, this one softer. She slowly stretches out and I mentally calculate how much longer this movie is going to last. I can't *not* have my hands on her much longer.

***

"Can Zero sleep with me?" Colt asks as he crawls out from the fort.

"I know you'd like that, but Zero is Tex's dog," I tell him gently.

"Tex, can we have a sleepover?" Colt skips the middleman and goes right to Harper. Smart kid.

"Sorry, Colt, but I don't like sleeping all alone at my house so I need Zero with me," she replies, ruffling his hair but keeping her eyes on me. "How about if you, Zero, and I hang out tomorrow while Uncle West goes to work and we can have a sleepover then? Colt and Tex's Big Day Out! We can play all afternoon and then you and Zero can snuggle all night long while I snuggle with these amazing blankets on the couch until Uncle West gets home. Then I'll go have a sleepover with Avery! If that plan's okay with Uncle West?"

Colt turns to me with puppy dog eyes and I give him a smile and a nod.

"Yay! We get a sleepover, Z!" cheers Colt, giving the dog a hug before launching himself at Harper. "You can have a sleepover with Uncle West so you're not lonely. Then we could have our sleepover right now!"

Harper's eyes have never been wider. This kind of panic is amusing though. I try to hide my smile as she visibly attempts to pull herself together as she continues to hug Colt.

"I don't even have a toothbrush with me and now I'm super excited to hang out with you all afternoon tomorrow. I'll even order us pizza from Sarah and we can make s'mores," Harper promises, her voice higher than usual.

"Okay bud, time to brush your teeth and get to bed so you have enough energy to keep up with Zero and Tex tomorrow," I tell him. He skips down the hall toward his bathroom with Zero following him, leaving Harper and I alone in the living room.

"Well that escalated quickly," I offer, rubbing the back of my neck.

"I hope that was okay?" Harper asks, suddenly looking worried. "I know you work late tomorrow, I was just trying to help."

"It's more than okay, he loves hanging out with you. Can you wait a few minutes while I tuck him in and extract your dog from his room?"

She smiles and nods, reaching for a blanket from the fort, so I pad down the hallway, hoping it's an easy bedtime.

I read Colt a story but he barely makes it through a few pages before he falls asleep. He always looks so peaceful in sleep, especially because he rarely holds still when awake. Even though I'm in a hurry to get back to Harper, I take a few seconds to watch him sleep so peacefully, his chest rising and falling in an easy rhythm. He played hard all day today, taking his job babysitting Zero very seriously. Glow tag at the bonfire followed by movie night really finished him off. I quietly tell Zero it's time to go and she slowly gets down from the bed, glaring at me the whole time. I follow her out, turning the light off and flipping the night light on as I walk by.

Back in the living room, Harper is taking down the fort, stacking the pillows and folding the blankets. She gives me an unsure smile and Zero beelines for her side. Her hand drifts down to scratch Z's head, and I see her rubbing her tattoo.

"I had fun tonight, thank you for inviting me," she says quietly.

I remember Avery's words from earlier: accept the fact that she's awesome and do something about it.

Harper is obviously nervous, that finger rub gives her away. But is she nervous because she's feeling what I feel? Like I will lose my goddamn mind if I don't touch her, like I want to throw her over my shoulder and take her back to my bedroom? I want to make her moan my name. I want to hand her coffee in the morning after spending all night with her wrapped around me. Perhaps that's not what I should lead with though.

"I can't exactly walk you home, but would you like to take Zero out and sit on the deck for a bit?" I ask, mentally crossing my fingers like the awkward teenager that this girl seems to bring out in me.

"I'd like that, as long as we can bring blankets," she says, grabbing the one she just folded and finally looking me in the eye.

I flip the strands of patio lights on, open the slider, letting her and Zero out ahead of me, then leave the door cracked open in case Colt wakes up. Harper's wrapping a blanket around herself and I really didn't think this through because not only does she resemble a mini-burrito with only half her face showing, but my adirondack chairs are placed a few feet apart.

"I don't like being cold and I swear I've been cold at least once a day since I got here," she laughs from behind her burrito blanket that's pulled up over her nose. She walks to the edge of the deck to stare out toward the water.

I slowly lower into my favorite chair, watching her as she watches her dog explore the yard. I can still see her rubbing her finger, even with the blankets wrapped around her, and she's shifting her weight from one foot to the other.

"Harper, are you okay? Are we okay?" I finally ask, after a few minutes of silence. I see her shoulders tense. "I feel like you're nervous, or upset, or anxious right now, and I'm hoping it's not because of me."

She waits another few seconds, the silence between us growing louder, then turns. Her gaze lands on mine and those heart-stopping hazel eyes are on fire. Even in the dim light, I can see the gold flecks shining. Her hands are still, she releases her lower lip from between her teeth, and the blanket loosens from around her shoulders as she walks toward me. I stay frozen in my chair, mind racing, heart racing. She reaches her hand out cautiously, dragging her fingers through my beard like she did the other night, and lowers herself onto my lap. I pull her in with one arm wrapped around her waist, my other hand cups her face.

"Hi," she says softly.

"Hi, Harper," I reply, using my thumb to trace her lower lip.

"You feel this, too, right?" she whispers, moving her hand behind my neck, her fingers in my hair. Her eyes are glued to mine.

"Since the first time I saw you. I meant what I said earlier, it wasn't just to make you feel better," I tell her quietly, tipping her chin toward me, inching us closer.

"West," she whispers my name, still hesitating.

"I'm all in, Harper," I say. When she leans forward, I close the distance between us, tasting her lips before gently pulling away.

"West," she whispers my name again, this time urgently, before crashing her lips to mine.

I kiss her until we're both breathless, until I can't lose myself any further. We pull back slowly, eyes locked on each other. I slip my hand under her shirt and grip her waist gently, my fingers splayed up her ribcage. Her skin is soft, warm, and smooth.

"I've never done this before," she whispers.

Stop. Halt.

What. The. Fuck.

I freeze my movements and sit back slowly. Her eyes widen, then she bites her lip and tries to hide a smile.

"Um, no, not that, I've done that," she says, laughing at my expression. "I've never been all in on a relationship. I always have an exit strategy even if it's been just for fun. Even the more serious ones, I've now realized they weren't that serious. Just time-passers. I just want you to know, I'm all in, too, but I don't know what the hell I'm doing. I just know that I like you. I like you a lot. And I trust you when I don't trust anyone. I want to climb you like a fucking tree when you say my name in that deep voice you use. Your hand under my shirt, on my waist like this, is my new favorite thing. I can't stop thinking about you. I love your nephew like crazy. I never know what I'm doing. But I know I need to do this, I need you. That's what I decided, standing there on the deck, I need to try. Also, have I mentioned that I overshare when I'm nervous?"

"Harper, please keep oversharing but please don't be nervous," I whisper and steal another kiss as she tries to shift lower in my lap, away from my eyes. "I told you I'm all in, and that means I am all in. I've never done this either. Sounds scary as fuck. *You* scare me."

That draws a laugh, and her hand moves to my beard again. She looks into my eyes and I drink her in, wanting to wrap her up in my arms and carry her back inside.

"So we're both all in, both scared shitless, and neither of us knows what to do. Great," she says wryly.

I kiss her again, unable to stop myself. She sighs into me.

"I should go," she whispers, pulling away, then leans in and softly kisses me again. "This is a lot. But I'm not panicking and running, I just need to get some sleep. I've got a date tomorrow with your nephew."

I want to ask her to stay. I don't want her to go, even if it's only a few hundred yards away. All in doesn't mean all at once though, so I force myself to release her from my grip. I grimace and readjust myself as I stand, then walk her to the street after she whistles for her dog.

"Goodnight, Harper," I say softly, smiling when she turns back to stand on her tiptoes for one last kiss.

I watch until she walks up to her porch at the end of the block and then I head straight for a very necessary, very cold shower. When I get out, I see a text.

Harper:
wait, how old are you?

I laugh, but then worry that she really is panicking.

West:
Old enough to know you're going to wreck me, Harper.

No response.

137

West:
I'm 32.

       No response.

West:
Change your mind so soon?

Harper:
i can now see the appeal of older men. (wink emoji)

       Now I don't know how to respond.

Harper:
or at least one older man.

       Hell yes. I'll take it.

West:
I stand by what I said. I'm all in. Goodnight, Harper.

Harper:
goodnight, old man.

Chapter Fourteen
Harper

I am exhausted but in the best way possible. Who knew five-year-olds were so tiring? Parents, everywhere, I'm sure. But I did not. We've been on the go since lunch time.

First, Colt and I met Kelsey at The Green Door Garden where Colt narrated an "Explain it to me like I'm five" gardening how-to video. Colt hammed it up and, with Jessie's permission, we hope to turn it into a series. We kept Colt off camera but Zero made a cameo, enthusiastically swinging the garden hose around, soaking both me and Kelsey's phone. Our followers love Zero; Kelsey laughs every time we get a comment asking about her.

Our social media accounts are gaining followers and inquiries into when each rental will be ready are rolling in. I feel a sense of urgency to get the kitchenware unboxed and washed, thus one step closer to opening each rental, but I promised Colt a fun afternoon so a fun afternoon we had.

We raced borrowed bikes up North Road, explored the creek along the tsunami trail, shared pizza from the cafe with Avery, made gluten-free chocolate crinkle cookies for Betty, took Zero on a beach walk, and then got invited to make our s'mores at Avery's family's house with Jenn, Avery's mom, who showed up for a last-minute getaway. Colt is currently basking in the attention from Avery, Jenn, and I as we finish off our sticky s'mores.

Jenn hands me a glass of wine as Colt snuggles in my lap, reminding me of my first night in town. Zero is at my side, nosing Colt from under the armrest whenever his fingers stop fiddling with her soft ears. I zone out for a few minutes, enjoying the warmth of his small body on my lap, lulled by the quiet conversation between Avery and her mom.

"Tex?" Colt whispers suddenly, looking up at me, big brown eyes locking on mine.

"What's up, my man?" I whisper back, smiling down at his cute little dimples.

"I love you," he whispers shyly.

My heart bursts. "Oh, Colt, I love you, too. You're my favorite five-year-old in the whole wide world," I whisper, squeezing him tight. Don't cry, don't cry, don't cry. Do. Not. Cry.

Zero doesn't want to miss out on the snugglefest and tries climbing into the chair with us, making both of us giggle. I laugh harder when our chair almost topples over. Avery grabs my wineglass from me as I try to fit a child and a large dog in my lap.

"Okay, friends, I think this is our cue. It's time for Colt and Zero to get to their sleepover before we cause more chaos," I say, tickling Colt as I set him on the ground.

I tuck Colt and Zero into bed, switch the night light in the hallway outside the bedroom on, and collapse on the couch. How can the two cutest, wildest, sweetest little creatures be so exhausting? It's barely 10 p.m. and I feel like I ran a marathon and then got hit by a truck of emotions.

Settling in on the couch, I take a few minutes to check the various social media accounts, smiling when I read all of the positive, encouraging comments about the upcoming Fourth of July Festival. How Kelsey got our accounts to reach so far and wide is beyond me. I try to focus on the excitement, and not the pressure I feel building to make this event one for the record books. Luckily, my support team keeps growing.

I have the volunteer fire department hosting the bonfire the weekend before the holiday as the Fourth falls on a Tuesday this year. I know there will be both locals and tourists setting off fireworks all weekend so I asked Brian and Nate, one of the younger guys, to take over hosting duties. I lived in Texas long enough to thoroughly enjoy blowing things up, but I also know my limits. Brian has assured me that he'll have everything handled.

We will have a farmer's market on Saturday with lots of local vendors and a book sale Sunday that will benefit the local library. Marabelle took the lead on the farmer's market as she's friendly with a lot of the local farmsteads. Her list of vendors grows by the day.

Lucas shocked me when he put me in contact with the head librarian in Rock Beach, who is his good friend. And seventy years old. And female. I have since noticed that he always has a paperback novel in the back room.

I haven't decided on any community event for Monday, but Tuesday will be a blowout party. The 5k will start us off at 8 a.m. followed by the parade at 10 a.m. Sand castles and kites start at 2 p.m., and fireworks after sunset. With Brian in charge of fireworks, I will be officially off duty after the sandcastle and kite contest award ceremony.

I switch over to the rental accounts and admire the new pictures of the flowers at The Green Door Garden, the sunset from The Glass House's floating deck, and a bald eagle soaring over North House. Kelsey is damn good at both social media and photography. And really, everything she sets her mind to. I send her a quick text thanking her for kicking ass, then pull up the text thread between West and I. Before I overthink it, I snap a selfie with my favorite blanket from the back of his couch wrapped around me and send it without any words.

Now that I'm finally settled in for the night, nothing left on my to-do list, all I can do is think about him, about us, about what the hell I'm actually doing with a man like him.

When I decided last night that I was all in, I didn't realize how relieved I would feel. Relieved I wasn't fighting that damn unexplainable pull toward him any longer, that I could let myself fall into him, into his steadiness. I was expecting doubt, anxiety, a creeping sense of dread, claustrophobia, you know, totally normal things like that. But a strange sense of calm has washed over me. I'm sure if I think too hard about it, I'll freak myself out, but for now, I'll take it.

I feel my phone buzz and smile when I see his name.

West:
You look like you belong there.

I bite my lip. I feel like I belong here, wrapped in this blanket, his nephew and my dog sleeping peacefully in the other room.

Harper:
this blanket smells like you, i want to stay wrapped up in it all night

Not exaggerating. I want to take this blanket home with me. I'm slightly concerned that it was a super stalker text to send, but I might as well go all in with honesty as well.

West:
Just had my last appointment walk in, might be a while. Take my bed, I changed the sheets for you. I'll sleep on the couch. Tell Avery you're staying so she doesn't worry. Extra toothbrush under Colt's sink.

Sleep in his bed? Yes, please. I bet even with clean sheets it still smells like him. So that for sure sounds stalkerish in my head, but again, I don't care.

I smile like a fool at my phone, shoot off a quick text to Avery, who sends a plethora of suggestive emojis back, then head down the hallway to peek in at Colt and Zero. Colt is flat on his back, one arm flung over his head, breathing deeply. Play hard, sleep hard. Zero is sprawled out next to him and she looks up at me but doesn't budge.

"Good girl, Z, you stay," I tell her quietly, closing the door.

After locking the doors, which I usually don't bother with, but having a five-year-old in the house makes it feel necessary, and snagging a Lightning McQueen toothbrush from under the bathroom sink, I let myself into West's room. It's clean, simple, and somehow reminds me of North House. I resist jumping on the king-size bed, but just barely.

There's a few pictures on the dresser so, of course, I walk over to look closer. West and Jessie as kids, arms slung around each other,

142

grinning widely. A happy couple, I'm assuming West's parents, on their wedding day. A selfie of West, Jessie, and Colt with a man I don't recognize. Liam, perhaps? His smile reminds me a little of Colt's.

I continue my way around the room. The bedside table has a mason jar of rocks and shells, I'm sure from Colt, as he gave me a similar one the other day. A small dish holds what looks like wedding rings. My heart nearly stops. Was he married before? I didn't even think to ask. Why would he keep the rings of a failed marriage? I glance back at the wedding picture on the dresser. The styles match. My heart feels heavy. That's enough to halt my snooping.

I step into the spotless, small bathroom and brush my teeth with my new, kid-sized toothbrush, thinking about how not only do Jessie and West not have parents, but Colt doesn't have any grandparents. Jessie told me that West and Liam bonded over losing their parents, so no grandparents on Liam's side either. I feel a twinge of sadness for Liam, a man I've never met, who I'd also like to punch in the throat. Turns out letting yourself actually feel your emotions is a wild ride.

I strip down to my underwear and tank top and climb into West's insanely comfortable bed. It does still smell faintly like cedar, citrus, and flannel. Who knew flannel had a smell? I stretch out, then curl onto my side, pulling the comforter around me. It feels weird to be in bed alone, usually Zero is burrowed into blankets beside me. I turn off the lamp, take in another deep breath of West-smelling sheets, and ease into sleep.

What feels like seconds later, but according to my phone is two hours later, I hear a door open. Unfortunately the bedroom door does not open. Damn him and his thoughtfulness, trying to let me sleep. I give it a few minutes and then wrap the comforter around me and walk into the dark living room. I very un-gracefully trip on the bottom of the comforter and knock into the end table when I see West pulling his shirt over his head. He drops his tee shirt and puts his hands out to stop me from falling all the way over and I end up pressed against his solid, bare chest.

"Hi," he smiles down at me.

"Hi," I reply a little breathlessly.

"I'd say I'm sorry I woke you, but I'm too happy to see you," he says, eyes roaming over me, hands not moving from my waist.

"He told me he loves me," I say, remembering the highlight of my day, as I smile and reach my hand up to feel the scruff of his beard.

"What?" West frowns in confusion.

"Colt. Colt loves me, and I absolutely, without a doubt, love him," I say softly with a smile.

"Of course he loves you. You have both of us wrapped around your finger," he says, placing his hands on either side of my cheeks and resting his forehead on mine.

"Kiss me," I demand, unable to have him this close without needing him closer.

His lips are immediately on mine, soft and slow. I've been waiting all day for this. I've been waiting since our goodnight kiss last night for this. I've been waiting weeks for this.

We only saw each other for a few minutes earlier when I picked Colt up. West had given me a secret smile, his eyes on my lips, as Colt flung himself at me. Now, with Colt fast asleep and West's warm, bare chest pressed against me, I want more.

No, I need more.

I deepen our kiss, dropping the comforter to greedily roam my hands over his chest. He responds immediately, nipping my bottom lip and groaning as I swipe my tongue along his lips in return. His hands are everywhere. He moves to trail kisses down my neck, then wraps his hands under my underwear-clad butt and lifts me up. I wrap my legs around his waist, humming my approval as I feel him hard against me.

"Harper," he whispers between kisses. "You're killing me."

I pull back, looking into his eyes. "I know we need to slow down, but holy shit, West, you're really fucking good at making out," I breathe.

He laughs, still holding me. Still shirtless. Still hard beneath me. I arch into him without thinking, tightening my grip with my legs. I run my fingers through his hair, unable to stop touching him.

"Please, take me to bed. Your sheets smell good, but they're not the real thing." I rub my nose into his neck and breathe him in. I just want him next to me all night. I want to stretch out and feel the bed dip under his weight. I want to tuck my feet under his calves.

144

"That sounds amazing," he whispers into my neck before dragging his beard along my collarbone, the gentleness of the motion contrasting deliciously with the roughness of his beard. "But also a little like torture. I want all of you, Harper."

"Hmmm," I hum, knowing he's right, it does sound like it's own kind of torture. "Can I interest you in letting me use you for your body heat all night?" I wiggle around until he slowly lowers me down to the floor. I keep my hands around his neck as I find my feet, my legs shaky.

"You can use me for whatever you want as long as you're in my bed." He grabs the comforter I dropped, takes my hand and practically drags me down the hallway.

I gently close the door behind us and as soon as I turn back, he has me caged in, hands on either side of me. I tip my head back to look up at him and he kisses me softly before pulling away a centimeter. Immediately I picture a much different scenario, with my legs around him, back pressed against the door, and a lot less clothing.

"I've wanted you in my bedroom for weeks, Harper. I can't think straight with you here," he says against my lips. "And these are going to be the end of me." He brings one hand down to gently snap the waistband of my underwear, the backs of his knuckles skimming my stomach, sending jolts of electricity through me.

I have never felt this level of need. Need for him to touch me, kiss me. I put my hands on his chest and gently push him toward the bed. Suddenly we've switched spots, the backs of my legs are against the bed, his mouth is on mine, swallowing my surprised gasp. With gentleness a man his size should not possess, he wraps his arms around me and slowly lowers me onto his bed.

"Harper," he whispers against my neck, his breath sending shivers down my spine.

I wrap my legs around his waist, loving how big every part of him is, how small he makes me feel. How safe. I close my eyes and shake my head. "Please don't say what I think you're going to say."

"My turn to slow us down I think," he says, slowly pulling away.

I open my eyes, he's staring down at me, jeans unbuttoned, broad chest rising and falling. He shifts to the side and I unhook my legs from his waist.

"Time out?" I ask, trying not to pout.

"Time out," he confirms, as his eyes continue to roam my body. They settle on my breasts, which are straining against the thin tank top. He sighs heavily and closes his eyes. "Killing me, Harper, slowly killing me."

He stands and unceremoniously throws the comforter all the way over me, leaving me in darkness. I laugh and alligator roll until I'm completely engulfed in his scent. I can hear him going into the bathroom and soon the sink turns on.

This is going to be the longest night ever if I have to keep my hands to myself. Which I do.

Chapter Fifteen
West

Harper's still hidden under the heavy comforter when I come out of the bathroom. I turn on the bedside lamp and climb in beside her, ducking under the covers with her. She wiggles her way across the king size bed until we're face to face.

"Hi," she says softly.

I lift the covers slightly until enough light filters in that I can see her smile.

"Hi, Harper," I say, bringing my thumb up to trace her lower lip. How I ever thought I could resist her is beyond me.

"I have a confession," she says, trying to duck into my chest to avoid eye contact.

"No hiding, come back." I gently run my fingers through her hair. "Tell me."

"I had a dream about this. About you, about being in your bed," she whispers.

"You can't tell me that," I groan, reaching out and pulling her flush against me. She automatically hooks her right leg over my hip. "I'm trying to be a gentleman here." I push the comforter down, needing to be able to see her, then move my hand back up to her cheek.

She grins wickedly at me. "So I shouldn't tell you that there was a lot less clothing involved?"

I hook my finger under her chin and crash my lips to hers, licking into her mouth as soon as her lips part. She presses herself into me, pulling me closer using her leg that's hooked over my hip. I run my hand down her side and she gasps when I slide my hand under the hem of her tank top. I grip her waist and rub my thumb over her soft skin.

She wrenches away from my kiss. "Your hand, right there," she whispers, bringing her eyes to mine. "It's my favorite thing."

I squeeze her waist. "You in my bed is my favorite thing," I tell her, getting lost in her eyes once again. I can just make out the gold flecks and there's a hint of green shining through.

With a smile, she pulls my mouth back to hers. We kiss lazily, slowly, like we have all night, which we do. I let my hand skim down her hip and over her thigh that's thrown over my side. She whimpers when I bring it back to her waist, my hand spanning her side. I already know I'm going to dream about that breathy whimper.

Harper slowly pulls back, looking dazed. "I really did just want your body heat, but this is good, too."

I gently pinch her side and her shoulders shake as she tries to contain her laughter. She rolls away from my pinch and I snag her waist and tuck her against me, her back to my chest. She fits perfectly, just like I knew she would.

"Goodnight, Harper," I whisper against her neck.

"Goodnight, personal body heater," she whispers back.

"I'm all in, Harper," I whisper as her breathing evens out.

She falls asleep quickly and I slip out of bed to check on Colt and Zero. When I slide back in behind her, she automatically pushes back into me, her body searching for mine. I turn off the lamp and once again wrap my arm around her, push my guilt aside, and lose myself to sleep.

***

"Tex! You're still here!" Colt throws himself at Harper when he finds us sipping coffee on the deck.

Zero trots out into the yard after nosing Harper, who pulls Colt into her lap and ruffles his hair like she always does. "Did you two sleep good?" she asks.

"Zero wants to sleep with me every night now," he informs us.

"Oh, she does, does she?" Harper smiles over his head at me and I want time to stop, with both of them happy and grinning at me.

148

"Yep, and you can spend the night every night with us, too," Colt tells her. "And then Uncle West will get you special hot chocolate."

She sneaks another look at me over his head and raises her eyebrows. He's right, I'd get her special hot chocolate, or more likely an extra-hot vanilla latte with almond milk, every morning if I could wake up like I did an hour ago.

I'd opened my eyes as Harper was trying to quietly sneak out of bed. I let her think she was getting away with it and then pulled her back at the last second, causing her to fall on my chest. She had retaliated by gently biting my shoulder, laughing quietly as I rolled us so she was under me. She pinched my side and made a run for the bathroom as soon as I shifted my weight. When she returned, smelling minty and with her hair slightly less wild, I had taken my turn in the bathroom, quickly brushing my teeth, and then returned to find her stealing one of my flannels from a pile on the chair in the corner, her back to me, only a bra and those tiny panties still on.

"Harper, if you put my flannel on, I cannot be responsible for my actions," I had threatened playfully.

She froze, then slipped it around her shoulders. She turned, slowly buttoning it, eyes locked on me as she took her sweet time, letting my eyes peruse the skin she was showing. Fuck, she had looked so fucking good I couldn't help but cross the space between us, sliding my hand under the flannel and gripping her waist lightly as I leaned down to kiss her gently. Then I had unceremoniously lifted her over my shoulder and carried her into the kitchen, setting her on the counter next to the coffee maker. After I started the coffee, she pulled me in and kissed me until I couldn't remember why we weren't still in bed.

So, yes, please, on the sleepovers.

"I'm glad you had so much fun with our sleepover, little man, I had a blast with you yesterday. And you know I'm always up for a walk to The Mercantile for special hot chocolate. Should we get ready to go?" she asks him.

"Race you!" he hollers as he scrambles down.

I turn to Harper to tell her that we can take our time, but she's already up and tearing after Colt. I hear a crash in the hallway followed by giggling and I shake my head at Zero, who has her head tilted, trying to figure out just what is happening inside.

I grab our coffee mugs and let the dog follow me back inside. I rinse the mugs and head for my bedroom to change out of my joggers. Harper skids around the doorframe just as Colt bursts out of his room. Harper is still in my flannel, having added black leggings earlier before Colt got up, and now has wool socks, and a "BREAKERS" hat that I've seen Kelsey wearing. Colt is barefoot, holding mismatched socks, and his shirt is on backwards.

"Okay, speed racers, why don't you two sort yourselves out a little more while I get changed." I duck into my bedroom feeling lighter than I have in ages.

When I return to the living room, Harper is patiently helping Colt tie his shoes. His tongue is poked out in concentration as he fights with the laces.

"You did it!" Harper gives him an enthusiastic high-five and pumps her fist.

"Yes!" Colt copies her, making both of us laugh.

Harper grabs Zero's leash and we head out the door. Colt and Harper jump over puddles the whole way to The Mercantile.

"Well, good morning, all three of you," Avery says, eyeing my flannel that dwarfs Harper.

"Four! Four of us. Zero is outside! We had a sleepover!" Colt tells her excitedly.

"That must have been *so* fun," Avery replies, raising an eyebrow at Harper.

"Colt, go ask Lucas for your hot chocolate, I want to see if he knows how to make it the right way," Harper tells Colt. As soon as his back is to us, Harper reaches for me, putting her hand under my shirt and winding it around my back, pressing herself next to me, other hand on my chest. "So much fun," she says, licking her lips and looking up at me with bright eyes.

"Ugh, get a room," Avery says with a smile, moving behind the counter.

150

Harper stands on her tiptoes and presses a quick kiss to my lips, shocking the shit out of me. "All in, right?" she whispers with a shrug.

I glance over to where Lucas and Colt are deep in conversation about the correct amount of whipped cream and then lean down to whisper in her ear. "All in on us, or all in on messing with your best friend?" I ask before kissing her lightly on the neck. She shivers.

"Both?" She continues to stare up at me and I'm swimming in her eyes.

A throat clears. Loudly. We both jump. Harper laughs at the expression on Avery's face.

"Take my advice?" Avery asks me, handing me my coffee.

"Oooh, what advice?" Harper asks, as she turns to check on Zero outside.

"It was good advice," I tell Avery, rubbing the back of my neck.

Avery is putting a lid on Harper's latte when I hear the door fly open.

"Jessie?" The tone of Harper's voice is all wrong.

I turn and she's catching my sister at the door. Reality crashes into me.

Jessie's obviously been crying, her face is tear-streaked and splotchy, and she leans heavily into Harper's embrace. Harper quickly herds her outside before Colt catches sight of his mom looking so upset.

"Where's Tex? Did she take Zero? She forgot her hot chocolate!" Colt goes to chase her out the door but I catch him before he can make it outside.

"She asked me to take it to her back at home, she had to go get something for Avery," I improvise, looking over at Avery behind the counter to back up my claim.

"Want to put some special sprinkles on it for her?" Avery asks, grabbing multi-colored sprinkles that definitely do not usually go in Harper's latte.

While Colt enthusiastically adds an alarming amount of sprinkles to the latte, I ease my way toward the door to see which way Harper took Jessie. Zero is whining as she looks toward the bridge. I see Harper and Jessie disappearing toward her cottage.

"I'll tell her you guys have her drink when she brings me those papers," Avery tells Colt cheerfully. "Check your phone," she adds so quietly I barely hear her. Confused as fuck and also concerned, I give her a slight nod.

"Okay, bud, can you take Zero's leash and your hot chocolate?" I ask Colt, pushing the door open.

As we walk home, I balance my black coffee and Harper's excessive-sprinkles latte in one hand and work my phone out of my pocket with the other.

Avery:
I helped Jessie with divorce papers this week. She was going to serve
Liam yesterday at the shop.

That explains a lot. But it doesn't explain why Jessie wouldn't have shared that with me when she called to tell me she couldn't make it out. What kind of brother am I if she can't tell me something so important, so life-changing? I had hoped things were better between us. I look at Colt, walking beside me, carefully balancing his drink in one hand and holding Zero's leash in the other, and I tell myself that it's time to do better, not just hope for better. It's time to mend fences, forge new paths, and whatever other metaphors are out there for fixing shit and moving on.

***

"Look who I found!" Harper calls out as she slowly opens the door after knocking lightly twice.

"Mom!" Colt runs to hug Jessie as she and Harper walk in the door.

Jessie's eyes are no longer red, she's holding a cup from the Mercantile as well as a small bag that must contain pastries. She gives me a shaky smile as she holds Colt tight.

"We had a sleepover!" Of course that's the first thing Colt feels the need to share. "All four of us! Me and Zero and Uncle West and Tex!"

152

"Oh reallllly," Jessie's smile goes from shaky to knowing as she looks between Harper and I. "Well, isn't that fun. How lucky are you?"

She might be talking to Colt, but all I can think is 'really fucking lucky' as I look at Harper, whose cheeks are slightly pink. She catches my eye and bites her lip, trying to hide the smile that I know I don't deserve.

Jessie doles out pastries and Colt tells both of us all about he and Harper's Big Day Out. Jessie's phone keeps buzzing and every time it does, she gets more fidgety. Harper shifts and I see her squeeze Jessie's hand under the table.

"Zero and I didn't get our morning beach walk. Colt, do you want to go with us now?" Harper asks. Colt is scrambling for his jacket before she even finishes her question.

"Thank you," I whisper, kissing her gently after checking that Colt is on the deck with Jessie. I grab my beanie off the hook by the door and pull it onto her head.

"Just be patient, kind, and steady, like you always are," Harper says, running her hands through my beard, then kissing my soundly again.

Jessie and I sit on the deck, watching Harper, Colt, and Zero run down the beach path together. As soon as they hit the sand, Zero sprints for the waterline. The three of them start playing a game of chase, endlessly energetic as always.

"I'm sorry," Jessie says, after a few minutes of watching their antics. "I should have told you why I needed to stay in town another day. I served Liam divorce papers last night at the shop. Well, actually, Grant did. I was going to use the sheriff's department but Grant offered to do it. Liam didn't react well."

"Why didn't you ask me to help? I would have done it," I say, clenching my jaw.

"West, I can't ask you to do more. You're doing so much already. You've done so much since the day Colt was born. Also, I needed to handle this on my own. I mean, I guess with Grant, and also Avery's help, but just let me do this, okay?" Her eyes are filled with tears and when she blinks, they spill over. She angrily wipes them away. Her phone buzzes again and she looks at it warily.

"Is that him?" I ask, indicating the phone that sits on the table between our chairs. When she nods, I have the sudden urge to throw her phone in the ocean. "What can I help you with? Do you need money?"

"I need a fucking life plan," she says with a self-deprecating laugh.

"Why isn't step one of the life plan to stay here for the week? I'll take the couch," I offer.

I can see some of the tension leave her body at this suggestion. She takes a deep breath, reminding me of Harper, and nods. Another deep breath. Did Harper teach her that? When she looks up again, it's with a glint in her eye.

"What about this sleepover situation you have going on though, big brother? Won't I be interrupting?" She bursts into laughter at my expression. Then she holds out her hand, pulls me up, and shoves me toward the path to the beach.

Chapter Sixteen
Harper

Thanks to Colt, my walk home is actually a classic example of a walk of shame, but without the sex or the shame. Walk of non-shame, down the entire street. It would be a normal walk home, but Colt yells after me that I forgot my toothbrush in Uncle West's bedroom. He sprints down the street to hand it to me and then loudly asks why I'm stealing West's flannel.

"It's too big for you!" he tells me with a shake of his head. I stifle a smile and give his hair a ruffle.

I call out good morning to the neighbors and own it. At least Betty doesn't live on this street; I'm sure she'd have *a lot* to say to me right about now.

I make sure Zero's water bowl is full, mop the floor after she sloshes water all over, refill her bowl, and flop unceremoniously on my couch. Two days ago at this time I was having a panic attack in fucking Ikea, counting down until I got to see West for movie night. Now I'm again having too many feelings, not of the panicky kind, and again counting down until I get to see West.

I dip my nose down and take another whiff of West's flannel, like the addict I am. We didn't have any time to ourselves after Jessie showed up, so all I know is that the man has me all out of sorts, thinking all sorts of dirty things, and having so many feelings. But also, I'm calm. Like oddly calm. The quick goodbye kiss we snuck in will have to tide me over until tomorrow. He has shop hours this afternoon and his sister and nephew at home. Instead of laying here on the couch daydreaming about

West, I should get my ass up and finish the rentals. Make up for my Big Day Out with Colt yesterday.

After a quick shower, I put West's flannel back on, find my notebook under my bed, "not today" pen shoved in the middle pages, and walk down the street with Zero toward The Green Door Garden. All this rental needs is for me to unbox and wash the Ikea kitchenware, put together the new reading lamp, and sort linens. If I move fast enough, I'll have three rentals completely ready to go by the end of the day.

Tex:
ya'll. lessssgo. send 'em live, kelseylove. garden, golf course, breakers.

KelseyLove:
hells yea boss

Aves:
I am surrounded by children.

Tex:
oh, shit. garden plant emergency. who has a green thumb?

Somehow, since Friday evening when we unloaded boxes, three of the raised beds have up and died. Or more accurately, they've been murdered. There are suspicious hoof prints leading to and from the crime scene.

KelseyLove:
not it

Aves:
I would assume someone at Rock Beach Nursery.

Tex:
(eye roll emoji)

156

No shit, Sherlock. I'll deal with the dead later, may they rest in peace.

With my "rage cleaning" playlist blasting from the small speaker in the corner, it takes no time to get this house ready, despite my constant daydreaming about a large, bearded, hot, older lumberjack tattoo artist. I look around the finished space and smile.

A few days ago I carefully gave a bubble bath to a garden gnome I found hidden in the yard and he now stands guard on the kitchen counter. There's small flower or garden accents throughout the entire house. Coffee mugs, throw pillows, and even toothbrush holders have small flowers or vines, and the windowsill has miniature seedling pots so guests can start seeds to take home. I'll swing back by to unload the dishwasher and it will be ready for the first guests. Other than the whole plant massacre out front.

The golf course house, which is still just named "The Golf Course House" despite my best (mediocre) efforts, goes just as quickly and does not have any plant related emergencies to contend with. Beds are made, bath towels laid out, dishes and glasses in the dishwasher.

Tex:
name ideas-the back nine, the beach nine, the sand trap, tee time/sea time, bunker bliss

KelseyLove:
bunker vs breakers bliss, unsure on that

Aves:
Getting closer, not there yet.

Tex:
this house will never have a name.

I'm not going to lie, Breakers Bliss has become my favorite rental. I love North House as a home and The Glass House for a rental, too, but Breakers just has shenanigans written all over it. And I love shenanigans. Kelsey has been pushing it hard on all of our social media accounts and I know it'll book fast.

The pink chalkboards inside the cupboards have "Welcome, Breakers!" and "be fucking unstoppable" written on them in Avery's swirly handwriting. The indoor plants on the corner shelves are alive and well, all in cute mismatched pink planters of all shapes and sizes. We are nearly ready to go.

I take the box of pink champagne and sparkling cider out of its hiding spot in the closet and put a couple bottles in the fridge. As soon as we get our first booking, we are celebrating. The rest of the bottles go to the front porch with the small stash of "BREAKERS" hats. They'll have to be stored at my cottage or in the back room at The Merc until we have renters. I sit on the porch swing, trying to figure out what else needs to be done.

"Tex! Hi! You're at the pink house!" Colt skips up the steps, Jessie following.

"We were out for a walk. Colt sure seems to know everyone in town," Jessie smiles at her son, who commandeers my swing and has us swinging haphazardly within seconds.

"I just finished up here. I need to go unload the dishwasher at The Garden though. What are y'all up to?" I ask.

"Garden?" Jessie asks, running her fingers through her hair. "I used to love gardening."

"You might be my new best friend then, because our raised beds were destroyed last night. I think the deer got them. Or a werewolf, based on the amount of damage. It was a complete massacre. I don't know if anything can be saved," I say.

"A werewolf? Cool," Colt breathes.

"Want me to take a look? I'd love a project for the next few days," Jessie offers, looking hopeful.

Sorry, Avery, move over for my new best friend. We swing Colt between us as we walk the block back to The Garden. Jessie's already so much lighter on her feet, the difference is amazing. I feel a little murder-y toward Liam all over again.

158

"Well, I think the nursery really set you up with a good selection of plants, but I'm not going to lie, they're all in the wrong places. These guys want more sun but they're stuck here in the shade. They should switch with those," Jessie nods toward the still-standing planter nearest the gate. "And I bet these little guys here would be happier over there." Her eyes scan the yard, taking in the entire space. She tests the soil in one of the planters, rubbing it between her fingers.

"Okay, I'm going to be honest, this is not my thing, at all. Teach me your ways?" I ask hopefully. If I'm going to keep this house to Grandma Georgie's standards, which is my goal, I need a lot of help.

"Yes, please! I'll rescue these guys now if Zero can keep entertaining Colt," she says, smiling brightly.

"I'm in!" I say, reaching for my phone that won't stop buzzing. "Give me one sec, then I'll get us into the shed for the limited amount of gardening tools I picked up."

KelseyLove:
FIRST BOOKING!

KelseyLove:
SOMEONE ANSWER

KelseyLove:
SECOND BOOKING!

Aves:
Really? That was so fast!

Tex:
that's what she said.

Aves:
(eye roll emoji)

Tex:

holy shit, three bookings! just logged in.

KelseyLove:
I AM SO EXCITED!

Tex:
team meeting. breakers in twenty?

KelseyLove:
YES

Aves:
I'll be there shortly.

"Hey Jessie, can we do this tomorrow? We've got a Team Merc celebration back at the Breakers, AKA the pink house. We got our first renters booked after posting them a couple hours ago. You should come! I'll bring Zero and she and Colt can play out back, it's totally fenced."

I don't want to bail on her after she's agreed to help but I want to celebrate with Aves and Kels. I also think including her in my new girl gang would be helpful. She needed Grant, who she had only known what, like a day, to help her serve Liam. I really think she could use a better support system. Also, she's my favorite five-year-old's mom. And my favorite thirty-two-year-old's sister.

"Oh, I don't want to intrude, I can finish up here though," she says.

"Please join us, don't make me channel my inner Emmy," I jokingly threaten.

"Okay, well that's a threat I want nothing to do with," she laughs. "How about I save a few of these guys and then join you guys after I wash up?"

"I'm not going to be able to drag Zero away from Colt, look at them," I tip my head toward the two, they're locked in an intense game of tug-of-war, both playfully growling. "So tell me what to do to help."

160

Jessie rolls her sleeves up and gets the plants back in the dirt before I even find the key to the storage shed. I manage to take a quick video and snap a few pictures but that's all I contribute toward the plant rehab. As we walk to Breakers, Jessie asks about the other rentals and the state of their gardens.

"I would love for them to stand out, even among the houses like these," I point out the massive flower garden that has overtaken John's front walk, "but I just don't have the green thumb for it. The house by the golf course could really use some better curb appeal, but I just can't quite figure it out." I pull up the Instagram page for the house and let Jessie flip through the pictures. I can see the wheels turning in her head. They start turning in mine as well.

***

A massive group hug greets us as soon as we step inside Breakers. Kelsey has Colt take pictures and multiple videos of us hugging and jumping around like fools. She puts it up on a story and continues documenting our celebration. We pop the pink champagne (sparkling cider for Kelsey and Colt) and start making toasts.

"To hard work!" Avery says, looking right at me.

"To our followers!" Kelsey says, winking at the camera.

"To all y'all!" I'm feeling a little overwhelmed and like my feelings journal might get put to use tonight.

"To new friends," Jessie adds, looking as overwhelmed as I feel.

"To Zero!" Colt adds enthusiastically, making both Jessie and I smile again.

Kelsey takes Colt and Zero to the backyard while Avery steps out front to take a very lawyer'ish sounding call. I give Jessie a quick tour of the house, showing her the "Easter eggs" we've hidden around the house. Besides the chalkboards inside the cabinets, I've added poetry magnets to a magnetic mirror that's on the inside of the linen closet in the bathroom. There are sand dollars painted pale pink on windowsills, bookshelves, and dresser drawers. I even hid heart-shaped rocks in the fire pit that I painstakingly built. It was a real life 3D puzzle that might have gotten the better of me, but the finished product is amazing, especially when you notice the hearts.

We reconvene around the fire pit, everyone complimenting my building skills, and refill our champagne flutes. Kelsey checks the rentals again and we have a dozen bookings between the three houses we've listed, all between now and the end of July. She squeals excitedly.

"I bet you I can get this house rented by this next weekend," Kelsey says, squirming in her chair like the excited teenager she is. She looks back and forth between Avery and I and attempts to raise one eyebrow like Aves always does.

Avery and I grin at each other, our silent communication still strong after decades, and I can tell we are both amused by Kelsey's enthusiasm. Also, she's killing social media for us. I can guarantee that's why we've had so many bookings within a few hours. She's like a little sister to both of us at this point and we are proud as hell of her.

"Deal. If you can get renters in this house within one week, so by next Sunday, I'll pay for your course materials for your first semester at college," Avery says.

"Okay, well that trumps anything I could wager," I say. "I was just going to buy your coffee for a week."

"Wow, Tex, we already get that coffee for free," Kelsey says with more than a trace of sarcasm. I crack up at her expression. "If I win, you have to do all the ridiculous TikTok ideas I have, with no power of veto, until the Fourth of July."

I glare at her. I can tell she already has something way over the top and probably genius planned. "Deal."

Jessie takes Kelsey's phone and takes a picture of the three of us shaking hands, then Kelsey disappears inside to work her magic. She hollers out the open window to ask if she can use Zero and Colt. After Jessie gives her nod, I shoo the two of them inside.

"I'm going to pay for her course materials no matter what," Avery tells us once the door closes once again.

"I know," I say, rolling my eyes. There was never any question.

"You can't read me that well," Avery retorts.

"Really? How about summer after ninth grade?" I say with a smirk. Avery glares at me. I glare right back.

"Uh, what happened during summer break?" Jessie asks curiously, her eyes darting between the two of us.

"Avery met this cute summer boy, they fell hopelessly in love like you do when you're fifteen, didn't exchange last names or numbers because, again, they were fifteen and teenagers are idiots, and she denies it to this day," I tell her.

Aves and I continue to glare at each other, the way only lifelong friends can. Jessie is silent, unsure what to make of this standoff. She shifts nervously.

"So. Harper. How was your sleepover?" Avery asks, looking pointedly at Jessie. She attempts a shock and awe, but that ship sailed the second Jessie burst into The Merc this morning.

"Don't worry, Colt already told me," Jessie laughs. "I don't mind, I trust both of you, you obviously both put Colt first. I appreciate all you've done for my son, and me, too, and I think you're good for my brother. He's lighter since he met you. Maybe you'll help him finally move on from his guilt over Liam, all the shit that happened."

I'm sure my cheeks are red. "He's good for me, too. We met at a really strange, stressful, overwhelming time in my life. It's been a lot. Luckily we had Colt to bring us together. Between him and Avery, I don't think West and I had a chance of keeping our distance."

I think back to the first night when I invited Colt, and therefore West, over for s'mores. The first morning that Colt came stomping past my house. My panic attack at The Glass House. My tattoo. Front porch dancing. The night at the bar. All the times at that little spot in the sand.

"I'm just glad he stopped being a stubborn idiot, accepted that you're the best thing that will ever happen to him, besides Colt, and did something about it." It's Avery's turn to roll her eyes.

"Is that what your weird standoff was the other night at the bonfire?" I ask, remembering their interaction as we had said goodnight. I refill our glasses one last time.

"I might have told him some things," Avery says, taking a sip of champagne.

"I'm just trying to remember the last time I saw him really date anyone," Jessie says, frowning. I'm instantly jealous of anyone who ever had his attention in any way, shape or form. Which I realize is ridiculous.

"It hasn't been since he moved here, that's for sure," Avery says. I breathe a little easier.

"I think it was before our parents died, maybe when he was in college. There were definitely girls, but not important ones," Jessie says thoughtfully. "That was when he and Liam were tight."

"While I appreciate your honesty, thinking about him with someone else, even if it was a decade ago, makes me want to murder the poor girl," I say, making Avery and Jessie laugh.

I also don't feel right talking about this without him. I know he and Avery are close, which I love, and Jessie is his sister, but I just don't like this. I wouldn't have cared if Ethan's friends spilled his past, why is this different? How am I even comparing the two? Not only are they as different as they could be, but the impact of this two-day-old relationship already eclipses what Ethan and I shared over eight months. There's also a weird, prickly feeling coming over me, an uneasiness about West's past, things he hasn't let go.

"You guys!" Kelsey bursts out the back door with a crash, Colt and Zero with her. "It's booked! Tomorrow! Pay up, b-witches!" Kelsey remembers Colt is next to her and covers her swearing.

"Shut up, how did you do that?!" I fumble for my phone to pull up the accounts. I find the Breakers Bliss Instagram and click on the story.

Kelsey's face fills my screen. "Hi, everyone, Kelsey here. Big news! Breakers is open for business! My friends Colt and Zero are here with me to give you an update on the space." Colt pops up next to Kelsey wearing Kelsey's "BREAKERS" hat with Zero next to him. She gives his face a lick and he giggles. "Colt, let's take our followers on a tour."

Rapid fire pictures and short video clips follow. Colt jumping on a bed. Zero sitting on the porch swing. Kelsey holding the sparkling cider bottle. Zero holding the sparkling cider bottle sideways in her mouth. All three dancing and jumping in front of the full-length mirror in the main bedroom.

164

Kelsey is back, sitting on the front porch swing with Colt and Zero on either side of her. "Breakers is within two hours of Portland, just over an hour from Salem, and we can't wait to host you. We have tons of surprises planned for all of our guests, our town is one of a kind, and I can't wait for you to get here." Her voice drops to an exaggerated stage whisper. "Now, here's the deal, friends. My two bosses have bet that I can't get guests out here within the next week. Who is up for a last minute girls' night? I'd love to work with you on a Breakers social takeover, you'd get to show the world the hidden secre-"

"The hidden shel-" Colt blurts out the secret, but Kelsey clamps her hand over his mouth. His eyes widen and he starts giggling behind her hand. She bursts into laughter as well. The video cuts.

"Anyway, the first guest or guests will get to do a full social takeover, but by full I mean edited by yours truly," she bats her eyes. "Ain't no one trying to get fired around here. You'll also get a welcome gift basket, I'll add in coffee from The Town Mercantile which is our local coffee shop, and I'll even get you a meet and greet with the Instagram-famous Zero. Airbnb link is in bio! Let the games begin!"

She fucking did it.

Avery, Jessie, and I all stare at Kelsey.

"And this worked? We really have renters tomorrow?" I ask in disbelief.

"We have a group of four girls from Portland checking in at 3 p.m. tomorrow," Kelsey confirms. "One of them has a big following, she's a fitness lifestyle influencer."

"Influencer," Avery snorts.

Kelsey is buried in her phone. "Say what you want, I bet this girl makes or breaks us, she has millions of followers, how she found my tiny account I don't know," she looks up uncertainly. Her face pales. "What have I done? Are we ready? How am I supposed to edit the takeover with someone that has a following like that? I'm eighteen! I've lived in a town of like twelve people my whole life! And Avery, you don't want your name out there and you're all over the stories today with this impromptu celebration." She's spiraling just like I do.

"Hey, Kels, whoa. This is exactly what you were supposed to do. You got us renters, you showcased the houses and the town perfectly. You're talented and smart and I'm so fu-dging proud of you," I say, sideways glance at Colt. "You crushed it. You took my vague idea and ran with it."

"Kelsey, you're doing the job I, we, hired you to do. You got a group to rent this house within, what, ten minutes, of our bet. That's incredible," Avery jumps in to reassure her as well. "I'm in maybe three pictures that won't be up for long and I don't think anyone will put it together. There's never been any proof I'm the author behind my books. I'm not worried."

"You guys are amazing, the support you have for each other, pulling me into this, I'm so grateful," Jessie whispers, looking between us. "Don't judge my tears, it's been an emotional twenty-four hours. Slash week. Slash month-year-decade."

Colt is looking wide-eyed between us. I reach my hand out and he climbs in my lap. As soon as he's in my arms, I stand, and motion for everyone to do the same. We gently crush Colt in the middle of our group hug. As he laughs and Zero dances around outside our circle, I tighten my arms around the emotional group hug. This *has* been an emotional day-slash-week-slash-month.

"Okay, okay, guys. I gotta get this place ready!" I pry myself and Colt out of the hug. "If you don't want to be put to work, y'all better get outta here quick!"

Colt runs for the backdoor, Kelsey and Zero follow.

"I'd like to help now, but I need to get Colt dinner," Jessie says. "Can you text me about the nursery and gardening? I'd love to help you with that."

"Absolutely. I really don't have much to do, I just need to unload the dishwasher, straighten linens, and then have a small meltdown," I tell her, smiling so she knows I'm joking about the last part. She sends Zero back out to me when she heads inside to take Colt home.

Avery looks at me and sinks back into her chair. I do the same. She breaks the silence first.

"You've had quite a weekend. Lots of ups and downs. You okay?" She watches me closely.

"You know what? I'm really fucking good," I tell her. "I'm sitting here with my best friend, my best dog, and we have our first renters showing up tomorrow after opening the rentals just a few hours ago. I'm going to watch the sunset from my favorite beach, my fucking feelings journal and a glass of wine in hand, after you make me dinner." What I don't say is that I might still be on a high from my weekend with West.

"I'm making you dinner?" She shakes her head at me, smiling so I know she's really going to do it.

"Yep," I put my hand out to pull her out of her chair. "Get your ass up to your hilltop retreat and start cooking, woman."

Chapter Seventeen
Harper

I make my way down to the beach, journal and wine in hand, pen stuck under my hat, dog by my side. I've barely settled into our spot when a blanket lands beside me.

"Hi." West's deep voice sends shivers down my spine. I'm immediately craving his touch.

"Hi, I was hoping you'd be down here." I scoot sideways to lean against him as soon as he's settled in the sand. "I didn't want to bug you at work; I figured you'd know where to find me." Zero noses the blanket and I move it so she's buried underneath. Three days straight of playing with Colt all day and she's finally tired.

"I've been thinking about you all day," he says in his easy and honest way, reaching for my notebook. He flips to a center page and pinches the pen from under my hat. "Jessie says you're letting her help you with gardening? And that you guys had a celebration?" He moves the pen across the paper and I can't take my eyes away. His hand dwarfs the pen, his strokes are quick but sure.

"We have our first guests at Breakers tomorrow! Kelsey did some magic and it's a group of four girls, one of which is some social media influencer, so stakes are a little high," I tell him, suddenly nervous, eyes still on the pen. His hand stops moving.

"Hey," he moves his hand to lift my chin, bringing my eyes to his. "You've done an amazing job with the house, they're going to have a great visit. I mean, just introduce them to Betty."

I smile at that. Betty is included in the scavenger hunt, I still need to bribe her with new yarn to play nice though.

"You've been talking to Betty? Does that mean you've heard that my ex-husband was in the mafia?" I move closer, eyes on his lips.

"Was that before or after the rodeo clown fiance?" he asks. I laugh and run my hands through his beard, a sensation I can't get enough of. "As long as you're here now, all the stories Betty has been telling could be true, and I wouldn't care." He gives me a slow kiss then returns to his drawing.

I slide my right hand onto his solid thigh, unable to help myself. He glances at me with a smile and slightly shifts the notebook away from me. Instead of trying to sneak looks at his drawing like I'm sure he's expecting me to, I just lean my head against his solid shoulder and run my hand up and down his thigh, absentmindedly playing with the seam on the inside. I watch the sun sinking lower, I feel Zero sigh under her blanket, and I just enjoy the peace that this place and this man bring me.

The notebook slides into my lap and West reaches for my hand that's still on his leg. He threads his fingers through mine and kisses my temple. "I haven't been able to get this out of my mind all day, from the moment I woke up to right now."

It's a rough sketch, an outline, the curve of a hip, a large hand on a tapered waist. A lacy waistband, legs disappearing under a sheet. Tank top strap falling off a shoulder, *my* shoulder. His calloused carpenter hand, partially hidden under my shirt. Hair falling over my face. What he would have seen, last night.

I look up at him, unable to put into words what is in my head, my heart.

"You said me touching you there was your favorite thing," he whispers, eyes holding mine. "Why are you crying?"

I'm crying? I'm crying. Of course I am. I just shrug helplessly. It's been over a month of roller coaster emotions. I don't know what's up and what's down. I only know that this is more than I've ever felt for a man.

170

"Hey," he shifts and gently wipes my tears with the pad of his thumb, other hand still holding mine. He frowns slightly. "What's going on in your head right now?"

"I don't even know," I whisper, and lean forward to kiss him. I dig my wineglass into the sand, set the notebook in my lap and reach for him. "I'm just happy."

"Me, too, Harper, me, too," he says, resting his forehead on mine.

I shift us again, so I'm once again leaning against his shoulder. As the sun sinks behind the horizon, I squeeze West's hand. "Stay with me tonight? I'll try not to cry again."

He chuckles. "You can cry, Harper, and I'll still be there."

"You're like one of the trees at North House," I tell him suddenly. I sat under one of them the other day, my back to the trunk, journaling and watching Zero and Colt explore the yard and dunes, and added that moment to my happy list. The wind moving the sea grass, the faint sound of the ocean, and the peacefulness of it all in the middle of a hectic day.

West gives me a quizzical but amused look. "I don't know what that means, but I'll take it as a compliment, because I like that little copse of trees."

I keep my eyes on the fading sunset. "It means that since day one, when we met, you've been this steady, solid presence. My storms don't move you, they don't push you away. You've seen a lot of me, more of me than people I've known for years have seen, and you just stand strong, and let me lean on you if I need to."

West is silent. I make myself look over at him and his blue eyes are almost too intense. They see too much of me. There's also something I can't quite define in them, a flash of uncertainty perhaps.

"Please say something," I whisper. I feel my eyes welling with tears again.

"Your storms won't move me, Harper," he gently captures my lips, kissing me slowly. "Tears, anxiety, mafia connections, I'll still be here."

I laugh against his lips. "I've got the mafia under control, it's the tears and anxiety that keep wrecking me."

"Nothing can wreck you." West kisses me again before standing. He holds a hand out to me and pulls me to my feet. "Except Betty, when she finds out about us from someone else. And after you mauled me at The Mercantile this morning, followed by Colt yelling down the street, that could be an issue."

"Mauled you?" I laugh. "I don't think that's what it was, you haven't seen mauling yet." I lean down to grab my wineglass and notebook, putting the pen back under my hat.

"Let's fix that, then," he grabs the blanket off Zero, who glares at us both. "Come on Zero, let's go tell Colt goodnight!" At his name, she gets up and starts toward the path.

"Hey, what do you think about leaving Zero with your sister and Colt tonight?" I hate being separated from my dog, but I don't know much about Liam and it would make me feel better if she was there since I'm taking West from them.

"I know Colt would be ecstatic and I think it'd make Jessie feel better, having her there," he says, squeezing my hand in silent thanks.

Colt is already in bed, but we let Zero into his room and she quietly climbs up next to him. Jessie reassures us that she's okay without West there and promises to take Zero for a walk in the morning since I have the early Merc shift with Marabelle. West tucks me under his arm, an overnight bag slung over his other shoulder, as we walk the block to my cottage.

"About that mauling," he whispers. Shivers run down my spine. "Really looking forward to it."

I snake my arm around him, slipping my hand beneath his shirt. I reach up with my other hand to pull his arm tighter around my shoulders before weaving my fingers through his. I use my thumb to gently rub the palm of his hand.

"I can't wait to have these hands on me again."

And those rough, calloused hands are on me the second we step inside. His bag hits the floor as the door closes, then he's on me. My back is pressed against the door, one of his hands is braced above my

172

head. His other is in my hair, gently tilting my head toward his, until his lips find mine. His beard scrapes along my neck as he trails kisses to my collarbone. My hands are frantically undoing the buttons of his flannel, pushing it off his broad shoulders, sliding under his tee shirt.

"In a hurry?" he whispers, kissing back up my neck.

"Yes," I practically pant. "You said mauling. This is it. Shirt off, please."

"I love how demanding you are," he says. "But what if I want to slowly peel your layers off, one by one, like I'm opening a present?"

"Just tear the wrapping paper, West," I demand. I need all of him, right now.

He huffs a laugh but reaches over his head and pulls his tee shirt off, taking a step out of my reach as he does. "Better?" he asks.

I trail my eyes over his broad shoulders, down the hard planes of muscle hidden beneath the smattering of hair that covers his wide chest, over the tattoos along his ribs. He's so big he should be intimidating, he absolutely dwarfs me, but all I feel is want. Need.

"Better," I confirm as I reach for him. He smirks and steps sideways, staying just out of my reach as he kicks off his boots. I ditch my flip flops as I unbutton my shirt, technically his shirt, slowly. If he wants slow, game on. I give him a glimpse of my hot pink bra but keep the flannel closed, even as I unbutton it. Slowly. So slowly.

His eyes are glued to my hands as I work my way down the buttons. I take a step back as I let it fall open. His eyes darken as I dip my hands on the sides of my leggings, like I'm going to discard those next but I pause, having moved them just enough for him to catch sight of matching lace. With a dip of my shoulder, his flannel falls partway down my arm, exposing more hot pink lace and skin. He steps toward me but I backpedal.

"Slowly, West, you said slowly," I tease, putting the couch between us.

"Harper," he says, voice rough with need. He's working out of his socks using his feet, his hands on his belt. "I wanted to open my present by myself. Slowly."

"So you don't want me to take this off?" I ask innocently, turning my back to him and slowly sliding the flannel down off my shoulders, walking toward my bedroom.

For a big, burly man he is fucking fast. He's over the couch and his hand is on my waist in what feels like half a second. My heart races as he spins me, pushing the flannel the rest of the way down my arms. It drops into a puddle on the floor. With one hand, he pushes open my bedroom door, with the other, he scoops me off my feet.

Being manhandled was never on my to-do list, but holy fuck. Yes, please. My back hits my mattress and he stands before me, tall and broad and *big*. I squirm under his gaze as he slowly peruses my body.

"Fuck, Harper, you're so goddamn beautiful," he breathes, finally moving, landing a kiss on my hip before he gently urges me further back on the bed.

He continues to kiss his way up my body and the roughness of his beard combined with the soft, open mouth kisses peppered on my stomach makes me gasp his name.

"So fucking beautiful," he whispers against my lips before kissing me like it's the end of days, like he'll never stop.

His hands roam my body, the scrape of his callouses leaving my skin tingling, aching for more. His hands find my leggings and he pauses. He pulls back, breathing hard as his eyes meet mine. I bite my lip and smile, wordlessly giving him permission, and he slowly peels them off, leaving the hot pink lace.

Again, he stands over me, taking me in as he drops my leggings to the floor. I can see how much he wants me, his erection straining against his zipper. With his eyes on mine, he gently lifts my leg and kisses the inside of my ankle. The gentleness, the tenderness of that single kiss makes me shudder.

His knee lands on the bed between my legs as he kisses his way up the inside of my leg, over my hip, my belly button. He groans as he moves his mouth over my breasts, then he kisses directly over my heart. He lays his cheek on my chest, still breathing hard. He moves to lay next to me, pulling me to my side with his hand on my waist, gently squeezing.

174

"Hi." He grins at me when I arch against him, unhappy with the loss of his hands and mouth on me.

"Hi." I can't help but drag my fingers through his beard once again. "Have I told you how good your beard feels against my skin?"

"You haven't mentioned it," he says with a smirk. "But those little noises you make give you away."

"West, what is this torture?" I moan. "You're the one killing me right now." I nip his bottom lip to show my impatience. He stills, suddenly serious, unsure.

"Are you sure about us? Me?" he asks quietly between kisses. "You deserve so much more, so much better than me."

"You're the one that I want, West," I whisper. "I want us."

I kiss him hard, pressing myself against him, roaming my hands down his chest. I know he feels what I feel, I've seen it in his eyes. I can feel the shift, when he accepts my words, my reassurances. He kisses me back, our tongues tangling. His hands are everywhere again, he buries his face in my neck and rubs his rough beard against me, then kisses away the prickly sting. I can't help but whimper.

"Harp," his tone makes me freeze. He closes his eyes and his jaw clenches. "I don't have a condom."

"No, this can't be happening." I bury my hands in the hair at the nape of his neck.

"Fuck, I want you so fucking bad," his eyes open, finding mine.

"We have time," I sigh, knowing it's true but also wanting, needing him. I kiss him gently, trying to bring myself back down.

"Time I can work with, no condom I can also work with." He gives me a wicked grin and works his way down my body slowly, methodically.

He's not lying and it doesn't take long for me to forget about anything except his mouth and his hands, how fucking good he can make me feel. When I cry out his name, I want to stay in this bed forever.

He pulls me to his chest as we both catch our breath. I can hear and feel his heartbeat slowing under my cheek. My fingers trace the tattoos on his ribcage. He catches my hand as it strays lower.

"That was more than enough for me," he whispers, bringing my hand back to his chest, feeling his heartbeat. "I could do this every day and be perfectly happy."

"But what if I want more?" I ask, fully aware that I'm pouting.

"What did you say about having time?" he asks, voice teasing.

"I'm too tired to argue," I tell him, once again tracing the tattoos along his ribs.

"Let me take you to dinner Tuesday, celebrate after your first guests leave," West says softly as he plays with my hair. "I don't have hours tomorrow or Tuesday, Jessie will still be here with Colt, just you and me, a real date. I should have asked you weeks ago."

"I like our beach dates, but dinner sounds nice," I say, smiling. "But only if you go find your tee shirt and let me sleep in it."

"Deal," he stands to retrieve his shirt from the living room and I step into the bathroom to brush my teeth.

"Like the view?" I see West leaning against the bedroom door, watching me as I stand in my underwear, brushing my teeth.

"Very much," he says as he crosses the room toward me.

He moves behind me, wrapping an arm across me as he pulls me flush against his chest, and grins at me in the mirror. I elbow him lightly in the ribs, but he just kisses my shoulder. He holds up his shirt and bunches it to pull over my head. I hold my toothbrush in one hand as he pulls it over my head, then I slide one arm through then the other, switching the toothbrush back and forth. He shakes his head, laughing at me in our reflection.

"Almost perfect," I say after I spit and rinse, looking down at his shirt that hits mid-thigh. I dip my nose in the neckline and breathe in his delicious smell. He groans as he watches me remove my bra and drop it to the floor, then step out of my underwear. "Now it's perfect."

West joins me back in bed after brushing his own teeth, and immediately wraps himself around me. His hand reaches under my shirt, his shirt, and finds my waist. He kisses my shoulder blade, rubs his beard against my skin, and whispers goodnight.

***

176

I'm awake before my alarm and take a moment to appreciate the large, warm body that's still asleep next to me. I've wiggled my way out of his arms but his hand still reaches for me, giant paw on my waist. I chew on my lip, debating my options. It's barely 5 a,m, and I have to be at work in an hour.

I slip out of bed, quickly use the bathroom and swish some mouthwash. I slide back in bed, and, feeling only slightly guilty at the 5:04 am time showing on my alarm clock, run my fingers along the waistband of West's briefs.

"Mmmm," he mumbles, rolling to his back.

I inch closer, dipping my fingers beneath his black briefs. I kiss his chest and his arm wraps around me, pulling me flush against him. I wrap my leg over his, continuing to work my hand into his briefs. When my hand finds what it's looking for, he groans my name.

"Good morning," I whisper, feeling his hand tighten around me, trying to pull me even closer.

"Very good morning," he says, his voice rough with sleep.

"About to be better," I say, moving to straddle him. I kiss my way down his chest and disappear under the comforter, enjoying every inch of his body as I go.

Nothing about West surprises me, from his size to how gentle his hands are in my hair, from the delicious way he groans my name to the quiet curse words he utters when he finds his release.

"That's quite the way to wake up," he says as we catch our breaths.

I'm sprawled on top of him, my cheek to his heartbeat, his arms holding me in place.

"I'd love to stay and snuggle all morning, but I have to go to work," I check the clock, "And right now I need a shower."

"Are you busy all day?" he asks, his chest vibrating under my cheek with his words.

"Unfortunately, yes," I say, thinking through my schedule. "But you promised me a date and I'm holding you to that."

"I can't wait," he says, hands roaming my body.

I kiss him slowly, then get up to turn on the shower and the coffee pot. I'm dressed and ready for the day within twenty minutes.

West walks me to work even though I told him to stay in bed. He kisses me, hand on my waist, at the door to The Mercantile.

It's my last peaceful moment for the next twelve hours.

Chapter Eighteen
Harper

I help Marabelle with the fresh pastries, make coffee while bantering with the regulars, and start to put together the welcome basket for our first guests during down times. Marabelle quickly whips up a batch of pink sugar cookies, a dozen for the basket and the rest for the store. I'm sliding them into the pastry display when Marabelle pops her head from the back and tells me that my phone is going crazy.

KelseyLove:
emergency can't work

KelseyLove:
someone check rentals, socials. my merc shift is 10-2. lucas/ katie aren't responding to cover me

Aves:
I'm headed to Merc. Call me when you can.

Tex:
we got you, KL.

"There's a commotion down at Mrs. G's house," Tom says in greeting as he walks in. I'm staring at my phone, willing Kels to reply or call. She's not the kind to bail on work.

My heart starts racing. "What do you mean?"

"There's a truck parked sideways in the yard, looks like Brian's," Tom replies.

Brian. Who is Brian? My mind is blank, my rising panic turning it into a black hole. Brian, the regular that orders a mocha, extra whip. Firefighter Brian. Brian, who I've had multiple meetings with about the Fourth. Dad-type, mid-50s. One of two non-volunteers on the crew. Paramedic. I don't even yell for Marabelle, I'm already out the door, sprinting up the street and over the bridge.

I run directly into Brian as I skid around the front door into Mrs. G's house. He catches me with a hand on my shoulder. "I got you, Tex. Breathe."

"Brian, what's happening?" I ask, gulping in air.

"Mrs. G is having some worrying symptoms so Kelsey is taking her to the ER in Rock Beach, they're gathering a few things," Brian says. "She's okay, but Kelsey was smart to call me. I'm on shift at ten so I can't take them. And Kelsey refused help."

Avery walks in the open door behind me. "Brian, what's going on?"

In case of emergency, you want Avery. Cool, calm, and collected; I'm certain her brain never turns into a black hole of nothing.

"Kelsey called me in a panic, thinking her mom was having a stroke. You know how long dispatch takes around here. I called them on my way, I'm waiting for transport to call back." He holds up both his phone and fire station radio. "I'm almost sure that it will be faster for Kelsey to drive her, and I'm almost sure it wasn't a stroke, but she does need a doctor." His phone rings and he holds up a finger and steps outside.

"Kels! Aves and I are here, what do you need?" I call into the back hall.

"One sec!" comes her shaky reply.

breathe in two three four, hold two three four, out two three four

"Brinley confirms the closest ambulance is at least twenty minutes out, probably more," Brian says, walking back in. "She's calling ahead to the ER for us."

180

"Thanks, Brian," Avery says. "Harper, I'm handling this. You're handling everything else. I'll call or text as soon as I can. You're going to go give Kelsey and Mrs. G a hug, and get your ass back to The Merc. Brian, what do I need to know?"

Cool, calm, and collected. I try to channel my inner Avery.

breathe in two three four, hold two three four, out two three four

"Kelsey said that her mom woke up with vision loss, weakness and numbness on one side of her body. She was overly tired all weekend and Kelsey has noticed some clumsiness lately. Mrs. G is still struggling with her vision and possibly some vertigo. She's stable. I've checked her heart rate, blood pressure, O2," he continues on, but I stop listening. Instead, I head down the hall.

"Kels, Mrs. G?" I call, peeking in rooms as I pass.

"In here," Kelsey says as I reach the last door.

I walk into the master bedroom. Kelsey is unsuccessfully trying to shove an extra long phone charger in a backpack while Mrs. G sits on the edge of the bed. I gently take the charger from Kels and quickly wind the cord around my palm, then tuck it into a side pocket. Kelsey is shaking.

"Hey, slow down, I got you," I tell her. "Hi, Mrs. G, let's go see Brian and Avery."

Kelsey moves to one side of her mom and I sit down on the other. Kelsey and I put our arms behind her and we all stand up together. We slowly make our way down the hall to Brian and Avery, who takes my place.

I grab a few granola bars and a banana from the counter, a hoodie off the back of a chair, and track down Kelsey's glasses on her nightstand. I give Kels a hug and settle her into the backseat of Avery's Subaru, handing her a bottle of water. Avery gives me a reassuring nod and they're off.

Brian and I stare at each other for a second after he finishes calling off Brinley's transport request.

"I didn't know your name was Harper," he says. "Sorry, that was random."

"Avery gave me the nickname a long time ago. Long story short, I was moving to Texas, the name stuck. She started introducing me around town as Tex and now here we are. And she says I'm the stubborn one in this relationship," I say with a shrug and a forced smile.

"Are you okay, Tex-Harper? Can I at least walk you back to The Mercantile?" Brian asks with an easy smile. Such a dad. "I'll get my truck later."

"I'm okay," I say, partly to convince myself it's true. "I'd love an escort, it'll give me a chance to make you your usual mocha, extra whip. Marabelle made extra cookies this morning, I'll send some to the station with you."

We walk toward The Mercantile, both lost in thought. Brian is sending a few texts, probably to his wife whose name I can't remember right now. My mind is a scramble of daily tasks and worry for Kelsey and Mrs. G.

Breakers has guests arriving. Is the hospital here big enough? Weekly Merc orders. Hardware store paint samples. Did Kelsey have socks on? Hospitals are cold.

"I think what you and Avery are doing for this town is really great," Brian breaks the silence once again. "I grew up coming here as a kid and was lucky enough to move here full-time after I put some years in on a wildland crew in Bend. It's a special place and I can already tell you two are making such a difference to this community. The Friday bonfires have been fun, just like I remember. The whole station is looking forward to hosting the Fourth."

"Thanks, Brian, that means a lot," I tell him honestly. "We have Kelsey to thank for a lot of it, she's the one getting the word out beyond the local rumor mill at the Mercantile."

"Kelsey's a great kid, I've watched her grow up. Us full-timers are pretty tight knit, and I actually taught her to ride a bike, way back in the day. My wife and I couldn't have kids, but we had Kelsey running around town," he says with a laugh. "I guess she's not much of a kid anymore, really hasn't been for years. She's more mature than half the firefighters I've worked with over the years."

So he's not a dad, but he is a bonus dad. Everyone needs a bonus dad or two.

Brian holds the door open and there's a small crowd in the store.

"Oh, gosh," I say, looking around the store.

"Speaking of the local rumor mill," Brian murmurs quietly to me as silence descends, everyone turning to look at us.

"Hey, ya'll, guess you're just here for coffee, right?" I ask with a small smile. "I'm kidding, I've already seen half of you this morning. Brian here could use his usual, Marabelle, and we're sending the extra Breakers cookies to the station."

I work my way through my neighbors, smiling at each of them, to box up the cookies as Marabelle starts his mocha.

"We just wanted to make sure Kelsey and Mrs. G didn't need any help," Sarah says with a smile.

I love this community. I joke about the rumor mill but I've noticed how they all show up for each other time and time again.

"Avery is taking them to Rock Beach Hospital, I'm guessing Tex here will be the one Avery calls first. I'm also guessing that Rebekah will stay overnight for observation," Brian tells our concerned friends and neighbors.

I don't think I've ever heard anyone call Mrs. G by her first name. Also, why is it Mrs. when there's no Mr.? Why is my brain thinking this right now?

"I'll check on her flower beds, maybe bring my mower around if the yard needs it," Tom says with a decisive nod.

"I'll make a breakfast casserole to put in the fridge for Kelsey tomorrow morning," says a woman that looks familiar yet I can't quite place.

"And Tex, you just let us know what else we can do, or if you need anything," John's wife Liz tells me, putting her hand on my arm as I come back around the counter with the box of cookies for Brian.

"Y'all are the best friends and neighbors, thank you," I tell the small crowd sincerely, my voice cracking slightly. "Now, if you'll excuse me, I've got some things to sort out since Team Merc is down two people."

Without another word, I duck into the back.

breathe in two three four, hold two three four, out two three four

Work now, freak out later. I make a mental to-do list for each facet of my job.

Find Lucas and/or Katie to cover Kelsey's Merc shifts for the week. Refresh the help wanted ad. Inventory/orders for the week. Apparel order. Backup host for Friday bonfire if necessary. Check Airbnb for arrival time today, any new or upcoming guests. Figure out social media takeover for Breakers. Welcome basket to Breakers. Green Door needs new plants.

My phone buzzes and I jump.

Lucas (Merc):
Just heard what happened, on my way in. Give me 20 min.

Not Avery or Kelsey with an update. But, helpful nonetheless.

Tex:
thanks, see you soon.

I open the Airbnb app, which is actually fairly user-friendly and definitely more my thing than the social media side of Team Merc. We have a booking request for The Garden, starting Friday through the weekend. I mentally move "plant massacre" up my priority list and accept the request.

Aves:
Arrived at ER, checking in. Tell Brian thanks for the call-ahead.

Tex:
keep me updated, please. let me know what y'all need delivered. KL's car?

KelseyLove:
that was scary, thnx pretend big sisters
184

KelseyLove:
need help w socials?

Tex:
i'll figure it out, you just focus on you and your mom. i got this.

One look at the various social media accounts tells me I do not got this. I do not got this *at all*. I look up the social media influencer who booked Breakers. ZoeSaysSoFitness. Her feed is filled with beautiful pictures of outdoor yoga classes, green smoothies with recipes, organic partner brands, and I decide right then and there that I want every pair of workout leggings she owns.

Based on her story, her group is already at the coast and out on a hike. I move back to the Airbnb app and send her a message. I quickly explain that we have a family emergency on our team and give her the door code, telling her she can check in early as long as it's after noon. I tell her that I will be at The Town Mercantile most of the day and if she could stop by, I'll just hand over the reins to the Breakers account because she's clearly much more qualified than I am. Too trusting? Maybe. But I'll take the gamble. I'm unsure what other choice I have. I don't have the time or patience for a crash course in social media management and marketing.

An hour later, I'm fairly confident I've responded to all rental inquiries (holy shit there's a lot, thanks Kels!), have put confirmed dates into a shared calendar with Aves and Kels, and sent Jessie a text about gardening. I'm putting the finishing touches on the welcome basket and feeling quite pleased. Pink champagne, sparkling cider, "BREAKERS" hats, s'mores kit with vanilla, strawberry, and coffee flavored marshmallows, Marabelle's cookies, pink sea salt shower scrub made locally, four small candles, and the first clue for the scavenger hunt.

Shit.

Betty.

I haven't bribed her yet. And I still have to place the other clues.

"Guys, I gotta bribe Betty to be nice to our renters that show up this afternoon. What do I take her?" I ask Marabelle and Lucas, starting to panic.

They look at me blankly.

"She's usually nice to strangers, but how you get her to not be inappropriate is another story," Lucas says, shaking his head.

Marabelle swats his arm and laughs.

"She propositioned me the other day!" Lucas exclaims, laughing.

"Mini basket! I'll make her a mini basket. Help, please!" I run to grab a bottle of sparkling cider as Lucas glances at the large basket and heads for the s'mores supplies.

"Tex! Phone!" Marabelle tosses my vibrating phone at me.

"Aves, is Mrs. G okay? Kelsey?" I don't even say hello.

Lucas gives me hand signals that I can't decipher so he just gently pushes me into the back as the front door opens.

"They have a bunch of tests they want to run, they're already saying she'll be here overnight. She's still quiet but not as nauseous. The vertigo seems to be better. At this point I feel like she's in good hands here. If she needs more specialists, I'm going to push for a transfer to Portland, or even just Salem," Avery says quietly.

"Is there any other family to call for Kelsey? I know it's just her and her mom here, but do they have extended family anywhere close?" I ask, chewing my bottom lip.

"Mrs. G's parents passed away and she doesn't have siblings. It's just the two of them," Avery tells me, still speaking quietly.

"Okay, what's our plan?" I blow out a slow breath.

"I'm sitting in the waiting room, Kelsey is back with her. If you could get Kelsey's laptop and mine and somehow find time to get them here, that'd be amazing. I can work from here today and I know that at some point Kels will want hers. I'll run out and grab us lunch in a few, so we're good there. Are you good with everything today?"

Like I said, cool, calm, and collected.

"Yeah," I glance at the time. "I gotta go though, give Kels a hug from me. I'll text you soon."

My heart hurts knowing it's just Mrs. G and Kelsey. I'm not the closest with my parents but our family reunions with my cousins are always a wild time and I know if something happened, half of them would show up within twenty-four hours.

As soon as I walk out from the back, Marabelle is making eyes at me. She looks pointedly at Lucas, who is surrounded by…shit, our renters. That's definitely the Instagram girl smiling up at Lucas. I take a deep breath and walk over.

"Hi! You must be Zoe! I'm Harper, known around here as Tex," I smile warmly and reach my hand out. She's stunning. Wavy dark hair tucked under a Trailblazers hat. Long eyelashes, bright eyes, glowing skin, not a stitch of makeup.

"Tex, so nice to meet you, I know we're here a little early, we absolutely don't expect to get in the house yet!" Zoe says as she shakes my hand. She's just as bubbly in real life as she is on her page. "Lucas was just telling us about the cafe next door. We'll grab lunch first. This is Kristen, Abby, and Casey."

"I'm happy you guys are here. Obviously this morning went a little sideways but I'll go get everything set for you at the house now. Kelsey is our social media manager but will not be available so, even though I joke that I only trust two people and my dog, I'll trust you with the account takeover," I tell her, mentally crossing my fingers.

"I was blown away when I saw how quickly Kelsey had grown your accounts, and is she really only eighteen?" Zoe asks curiously.

"She's about to turn nineteen and then abandon me for Oregon State; you actually helped her win free books and class supplies from Avery, our boss slash my childhood best friend," I proudly tell Zoe.

The other three girls are looking at the local handmade jewelry display, exclaiming with Marabelle over the earrings. Zoe glances over at them and drops her voice, leaning toward me slightly.

"Is Avery really A.Marino, the author? I thought I recognized her in one of the stories Kelsey posted, but I know how private she is so I didn't even tell my friends. We all love her books!" Zoe tries to keep a hushed voice but she's obviously beyond excited at the possibility.

I just smile. Zoe squeals. She does a little dance and I can't help but laugh with her. It's been a shit show of a morning but her energy is contagious. I absolutely trust her with the account for the day.

After she explains the easiest way for her to have access to the account, I give her my cell number in case they need anything, then it's time to get the house ready and try to convince Betty to behave.

"Tex! Hi! Zero had a secret sleepover!" Colt nearly trips me as I balance the two gift baskets and navigate the steps out the front door. "I woke up and she was in my bed!"

"Hi, Colt! I knew you'd like Zero to have another sleepover, I bet she liked it, too!"

Jessie grabs the bigger basket from me just as it tips sideways. "Hey, we came to check on you. Brian called West and then Tom stopped by, so Tom and West are at Mrs. G's doing yard work. I'm supposed to ask you if you need anything."

Zero spots me from where she's laying outside the door and whines for my attention.

"Hi, Z, good girl," I shift the basket so I can give her ears a scratch. "Uh, yes, but my brain is overwhelmed. Can you walk and talk?"

"Of course! Colt, grab Zero's leash, let's go for a quick walk," Jessie says. Colt happily grabs Z's leash and leads the way toward the bridge.

Fifteen minutes later Breakers Bliss is officially ready for our first guests. I snap a quick pic of the gift basket on the counter and send it to Aves and Kels.

"They're going to love it," Jessie reassures me as I hesitate at the door.

"I know, I just wish Aves and Kels were here, especially Kelsey," I say quietly. "She's the one that got them here today, she was so excited yesterday."

Jessie takes Betty's basket from me and sets it on the porch. She motions for Colt and the two of them wrap me in a hug. Zero takes the opportunity to wrap the leash around us, which makes Colt laugh. His giggles are contagious and soon all three of us are laughing as Zero jumps around us.

188

"Okay, I'm good. Let's go see what Betty thinks about the world today," I say as I lead us down the porch steps.

"I haven't met Betty yet, I'm oddly nervous," Jessie says, grinning over the basket at me. Colt and Zero run ahead of us, happy playmates as usual.

"Just ignore anything she tells you about me and we'll be fine," I tell her. "She's a loose cannon and apparently her new hobby is making up a sordid past for me; her imagination is a wild place."

"I cannot wait for this," she replies. Jessie is a whole different person today than the one I caught at The Mercantile door yesterday morning.

"If we survive Betty, can you help me for a few hours? I need to get laptops to the hospital, set up the rest of the scavenger hunt, the plant massacre still needs to be fixed and that house now has renters at the end of the week. I have a ton to catch up on at the store and depending on what Aves tells me, I'd like to try to have dinner at the hospital." I don't even know what time it is right now, but it can't be much past noon. My mind trips ahead. "The Mercantile is getting busier and I haven't found a new hire yet so Kelsey has been working extra hours. Avery took a couple shifts last week, it's crazy. And I'm not letting Kelsey be alone tonight, whether she's at the hospital or her house."

"Of course I'll help, just let me know what you need," Jessie says.

She looks up and gulps, I follow her gaze and see Betty already on her porch, standing with her hands on her hips and glaring down at us. Zero and Colt stand beside her. Colt looks at Betty and puts his hands on his hips, mimicking her stance.

"Am I the last to find out?" she demands.

"Good morning, Betty, this is West's sister Jessie, also known as Colt's mom." I make the introduction and Jessie smiles nervously.

"Nice to meet you dear, your son is adorable," Betty says sweetly with a smile. Colt beams. Then she turns her glare back to me. "Am I the last to find out?"

"I was going to talk to you after Avery gave me an update, I didn't want you to worry," I say quickly.

"Tom already told me about Rebekah, I'm talking about you and her brother!" Betty exclaims as she tilts her head toward Jessie. Ah, yes. That.

"Yes, you are the very last. We made the rounds to inform everyone else, one by one, in person, purposefully keeping you in the dark," I tell her solemnly. I take the gift basket from Jessie and set it on the porch railing.

"I knew it, I knew you'd be the one to finally break that boy." Betty shakes her head at me. Colt shakes his head. I swear Zero shakes her head. Jessie's wide, amused eyes dart back and forth between us as she tries to hide her smile.

"As you know, breaking boys is my specialty; West was no problem after my mafia experience," I deadpan. "Now, can we talk business?"

"I don't talk business after noon." Betty is extra feisty on this stressful Monday.

"Well then I'll talk. We have our first renters at Breakers Bliss and they might be looking for you. If you see a group of four young women in hats like this," I pull the hat from the gift basket on the railing. "They might be on a scavenger hunt. Their last task is to get a picture with someone wearing a matching hat. I thought you might have fun harassing someone new since I'm really busy today, breaking hearts and all. One of the girls is a little bit famous on social media, I thought you'd enjoy that, too. So, wear the hat or leave it here on the porch where it can be seen and I'm pretty sure they'll find you." I hold my breath.

"Social media star, well, I like the sound of that," Betty says, placing the bright pink snapback over her gray curls.

Thank you, eight-pound, six-ounce, newborn baby Jesus. And Ricky Bobby.

Betty starts looking through her gift basket, setting a candle and the homemade marshmallows on the railing.

"Can I have a hat, too?" Colt asks eagerly.

"Of course, my man, let's go grab one from The Merc. Lucas can make you a special hot chocolate while I beg your mom to work for me."

190

I ruffle his hair. "Thanks, Betty, don't go too hard on the poor girls if they show up!" I give Betty a wave as I back off the steps.

She ignores me and instead gives Colt a pat on the head, Jessie a quick squeeze on her arm, and Zero a scratch. I snort. I hope I am Betty in the future.

Chapter Nineteen
West

I clap Tom on the back as he finishes mowing Mrs. G's small lawn. He had already watered all the plants when I showed up so I took the chance to fix a portion of her porch railing that was rotting. I've been meaning to do it for weeks. I don't have the key to her storage shed so I can't get the deck stain, but it's a start.

"You'll let me know when Tex hears from Avery?" Tom asks, wiping his brow with the bandana that always sticks out of his back pocket.

"I'll let you know as soon as I hear anything. I'm going to check in at The Mercantile now that we've finished here," I tell him. He gives me a solemn nod.

Kelsey has been raised in this town since she was a few months old; everyone knows her and her mom. Tom and Brian both stepped into fatherly roles over the years, attending the dad functions when she was in the small public elementary school in Rock Beach. Mrs. G and Kelsey are like family to every single full-timer and a good portion of the summer residents.

"She's in the back," is how a harried-looking Marabelle greets me when I push open the door of The Mercantile. I give her a smile and step behind the counter to peek around the door.

"Hi," I say quietly, still making Harper startle. She's looking at spreadsheets on her laptop and chewing on her lip.

"Hi." Without warning, she stands and launches herself at me.

I pull her into my chest and feel her take a deep breath. I automatically slow my breathing, matching it to hers. I stay silent, knowing she needs a minute.

"Have you heard anything?" I finally ask quietly.

"No, just that I need to get their laptops to the hospital. Mrs. G is still waiting on more tests. Avery is on top of it, as usual. Was it still busy out front? Apparently Kelsey did too good of a job with Merc media, we've had a steady stream of tourists stopping in all day. Which is great, but I'm down an employee and up three open rentals," she says rapidly, her voice slightly muffled as she stays buried in my chest.

"It was busy out there but they've got it handled," I tell her, enjoying the fact that she's seeking comfort from me. "How can I help? Can I deliver laptops? I don't have shop hours today."

I slowly rub my hand down her back, like I wished to all those weeks ago when I found her in the midst of a panic attack. She melts into me further and I rest my chin on her head; she fits perfectly with me. I feel her take one last deep breath and reluctantly loosen my arms.

"I actually just asked Jessie to deliver laptops on her way to the nursery, which reminds me, I need to call the nursery and tell them to add Jessie to the account so she can charge us," Harper replies, stepping out of my embrace and reaching for her phone.

"I'll find Jessie and take Colt and Zero from her," I say, catching Harper's waist before she can pull further away. She pauses and I take the opportunity to tip her chin up, kissing her gently. "Let me know if there's another way I can help; otherwise, I have your dog."

"Thanks," she sighs. "At least the morning started out really freaking fantastic, right?"

And she's back, giving me her devilish wink. Just the reminder of our morning has my blood heating.

"Shit! The scavenger hunt, I gotta go!"

She's running out the door before I can say another word.

***

I'm sitting in our spot, watching Colt and Zero dig holes together, their all-time favorite pastime, also their sandiest, wishing Harper was sitting beside me. If my plan worked, Sarah should have walked dinner over to

194

her at The Mercantile just a few minutes ago. I'd stopped in at the cafe to ask Sarah to put together a to-go order for Harper, Avery, Kelsey, and Mrs. G.

Jessie's still working on the garden so my only responsibility is to tire out the dog and the boy before feeding them. Based on the size of their hole and the height of the sand they fling, we're not there yet. I feel my phone buzz and smile, knowing it's Harper, probably thanking me for dinner.

Liam:
I'm in a bad place man.

Shit, not Harper. I don't know what to do with this.

"Excuse me," says a dark-haired girl, probably between Harper and Kelsey's ages. "Is that dog named Zero?"

Startled, I shove my phone back in my pocket. I glance between the four young women standing in front of me, unsure how to answer. I mean, yes, the dog's name *is* Zero, but how the hell do they know that?

"Sorry, we're staying at Breakers Bliss, and we get bonus points on a scavenger hunt if the dog we take a picture with is Zero," the blonder one says, smiling at my confusion.

The third one turns to face me and I realize that her pink hat says "BREAKERS" on the front. Colt is currently wearing the same one.

"We don't know what the bonus points will get us, but we are fully invested in this scavenger hunt," the first, dark-haired girl says with a melodic laugh.

"Oh, yeah, sorry, it's been a weird day," I say, standing. "I'm West, and yes, that's the famous Zero."

"And Cutie Colt?" the fourth asks. "Okay, this must be so weird, strangers asking you about your dog and your kid."

I chuckle at that. Ain't that the truth. "Well, neither are technically mine, I'm just the lucky babysitter I guess."

"I'm Zoe, and this is Abby, Casey, and Kristen. If you know Zero and Colt then you must know Kelsey and Tex. They crushed it with this rental, we are having so much fun with the scavenger hunt! I feel like a little kid again. We love your town, the house, the store, everything. You're so lucky to live here!" The first one introduces herself and the group. Her name rings a bell. She's the Instagram one.

"Besides babysitting, what do you do for work?" the blonder one, Abby I think, asks. "Because I am ready to move here. But, you know, money. Adulting. Bills."

"I own the tattoo shop in the next town, bigger town, over. Rock Beach Tattoo. I also do carpentry work. And," I nod at Colt and Zero who are now chasing seagulls, "babysitting. But that doesn't pay well, or at all."

"No fucking way," Zoe breathes, eyes immediately tracing the tattoos visible on my arm.

"Uh, yes fucking way?" I reply, confused but amused. She reminds me of a dark-haired Emmy.

"We looked you up earlier but it said you don't have hours on Mondays and Tuesdays; we wanted to get tattoos this trip," Zoe says, ponytail swinging.

"Well, as long as my two charges have a different babysitter tomorrow, I can do that. I know Harper told you about the family emergency today, so let me check on the plan for these two," I tell her. I whistle for Zero who obediently trots over, Colt trailing along. "Hey bud, remember Tex's scavenger hunt? These ladies are hoping for a picture with Zero, can you share her for a minute?"

"I love your hat!" says the girl wearing the matching "BREAKERS" hat, tapping the bill of Colt's.

"Miss Betty has one, too, you're supposed to find her," Colt informs the group. "But that's a secret."

"Your secret is safe with us," Zoe says, smiling down at Colt. "Thanks for sharing Zero with us! Looks like you were having a lot of fun together."

I step away to text Jessie about tomorrow's schedule while Colt and Zero happily pose for selfies. They both love the attention from the girls, Colt showing off his beach treasures he has stashed in his pocket and Zero licking everyone's faces enthusiastically.

196

Colt asks them to race him to the waves and Zoe looks at me before agreeing. I give her a nod and smile and they take off. By the time they walk back, Jessie has texted and confirmed she can have Colt in the afternoon.

"I can get you guys in at 1 p.m., does that work?" I ask, looking between the group.

"Perfect! We're supposed to check out by 11 a.m., but I think I'm going to text Tex and ask if we can book another night. I need to make sure we have enough time to get all the selfies for the scavenger hunt," Zoe laughs.

Zoe and I exchange numbers in case anything comes up, then the girls are off in search of Betty. I don't think they know what they're in for.

***

"Hi, thanks for dinner," Harper says as she appears on my deck just as the sun is sinking into the ocean.

I shove my phone back in my pocket; staring at Liam's text isn't doing anyone any good. I look back up and smile at Harper. With the sunset behind her, she takes my breath away. The soft light accentuates her gentle curves and her hair moves slightly in the breeze. She gives me a small smile but her thumb is on her tattoo.

"Hi, how is Mrs. G? And Kelsey?" I ask, standing and pulling her into a hug. I breathe her in, feeling the tension slowly leave her body as I rub my hand on her ribcage.

"Can we sit? I'm exhausted," she says quietly.

I motion to the chair next to mine. Instead, she puts her hand on my chest and lightly pushes me into my own chair, then sinks sideways into my lap. She leans into my chest and buries her nose in my neck. I keep my arm around her waist, hand splayed on her thigh.

"Mrs. G is staying overnight for observation. Kelsey is freaking out. Not going to lie, I am, too," she sighs and I tighten my grip on her.

"What can I do?" I ask softly.

"This. This is helping," she says, laying her hand on my chest over my heart.

I turn to tip her chin up, bringing her lips to mine. She hums contentedly and I wish we could stay like this.

"Where are you all staying tonight? Where's Kelsey?" I ask, knowing Harper and Avery won't let Kelsey stay alone.

"They're at Kelsey's, packing a few things, then we are meeting at Avery's cabin. I need to steal my dog back and head up there," she says. "Zoe texted and said she met a hot, older lumberjack that's going to open his tattoo shop for them tomorrow, know anything about that?" She huffs a small laugh.

"She didn't mention muscles? Sexy beard? Deep voice? Broad chest?" I joke, wanting to hear Harper's real laugh.

"No, it was more emphasis on 'old' if I was reading her tone correctly," she says, hazel eyes shining with laughter.

I stand abruptly, pulling her with me, then shift her so she's thrown over my shoulder. That gets me her real laugh, and I hold her steady with my hand on the back of her thighs as I carry her inside.

"Tex! Are you okay? How's everyone? Did you see the pictures I sent of the garden? Zoe's killing the socials for you right now! Her video with Betty is hilarious," Jessie rushes over after I drop Harper gently on the couch.

"Tex! Zero misses you!" Colt barrels down the hallway in his pajamas, quickly overtaken by Zero, who does excited couch parkour before wriggling her way into Harper's lap.

"Hi, everyone!" Harper laughs happily, and seeing her sitting on my couch, her head on my sister's shoulder, my nephew and her dog fighting for space on her lap, my heart squeezes. She must sense something, because her eyes lock on mine, and she smiles before giving me a wink.

I lean against the kitchen counter and wonder how this is my house. It was what, six, maybe eight weeks ago, when my house was silent, empty. I thought I had been content with that, but now, with my eyes on the chaos on my couch, I know what content really is. It's a funny, smart, beautiful girl you don't deserve, your sister that you let down, and your nephew you walked away from, all sharing the same space.

198

"Do you think this could be the right place for Colt and I?" Jessie asks, sitting down next to me with her hot tea, Harper long gone and Colt tucked into bed. "Right now it just feels like an escape, but I see how happy Colt is, how this town pulled together for Kelsey today, how it's changed you, and I wonder if it's possible for me."

I weigh my words carefully. I had begun to think she'd never leave Liam, but she did, all on her own. It obviously wrecked her in a way that I don't understand, but she did it. I want Colt to stay, Jessie, too, but it can feel isolated during the winter months. Or was that my own doing, my own isolation?

"If you want to make it your place, it could be," I finally offer. "It's a different life than Portland, one that works for me. Winter months are long and dark. There's only a few dozen people that stay here year round and finding winter work can be hard in a summer town. Rock Beach has a great public school, Kelsey went through middle school in the district and you can see how amazing she turned out."

"I just see how happy you are and I want that," Jessie says quietly. "I'm realizing that I've been in fight or flight mode for so many years with Liam, never knowing what his addiction was going to bring. I tried so hard to keep my family together, but that wasn't healthy for any of us. I need to do better for Colt, for myself. I feel like I can finally breathe when I'm here." She has tears silently streaming down her face. I reach my hand out and grasp hers.

"We've both done a bit of a shit job dealing with things, haven't we?" I ask her.

"But you're so happy!" she sobs. She pulls her hand from mine furiously wipes her tears and then buries her face in her hands.

Does she think I've been happy here all these years? Without her and Colt in my life? I've been happy at times, but what she sees now, this has not been my life.

"Jessie, this happy that you see, it's new. When I left Portland, I basically put myself in isolation out here. I worked, I sat in my cold, empty house, and I blamed myself for everything, every single mistake. I told myself I wasn't worthy of happiness. I was living under a dark cloud," I tell her honestly when her crying slows. "It took Avery a year to break through my walls. Then it took both Colt and Harper showing up here to give me any sort of reason to try to live a real life again. Now I want to live a happy life. I'm still not sure I can, that I know how, but I want to try."

"Those three really refuse to take no for an answer, in very different ways, don't they?" Jessie asks, sniffling.

"That's a good way to put it," I tell her.

"I guess the good news is that I have a part-time, temporary job this week," Jessie smiles through her tears. "And gardening this afternoon was amazing. I've missed playing in the dirt so much." She fumbles with her phone and then hands it to me.

"Damn, Jessie, that looks amazing, Grandma Georgie would be proud," I tell her as I swipe through the pictures of The Green Door Garden. Bright colors burst from the planters I repaired and the new flower beds that line the walkway. The pots on the front porch welcome visitors with colorful blooms.

"I want to ask Tex if we can add a vegetable garden in that side bed, and that house on the golf course desperately needs new landscaping," Jessie adds. "She asked me to send a few pictures so they could add them to the stories, want to see?" I hand her phone back and she navigates through her apps.

"Um, this is not a garden," I tell her, watching a video of Zoe and friends arriving at the Breakers house. House tour. A giant gift basket with pink champagne. They suddenly all have those pink "BREAKERS" hats on.

"No, but it's great advertising for Team Merc rentals. Watch the part with Zero on the beach," Jessie's tears have dried and now I think she's near laughter. "Just wait."

Zoe's put together an amazing variety of pictures from the Breakers house as well as around town. Some of the handmade "go slow" signs are featured, a menu from the cafe, salmon berries ripening along the tsunami trail, the flowers in front of the cafe. A short video where Zoe explains that they're starting a scavenger hunt. A clue leads them to the golf course, another to one of the tsunami evacuation routes.

200

Back to the cafe, then to a fence post along the far beach path. Harper really had them running all over town. Now it's a piece of paper with a list of selfies they need to take.

*Rejection Rock
*Sea anemone
*Flying kite
*Someone golfing
*A seagull
*A house with pink flowers
*Frisbee game
*Starfish
*Dog on the beach (bonus points for Zero)
*A stranger in a "BREAKERS" hat (bonus points for Betty)

"Okay, we're walking down the path to the beach and we think we see Zero," Zoe whispers as she films. "There's a cute little boy with her so we won't film until we get permission, but there's only this hot, older, lumberjack guy on the beach with them. Please hold for more."

Jessie cracks up next to me. She's legitimately gasping for air. "Oh my god, you should see your face," she crows.

"Harper said Zoe texted her that, didn't realize she put it out there like this though," I say, amused by Jessie's reaction. Zoe really is a little, or a lot, like Emmy.

Zoe doesn't post any of the pictures with Colt, but she does have a couple with Zero. And now we cut to Betty. All five women are in "BREAKERS" hats. This should be good.

"Well now, dear, back in my day, if I would have had this fancy Instabook, I would have had *all* the boys looking at my pictures, if you know what I mean," Betty says in the video, waggling her eyebrows at Zoe's camera. "Tex says you're famous on Instabook, so let's make me famous, too. I got rid of my last husband, good riddance, but I'm not looking to marry, I just like the attention."

The video cuts to a selfie of Betty with Zoe and her friends, and then another, and another. Betty is glowing, surrounded by the four young women. Their smiles are big, laughter in their eyes. The angle changes, Betty has the phone now. One and a half of the girls are cut out. The angle changes again and the last selfie is only Betty, ear-to-ear smile.

"I love that I was a tiny part of that today," Jessie says, nodding at her phone that's still in my hand. "Those girls are having a great time together, it must make Team Merc pretty happy, despite the tough day, to see that."

That's an interesting way to look at it. Being a part of someone's happiness. There are definitely people that can add to your happiness and being a part of someone else's happiness can make you happier. I think I've forgotten that in the last few years.

A text buzzes on her phone in my hand and I glance down as I hand it back.

"Grant?" I ask, giving her my big brother look. She merely shrugs. She seems to think I don't notice her small smile as she walks down the hallway to bed. It seems he might be a part of her happiness today.

I pull out my own phone and look at the text from Liam again. I don't know what to do with this. Jessie and Colt are my priority in this triangle, but the guilt I've pushed down threatens to reemerge, dampening the happiness that I felt earlier.

Chapter Twenty
Harper

My phone buzzes with a text notification on my desk and I grab it, hoping it's Kelsey or Avery. They're back at the hospital with Kelsey's mom and no one has heard from either of them all day.

Zoe Campbell:
(photo) new tat, who dis?

A selfie with West loads, Zoe holding up her hand awkwardly. I laugh, her wrist tattoo is upside down with how she's angled her arm. West's giving his half-smile, clearly amused. I swear his eyes twinkle at me through the phone.

Zoe Campell:
photo fail

Harper:
hope to see it in person and not upside down.

Zoe Campbell:
west says you should ditch him and hang with us tonight. and bring kelsey and avery. not just bc i'm avery's biggest fan. promise not to fangirl. much.

Harper:

waiting to hear from the girls still

Zoe Campbell:
no pressure at all, you know where to find us. thnx for letting us book extra night very last minute.

An hour later, I still haven't heard from Avery or Kelsey. I'm finished with my Merc apparel order, inventory is restocked on the shelves, brand/logo goodies for Breakers are awaiting final approval, I've confirmed that Jessie and Colt have Zero, all volunteers are confirmed for the Fourth Festival, and I've opened the calendars for the other rentals. The Glass House and North House are officially open for business. Team Merc should be on a high right now. Apparently our BFF telepathy is still strong. My phone rings immediately.

"Hello?" I answer nervously, reminding myself to breathe.

"Hi, we're all on our way back to Three Rocks!" Avery tells me immediately. "Well, we will be shortly, waiting on discharge paperwork."

"Great news!" I exclaim. "Want some good news in return?"

"Yes, please! Wait, is this Team Merc good news? Speakerphone good news?" she asks.

"Yep, Team Merc crushing it," I tell her. "Okay, ready….all rentals are live!"

"Hell yeah, boss!" Kelsey cheers.

"Great job, girls, I'm so proud of all three of you," Mrs. G says in the background. Her voice gets louder; I'm assuming Avery moves closer or hands the phone off. "And Tex, I have already told Avery, but want to tell you as well, thank you so much for your support the last couple days. I'm so glad Kelsey has both of you in her life."

"Aw, Mrs. G, of course we're here for her," I say, wishing I was with the three of them. "As Avery and I say to each other: anything and everything, always."

"We better go, just wanted to let you know we'll be home shortly," Avery says as I hear a door open and someone greet Mrs. G in the background.

"Real quick, we have an invite to hang with Zoe and her friends tonight, they booked Breakers for another night, either of you interested?" I ask quickly. I laugh when Kelsey shrieks. "I'll take that as a yes. See y'all soon!"

***

While I'm excited to have a girls' night, I was really looking forward to a date with West. I missed him sleeping next to me last night. Two nights with the man and I can't get enough. Ridiculous, I know. I just want to sit across from him and let him take away the stress of the last two days. I check my watch. It's early, so this should work. I holler to Lucas that I'm cutting out early, text Aves and KL that I'll meet them at 7 p.m., and jog back to the cottage to jump in my Jeep.

Then I start the overthinking part of my day. Driving and overthinking go hand in hand for me. The drive isn't long but I have more than enough time to wonder if I'm getting in too deep, too fast. This is why I always revert to half-in, good-times-only, easy relationships. Things with West feel *too* easy though, but in a very different way. Instead of no thoughts and no emotions easy, it's just plain easy to be with him, to let him in, allow him to see the real me.

I've nearly chewed a hole in my cheek by the time I pull up in the small parking lot behind Rock Beach Tattoo. I park between West's truck and a red 4Runner and walk around the building. I can hear Zoe's contagious laughter from here.

"Harper!" Zoe exclaims as soon as I peek around the wall just past the front desk. "Or Tex? I can't tell which one you go by or which I should call you. But hi!"

"Hi! I was hoping I'd catch y'all. I took the gamble that you got your tattoo first and I had time," I say, giving her a quick hug. "I go by both. Most people in town call me Tex, thanks to Avery, but West started calling me Harper when he did my tattoo and saw my ID." I show her my tiny wave.

West's eyes are on me, concerned and steady. I give him a smile and a wink, hoping that'll reassure him that I'm here for good reasons, not bad. I just realized that he probably hasn't heard that Mrs. G was released today. He gives me a slow smile then returns to Casey, who is stretched out on her side. She gives me a wince as the tattoo pen buzzes.

"Only Casey is left!" Kristen chimes in, holding her foot up awkwardly for me to see, sunset tattoo on the top.

Abby dips her shoulder to show me her shoulder blade, and Zoe holds her hand up.

"Oh, it's not upside down!" I tease. "For someone who makes their living taking pictures, that was not your best work earlier."

"I was too excited!" she exclaims, laughing. "But look at the real ones we got."

Zoe shows me the pictures and videos she and Abby took while she was getting tattooed and she briefly outlines how she'll put them all together. I have no doubt it's going to be amazing.

"So, just to warn you, Team Merc is in for tonight since Mrs. G is on her way home from the hospital. Kelsey is probably going to ask you a million questions, maybe a million and a half," I tell her. "I'm going to make the hot, older lumberjack take me to an early dinner first, though."

"Oh my god, did you see my story?" Zoe says, covering her face. "I did not realize I'd now be spending time with the hot, older lumberjack or that he was...with you. But gotta say, Abby is fielding questions left and right about him already and we haven't even shown his beard."

I risk a glance at West, who I'm sure can overhear us, and he's carefully covering Casey's rib cage. I can see the corner of his mouth turned up, so he's definitely heard at least part of this conversation. He does give off rough, lumberjack vibes, but watching his gentle hands work is one of my favorite things.

"Uh, I don't think I want to know what you're thinking right now, Tex," Casey says, catching me watching West.

West's hands pause and he looks up at me. My cheeks flame and he gives me his full smile, probably knowing exactly what I'm thinking.

"Holy hell, girls, we gotta go!" Zoe says, fanning her face.

"I'm just going to go splash some water on my face, I'll catch y'all back at Breakers," I tell them, nearly sprinting past them to the door that I really hope is the restroom. Laughter follows me.

Zoe is right: holy hell. I look at myself in the mirror. My eyes look a little wild, my cheeks are pink, and I can't stop smiling. It's official, I've lost it. I run my hands under cold water, willing myself to pull it together. Who am I kidding, I can't. I splash water on my face and open the door.

"Hi, Harper," West says, smiling at me from where he's cleaning his station.

"Hi, hot, older lumberjack, I was hoping I could cash in on that date."

"Can we lose the 'older' part of that?" West asks, stepping toward me with a predatory look in his eye.

"Hmmm," I hum, tilting my head as I consider it. "No, I like the older part. A lot."

All of a sudden I'm pressed back against the wall and his mouth is on mine. I wrap my arms around his neck and spider monkey my way up his body until my legs are wrapped around his waist. He's so much taller, so much bigger, he easily holds me without trying. My mind briefly flashes to other things he could do with his strength and my body. If someone would have told me two months ago that I'd date a bear-sized lumberjack, I would have thought they'd lost their mind. But damn.

"I missed you in my bed last night," I tell him as he kisses down my neck and across my collarbone.

"And it sounds like I don't get you tonight, either," he whispers, his lips brushing my ear and making me shiver.

"You can have me right now," I pant, no shame in my game, as I arch into him.

"Harper," West groans. "I'm not going to pretend that you splayed out on my table isn't a fantasy that plays on repeat, but our real first time is going to take me all night. All. Night."

"I can't decide if I just got shot down or if that's *my* new fantasy," I whisper, tightening my legs around his waist.

"You test every fiber of my willpower," he says between kisses. "Every time I see you, I want you. Every time I think about you, I want you."

He tangles one hand in my hair, his light grip around the back of my neck helping him maneuver my mouth for better access. I forget about dinner, I forget about my night with the girls. I think I even forget my name. I whimper when his hand finds its way under my shirt, gripping my waist, calloused hand rough on my skin, the other gripping my thigh, holding me up.

"Harper," West whispers, pulling back just enough to rest his forehead on mine. "Let me take you to supper."

"God, you really are old, supper isn't a thing," I murmur, pressing my lips to his again, not willing to concede defeat.

"I meant what I said. All night, Harper," West pulls back again. He presses his hips forward and I'm ready to beg. "I want to show you in every way possible, I'm all in on us, on you."

I look into his eyes, and I see it. I see him. He's just as overwhelmed by this as I am. Isn't this what I always do? Enjoy the physical side to avoid the emotional? What will happen if I follow his lead, slow everything back down, and take my time? The thought is terrifying. But his blue eyes are steady on mine and his thumb is rubbing gently on my waist.

"Supper it is," I whisper.

"Don't think for one second that this scenario here is put to rest, this is merely to be continued," West tells me, pressing another kiss to my lips before slowly, so freaking slowly, letting me slide down his front.

"Promises, promises," I reply, staring up at him.

His eyes rake over my body, making me feel wanted, no, needed, despite the brakes we just put on. He reaches his hand out for mine, pulls me in for a sweet kiss, and then leads me out the front door and down the street to supper, which might be my new favorite meal.

***

"First, oh my god, I told Harper I wouldn't fangirl but I am a liar because holy shit, you're A.Marino!" Zoe whisper-squeals. "I swear I didn't tell anyone else, not even my girls. But, oh my god! Second, hi! Come on in!"

"It's so nice to meet you," Avery says, smiling. "I actually heard from Tex that you love my books so I brought you the trilogy, hardcover, and I signed them about ten minutes ago."

"Shut up, you're A.Marino?" Kelsey is frozen on the front step.

"Oh my god, I'm so sorry, Avery, I just assumed she knew!" Zoe says, looking between starstruck Kelsey and Avery.

"Don't worry, I brought more pink champagne, she'll get over it quickly," I say, holding up the bottles I grabbed from the back room at The Merc.

"I actually thought you already knew," Avery says, looking at Kelsey and shrugging. "I guess your mom keeps secrets."

"She's a fucking vault," Kelsey grumbles. Obviously that hit a nerve. Aves and I exchange a glance. Kelsey grins. "But actually, I was just trying to cover for all of us. Basically the whole town knows. Like, we *all* know. And have since you moved here."

"Kelsey!" Avery exclaims, laughing. "You totally had me going!"

"I did star in the third grade spring play," Kelsey deadpans. "Kind of a big deal."

I try to swallow my laughter as I look between them. I fail and double over in laughter.

"Ugh, you two," Avery says, pushing us inside. "Zoe, please take them away from me."

Zoe makes the introductions as I pour champagne for everyone but underage Kelsey. She happily takes a sparkling cider and we toast to new friends.

The girls break into chatter about Betty and everything they've done while in town. They show off their tattoos and show us the story Zoe posted about their experience. Kelsey points out that Rock Beach Tattoo already has a few hundred more followers than it did before Zoe posted her story. She launches into a line of questioning and Zoe patiently answers each question. Abby chimes in often, as she's co-creator for most of Zoe's content. Casey falls asleep nearly immediately, which makes Kristen crack up.

"She can fall asleep anywhere! The account we need is a 'Casey sleeps' page," Kristen tells us. "Also, we are so well versed in ZoeSays that the subject puts us to sleep."

"This is why my publisher runs mine," Avery says. "Shit." She closes her eyes.

"I knew it!" Kristen crows. "I wasn't going to say a thing, but I knew it the second we met. How Zoe hasn't fangirl'ed is beyond me. She is your biggest fan."

"Oh, I did!" Zoe catches our conversation. "Absolutely acted and felt like a fool, but I couldn't help it."

"I knew, too," Casey says, rubbing her eyes and stretching.

"Well, thank you for not making a big deal," Avery smiles, relief evident.

"Hey guys," Kelsey says suddenly. "I have an idea."

"Just to warn y'all, this is exactly what she says when she's about to make me do something ridiculous," I tell the group.

"I love it, I'm in," Zoe says immediately, eyes sparkling.

"Grab the other bottle of champagne, let's go," Kelsey says, leaving no room for argument.

We obediently trail behind her and when she takes a right on the street, I have a feeling I know where we're headed. She really is a genius.

"It's definitely low on the scale of one to ridiculous, but this soaking tub is definitely made for two, not four," I say five minutes later, laughing as Zoe, Kelsey, and Abby all pile in with me.

"No, have Kelsey and Abby trade spots," Kristen directs.

"Who put her in charge?" Zoe jokes, leaning sideways as Abby climbs back into the tub.

"Perfect!" Kristen says, taking a handful of pictures of the four of us crammed into the tub.

Kelsey had waited until we were standing inside The Glass House to pitch her idea. She had nervously eyed Avery and I when she offered a free night stay to Zoe in exchange for helping push the new rental on all social media platforms. Zoe had jumped up and down in excitement, grabbed Kelsey's hand, and demanded a tour.

"She needed this," Abby tells us, nodding to Kelsey and Zoe who have retreated to the floating deck with their phones. "Not just this quick getaway, but Kelsey's energy. I think Zoe is burnt out."

Casey and Kristen nod their agreement. I briefly think back to my last few months in Austin. I wasn't necessarily burnt out, but my mental and emotional outlook was definitely in a slump. Not even Emmy could pull me out of it.

"Then this was perfect timing, Kelsey is beyond excited about how well Team Merc is doing and there is no way you can spend time with Kelsey and not have at least a little bit of her joy rub off on you," I tell them.

"So true," Avery nods her agreement. "We might be biased as proud, pretend big sisters, but she's amazing."

"I love the girl gang vibe," Casey says, motioning between Zoe and Kels on the other deck and the four of us. "It's easy to get a little lost in day-to-day life, or who you're dating, or even your family, which if it's anything like mine, has drama. You need some kickass female friends to get you through."

She's right. That's all there is to it. I miss Emmy like crazy, but this town is a girl gang in and of itself. Avery, Kelsey, and Jessie, they're just the beginning. Mrs. G and Rachel, best friends as long as they've lived here. Sarah, always feeding us when we need it most. Quiet Katie, still working on finding her place, but willing to put herself out there a little more every day. Marabelle, master of life-changing pastries. And never forget Betty.

No wonder why I'm happier. So many amazing women, all right here for me every day.

Chapter Twenty-One
Harper

Kelsey and Zoe's badassery is officially proven the next morning when The Glass House goes viral. Much to West's surprise, so does Zoe's video on her tattoo experience. Team Merc is overwhelmed with booking requests for both The Glass House and Breakers Bliss and West is swamped with Zoe's followers requesting appointments. It appears a lot of the dates and names line up. One of us is much happier about this than the other. Then again, only one of us works completely solo.

I immediately call Jessie, offering her a job with Team Merc. She happily agrees to morning shifts at The Merc and afternoons helping with all things having to do with our short term rentals. I can permanently cross gardening off my list, a relief to everyone involved.

I talk to Katie and Tammy, our newest hire, about picking up a few more hours at the store, which I hope will free up enough of my time to keep up with rentals. Although at the rate we're going, I should probably renew our help-wanted ad. Again.

By the end of the day, I feel like I have a handle on Team Merc. Or at least I have a lot of sticky notes and lists left all over the place, which is basically the same thing. I fall into bed with Zero, happy and almost content. I just need one more large body in this bed with me.

Harper:
if i leave the door unlocked, will you come here after work?

No reply, I'm sure because he's busy. He's a night owl, even if he doesn't have a client sitting in front of him, he likes to work on upcoming designs in the shop. According to Instagram, he's going to have a lot of designs to work on in the coming weeks. I fall into a restless sleep, Zero keeping my feet warm, but the rest of my bed empty. I wake up with my entire bed empty.

"Shh, good girl, Zero," West whispers, using his phone flashlight to maneuver around the room as Zero circles his feet, seemingly herding him to bed.

He slides in next to me and I feel the bed dip again when Zero jumps back up. I roll over and tuck myself into his chest. It's like the chaos of the day finally melts away when his hand lands on my waist.

"I missed you," West says quietly, kissing the top of my head.

"It was only a day," I mumble. I missed him, too.

"Still did," he replies, running his hand up and down my back. "Go back to sleep, Harper, I know you have an early day again."

"Not tired," I whisper, tangling my legs with his.

His chest rumbles with a laugh and I close my eyes to breathe him in, enjoying how he wraps around me so fully. It's the last thing I remember.

When I wake up before my alarm, I can tell I've slept hard. Instead of reaching for West like I really want to, I slip out of bed and take my dog for a walk. Self-reflection game, still strong.

Of course I self-reflect on how I'm going to balance my ever-changing job with Zero, Colt, and West. Is this why I've never had a real job? A real relationship? Why I run from commitment? Because I can't do it all? Am I the asshole when it comes to Ethan, his job, and our failed relationship? Is this what he felt? Am I now going to be Ethan?

"Hi, Harper."

I startle, having been lost in my overthinking. West sits in our spot at the base of the rocks near the path, holding my bright pink "fucking ray of sunshine" mug, steam swirling off the dark liquid inside.

"Hi, West," I say, smiling down at him. It just takes looking into his bright blue eyes to feel calmer.

"Join me?"

214

I check the time on my phone before sitting down in the sand next to him and leaning back against the rocks. He hands me the mug and I take a sip, watching Zero sniff her way back down toward the ocean, happy to have more time on the beach.

"Based on my day yesterday, and I think yours, too, we're about to be really busy," West says. I merely hum my agreement, sipping the hot coffee and letting the mug warm my hands. "So, before you overthink it, I want you to know that I'm still all in. No matter how busy we are, I'm here. I'm in."

"I already overthought it," I admit. "Is that a word? Overthought? Overthinked? I did that. Just now."

"Can you unthink it?"

I laugh and take another sip before wordlessly handing the pink mug to West when he holds his hand out. Why does it feel so intimate to share coffee like this? He keeps his eyes on mine as he takes a swallow. I can feel him reading me.

"I'll try," I finally say.

"Me, too," he says.

To unthink his own overthinking? What was he overthinking about? Should I overthink about his overthinking? Am I overthinking his overthinking? Why is my brain like this?

breathe in two three four, hold two three four, out two three four

West reaches his hand to my lap, covering my hand with his. I look down and realize my thumb is on my tattoo.

"I mean I'm going to try every day, even when we only have a few minutes together like right now, to make sure you know that I'm still here, still all in, still patiently waiting for things to settle down for us," West says, his eyes never leaving mine.

I hold my hand out for the coffee and he silently hands it over, patiently waiting for me to process his words. They're already processed. I set the mug in the sand and climb into his lap, bringing my hands to cup his jaw as I rest my forehead on his.

"Hi, Harper," he whispers.

"Hi, West," I whisper back, before gently bringing my lips to his.

215

The coffee is on the colder side of lukewarm before I remember that I'm working the early shift, and I jog to The Merc in my sandy clothes, ready to take on another day, leaving my dog with my bearded lumberjack.

***

Somehow we make it to the Fourth of July Celebration but sleep deprivation is no joke, I swear my short term memory is shot. I don't know what I did yesterday, let alone last week. I need to order more sticky notes at the rate I'm going through them. Some days I wonder if I need to write "brush teeth" on a sticky note. That's a lie, I'm obsessive about brushing my teeth. Maybe "brush hair" though, because that ship sailed about the time the "BREAKERS" hats came in. Beach hair, don't care.

I'd like to say I make sleep a priority, but I don't. I still wake up at 5 a.m. and quietly untangle myself from West's arms. Sometimes I manage a quick morning beach walk with Zero, but more often than not I find myself sliding back under the covers and reaching for West. Luckily Zero spends her days with Colt, so she's not hurting for exercise.

West and I's schedules are the complete opposite, most days our only time together is 5 a.m. before I leave for work or nearly midnight when he's home from work. Home. How does my cottage only feel like home when he's here? Luckily he's here a lot, having basically turned over his bedroom to his sister.

Despite our schedules, I'm happy. Really fucking happy. Some mornings I'll wake up to a sticky note sketch on the bathroom mirror or stuck to my phone on the nightstand. Those are definitely slide-back-in-bed mornings. We still haven't crossed the line in the sand, but West whispering "our real first time is going to take me all night. All. Night." basically runs on repeat in my head. It's probably a good thing my days are so busy, otherwise I'd just be staring off into space, daydreaming.

I love the mornings I get to make Colt his special hot chocolate when he, Zero, and West walk Jessie to work, which earns me a hug from Colt and, if we're sneaky, a lingering kiss from West as we hide in the

216

back room. Shout out to Lucas for always asking Colt about new beach treasures and to Jessie for turning a blind eye.

Today, The Merc is slammed. There's no way for me to get away, even to the back room, until well after noon. Even then, it's just long enough to inhale my lunch. Jessie volunteers to do the final check of the rentals, one of which I cleaned until 10 p.m. last night. Kelsey has already refreshed the welcome baskets and Lucas delivered them between the morning coffee crowd and the lunch rush.

I love busy days, I really do. I love seeing my friends and neighbors, welcoming new tourists into town, answering questions, and planning our community events. I especially love the buzz in the air over our Fourth Festival. Brian stopped in for his mocha (extra whip) this morning and reassured me that he has everything handled for the Friday bonfire tonight. If I'm lucky, I'll have all rentals checked in and be able to sneak in dinner with Avery, West, Colt, and Jessie before we all head down.

I'm not lucky. I mean, I am very lucky, but I don't get dinner with everyone. I do get dinner with Avery, sitting in the back room at The Merc, color-coding our calendars. And any dinner with my best friend, even a working dinner, is a good dinner.

***

"Surprise!" a vaguely familiar voice calls.

"Zoe!" shrieks Kelsey, darting out from under Brian's arm slung around her shoulder and down the beach. She and Zoe crash into each other in a hug.

"Surprise," a deep familiar voice says before wrapping an arm around me. West's scent surrounds me as he pulls me into him, my back hitting his solid chest. He leans down and kisses my neck.

"What? Hi. What?" I'm obviously not firing on all cylinders. See: sleep deprivation. I turn in his arms to face him. "You brought Zoe here?"

"Zoe wanted to surprise Team Merc with a visit," West says, smiling. "I know it's not really what we're supposed to do, but she rented The Garden using her friend's account. Sorry." He shrugs, not looking at all sorry. I knew he and Zoe had been in contact after her followers went crazy for the tattoo stories and reels, but I had no clue he was helping to get her out here again.

"You helped with this?" Kelsey asks, her arm tucked through Zoe's as they approach the bonfire that Brian's about to light.

"He did," Zoe confirms. "He offered to let me stay at his house, or yours, Harper, but I wanted to support your business." She smiles brightly at both of us before Kelsey pulls her away to introduce her to her mom.

I stand on my toes and give West a soft kiss.

"Hi, Harper," he says, smiling down at me.

"Hi, Lumberjack," I reply, wrapping my arms around his neck.

"I don't know if you can call me that anymore, Zoe has me so busy with her followers that I don't even have time to do any woodworking, and have you ever even seen me chopping wood?" he says, dipping down to plant another kiss on my lips.

"Hmm," I hum. "I haven't, but that's definitely a sight I want to see. Can we fit that in the schedule soon? And you're really hot in your flannel, plus your beard really fits the theme."

"Honestly, Harper, you can call me whatever you want, as long as one of those things is yours," he whispers. "And my flannels look way hotter on you."

Damn this patient, kind, gentle, funny, really fucking hot, older lumberjack and the things he says. He claims he's not good with words, but the ones that run on repeat in my head are more than enough for me. I'm beyond ready for some slower days, days when we can sink into our spot after having dinner together, watch Colt and Zero race on the sand, and then have all night together, no 5 a.m. alarm. I'm going to find a way to make that happen, sooner rather than later.

For now though, I'll lean back into his chest and enjoy an evening with our friends and neighbors. And hope Brian doesn't let anyone blow themselves up with fireworks.

***

The next two days are a blur. Marabelle and her vendors pull together an amazing farmer's market on the front lawn of The Merc. We nearly sell out of Mercantile branded hats as the sun comes out first thing Saturday

218

and shines all weekend. Heritage Farms, a flower farm, leaves us a huge bouquet that takes up a quarter of the coffee counter. I have Katie deliver it to Mrs. G when her shift is over.

Lucas and his librarian friend, Nancy, with an assist from Zoe of all people, hold not only a book sale but a family craft and story time late Sunday morning. Mrs. G reads the kids a Llama Llama book and receives a hug from every child in attendance. Two from Colt. I run inside The Merca and grab the strawberry and powdered sugar donut holes that I helped Marabelle make early this morning. I drew the line at blue balls, I mean blue donut holes, even if they would have completed the red, white, and blue theme. Kelsey helps me hand them out to every family on the lawn.

"You really did it, Tex," Avery says, looking out at all the happy families. "You helped make this a real community again."

"*We* did it, Aves," I tell her. "The three of us, with a lot of help. We fucking did it."

"Hike with me tomorrow? Luke says there aren't any community events," Zoe pops up beside us, licking powdered sugar off her fingers.

Having looked fairly closely at her social media before her first visit, I can say with one hundred percent certainty that she's never posted any picture that includes sugar. She's also somehow even bouncier than ever and she's the only person I've ever heard call him "Luke."

"I'll cover your shift," Lucas says, walking up, also licking sugar from his fingers. My eyes dart between them and he gives a small smile and a shrug. Sneaky *Luke*.

"I guess I'm available in the morning, then," I tell Zoe.

"I'm in!" Kelsey says eagerly, always up for an adventure.

"Definitely in," Avery agrees.

"Great, meet here at eight?" Zoe says, squeezing my arm before walking away with Lucas.

"Hey, North House is checking out early, that's weird," Kelsey says, looking at her phone. "Nothing is wrong with the rental, they just booked through the Fourth but they're going back home."

"Tex! Kelsey! Miss Avery! That was the best story time ever!" Colt says excitedly as he rushes over.

"Oh man, didn't Mrs. G do the best voices?" I ask him, laughing as he jumps on Kelsey. I see West approaching out of the corner of my eye and an idea forms. "Why don't you have Kelsey walk you inside to see your mom, tell her I'll be there in five minutes to take over for her."

"You have to work?" West asks, his hand landing on my waist and squeezing gently. "I was hoping we could take Colt to the beach together."

"Well, I have this idea, which requires me to bribe your sister a little bit, and also for you to keep Tuesday night and Wednesday morning open for me," I say, smiling up at him. "Please?"

"Do I get a hint as to what this idea is?" he asks.

"Nope, you just have to blindly agree," I tell him, biting my lip to contain my smile.

"Bite your lip like that and I'll do anything you say," he whispers in my ear, gripping my waist tighter.

"Promises, promises," I sing, turning out of his grip and walking toward The Mercantile.

I look back over my shoulder and see him watching me with an amused expression. I give him a wink and he shakes his head at me.

Chapter Twenty-Two
West

I grab the back of Colt's shirt as he nearly darts in front of the fire truck being driven by Brian. He's a little too enthusiastic about the candy being thrown. I hope Harper can see how happy this town is at this moment, nearly all thanks to her tireless work. Avery closed The Mercantile for two hours this morning so everyone could enjoy the parade, as well as help Harper with any last minute needs. I'm sure lining up the parade participants closely resembled herding cats.

Colt and I wave to our friends and neighbors as they pass. Kids pedal decorated bikes, trucks pull flatbed trailers being used as floats, and there's even horses from the stables a mile up 101, their manes and tails braided with red, white, and blue ribbons. It's a toss up if there's more kids in the parade or watching the parade. Colt is in heaven and not just because his sand bucket is now filled with candy.

I'm a little worried about when, or if, he's going to come down off this high. He woke up with the sun and was the official starter of the 5k race which Avery, Harper (with Zero), Kelsey, and Zoe ran together. Jessie was the timer, Lucas had a table at the halfway point filled with water bottles and red, white, and blue Gatorade, and Marabelle had themed cookies at the finish. The sugar rush started early for Colt and he shows no signs of coming down anytime soon.

"Tex! Grant!" Colt yells, making a run for Grant and Harper, who are following along the end of the parade. He launches himself at Tex, who swings him around. "This is the best day ever!"

"Just wait, my man, there's so much more to come!" Harper ruffles his hair after she sets him down. She grins at me as Grant kneels down to Colt's level to hand him a rock.

I shake Grant's hand when he stands, glad to see him. He adds happiness to Jessie's life, as well as Colt's, and he seems to have no expectations other than spending time with them.

"Hey, West. I couldn't stay away when I heard how much work Jessie and Tex put into today, along with the rest of the team," he says in his easy way. "Grabbed a room in Rock Beach at the last minute, hoping Colt will let me help with the sandcastle contest."

"Yay!" Colt cheers and does the fist pump Harper taught him.

"Jessie reopened The Merc but she'll be off in time for sandcastles," Harper says as she wraps her arm around my waist. We've continued to slowly ease Colt into seeing us closer, so I pull her into me with an arm around her shoulder and give her a kiss on the temple.

"You've done an amazing job," I tell her quietly. "I've never seen this town happier in the years I've been here."

I've also never been happier myself.

***

Grant, Colt, and I retreat to my house and have a quick lunch together on my deck, inhaling the sandwiches that Grant brought. We can see Team Merc on the beach setting up the canopy for the sandcastle and kite contest check-in, but they refuse all of our offers to help so we stay on the deck, trying to let Colt have some down time. All that does is give him more time to come up with outrageous sandcastle ideas.

When the opening bell rings, he enthusiastically starts building his dinosaur castle that is being attacked by sharks. On land. Because his imagination is bigger than he is. Luckily Harper and Jessie join in and seem to understand his vision because Grant and I are not much help, we didn't even make it past the moat and bridge.

Judge Avery and Assistant Zoe start making their rounds with a clipboard and sand flies faster as Colt directs his own assistants. There are stegosaurus type spikes along the castle roof and shark fins made with shells in the moat. By the time their dino castle is finished, all three of them are covered in sand and have stripped down to swimsuits. They

222

toss their shovels aside when Zoe blows the air horn that signals the end of the contest, then bolt for the ocean. They shriek as the cold water hits their feet and swing Colt between them up and over the small breakers.

After splashing the sand off, Jessie and Colt veer off toward the awards ceremony. My heart thuds loudly in my chest as Harper walks back up the beach toward me. Her eyes are glued to mine as she weaves her way through the sand masterpieces. Water glistens off her shoulders and while her red, white, and blue bikini could stop a man's heart, it's her happy smile that makes it hard to breathe.

Grant's hand on my shoulder startles me. He claps my back and gives me a knowing look as Harper approaches.

"I'll go help with awards, Harper, you deserve a break," he says as he stands, giving Harper a smile.

"Thanks, Grant," Harper says as she lowers herself onto the oversized beach towel next to mine.

"Nice castle," I tell her. "I wasn't sure how you guys were going to pull it off, but you really nailed it."

"The kid had a vision, I respect that," she says, leaning forward to give me a quick kiss. Her lips taste like saltwater and watermelon chapstick.

Harper's abs flex enticingly as she slowly lays back on her towel. She stretches her arms above her head and sighs. The beach disappears and all I can see is Harper, her heart-stopping bikini, and salty watermelon lips turned up into a smile.

"You're so fucking beautiful right now," I say, rolling toward her and reaching my hand out to run a finger down her side. She squirms under my touch and rolls toward me. I barely manage to keep my eyes on hers as I see her bikini top shift out of the corner of my eye.

"It's been a good day," she says, her eyes burning into mine. She reaches out and runs her fingernails through my beard. She bites her lip and glances around and then slowly leans forward brushing her lips to mine. "And tonight's going to be even better."

My body responds to her lips and her words while my mind races at what this surprise she has planned could be. While I'm looking forward to dinner at Jenn's house with our whole group, and of course the fireworks after, I desperately want to be alone with Harper, no matter what this surprise is. I want to show Harper with everything in me just how much she means to me. How she's brought me out from under my dark cloud, how she brings pieces of happiness to me every day.

"You're killing me, Harper," I whisper against her lips. "Your smile, the light in your eyes, and this fucking bikini, absolutely killing me."

"Mmmm," she hums, kissing me again. "I guess it's going to be a slow death, because I need to go hand out kite awards and then help Avery's mom with dinner."

She rolls away from me, stretches out on her back one more time, toes pointed, arms above her head, and perfect breasts straining against her bikini ties. A slow, painful death, indeed.

***

"I don't get one single little hint?" I whisper in Harper's ear. I feel goosebumps erupt along her skin. "Even if I say please?"

She leans back into me, nestling in, her hands running along my thighs. Her head tips back onto my chest as fireworks explode overhead. She's been torturing me all afternoon with that look, the one where she bites her lip as she eyes me like I'm candy, and her little touches seem to linger longer than usual.

"The only hint you get is-" she starts.

"Tex! Did you see that one?!" Colt launches himself at Harper, who laughs and pulls him into her lap.

She sits forward so she's no longer leaning against me, although she stays sitting between my legs. I rub her low back, knowing she must be exhausted after all she's done today. I can feel her push back slightly, wordlessly asking me to continue.

"Isn't Brian doing an amazing job with the fireworks?" she replies to Colt. "I'm so happy tonight." I can see her give him a squeeze-hug, his favorite.

"Me, too!" Colt exclaims, his face to the sky as more fireworks boom overhead.

I look around the small bonfire, wanting to keep this memory forever. Kelsey and her friend Annie are sprawled in the sand next to

224

Mrs. G, Jenn, and Rachel, who brought chairs down. Avery, Jessie, and Grant are sharing a beach towel and the two girls have a heavy blanket wrapped around their shoulders. A Colt-sized space is between them.

My heart squeezes in my chest, I feel like The Grinch when his heart grows. Avery catches my eye and smiles, she must know exactly what I'm thinking. I smile and shrug at her. We both look back up as the finale starts with the loudest booms yet.

The sky lights up with fireworks set in rapid succession, the outline of Rejection Rock and her two sister rocks hazy in the smoke. I slip my hand under Harper's layers and wrap my big hand around her slender waist, needing to feel her skin under my fingers. I can feel her sigh at my touch, even as she oohs and aahs with Colt.

Cheers break out along the beach when the finale winds down, two red flares sent up to signal the end of the show, as everyone shows their appreciation for Brian and his crew. Whoops can be heard from all directions, and someone, probably Tom, hollers Brian's name. More cheers erupt.

"Well done, Team Merc," Rachel tells Avery, Kelsey, Jessie, and Harper. "We haven't had a celebration like this in years. What a day."

"Best day ever!" Colt cheers, jumping out of Harper's lap and fist pumping, making everyone laugh.

I squeeze Harper's waist and think to myself that, no matter what Harper's surprise is, Colt is right. Best day ever.

Chapter Twenty-Three
West

When Harper pulls up in front of North House, I can just barely make out her smile in the darkness that surrounds us. She puts the Jeep in park but doesn't move. I stay still as well, studying her profile. She's biting her lip and even though I can't see her hands in the dark, I know her left thumb is on her tattoo.

"Hi, Harper," I say, reaching for her hand. I bring it to my lips and kiss the inside of her wrist gently.

"Hi, West," she replies.

I wait patiently, gently rubbing her thumb, letting her gather her words. I can feel her turning them over in her head.

"Okay, I'm suddenly a little freaked out because I planned this surprise for you, for us, and it suddenly feels big, bigger than I realized," she says quietly.

"Will it help if I tell you that what I feel for you has felt big since day one?" I ask, turning in my seat and reaching into Harper's duffel bag.

I find what I knew would be in there, her notebook, looking slightly worse for wear, and flip through the pages in the dark. I hit the dome light and hand her the notebook, open to a page in the middle.

She looks down. I can hear her sharp inhale and her hand moves to the sketch.

"The first night you were here," I tell her, nodding to the page. "I remember every detail. Big from day one. I'm all in, Harper."

She blows out an unsteady breath. She moves her eyes from the drawing to me, and the air leaves my body. Her eyes are somehow just as startling in the dim dome light as they were that first night by the fire.

"I just wanted a night for us. No Colt, no Zero, no early morning alarm, just a little bubble of our own for once. I thought about The Glass House, we've both put a lot of work into that house, but it didn't feel quite right. This feels like us. Plus, I know the manager," she says, adding the humor to the end like she always does when she's nervous.

"Harper, this is perfect," I whisper.

Silence. Does she know that I will take her in any way, shape, or form I can? Every quick kiss at The Mercantile, every glance from across the bonfire, I want all of those moments.

I turn the dome light off, plunging the car back into darkness. I shove my door open and am around the hood and opening her door in record time.

"Promise?" she asks, turning in her seat.

I rest my hand on the roof of the Jeep and lean in, kissing her gently. "Promise."

She wraps her arms around my neck so I tug her from her seat, lifting her as she wraps her legs around my waist. I shove the Jeep door closed and stalk toward the house, one arm around her waist and the other firmly planted on her butt.

"Our bags!" She laughs into my neck as I carry her up the steps.

"Later," I practically growl, pressing her back against the front door. She tightens her grip around my waist and arches into me. "Where's the key?"

"It's unlocked," she says, shifting sideways to turn the knob. With a jolt I remember that she's pushed up against the door. I stumble forward when the door flies open, catching her weight as I step over the threshold. I turn and push her against the closest wall as I kick the door closed.

"Too fast?" I whisper as I kiss her neck. She shakes her head and whimpers as I find the spot at the base of her neck that she likes. I groan and catch her mouth in a searing kiss.

"West," she gasps between frantic kisses.

228

Her eyes burn into mine. There's a pause in movement, we're both staring at each other, unmoving. My heart races, pounding against my ribs, and my fingers itch to have her soft skin under them. I've memorized every inch of her body but we've held back one thing. For some unspoken reason, we've waited. I want to savor this first time. But I'm desperate. I need her. Now.

Seeing my need mirrored back in her eyes, I tuck my hand under her shirt, gripping her waist. She sucks in a halted breath and grabs the hem of my shirt. I hiss as her hands skim my abs, trying to control myself. She pushes my shirt up my chest and I brace her against the wall before reaching one hand above my head. I rip my shirt off and let it fall silently to the floor.

"I need you," she whispers, her hazel eyes dark with need, hands tracing the tattoos on my ribcage. "Please take me to bed."

I trail kisses down her neck as I carry her across the room, pausing when I realize I don't know which direction to go. She takes advantage of the falter in my step to crash her mouth to mine once again, tongues tangling, her hands in my hair as I pull her as close as possible.

"Main bedroom," she pants.

I'm really fucking glad she said that, no time for stairs. I need her writhing beneath me, now. Her legs tighten as I turn down the hall and she leans to press a lightswitch as we pass. The light makes a path straight down the hall and into the bedroom, the bed shining like a beacon.

I slowly lower Harper onto the bed, pausing to search her eyes as I hover over her. Does she feel this, too? This moment? She's the burst of sunshine that rid me of my darkness, she's the one that brought joy back into my life. But no matter how amazing she is, or how perfect this feels, I've never done one hundred percent with anyone. And this feels like a one hundred percent night. All in.

"Please," she begs.

"Harper," I whisper, leaning down to taste her lips once again, unable to put my thoughts into words.

I kick out of my boots as she fumbles with my belt. I divert her efforts when I pull her shirt over her head. And then her other shirt.

Fucking cold Oregon weather. There are still way too many pieces of clothing between us. I kneel in front of her and pull her leggings down, nearly ripping them off her. I quickly shed my jeans, pausing to drink her in as I stand. She's a fucking vision, matching black lace, lean legs stretched before me, wavy hair floating around the white sheets.

I kiss my way up her body, chasing her as she shifts backwards toward the top of the bed. When my mouth finds the lace edge of her bra, she moans my name. I nearly lose it right then. I press myself into the apex of her thighs, feeling her need.

"Hi, Harper," I murmur when I finally end my wandering and bring my mouth back to hers, smiling as she arches her displeasure when I still my hips.

"Hi, West," she whispers into my lips, biting my lower lip in retaliation.

"I'm just realizing that my wallet is in the car," I whisper, burying my face in her neck.

"No, West, I just want you," she says quietly, her hands roaming my torso, dipping lower toward my waistband. "I'm on birth control, I'm all in on us, I trust you."

I stop moving altogether. I pull back slightly to look into her eyes.

"You're sure?" I ask. At her nod, I groan her name and take her mouth in a searing kiss. "You're perfect."

All I want is to be inside her, but I'm determined to draw this out. I lower myself to run my rough beard over her lace bra, groaning again when I realize her bra snaps in the front. When I use my beard on her skin, bra thrown somewhere behind me, she arches into me and I kiss the sting away.

I work my way back down, kissing every inch of skin along the way, and slide her panties down her lean legs. I stand at the end of the bed, lace in my fist, and my mouth waters at the sight of her spread before me. Even though I've seen her in this exact position before, everything feels different.

When I sink inside her, nothing between us, I know everything is different. I know, in this moment, as her eyes hold mine, that I'm in love with her. There was no other end to our story, no other place we could have ended up but here.

We move together and it's like nothing I've ever felt. She knows my needs before I do. When she falls over the edge, shuddering beneath me, I fall with her, her name on my lips.

"Harper," I whisper as I pull her onto my chest, both of us breathless, heartbeats slowly returning to normal. "You win. I'm ruined. Wrecked."

I can feel her smile and her hand drifts to my ribcage. I am so content with her tucked into my side, leg wrapped over mine, that all I can do is savor this moment, memorize how her fingers feel as they trace circles over my tattoo, how her breaths slowly even out until she sighs in her sleep, her hand finally still over my heart.

***

The morning light is barely filtering through the curtains when I open my eyes; I have no idea what time it is, all I know is Harper is still pressed up against me. I must have shifted as I came to because I feel Harper stir on my chest. Her hands drift down my ribcage, lazily tracing my tattoos. My body responds immediately.

"Good morning," I say, my voice still gruff with sleep.

"Good morning," she whispers back, reaching up to run her hand through the scruff of my beard.

I gently catch her hand, bringing her wrist to my lips. I softly kiss the thin skin and feel her shiver.

"Best morning ever," I tell her, using the arm that's gently wrapped around her to pull her on top of me.

"Can I make it even better?" she asks, sitting up, letting the sheet fall into a puddle on my thighs.

"You just did," I tell her, reaching forward to grasp her waist. "You're perfect."

She slowly rolls her hips and I'm mesmerized by the movement. I rake my eyes down her body, taking in every inch of her, from her bright, clear eyes to where my hands dwarf her waist.

"I'd feel self conscious, but I can feel your need for me," she says, rolling her hips again, giving me a wicked grin.

She places her hands on my chest and leans down to give me a slow kiss before shifting to slide over me. The next time she rolls her hips, all I can do is groan her name. When she finally takes me fully, I have to bite my tongue so I don't tell her I love her.

She moves slowly, keeping her eyes on mine, and shudders when I whisper her name. She's beautiful, beyond beautiful, and I don't know how she's mine. She works us both to the tipping point and we find our release together.

"You're fucking incredible," I tell her, lightly running my hands down her back.

"I think it's us, together," she says from where she lays collapsed on my chest.

"I think it's you," I tell her honestly. I know it's her.

"Is this the part where things are too good to be true?" she asks in a timid voice.

"Can't they be too good and true?" I ask her in return.

"It just feels like a lot," she says, rolling off me. "In a good way, but still a lot."

"I'm crazy about you, Harper," I tell her, again swallowing the urge to tell her I love her as I pull her toward me.

"I just want to stay here forever," she whispers, pulling my arm around here as she curls into me.

***

This newfound realization that I'm in love with Harper has me wide awake, unable to fall back asleep, although she sleeps deeply with her back pressed against my chest. When the morning light can no longer be ignored, I slowly uncurl myself from around her. She doesn't stir.

I find my jeans at the end of the bed and pull them on, taking one last look at Harper stretched out on the bed before me. She shifts, seemingly realizing that I'm no longer her pillow. I take a deep breath and fight the urge to climb back up her body as the sheet dips low, exposing more skin than I can resist. With a soft sigh, she turns onto her side and pulls the comforter around her. A million thoughts run through my head, flashes of her, of us. I force myself to retreat, to let her sleep.

232

After I grab our bags from the car and find a clean tee shirt, I make a pot of coffee and settle into one of the chairs that overlook the backyard. My phone vibrates on the table and I frown at the text.

Drake:
Hey man, have you heard from Liam? He's in bad shape.

What is it with chaos finding us the morning after we take new steps in our relationship? I choose to ignore it and instead stare out over the backyard, thinking of Harper, of how I've gotten in so deep. I dig out Harper's notebook and find an empty page. I'm not always good with words, but my pencil flies across the page. Those flashes of us that I saw fill the pages.

The two of us tangled under sheets, her eyes closed in pleasure. Harper asleep in bed, hand reaching for me. Harper sitting on the kitchen counter drinking coffee. Harper running with Zero and Colt on the beach. Harper in my flannel, lacy underwear underneath.

I don't stop until I hear the bedroom door creak open. I set the notebook on the table and turn to her. She's an adorable sleepy, stunning mess.

"Good morning," she says as she walks toward me, the exact replica of my current sketch, down to the mouth-watering lace I glimpse as she drops into my lap, no bra peeking through.

I dip my hand under her shirt, my shirt, and my hand easily spans her ribcage. She says it's her favorite thing and it's quickly becoming one of mine. It feels possessive but soft, just for her. I gently squeeze her waist as she leans in for a soft kiss, then pull her into my lap.

"Good morning, want me to make you fresh coffee?" I ask, searching her eyes.

"Mmmm, coffee sounds amazing, but I don't want to get up," she replies, tucking her small body further into my chest.

"Here, have mine, I just refreshed it," I say, handing her the mug that's on the table between the two chairs. "No dairy, just black."

I let my hand wander down her side until it's on her hip, holding her close to me. My other hand splays on her bare knee, rubbing small circles in her soft skin.

"What have you been doing out here while I was sleeping the day away?" she asks as she takes a sip. She hums her pleasure as she takes a swallow. I shake my head to clear the dirty thoughts that entered the second she hummed.

"Want to see?" I ask, wondering just how freaked out this might make her.

"Yes, please," she says, taking another sip of coffee.

I reach back over to the table and hand her the notebook. "In the middle," I tell her, taking the coffee mug from her as she flips the pages.

This could backfire spectacularly. What if she's not here with me? I know she feels some of what I do, I can see it in her eyes and feel it in her touch. Is this going to ruin everything?

"There," I tell her nervously when I see the first sketch of the morning. She pauses at my tone and gives me a soft, slow kiss.

"Hey, I'm going to love it, I can guarantee it," she whispers against my lips.

She looks down at the drawing in her lap and takes a sharp inhale. She flips the page but doesn't get any further. Her mouth is on mine, notebook forgotten.

"I'm sorry, I'm not good with words," I murmur as the notebook falls to the floor.

"West, I fucking love your words *and* your sketches. I'm sure there's more because you've probably been up for hours, and I promise I'll look at them later, but right now," she trails off, shifting to straddle me.

I dip my pinkies under her lace underwear as she greedily presses into me. I grip her tight and pull her flush against me and she moans when she feels my reaction to her. Her lips meet mine in a frenzy.

"Right now, I need you," she tells me, finishing her sentence, when we come up for air. She tugs at the hem of my shirt in a silent plea.

"I always need you," I whisper back, eyes catching hers before I reach over my head.

234

Her flannel hits the floor at the same time my tee shirt does, and her bare breasts get my attention. Her fingers make quick work of the buttons on my jeans, I barely shift and she has me in her hand. When she sinks down on me, I'm lost. There is no return from what Harper has done to me. What she is to me. What will come.

I reach up and brush my thumb over her cheek then my hand is behind her neck, gently pulling her lips to mine. She kisses me with renewed urgency as her hips move faster. My hands roam her body, giving attention to her most sensitive parts. Her body reacts, arching to push her breasts closer. She gasps when I rub a finger between us. She pulls away from the kiss and our eyes are locked together as we tumble back over the edge together.

"I will never look at these chairs the same way again," she whispers, still on my lap, flushed and breathless.

"I definitely need to get one of these for my living room," I say, tracing her bottom lip. She huffs a laugh and bites my finger playfully.

We shift back to our original positions, clothing partially readjusted, her nestled in my lap. I kiss her temple and then reach for the lukewarm coffee. She scrunches her nose and shakes her head when I offer it to her. She only likes her coffee ice cold or tongue-burning hot.

"I wish we could stay here forever," she says wistfully. "For so many reasons. I love this house."

I nearly tell her that I love *her* in this house, in any house. I catch myself in time.

"Did you find the false door in the cabinet when you were getting it ready?" I suddenly ask, remembering my last time here with Eldon.

"Uh, no, and I love secrets!" she says, eyes gleaming. She scrambles off my lap and pulls me up. "Lead the way! Wait, do I need pants?"

"No pants," I tell her. I give her a playful swat and gently push her toward the staircase that leads down to the garage. She veers for the bathroom first and I pour her a hot cup of coffee, which she nearly spills as she rushes down the stairs.

I bite back a smile as I watch her search the garage, opening and closing the cupboards above the small workbench. There's no way she finds it.

"Here!" she exclaims, after opening and shutting the same cupboard door three times. "I can hear it." She sets her coffee mug down and climbs onto the counter, flannel riding up just enough to show me the lace underneath, as she reaches into the dusty cupboard and shakes a shelf.

"Uh, I'm loving this view, but you're definitely in the wrong spot," I finally tell her.

"Got them!" she pulls out a stack of papers with a flourish.

"What? That definitely was not the cabinet I was talking about," I say, frowning. I open the cabinet behind me, and sure enough, I can press my hand into the back and open a hidden compartment. All that's in it is dust.

"Well this one has these drawings, I think they're building plans," she says slowly, sitting down on the counter to look through the loose papers.

I walk over and stand between her legs, both hands drifting to her thighs. I'm looking at the papers upside down but she's definitely right, they're building plans. I bet I know what they are. I tilt my head to confirm.

"It's the workshop he was going to build; these are the plans he showed me," I say, a catch in my throat. "He asked me to help him with it, then we'd build furniture together in the winter when things were slow. He died before we even ordered materials."

Harper looks up at the change in my voice and gives me a gentle smile. She sets the papers beside her and leans forward, her hands on my chest for balance. I tug her hips forward until she's at the edge of the counter and she wraps her legs around me.

"I'm sorry, West," she says, and gives me the softest kiss.

"He was a good man," I tell her. "Maybe someday I'll see that dream of his through."

"Good thing your amazing girlfriend found these plans then," she says, leaning back and winking at me as she holds the papers out to

236

me. When I go to take them, she snatches them back and hides them behind her back.

"Guess I'll just take the whole thing then," I tell her and stoop low into her middle, throwing her over my shoulder. I grab her abandoned coffee mug and head for the door.

She laughs as I stalk back up the stairs and into the house, setting her on the counter before finally making her fresh coffee before we go back to reality.

Chapter Twenty-Four
Harper

"Good morning," West's gravelly morning voice comes from the doorway right after I climb back in bed.

"It would be, but you're not in bed," I say, stretching, letting the sheet fall down my body.

"Your dog wakes up early," he replies. His eyes roam my body and I kick the sheet down further in invitation. "I was going to offer to bring you coffee in bed, but…"

"But?" I ask when he trails off.

I know that look in his eye. It tells me I have approximately four seconds before he's on me. I'm glad I already got up to pee and brush my teeth. I'm hoping, if he's already let Zero out and fed her, we can spend the rest of the morning in bed.

This past week and a half has been a happy blur. With the Fourth celebration behind us, I've found a slightly more manageable schedule. I'm still awake with the sun, untangling myself from West's heavy arms, stumbling out the door to walk Zero on the beach. Some mornings he joins us, but others he seems to sense I need space. And others I just end up right back in bed with him. But we are still short on time together. I'd like to take full advantage of our morning off together.

I was wrong, it's three seconds before he's hovering over me, his blue eyes on mine as I run my hands through his beard before pulling him down for a kiss. After he wrings every ounce of pleasure possible from me, he pulls me to his chest and we lay in comfortable silence. I trace the tattoos along his ribs and his hand skims over my back.

"Harper," he says, his chest vibrating under my cheek as he speaks.

When he doesn't continue, I prop my chin on his chest and look up at him. His eyes don't meet mine. My thumb touches my tattoo, reassuring me.

"I just," he says and then stops again. "I don't deserve you, I don't deserve this, this happiness you've brought into my life."

I rub my tattoo. "Where is this coming from? You're an amazing man, I'm lucky Colt and I guess Avery, and probably Zero, too, pushed us together," I tell him.

It's true. The way he quietly supports not only me but all of Team Merc, plus his sister and nephew, on top of running a business, all of that is just the tip of the iceberg. He's patient, kind, funny, talented, and makes me feel wanted every single day, even if we only see each other for less than an hour.

"I've gotten a couple texts from my old life," he says. "Liam, and Drake, who bought me out. I think Liam's in a bad place."

"Okay," I say slowly, trying to figure out where he's going with this.

"I just feel like I abandoned him, or that I owe him something. I don't know, it's just weighing on me," West says, his hand still rubbing my back. He pauses before adding, "You make me want to be a better person. You're always stepping up for other people, bringing happiness to others. From the little things like knitting with Betty, to the big things like always being there for Colt. Bantering with Tom, which makes his day, taking Kelsey under your wing. You do it all."

"You do those same things, West. But if you think you need to try again with Liam, I will absolutely support you," I tell him. What I don't say is that I'm still firmly on Team Throat Punch when it comes to Liam, because apparently I'm not quite as good of a person as West thinks I am.

"He was my best friend," West replies. "And, even if he and I never get back to that, he's Colt's dad."

240

"I love Colt, and I love the way we basically get to share custody of him with your sister; I really do hope that someday his dad is back in his life," I admit.

"Me, too," West says quietly.

I let him stew in silence as I know that's his way. My hand continues to roam his torso as I also stew in silence. What a complicated mess.

I wish he didn't carry this guilt and that he could see himself the way I see him. He didn't abandon Liam, he saved himself. My heart aches thinking about having to make that decision, picturing Aves or Em in Liam's spot. Would I be able to separate myself? The difference between supporting someone and enabling their addiction is a fine line. A very blurry line, I'm sure.

I can feel the heaviness of his past weighing both of us down as we lay in silence. My thumb finds my tattoo again. West immediately notices and threads our fingers together, resting our hands on his chest. I feel his steady heartbeat under my hand and match my breaths to his. Our chests rise and fall together.

Eventually we make our way to the kitchen and make fresh coffee. And then I take his hand and tug him right back to bed.

Over the next few days, I sometimes sense he's holding something back, some part of himself, but I'm also sure of our future. Even as he wrestles with his past, he still finds little ways to show me he's with me. I wake up to a new notebook on my nightstand one morning after he worked late; the first page already filled with a full color drawing of Rejection Rock at sunset.

I let myself fall further into him.

Colt, on the other hand, holds nothing back. He is ecstatic that West and I are together and has announced it to anyone that will listen. I know he loves and adores me, but I'm pretty sure he thinks the best part of this arrangement is canine related. He and Zero, best friends forever, spend every day together. Some days Zero refuses to pass West's house, now basically Jessie and Colt's house, on our way home from our morning walk, and I have to sneak her in the back door so she can wait for her boy to wake up. Jessie, West, and I really do seem to share custody of the tireless duo at this point and I wouldn't have it any other way.

If I'm lucky, we'll adopt Betty next.

***

"I reached out to Liam today," West tells me as we sit in our spot another blissful week later. "Haven't heard back. But it felt like the right thing."

I bring my head up from his shoulder and use my hand to tip his chin my way. His eyes are bright blue and clear, piercing into mine. He leans down and gives me a kiss, a small reassurance that he's feeling better about what's been weighing on him.

"Have you told Jessie anything?" I ask, glancing down the beach to where Colt and Zero are digging together.

Jessie offered to clean The Why Can't I Come Up With A Name Golf Course House after she did her gardening rounds this afternoon, I'm wondering if she needed to rage clean the way I sometimes do. She seems happy and settled, spending a lot of time with Mrs. G, and I thought her texting was with Grant, but maybe I was wrong. I chew my lip in worry.

West reaches over and uses his thumb to gently pull my lower lip from between my teeth. "I didn't tell her anything, I didn't want to worry her or get her hopes up."

I yawn, still tired from whatever bug Colt gave me. Kids are germy. "I haven't said anything either, I just thought it was weird she offered to take my cleaning this afternoon."

West gives me a smile. "I know why she did," he says, looking at his watch. "So does Avery. Maybe you should stop by The Mercantile while I get these two hosed off before dinner."

He stands and pulls me up, presses a kiss to my lips, then unceremoniously pushes me toward the path while he heads for the water. I don't know what to make of this and I'm sure Avery and West plotting together is no good.

Sure enough, Avery is grinning at me over the coffee counter when I walk into The Merc a few minutes later.

"I have a surprise for you," Avery says, leaning over the coffee counter that she's definitely not scheduled to be working behind.

242

"Is it the corn hole bean bags that I'm missing for the Block Party?" I ask, knowing it's not.

"Well, no," she replies.

"Is it coffee?" I ask.

"Uh, no, but I guess it could be," she says. "You do get free coffee and can make one any time. That'd be kinda a lame surprise."

"But it takes so much energy to make a latte," I moan dramatically, laying my head on the counter. I really am exhausted.

"You are impossible. It's nearly dinner time, you really want coffee?" she asks.

"I just want an emotional support coffee, just to hold in my hands and make me feel better," I tell her. "So, decaf, please."

She sighs and turns to grab a cup. "And do you want your surprise?"

"Well, duh, I want the surprise," I say, watching her make me a decaf almond milk latte. Why do lattes taste so much better when someone else makes them for you?

"With Kelsey, Jessie, and West's help, I think I secretly juggled your schedule enough to send you to see Emmy this weekend," she says, grinning at me as she hands me my latte.

"Wait, what?" I ask.

"You've kicked ass way beyond what I asked of you, so you're taking a paid mini vacation to Austin!" she says, walking around the counter.

"Aves!" I shriek, pulling her into a one-arm hug, holding my hot latte out of the way so I don't burn the person sending me to Texas. "Holy shit, best boss!"

"Drink this, then go do laundry, I'll cover here, you have bags to pack!" Avery says with a smile. "And John has the bean bags at the golf course already. They came in yesterday when I was here, triple checking the schedule. Colt and I took them to John."

"You're the best!" I tell her, practically skipping out the door.

Chapter Twenty-Five
Harper

"Miss, are you okay?" The nice older lady sitting next to me scrambles for the seatback puke bag as I fan myself. "My daughter gets airsick, too."

"I don't get airsick," I mutter, trying to breathe through this awful feeling.

Is jumping out of this airplane an option? Because skydiving is definitely not on my bucket list but it sure as shit would be better than this. My stomach rolls and I dry heave into the bag. I'm going to be pissed if Colt's stomach bug finally caught me and I'm sick the whole time I'm with Emmy. This explains why I've been so tired the last couple of days.

"Try a few sips of this," my seatmate says, handing me a cup with clear bubbly liquid and ice.

I don't even question her. Taking unknown drinks from strangers, a real solid decision. It's Sprite, which seems to help. She reaches up and turns to point her tiny fan and mine directly toward my face.

breathe in two three four, hold two three four, out two three four

I breathe my way through the entire three plus hour flight, barely hold it together during landing, and scramble off the plane as quickly as possible. I basically sprint to the nearest restroom and splash water on my face. I'm still nauseous. I flash back to sitting on the bathroom floor with Colt while he threw up, his sad moans breaking my heart.

"Which one is yours?" my sweet seatmate asks after finding me sitting against the wall at baggage claim. "You stay there, I'll grab it. Do you have a ride?"

"My friend is picking me up, I just need a minute, I got it," I try to reassure her. She levels with me The Mom Look which does its job. I relent. "It's a tan duffel bag with a hot pink ribbon."

I lean my head back, willing this feeling away. I can feel my phone buzzing but don't even move to check. It's gotta be Emmy, texting from the cell waiting lot. I ignore her. I just need to focus on not throwing up. So much for a triumphant return to Texas.

Dirty cowboy boots appear in front of me. A barrel-chested man with a large belt buckle gently sets my duffel down beside me as my seatmate lets go of his hand to crouch in front of me.

"You sure you're okay, hon?" she asks, concern obvious in her eyes.

"Yeah, my friend is here," I croak. "She'll pull around as soon as I text her." I fumble for my phone. The trash can a few feet away beckons.

"Oh, hon, you just can't shake that flight," Seatmate Mom is once again holding my hair.

Her cowboy silently hands her a bottle of water and she cracks the seal before handing it to me. I swish the water around and spit into the garbage can. She hands me a tin of mints and I pop one in my mouth. I would be slightly humiliated by this whole vomit-in-a-garbage-can-in-a-crowded-airport situation if I cared about anything other than not puking again.

"Harper?" No, this can't be happening. No, no, no. "What are you doing here? Are you okay?"

"Ethan," I groan, because this really is happening. "Can you text Emmy to pull around?"

Seatmate Mom, Cowboy, and Ethan all eye each other.

"It's okay, I know her and her friend," Ethan reassures the other two.

246

Cowboy gives Ethan a silent once over and looks at his wife. I'm assuming she's his wife. I don't know, nor do I care all that much at this point.

"Hon, are you okay with him?" Seatmate Mom asks gently, not willing to step away until she knows Ethan is friend not foe.

Which is he? We aren't exactly friends, but I don't feel he is my foe. I don't feel much toward him if I'm being perfectly honest.

"I'm okay, he's okay, he'll make sure I get to the right car," I tell her, sliding back down. "Thank you. So much."

She gives me an encouraging smile and shoulder squeeze. "Try Dramamine next time you fly, works wonders for my daughter," she suggests, waiting for her husband to retrieve my duffel from the last wall that held me up. They walk away hand in hand, looking back when they reach the doors. I give a feeble wave.

"Emmy's almost down here, you okay to walk outside?" Ethan asks, holding a hand out to help me up. "Fresh air might help."

Fresh air would probably help, but instead I'm slapped with humid heat combined with vehicle exhaust. It's an actual shock to my system, going from Oregon Coast weather to pukefest disaster to Austin heat. Ethan grabs my elbow when I stumble.

"Harper, are you sure you're okay?" he asks worriedly.

"I've never been airsick, but at this point I'd rather walk back to Oregon on Friday," I tell him.

The breeze, although sticky and freaking hot as hell, is better than airplane and airport air.

"If you have time, can we get coffee this week while you're here? I understand if you're too busy with Emmy and your parents or even if you don't want to, but I'd like to talk," Ethan says hesitantly.

"My parents aren't in town, they're off in their RV, somewhere up north. I'll make time, we should probably talk, seeing as I fled the state so quickly," I manage a smile. "Thanks for rescuing me in there."

"Harp, oh my gosh, are you okay?" Emmy is suddenly on my other side.

Thankfully there's no Emmy-tackle greeting involved this time. Instead she helps me to her passenger seat as Ethan puts my duffel and backpack in the backseat for me.

"Call me?" Ethan asks, smiling down at me as I settle into my seat. I nod. "Feel better, Harper."

"Well, you sure know how to make an entrance," Em says as soon as Ethan shuts my door. She glances over her shoulder and pulls away from the curb. "Let's see if Ethan's text recap is correct. You puke in the middle of baggage claim, which I'm assuming was super crowded, your ex-boyfriend who you literally ran thousands of miles away from finds you, and a mean cowboy had your bag? Is that what just happened?"

"I don't even know, Em, I feel so awful, this is my pre-apology for being a lame houseguest and probably getting you sick, too," I moan. It feels like days ago that I left Three Rocks. "I just want to go to bed."

What I don't add is that I wish I could go to bed with West wrapped around me, his reassuring hand on my waist, and Zero laying on my feet. I was so excited for this trip and now all I want is to be back home.

"Um, Harp, are those tears? What is going on?" Panic laces her tone.

She's not used to the new emotional mess Harper. And yep, those are tears.

"I'm just tired and nauseous but also I'm hungry but I don't want to puke and why is it one hundred degrees?" I'm quickly moving from kinda emotional to full breakdown. Holy hell, I need a nap.

"Patrick is already grabbing ginger ale, Gatorade, and crackers at HEB, we'll get you home and tucked in. It's probably just a twenty-four hour bug, you'll be back up in no time," Ems tells me as she merges onto the highway.

I lean my head back and close my eyes, glad I'm not the one driving through Austin traffic. Next thing I know, Patrick has plucked me out of the car and is carrying me into their house.

"Aw, my favorite pretend brother." I lean into his shoulder. "Is this better or worse than all the times you carried me out of a bar?"

248

"At least this time I don't have both of y'all to wrestle into submission," Patrick says, bridal-carrying me down the hall.

He deposits me in their guest room and Emmy tucks me in. The blackout curtains do their job and I wake up with no idea what time it is or even what day it is. All I know is I feel a thousand times better, maybe Seatmate Mom was right about the motion sickness.

***

Spoiler alert, it was not motion sickness. I realize this as I hug the toilet the next morning.

"Good morning, sunshine, how are you this hungover from half a margarita?" Emmy lets herself into the bathroom and piles my hair on top of my head for me. She rubs my back as I heave. Once my stomach is no longer trying to escape my body, I sit with my back to the shower door.

"Colt was sick last week, this must be some summer flu the tourists brought in," I tell her. "I thought for sure I was already over it, I felt fine last night!"

We had grabbed dinner at El Arroyo, both because their food and margaritas are consistently good and because their sign out front always cracks me up. My stomach was empty from the pukefest that was my travel day so I had downed maybe not my weight, but perhaps my volume in chips and salsa. A choice I never thought I'd regret until about twenty minutes ago.

"I've got to go into the office for the morning but Patrick is working from home, he'll check on you in a bit. Sleep this off and we can float around the pool later," Emmy says as she turns the shower on for me.

One life-changing shower later and I'm good as new. I grab my laptop and park on the couch in the living room. Although I know we've turned The Merc into a well-oiled machine, I still check in with Marabelle. It's early in Oregon but I can hear Tom telling tall tales in the background and Lucas's laugh. First check-in complete.

Tex:
Z proof of life, please.

Aves:
(photo of Zero running on the beach)

KelseyLove:
i did not run on the beach or anywhere this morning, fyi

Tex:
miss y'all already.

"Hey, Harper, how are you feeling?" Patrick walks into the living room, button down shirt paired with swim trunks. Work from home life. Business on top, pool boy on bottom.

"Much better, I must just be hanging on to whatever virus Colt gave me. I guess that's what I get for hanging out with a five-year-old the majority of my days," I tell him.

Patrick sprawls out beside me and steals the remote from my arm rest. When I try to snatch it back, he holds it overhead like the pretend brother he is. I give up the fight and he puts on The Office, which was our go-to on those bar nights when he'd haul Em and I home and toss us on the couch, knowing he was the third wheel in the threesome.

"I can't believe you're dating a guy with a kid, you're such a grown-up all of a sudden. I mean, the TikToks make you look like the immature dork I know you to be, but obviously they're working, Em says your rentals are slammed. I can't believe it, little Harper all grown up," Patrick teases me.

"First of all, I'm older than you, don't 'little Harper' me. Second of all, I am indeed an immature dork, that will never change. Those reels might be a teenager's idea, but I'm always fully supportive of jumping on beds and throwing paint. Third, Colt's not his kid, he's his nephew, but if he was his kid, I'd still be in," I retort.

"Ugh, little Harper all in loooove, never thought I'd see the day," Patrick has the annoying brother routine down pat.

"You saw me with Ethan all the time," I remind him, even though I now realize that was not love or anything close to it. But I did

250

live with the guy, and I'm sure everyone assumed we were in love, much like I did.

"I hate to break it to you Harper, but that wasn't love. That was like mild lust, a little bit of boredom, and a sense of responsibility you had going on. Ethan might have been in love with you, but I saw right through you," Patrick gives me A Look.

"Did everyone know that but me?" I am actually shocked by this.

"I've been in love with Emmy since I was eight years old and she put a live snake down Brayden Beckford's shirt at recess when he was being a bully," he tells me. "I know what love is."

"I can totally picture that," I tell him, snorting at the image of a tiny blonde girl standing up to the class bully by scaring the shit out of him with a snake. "God, your wife is a terror."

"Don't I know it," Patrick says.

"Wait, who was Brayden Beckford bullying?" I ask suspiciously.

"Me," Patrick replies cheerfully. "Hence the falling in love."

"You guys are relationship goals," I say, sighing.

"Actually, scratch that. I would have fallen in love with Emmy no matter what," he says, smiling to himself.

That sticks with me as we watch our show. And as Patrick makes me lunch (he really is the best). And as Patrick throws me in the pool (he really is the worst). And as we float around the pool (he really is the best).

Fuck, I've gone and fallen in love. And it would have happened no matter what. Even if Colt hadn't stomped up to my porch that morning and if Avery hadn't meddled. I'd still be here, floating around a pool, over two thousand miles from that man I've fallen in love with.

Chapter Twenty-Six
West

Liam:
im in a bad way man. i need help.

Liam:
fuck you

Liam:
i need help man.

Liam:
i need help.

Liam:
i know i fucked up big time.

Liam:
west. please. fuck.

Liam:
there is no one else, west. no one else for me to turn to.

I get back to Harper's cottage after taking Zero on a long walk before dropping her off with Jessie and Colt to a barrage of messages. It takes a minute for reality to sink in. I just spent over an hour walking the beach, thinking about Harper. How I should have told her I was hopelessly in love with her before she left. There's this little part of me that knows she saw her ex, who she said is not in the mafia and is not a rodeo clown, and never was any kind of fiance, just a regular guy, but he wanted to talk to her. I'd bet good money he realized he fucked up when he let her out of his life. I also know how much she misses Emmy and the man brave enough to call Emmy his wife. What if she regrets leaving Texas? What if she realizes that I'm not deserving of her?

Fuck. I am a mess. Reaching out to Liam really fucked me up. And now this. What do I do with this? I have to go, right? I know I have to go. It's the right thing. This is exactly why I reached out to him. But like the lovesick fool I am, all I want to do is take Harper to our spot on the beach as soon as she's back and tell her I've fallen madly in love with her. That I want everything with her. But if I want that future in Harper's notebook, we both need to be ready. I can't carry this weight with me any longer.

I call Harper as I start throwing things in a bag.

"Hey," she answers breathlessly. "Sorry, I was in the pool and almost didn't get it in time."

"Hey," I say, unsure what exactly I'm going to tell her.

"You okay?" she asks quietly. I hear water splashing behind her.

"Liam replied," I manage to say. "I have to go."

"Are you okay?" she asks again. "Do you want me to meet you in Portland? I fly home in a couple days or I could move my flight up."

"No, I need to do this on my own," I tell her. "I don't even know what's going to happen. I'm sure he's drunk and I don't know if he'll answer my calls when he sobers up. I don't know if I'll even be able to find him. He's really good at disappearing for days on end. If I do find him, I don't know what will happen. But I have to go. I have to try."

"You're a good man, West," she tells me.

"Harper, I l-appreciate you so much," I say, nearly slipping and telling her I love her for the first time over the phone. Fuck, I need to get it together. "I'll call you once I figure some of this shit out."

**

254

I don't even tell Jessie or Avery that I'm leaving. Asshole move but I don't want to get Jessie's hopes up, worry her even more, or send her into a breakdown. I turn my phone to 'do not disturb' and just throw my bag in my truck and leave. They'll think I took extra appointments at the shop.

Two hours later I'm walking into PDX Ink, Tattoo and Piercing. The memories are like a punch in the gut. My hopes and dreams, Liam's spiral into addiction, and all the mess in between. I only recognize one of the guys in here besides Drake.

"Hey man, thought you fell off the face of the Earth until I saw that video," Drake says, looking up from his workspace where he's drawing a new design. "That chick is fucking hot, wish she would have come here for her work instead."

How Zoe puts up with this kind of bullshit in real life and online is beyond me.

"Hey Drake, Liam around?" I ask, ignoring the rest of the stares I'm getting.

"Nah, haven't seen him in days. He no-showed his appointments, no one can get ahold of him," Drake replies, shrugging.

"Thanks, man," I say, turning to leave.

"Don't kick his ass too bad, he's been in rough shape since your sister took the kid," Drake says to my retreating back.

I don't turn, I just push the door and walk out onto the street. If you were an alcoholic in rough shape, where would you be? Apparently not at home, because there's no answer when I bang on the door to the apartment he, Jessie, and Colt used to share.

"Fuck!" I groan, giving the door a kick.

I take a deep breath and close my eyes, trying to think of our old haunts and which one he'd disappear to. A cough sounds. It's weak, but it's definitely coming from inside the apartment.

I jog back down to my truck, fumble around in the glove compartment and finally come up with the spare key that Jessie gave me years ago.

"Liam! Open up, asshole, or I'm coming in on my own!" I knock again. I really fucking hope this key still works.

I push open the door slowly, bracing myself for what I'll find. I don't see Liam anywhere, but the place is trashed. There's fast food wrappers and whiskey bottles all over, it smells worse than the dive bars I thought I'd have to search, and every window has the shades drawn tight. It's the dark cave of a depressed alcoholic.

I take my phone out, ready to call for a well-check or EMS or someone, anyone more qualified than me, when a fist flies. I drop my phone as I block Liam's cheap shot that comes as soon as I finally take a step inside.

"Fuck, Liam, it's me!" I grunt, ducking my shoulder and nearly lifting him off his feet as I pin him against the wall.

The fight goes out of him. I keep him against the wall with my forearm, making sure he recognizes me before I let him go.

"You're too late," he says. His breath reeks of booze and despair.

"What the fuck does that mean, man? I'm here, we're figuring this shit out," I tell him, removing my arm from his throat.

He immediately shoves me and I step back, hearing a crunch beneath my boot. I have him back against the wall in half a second.

"You done?" I ask.

I wait for his nod and let him go again. He stumbles past me, stepping on my phone for good measure, and collapses on the couch. I pick up my phone from the ground, and between getting dropped and the two of us stepping on it, it's never making it out of this apartment. I just hope I can get Liam out of here. He's pale, the hand that sits in his lap is shaking, and there's a Jack Daniels bottle in his other hand.

"Fuck, man, what the fuck happened to you?" I say, giving him a glare as he opens one eye to study me.

When he runs a shaky hand through his hair, I can see Colt in his mannerisms. My determination hardens.

"I didn't think rock bottom existed for me, but here it is," Liam replies, his voice weak. He motions around the apartment. "I found it, I finally found rock bottom. I live here in this pit of despair now. And it fucking sucks." He closes his eye again, shutting me out.

Well, now what? Despite his texts, this is not what I expected to find. I've experienced Party Liam, I've calmed down Real Fucking

Angry Liam on multiple occasions, but I have no fucking clue what to do about Rock Bottom Liam.

"You want a shovel or a hand?" I finally ask. "You wanna dig yourself deeper or pull yourself out?"

"I don't even fucking know. Even if I get out of this pit, there's nothing out there for me. I'll just sink back down. I can't fucking do this. I can't even get more than five feet away from this bottle. Maybe I should just take the shovel," he says. "That kid was right, man. It's now or never."

"Kid? You hanging out with kids?" I can only see Colt in my mind.

"No, that kid that brought Jessie's papers, law school guy," Liam says and finally opens both eyes. He sits up and shakily takes the top off the whiskey. I grimace as he takes a pull straight from the bottle. "He said I'm almost out of time, that Colt won't forgive me forever. I know your sister won't, and she shouldn't. I've fucked everything up, down, and sideways."

He leans back again, head dropped on the back of the couch, eyes closed, bottle of booze settled next to him.

I knew Grant served Liam divorce papers, but I did not know he also served him the hard truth. I guess I owe him another beer. Although, standing in this mess, I don't know if I ever want to see another drop of alcohol.

"Well, you gonna do something about it?" I ask. "Grant is right. He's a smart guy, law school smart. Your son won't forgive you forever. You want a place in his life, you need to earn it. It won't be easy. It'll be the hardest fucking thing you've done, but I'm here to tell you that he's worth it. You're worth it, man."

Liam is silent.

"Will she even let me see him?" he finally asks. "I know I don't deserve to."

"You'll have to prove yourself, and continue to prove yourself over and over," I tell him honestly. "But if you want to get sober and put in the work, I'll help."

Liam sits up again, elbows on his knees, whiskey bottle hanging from one hand, and stares at me. I stay silent. It has to be his choice, because the one thing I do know about sobriety and getting help, is the person has to want it. If I could choose for him, I would have zip-tied his hands behind his back and thrown him in rehab years ago.

"The hand, I want the hand. Keep your shovel for someone else," he says, holding eye contact.

I can feel the weight lift off my shoulders. I take a deep breath and give him a slow nod. But what the fuck do I do with him now? I look around the apartment and then at the state of his clothing.

"Take your bottle and go take a shower," I tell him. "But give me your phone, mine is out of commission."

He's far enough in that he's going to need real detox, doing it alone wouldn't just be hard, it'd be downright dangerous. I know Portland has services, I just don't know where. Or how. Or when. Or anything.

Since I don't have Harper or Avery's numbers memorized, I send Jessie a text, adding to the string of unanswered texts Liam has sent over the past months, telling her that I'm getting Liam help and please tell Harper I'll call her as soon as I have a phone. Then I start researching.

***

I have Liam and a new bottle of Jack in my truck at 5 a.m. the next morning. We're sitting outside the Hooper Detoxification Stabilization Center waiting for their inpatient admissions hours. I don't know what to expect and I'm honestly still waiting for him to bail, to change his mind, make a run for it.

"Hey, I just want to say thank you for showing up. I don't know why you did, but thanks," Liam says, watching as a line starts to form outside. "You don't have to wait, hopefully I'll be able to call you in a couple days."

"Nice try man, I'm coming with you."

I push my truck door open and walk around to Liam's side, waiting while he takes what I hope is his last pull from the bottle. When he steps out, he looks unsure. I can see a flash of Colt in his expression again and it hurts to think about my nephew. I can't believe I left without telling him.

"Let's fucking do this," Liam says with a nod.

A few hours later, I walk back out, leaving Liam inside. Now the real work, for both of us, starts. While Liam gets clean, I'm making a plan. Like he said last night, there's nothing here that will keep him from sinking back into addiction.

I use Liam's phone to find the closest iphone repair store and walk out two hours later with a usable phone. I have multiple missed calls from Harper, Jessie, and Avery. I call Harper but no answer. Same with Jessie and Avery. Fuck. I send the same text to all of them.

West:
I just left Liam at detox, please call me.

While I wait, I call and talk to Drake. When he asks me why I'm doing this, I just tell him that I've got to get my shit together and finally close this door once and for all.

"She must be something special if you're back wading through Liam's life," he says, somehow knowing the motivation behind my actions.

He has no idea. I look down and realize my napkin doodles have turned into a sketch. A sketch of Harper, of course.

"Can we grab coffee, talk about Liam's options for the shop?" I ask.

"Yeah man, come on by before we open, maybe around eleven," he replies. "And thanks for coming back. We were in over our heads with him."

Chapter Twenty-Seven
Harper

"Um, Harp, you've thrown up every day since you've been here," Emmy is once again holding my hair. I'm dry heaving, nothing quite willing to come up. "Is there any possibility you're pregnant?"

"What? No, I'm on the pill," I say. Suddenly I'm cold. Ice cold. "Wait."

"Wait what?" Em asks, rubbing my back.

"No, no fucking way," I say.

breathe in two three four, hold two three four, out two three four

No no no no no. That doesn't actually happen. Fake news.

"Uh, Harp, you're shaking, are you okay?" Em looks a little alarmed as I turn to her.

"I was so busy with planning the Fourth, and then the Block Party, I missed like two pills plus took one the next morning. That doesn't really happen though, does it? That's not real."

I'm starting to panic. My vision blurs. My hands tingle.

"Hey, breathe, I've got you," Em grabs my hand. "Harp, do the breathing."

breathe in two three four, hold two three four, out two three four
breathe in two three four, hold two three four, out two three four
breathe in two three four, hold two three four, out two three four

"No, Emmy, I can't, I can't be pregnant," I moan.

"Stay here," she demands, running from the bathroom.

Holy shit, what have I done? We've said we are all in, it feels like we are all in. I've pictured my future and he is always in it, but "oh hey I'm pregnant" is not the same thing. He was in self-isolation just a few months ago, now we share a bed every night and share a five-year-old and a dog every day. And now this. Shit shit shit.

breathe in two three four, hold two three four, out two three four

I realize I'm rubbing my tattoo with my left hand but I have my right hand on my abdomen. I don't even need a test to know it's true.

"Pee on this," Em skids around the doorway, pregnancy test in hand.

"Why do you have that?" I ask, stalling.

"We've been trying to conceive, now shut up and take the damn test," she demands.

"Em, I already know. I'm pregnant," I tell her numbly.

She hands me what looks like a Covid test. "Pee. On. This."

"Em," I whisper. I shake my head. I somehow know it's real, but a test is *really* real.

"Tough love, Harper Sage. Pee on the damn stick," she demands.

Three minutes later, it's *really* real.

I slide back down to the floor, leaning against the wall. Holy shit. Em settles down in front of me and sits cross-legged, holding my hands.

"At least now I know you didn't get a secret boob job," she deadpans.

"Em!" I manage a laugh. "Okay, they are bigger, aren't they?"

"Harp, it's okay. This is okay. You're okay," Em says, looking me in the eye. "We can sit here all day if you need to."

"I don't know what I need," I laugh-cry.

"Maybe your feelings journal?" She tries to hide a smile and fails.

"You're such an asshole," I moan. "Just for that, go get it."

I need to see the sketches that West always leaves on random pages. I need to see his handwriting. The stickers Colt plastered all over the front. My happy list.

Emmy is back in no time, my old, beat up notebook in one hand, a glass of water in the other. She hands me both and slides down the wall beside me. I drain half the glass of water and immediately feel nauseous.

"You're my best friend, Harper, and I love you," she starts. I immediately start sniffling as my eyes fill with tears. "If you want this baby, with or without him, you're going to be the best mom. You've spent years keeping me in line, taking care of me without even realizing what you're doing. How many times have you told me you're proud of me and you love me? Like a billion. How many times have you talked me through decisions, good and bad? Like at least half a billion. I saw you with Colt, you stepped into a parental role without knowing that's what you were doing. Don't even get me started on your spoiled dog-child. You took Kelsey in as a little sister. You stepped in when Avery needed you and got a handle on her life for her. You're amazing."

My tears finally fall and splash onto my notebook in my lap. It's open to a sketch of Zero and Colt playing at sunset. I can almost feel West beside me in our spot, backs to the rocks, watching the sun sink down. I wipe my tears and flip the pages.

"Whoa. To quote vintage Paris Hilton, that's hot," Em says, head tipped on my shoulder.

My cheeks flush as I see it's the drawing of West and I tangled together under the sheets, my eyes closed, back arched.

The next page is me asleep in bed, my hand reaching across to West's empty side of the bed. I had forgotten to look past these that morning.

Another page. Me sitting on the kitchen counter, sipping coffee.

Next page. Me running with Zero and Colt on the beach, bikini and backwards hat.

Next page. Me in West's flannel, lacy underwear peeking through.

Next page. Another I haven't seen.

"Em, oh my gosh," I sit up straighter.

"What? It's...a house? A treehouse?" She reaches down and turns the notebook slightly her way. "I don't get it."

I flip to the next page. The next. How have I not seen these? They're far more detailed than the others. He must have added these after I started my new notebook.

The treehouse we had both envisioned that very first week, complete with a pulley system and planter boxes under a small window.

The workshop that West found the plans for in the garage, Zero guarding the open door, West standing between my legs as I sit on a work counter, our foreheads pressed together.

The two of us standing together under a driftwood arch, flowers in my hair, gentle waves behind us.

My thumb finds my tattoo. My other hand returns to my abdomen.

breathe in two three four, hold two three four, out two three four

"Our future, he drew our future," I whisper.

It's going to be okay.

***

My phone buzzes beside me and I just stare at it.

"You going to answer that?" Emmy asks.

"I can't tell him over the phone," I groan.

I was worried when I didn't hear from him last night, but this morning it was a relief he didn't call, I needed time to process. I might still need time.

"Just answer the call, Harp, it's going to be okay," Emmy promises.

"West?" I manage to catch his call right before it sends him to voicemail.

"Harper, I'm so, so sorry if I made you worry," West says in a rush. "I sent a text to Jessie last night from Liam's phone after mine was broken, I'm guessing she had blocked him though. I should have found another way to reach you. I'm so sorry."

"It's okay, I'm sure you had your hands full. Is Liam okay?" I ask quietly, trying to push down my emotions. Tears fill my eyes. I don't even know why. General overwhelmedness is my best guess. Emmy reaches over and squeezes my hand. I grip her hand like the lifeline it is.

"I found him at the apartment. He was in bad shape, really bad shape. Rock-bottom bad. He took a couple swings at me which is when my phone broke, but he agreed to get help. To try again. He checked into medical detox this morning," he tells me, his tone devoid of any emotion.

264

"Okay," I say, blowing out a breath. I'm so caught up with my morning, I can't really comprehend what West has been through in the last twenty-four hours. But it's obviously been a lot. And it's even more obvious that now is not the time to talk about my news. "I'm glad he's safe. How are you doing? That's a lot to walk in on. Have you talked to Jessie?"

"I'm better now that I've heard your voice," he says, the smallest reassurance amidst all of this turmoil. "I didn't know what to do with him, seeing him like that. Fuck. It was bad. I'm so fucking glad he got into detox this morning, I don't know what I would have done with him otherwise. Now I need to talk to Drake and see what Liam can salvage there, if anything. I want to set him up to succeed."

"How long is detox? And how is Jessie?" I ask. Em squeezes my hand as I blink back tears.

"I texted Jessie, but she hasn't called me back. That's going to be a rough conversation," West says, emotion finally creeping into his voice. My heart aches for him.

"You're a good man," I tell him. The best, actually.

"I don't know about that, but this has been weighing on me for a really long time. This is my last shot and I want to make it count. I have some ideas after researching rehabs, sober living, and AA last night. He should be out in three to seven days and I'm the only contact they have for him. After that, I want him to have a clear path, the best chance possible, whatever that means."

"Wow, you've done a lot," I say. I don't think I've ever considered what it takes to overcome addiction.

"Are you feeling better?" he asks. "I'm sorry you've been sick your whole visit."

"Em is taking good care of me," I answer, avoiding the question. Shit, if West is gone another week or even more, when the hell am I going to talk to him? "Want me to meet you in Portland after I land tomorrow?"

I can't drop this on him tomorrow, but I just want to see him, feel his arms around me, bury my face in his chest. I want to hear his steady heartbeat, match my breathing to his. My heart aches for him in a whole other way now. A way I've never allowed myself to feel before. All in.

This is going to be fine. I just freaking realized I'm in love with the man, we've talked about forever, I saw the drawings. Why am I panicking? We don't do things in the right order, this is just another to add to the list. I absentmindedly put my hand on my stomach. I remember the picture of West holding baby Colt. It's going to be *better* than fine.

"I'm sorry, but I told Drake I'd meet him at the shop to talk options soon. Can we talk later, maybe once I have a little more info? I feel a little like I did when Jessie first left Colt with me. It's like parenting, someone is always counting on you and you have no fucking idea what you're doing, but you have to do it and the stakes are really fucking high. I don't think it's for me," he says, laughing a little.

I stop breathing.

Like my body actually forgets how to breathe.

"Yeah, I gotta go, sorry," I manage to get out, then hang up before he can say anything else.

My phone drops to the floor as I wave my hands in front of my face, trying to find air. Emmy is kneeling in front of me and I can't hear her words but I understand them.

Breathe.

Harper.

Breathe.

Chapter Twenty-Eight
West

It takes three days to come up with a rough plan. Three days of working in a silent apartment. No chatter from Colt, no Harper bursting in and out, no Jessie giving me shit, and no Zero sloshing water everywhere. I'm hit with the realization that I can't live like this once again. I have to put up a fight for the life I want, the life I promised Harper.

Harper. Fuck. Whatever this space is between us is killing me. I know she's busy but her texts are short and she barely has time to talk. No selfies, no pictures of Colt and Zero. This is not like her at all. She supports everyone over herself; a week ago I would have bet she'd be knocking on the apartment door to see me. She's told me to stay and see this through, but I'm really questioning it right now. Every time she flashes through my mind, which is a fucking lot, I find myself out of breath and reaching for the notebook I picked up on my way to talk to Drake. I sketch ocean waves, tall trees, the rocky spot where we sit. Zero and Colt. Beach grass waving in the wind. And Harper, Harper, Harper.

Is my plan really going to work? I know, deep down, that "fixing" Liam is not my responsibility, but I have to fight, not run. I have to fight for myself. I need to be ready to move forward, no holds barred, no missing pieces, loving Harper with my whole heart. I need to fight for Colt and Jessie, the only family I have left. I need to work through all of this and get back home to all of them, with or without Liam.

Flipping the page of the notebook, I start with step one of my plan. The person who was first able to break into my shell after my move. And the person who quite literally holds the keys to the future I want.

"West, you're a real asshole." Avery lays into me without saying hello. "You leave town without telling anyone, you're lucky I answered."

That's fair. And if that's all she's going to say, I'm getting off easy. But I really need her help. I hate asking for help.

"Don't hang up," I say in a rush. "Please. I need your help."

Silence.

"Avery?" I pull my phone away from my ear to see if the call disconnected.

"West," she says with a sigh. "You know I will always be there for you, but right now I'm pretty pissed. I also just learned that the lot next door is finally going up for sale, but Kent is being stubborn and says the land isn't calling to me. Neighbors, West, I'm going to have neighbors if I can't buy him out."

"Well, Avery, I might have a solution for you," I tell her, hope rising in my chest. This could actually work. "But first, is Harper okay? She's avoiding me, I know she is. And she's all I want, all I need. This is for her."

"Let me hear your plan, then I'll tell you my thoughts on Harper."

I take a deep breath, and lay out my plan, step-by-step, piece-by-piece. Avery stays silent, doesn't ask a single question.

"Well, that's it," I finish lamely, really thrown by her silence.

"Okay," Avery says.

"Okay?" I repeat.

"Okay," Avery repeats back to me. "I'm in. It's a really fucking good plan, not just because it also helps me."

"Is Harper okay?" I ask, needing to hear it from her best friend. "I'll throw the plan out the window and come back right now if you tell me to."

"She's okay. I promise. Let her work through her things while you work through yours. I promise she's okay. The only thing I'll tell you is that she looks at your drawings in her notebook all the time."

268

I glance down at my own notebook, pieces of the plan outlined in bullet points, Harper's Jeep drawn in the corner and a "BREAKERS" hat in another. Little pieces of her.

"The drawings haven't stopped, Avery," I tell her. "I know I sound like a crazy person, but she hit me hard from the beginning. I'm all in with her, have been since day one."

"Glad you're actually admitting that now," Avery says. "Now, let's work back through the plan, I have some ideas."

***

While Harper works through whatever Avery alluded to, I work my ass off on my plan. There are a lot of moving pieces and a lot of people involved, which, when I really think about it, is shocking. How did I go from my solitude to this?

I have a group FaceTime with Mrs. G, Jessie, Colt, and Kelsey. They reassure me that we're all on the same page. Colt gives a fist pump when he hears the plan.

Drake and I meet with the other artists at the shop and agree to a few options to present to Liam. They also agree that if Liam chooses to stay, they will all walk out the second he's no longer sober.

I invite Zoe to coffee, but instead, she FaceTimes me from a coffee shop that has a stunning mountain view.

"I needed a change of scenery," she says with a shrug. "But I still wanted to turn down your offer face to face."

"Well, thanks, I guess?"

"I think you should talk to my friend Abby though, she does at least half of the work for ZoeSays and her sister is an alcoholic, so she has more knowledge than me," Zoe tells me. "She'll smooth over your sudden closure as well as handle anything that comes up if Liam joins you at Rock Beach Tattoo. I'll text you her number. Call her."

"Thanks, Zoe. And I have to say, you look like you're enjoying your change in scenery," I tell her. I'm not blind, she's obviously beautiful but seeing her on my small screen, she looks truly happy. "Is it a permanent change?"

"It's an extended trip but I'll be back," she says, staring past her phone. "I'm hoping to find a house there someday soon."

"Interesting," I tell her. "I might know of one coming up for sale."

"Seriously?" she asks. "Send me the details, I'm going to call my accountant now."

Zoe throws a wrench in the original plan, but I call Avery and we revise. I'm pretty sure we are on Plan 17.0 by now. And it could all come crumbling down the second Liam walks out of detox.

***

The second Liam walks out of detox, he wants to attend the first Alcoholics Anonymous meeting we can find. I find myself sitting outside a church in my truck, waiting for him once again. I pass the time by adding to the design I started the same day I called Avery with my plan.

"What's that?" Liam juts his chin toward my notebook as he slides into the truck.

"Tattoo," I reply, shutting the notebook and starting the engine.

"Looks good," he says.

Silence descends upon the truck as I navigate us back toward his apartment. I have no fucking clue what to say, how to start the conversation we really need to have.

"Hey, West," Liam starts, hesitating only for a second before barreling on. "Thank you. For all of this. For coming back. For taking in Colt and Jessie. Not giving up on me. I would have stayed in that apartment and slowly drank myself to death. No lie."

"I'm glad we're here," I tell him, keeping my eyes forward, unable to look at him. "There's a lot more ahead of us, I'm not just dropping you off, I hope you realize that."

Liam coughs, then clears his throat. I cut a glance sideways and see that he's barely holding it together.

"Hey man, just breathe, we got time," I tell him as I turn into the apartment complex. "You tell me what you need. Sleep? Food? Or you wanna jump right in and hear my plan?"

"All of that," he says.

An hour later, I've got the paperwork for my plan laid out and our Door Dash driver is about five minutes out. I thought about going out to grab food while Liam showered, but I'm sticking with 24/7 babysitting until we've had a real talk.

"Am I starting or are you starting?" Liam asks when we sit down at the table, my papers scattered between us.

"You tell me. I took it upon myself to talk with Drake, so I know your options there," I tell him. "What do you need to stay sober? I guess that's the question."

"I can't stay here," he immediately replies, shaking his head. He takes another bite of his sandwich and chews before speaking. "I don't know how this is possible, but I need a job, a place to live, and a lot of AA meetings. A lot."

"You'll have to talk to Drake in person, but it sounds like you have a few options with the shop. You can either stay working, keep your part in the business, and know that if you fall off the wagon, everyone is leaving," I start, but Liam interrupts.

"I can't stay, man. I can't."

"The two younger guys, the brothers, they're interested in buying you out, and Drake is good with that as well," I tell him. "But you can also keep your stake in it and just be part-owner, not working. You'd obviously need another job, the shop isn't doing great right now, but if you have savings, that might be the way to go."

"I fucking blew through everything, I have nothing but debt," Liam tells me. "Fuck, I don't know how to do this." His hand shakes.

"Third option," I forge ahead, hoping that if I keep talking, he'll keep listening instead of going down a dark road. "Sell your half of the business to the Smith brothers and use that money to start fresh."

"There's nowhere else to go, I have no one," he says.

"You have me," I tell him. "And if you sell and start over, I have a job offer for you."

"Why the fuck would you do that?" he asks, finally looking up at me. "I still don't understand why you're here. I've put you through enough shit over the years, and that doesn't even count what I did to your sister and your nephew."

"Don't get me wrong, there'd be a lot of stipulations, but you're family. Not just because of Jessie and Colt, but you were the one that got me through my parents' accident. I left without much of a fight last time, but this time I'm fighting," I tell him. "You don't have to take my offer, but at least hear me out."

***

Three days later, we've sold all Liam's remaining furniture, Avery has looked over the paperwork for the Smiths buying Liam out, I've driven Liam to six different AA meetings, and we're about to lock the apartment for the last time.

"Fuck, man, this feels weird," Liam says, placing his hand on the apartment door.

"Forward, look forward," I tell him. "Let's go find you a better path."

I follow Liam to PDX Ink one last time. It's early, only Drake is here to meet us. He hands us coffees and we sit at Liam's station for a few minutes, silently contemplating each other.

"You sure?" Liam asks me, giving me a hard look.

"Only guy I want doing this," I tell him, giving him a nod as I roll up my sleeve.

He did the work on my other arm; it feels right that he does this one as well. Afterward, I start boxing up Liam's shit while Drake and Liam talk. I work quickly, my new ink making me desperate to get to Harper sooner rather than later. She's still been hard to pin down, quick, distracted conversations is all I've gotten out of her. Avery continues to reassure me that things will be okay. Avery's smart as fuck but I'm still worried.

"Good luck with your girl," Drake says, giving me a handshake and a clap on the back. "And I told Liam that I'll be out to celebrate when he hits a month sober. Better get a guest room ready."

"Looking forward to it," I tell him, glad to hear that he's giving Liam another chance.

Liam is quiet as we walk out. I have a trickle of fear that he's going to bail, but then he turns to me and gives me a nod.

"Let's fucking do this," he says, the same words he said when he walked into detox.

Chapter Twenty-Nine
Harper

Captain's Log: Day 8. It's been eight days since I took the pregnancy test and I'm still numb. I'm also hopeful, calm, sad, and determined. Oh, and nauseas. So, basically a hot mess, which could be considered normal for me.

Let's back up. A recap, if you will.

"I don't think parenting is for me."

His statement echoed in my head. As soon as I rushed him off the phone and got my hyperventilating under control, I stumbled to the guest bathroom and threw up the crackers I had managed to choke down.

"Want to stay?" Emmy offered. "Reverse run away? Run back?"

"No," I croaked out, laying my head on her lap.

"Want me to fly back with you?" she asked.

"No, I can do this," I whispered, trying to convince myself more than anyone else.

And I did. I flew home by myself, only throwing up when we landed and only crying once when I got to my Jeep in short term parking. In an effort to stay busy, I drove directly to The Mercantile to check in on the store.

Of course I was immediately nauseous as I looked at the rows of beautiful pastries.

Avery found me, I'm guessing thanks to Marabelle who peeked her head around the corner a few minutes after I threw up. Aves hauled my crying, blubbering ass up the hill to her cabin in the woods. I dry heaved in her bathroom, because apparently throwing up in as many locations as possible was (and still is) my new hobby.

"Want to talk?" she asked, rubbing my back as I hugged her toilet.

"No," I told her miserably, wiping my mouth with toilet paper and laying down right on the bathroom floor.

"Did you tell him?" she finally asked, after realizing I wasn't going to break the silence.

"Did I tell him what?" I asked, scrambling back to my knees to hug her toilet.

"Uh, that you're pregnant, Tex," she said and I laid my cheek on the toilet rim to peer at her next to me. "Wait, you are pregnant, right?"

"How do you know I'm pregnant? Did Em tell you?" I asked, confused as hell, and also so, so tired.

"No, but you've been really tired, pale and shaky, you didn't want beer at the bonfire before you left, even though I brought your favorite, and now you're hugging my toilet," she replied evenly. "Also, your boobs are bigger."

"Does everyone stare at my boobs? No, I didn't tell him. I can't tell him over the phone," I told her miserably. "What the fuck, Aves? What do I do now? He said parenting isn't for him. Like he actually said those words. I didn't even tell him I'm pregnant and he managed to make his thoughts on the subject known. He doesn't want to be a dad."

"Tex, you're my best friend. I've known you for twenty years. If you choose to have this baby, with or without him, you're going to be just fine," she told me, and because it was her, I almost believed it. "If you had told him and that's why he bailed, I would have tracked him down and murdered him myself."

"Thanks, Aves," I said with a snort. "You'll be the best almost-auntie."

"Anything and everything, always," she said with conviction. At that moment, I had no doubt she was capable of murder. "But Tex, maybe give him the benefit of the doubt here. Whatever context that was in, I don't think he meant it."

274

"Are you telling a crying, pregnant woman who is hugging your thankfully very clean toilet to calm down?" I asked incredulously.

"I'm Team Tex, all day every day. But I also knew West when he first showed up here. Going back to face Liam was probably very difficult for him and I don't think he meant for that comment to mean anything other than that he's overwhelmed," Avery said gently.

"Please stop being kind and logical and get on my hormone train," I moaned.

After making sure I wasn't going to drown in her toilet, Avery left me on the floor to go down the hill to fetch my dog, clothes, feelings journal, and laptop, effectively moving me into her guest room.

And now here we are. One of us as unflappable as ever, the other is hot mess. A pregnant hot mess.

It took a few days, but I caught my stride. Or at least picked myself up off the floor. The morning beach walks that both Avery and Zero insist upon seem to help my morning sickness. I've found a doctor in Rock Beach and scheduled my first prenatal appointment, which sounds terrifying. The healthy dinners Avery cooks are helping my energy levels. I'm still confused, sad, and angry, yet also hopeful, happy, and every single other emotion in the whole universe.

Team Merc is still crushing it, thanks to everyone but me. The Mercantile has a steady stream of visitors from open to close, our rentals gained popularity quickly thanks to our welcome baskets and activity add-ons, plus Kelsey's genius marketing. We've had to order new "BREAKERS" hats multiple times and Betty is ecstatic that she's well on her way to social media fame. Visitors to The Merc regularly ask about her, it's wild.

The Golf Course House (real name forever pending) and North House are nearly always bursting at the seams with happy families. The Green Door Garden is in full bloom thanks to Jessie, and The Glass House is booked every weekend through December. My favorite continues to be Breakers Bliss, and the magnetic poems and chalkboard notes left by our guests never fail to cheer me up.

We've all slid into our own roles and while none of us can do Marabelle's job with all of the baking, we've definitely played musical jobs a time or two. Lucas is surprisingly good at scrubbing showers and we've figured out that he's behind the amazing photos Kelsey posts, he just doesn't want the credit. Shy Katie wowed in her TikTok debut, belting out the lyrics to "Girls Just Want to Have Fun" when a Breakers bachelorette party was set to arrive. Kelsey is packing for college and Mrs. G has really bonded with Jessie, more so in the last week. Those two are not just a lesson but a whole course on single motherhood. The only time I feel like crying is when I'm in bed, Zero curled up at my feet, an empty space next to me.

During one of my wild emotional swings, I realize something. I'm doing this. With or without him, I'm doing this. I don't know that having kids was ever on my mind, but hormones really are powerful because, despite throwing up way more than anyone should, I'm excited. I don't know what will happen if West doesn't want this new future with me, with *us*, but I have a great life here, and I'm ready to go to battle. Not a real battle, or even a battle with West, but a battle with myself. A battle to move forward on my own.

I'm fucking doing this.

***

I glance up from where I'm folding new sweatshirts and see a tall man with dark hair walk into the store. Tattoos cover his hands and he looks vaguely familiar. He looks around nervously and I'm immediately on edge. Something feels off. He gives me a tentative smile when he notices me in the corner but heads for the coffee counter without a word.

Jessie turns and her face pales. "Liam!" she gasps, fumbling the cup she's holding, spilling hot coffee on her hand.

I stop and slowly turn to face the man that I've never met and want to hate. He looks broken, sad, and scared. I can see Colt that first morning he showed up on my porch. Damnit. I don't think I can hate him when his amazing son looks so much like him.

I gently take the cup from Jessie's hands and guide her to the sink to run cold water over her burn. She's shaking. I fill a new cup with coffee, snap a lid on, give her customer a bright smile and tell them it's on the house. When I turn back, Jessie is gingerly drying her hands and staring silently at Liam.

276

"I know you're at work, but I didn't want to show up when Colt was with you, that wouldn't be fair to him," Liam starts. "I'm clean, I have a long-term sobriety plan, and I'd like to talk to you sometime soon."

Jessie still doesn't move. I reach out and touch her arm, silently asking if she's okay. She closes her eyes, swallows hard, and raises her chin. She levels Liam with a look that I'm glad I'm not on the other end of.

"I'm willing to listen, but I don't have anything to say to you, and you can't see Colt," she says, her voice strong and steady. She covers my hand that's still on her arm, her fingers slightly digging into my skin. She glances around the now-empty shop. "You have two minutes, starting now."

Liam doesn't spare me a glance. Keeping his eyes on Jessie, he takes a deep breath. My hand twitches but Jessie shakes her head at me. I guess I'm staying for this.

"I'm so sorry for everything I put you through," Liam starts, his voice shaky with emotion. "I'm sorry for not asking for help sooner. I'm sorry for ignoring your requests, no, your pleas, that I get clean. I'm sorry for being a terrible husband, father, partner, and friend. I don't expect your forgiveness, nor do I deserve it, but I'd like to prove to you that I can be in Colt's life. Maybe not today, or tomorrow, or even next week but I want to work every day to get closer to the time that you'll let me be in his life, to the time that I *deserve* to be in his life."

The front door opens and West fills the doorframe. I think I gasp. Jessie removes my hand from her forearm and grips it, squeezing hard. West's eyes are locked on mine, but he doesn't move toward me. He stands just inside the door, waiting.

"West saved me," Liam continues, giving West a nod. His voice is clearer now, more determined. "He got me into a medical detox program, then we worked together on my short- and long-term plans. I met a man there, in detox, sixty years old, five daughters and two granddaughters, none of them in his life due to his drinking. He didn't even know where his youngest was going to college, where she was living. I don't want that to be me. I want this to be it. I know it's going to be the hardest thing I've ever done, but I have a plan, Jessie, and I'm really fucking determined. Shit, I didn't want to swear. I'm sorry."

"Time's up," Jessie says, clearing her throat. "Thank you for your apology. I'll let West know when I'm willing to talk to you again."

She releases my hand with a final squeeze and gives her brother I look I can't decipher before bolting to the back.

"I'm sorry for interrupting," Liam says, turning to me. "I'm Liam. West has told me all about you. I've been looking forward to meeting you, Harper. Thank you for everything you've done for my son, and for Jessie and West."

I give him a brief smile, unsure how to respond. Before I can say anything, he turns and walks out The Mercantile door, shaking West's hand on his way by. It feels like the air is sucked out of the room as the door closes heavily behind him.

West's eyes return to mine and he puts his hands in his pocket, looking nervous. I can see his chest rise as he inhales and his blue eyes widen when I start toward him. I stop short and there's a beat of silence.

"Hi, Harper," West says, the corner of his mouth lifting into a small smile.

"Hi, West," I say, my hands itching to reach for him.

I want to launch myself at him. I want him to catch me and hold me, let me bury my nose in his neck and breathe him in. I want to stare into his clear, blue, hopeful eyes. Instead I rock back and forth on my feet, unsure what to say or do. His words from that phone call echo in my mind. I rub my tattoo and quickly move my right hand away from my abdomen, unsure how it ended up there in the first place.

"I had a whole speech, but I forgot it the moment I saw you," he says, taking another tentative step toward me. "I just know that I love you. I'm madly in love with you, Harper. I should have told you weeks ago. I love you."

My heart lurches. Then my stomach lurches. I turn and sprint for the back, skidding around the corner of the bathroom and throw up everything I've eaten in the last seven years.

"Tex?" Jessie says, hurrying in behind me. "Are you okay?" She tucks my hair under my hat and puts a reassuring hand on my back.

278

When my stomach settles, I reach for the mouthwash I stashed under the sink my first day back. Swish and spit. I wonder how many times a day I've done this recently. I meet Jessie's worried eyes in the mirror. What a pair we are, her with red eyes and cheeks and me as pale as a ghost.

"Yeah, your brother told me he loves me and I ran away and threw up, things are going great," I say wryly. "Looking in this mirror, we've never looked better. Are you okay?"

My right hand drifts to my abdomen without me thinking about it. Jessie clocks my movement.

"Shut up," she says, eyes widening. "I mean, duh he loves you, that much is obvious, but shut up. Am I right?"

I stay silent.

"Holy shit, he doesn't know," she breathes. "Okay, everything is fine, this is fine."

"What is fine?" West's deep voice asks from outside the door.

Jessie's eyes fly to mine in the mirror. My stomach turns over once again.

Holy shit is right. Now or never.

Chapter Thirty
West

I only feel slightly guilty about letting myself into the back of The Mercantile. In all fairness, both my sister and my hopefully-still-girlfriend just had bombs dropped on them and then ran for cover. I had to check on them both. Shy Katie had given me a nod when I stepped behind the counter, that's permission enough for me. I just have to hope my heart isn't about to get ripped from my chest.

Jessie appears first, her eyes bright with tears. But she gives me a grin and a tight hug, whispering "be gentle, asshole" as she releases me.

"Harper?" I knock on the open door of the bathroom. When there's no answer, I peer around the corner and see her sitting on the floor.

She's pale, thinner than she was a week ago, and her eyes are filled with tears.

"I'm sorry," she says, her voice cracking.

"Hey, hey, what's going on? Are you sick?" I rush in and crouch in front of her. "Why are you apologizing?"

Her tears spill over. Tears like I've never seen, which is something, considering two of the first few times we met she was crying. A vice tightens around my chest. She furiously wipes away her tears and takes a shuddering breath. She's steeling herself for something, that much I know. Am I really about to get my heart obliterated in a back room employee bathroom? Why did Avery tell me to stay away? What the hell happened in the last week?

"I'm pregnant."

Silence. The silence is deafening.

I stare at her. I thought I was past the days when I was speechless around this woman. I was wrong.

Moments flash before me. My parents hugging me on Christmas morning, my mom with a red ribbon from a present worn as a necklace. My parents cheering in the stands when I graduated high school. Sitting beside Jessie at our parents' funeral, our hands linked tightly together. Holding Colt for the first time, tiny in my arms. The very first time I saw Harper. Harper's hand in mine, wave tattoo positioned perfectly above her scar. Harper next to me in our spot, Colt and Zero racing the sunset to the ocean. Harper at North House, walking toward me in my flannel.

"Please say something," she whispers, tears gathering in her eyes once again.

"This is amazing," I say, reaching tentatively for her. "Are you okay? But how?"

"Amazing?" she asks in a small voice, scooting closer to me.

"I want everything with you," I tell her, sitting down on the floor and pulling her into my lap. I kiss her temple, wrapping my arms gently around her. I can feel her melt into my chest. "I love you. I'm all in, all in on everything."

"But you said that you didn't think parenting was for you," she says, stiffening slightly in my arms.

"What? When did I say that?" I ask, confused as hell. When have we ever talked about having kids of our own?

"That very first phone call after you got your phone fixed," she says, her voice rising. "I found out I was pregnant about two hours before. I was freaking out about telling you, about how to tell you. Then you said you didn't think parenting was for you. How was I supposed to tell you that I messed up my birth control and your life?"

"Fuck, Harper, no. No, no, no," I say, shifting our weight so I can tip her chin in my direction. Her eyes search mine. "I was stressed, it felt like every decision I had to make for Liam was going to be the wrong one. I absolutely, one hundred percent, did not mean that. I'm so sorry you've spent more than a single second thinking that."

"I don't want to pressure you," she says, her eyes watering again. "But I also know I'm keeping the baby."

"We. We are keeping the baby, Harper. Is this why you've been so distant?" I ask, wiping the tears from her cheeks with my thumbs.

"I couldn't tell you over the phone, especially after that. I didn't know what to do," she whispers. "I'm sorry."

"This is the best news I've ever gotten. Today is the best day ever," I tell her, dropping a kiss on her lips. "I love you. I want everything with you. I have something to show you that will hopefully prove to you that I mean every word."

"Okay," she nods. "But I need a minute, I'm pretty sure if I stand up, I'm going to throw up."

"What can I do?" I ask her, wishing I could take away not only her nausea but the memory of the pain I caused her with my careless comment.

"Just stay, just for a minute," she says into my chest, leaning further into me.

I tighten my grip around her, move us so my back is against the wall, and hold her. I don't think I've ever liked a bathroom floor more.

***

"So you just copied my Fourth of July surprise?" Harper asks when we pull up in front of North House, shooting me a smirk.

I try to hide my grin as I hurry around to open her truck door. Zero jumps out and takes off for the dunes. I pull Harper flush against me and urge her to wrap her legs around my waist, just like she did that night.

"It's locked," she says when she leans sideways to try and open the front door, still secure in my arms. "And the keypad doesn't work."

"Weird," I say with a straight face. "Do you have your keys?"

She slides down my front and huffs impatiently as I jog back down to the truck to grab her bag. She rummages around and comes up with her rental key ring.

"The key doesn't work," she says, frowning. "It's definitely this key, why doesn't the stupid key work?"

"Try this one," I suggest, holding up the key that Avery slipped me in the parking lot earlier when Liam went into the store ahead of me.

"Okay, what is going on?" Harper demands.

"Just open the door," I tell her, not giving in to her cute pout.

The key turns smoothly and Harper timidly opens the door, obviously on high alert.

"Welcome home, Harper," I tell her, pushing the door all the way open.

"What?" she asks, frowning up at me.

"It's ours," I tell her. "I called Avery three days into Liam's detox and made her an offer. I knew it was supposed to be ours."

"You bought a house for us, without telling me, when we've only known each other for three-and-a-half-months?" she asks incredulously.

"Well, in my defense, you made us a baby in the same amount of time," I tell her with a grin. "Which is way, way better than just a house."

"Oh my god, you bought us a house," she says. "Can we go in?"

I lean down and scoop her into my arms and carry her over the threshold. I walk straight to our chairs by the big windows and gently sit down, keeping her in my lap.

"Oh my god, you bought us a house," she repeats. "This house."

"There's a few more things to show you," I tell her. "Are you feeling good enough for a tour?"

She gives me an uncertain look after glancing around, probably because it looks exactly the same as every other time she's been in here.

"So we can't just sit here?" she asks.

"We absolutely can, but Zero's at the door, so I have to at least get up and let her in," I tell her, kissing her nose as she scrunches it up.

"Okay, tour," she says, standing up. "Where do we start?"

I let Zero in the back door and then return to Harper, taking her hand. I start for the stairs, tugging her along, Zero happily following in our wake.

"So, my house already has a buyer, and Jessie and Colt already have a new house," I tell her as we climb the stairs. "But, I told Colt that he'd always have a room with us. Jessie brought him over a couple days

284

ago and we FaceTimed while he chose his room. This will be his, with the stipulation that Zero has a dog bed in here."

I push open the door to the bedroom at the very end of the hall and Zero immediately crosses the space and jumps on the bed, turning in a circle before lying down to curl into a ball. I'm unsure why Colt thinks there needs to be a dog bed, Zero's always sharing his bed and appears to have already claimed this one.

"Wait, they can't move!" Harper immediately protests.

I love her even more for how fiercely she loves Colt.

"They're not going far, they're actually moving in with Mrs. G since Kelsey leaves in a couple weeks. Mrs. G can help with Colt, Jessie can help with all the little things Kelsey usually does for her mom," I tell her, pulling her in for another kiss. "They're all really excited. They had already talked about it a couple times."

"Okay, that's actually a brilliant idea, I know Mrs. G was not looking forward to being an empty nester," Harper relents.

I retrace our steps and open the next door. This next part of the tour was a shock to me, but sometimes things really work out.

"And with your much more exciting news, I'm thinking this room should be a nursery," I tell her, repeating those words in my head as they still sound foreign.

"Ohhh," she breathes.

She walks into the room, puts her hands out, and spins in a circle. When she stops, she looks right at me. Her smile nearly knocks the wind out of me. She's so beautiful, standing in our baby's room. Maybe if I say it in my head enough times, it won't feel like someone else's life I'm living.

"Will you paint a mural on that wall?" she asks as she gestures to the wall to the right of the doorway, tilting her head as she contemplates the space.

"Absolutely," I tell her. "And I want to make the crib. And dresser. And whatever other furniture goes in a baby's room."

I don't know where that idea came from or why I said it, but it feels right. Harper slowly turns to me. She looks at me from head to toe and back up before locking her eyes on mine.

"I think that's the hottest thing you've ever said to me. I know that sounds crazy, but this hormone train is out of control," she says, throwing herself at me.

Her hands are under my shirt, her lips are locked on mine, and I need more. I slide my hand under her shirt and grip her waist. Her sharp inhale is my reward. God, I love that sound. She tugs impatiently at my shirt as she pushes me toward the hallway.

"But the tour isn't done," I whisper against her lips.

"What's this room?" she asks, slipping out of my grasp and into the hall, pushing open the third bedroom door.

"Guest room, boring," I tell her, watching as she pulls her own shirt over her head.

"Mmmm," she hums, undoing the button of her cut offs and nudging the last door open with her foot. "And this door?"

"Bathroom, boring," I say, undoing my belt and stalking toward her.

"Where to, then, West? We're out of doors up here," she says breathlessly, reaching for my waistband the second I'm within her reach.

"I guess we better head back downstairs then," I tell her, gently grasping the back of her neck with both hands, tipping her chin up so her mouth meets mine.

She gasps as I kiss her hard, needing her to feel my need, tongue sweeping inside her mouth. She slides her hand under the waistband of my briefs and it's my turn to gasp. I'm left reeling when she suddenly pulls away, giving me a sly smile as she takes off down the stairs. Her cutoffs slide off when she hits the landing. I'm frozen, watching her every move.

"Where to next?" she calls back up to me, giving me a wink.

That fucking wink breaks the spell that holds me frozen and I nearly trip down the stairs to get to her. She laughs and takes off toward the master, running through the living room in just her underwear, headed exactly where I want her to go.

She skids to a halt in the doorway.

"West," she breathes when she feels me behind her.

She's the one standing frozen now. I wrap my arm around her and pull her back against my chest, thoroughly enjoying the fact that she's in her underwear.

"I didn't even realize what I was doing, I'd look down and I would be drawing," I whisper, kissing her neck. "It's what got me through last week."

I release her and gently push her forward toward the bed, leaning on the door frame to watch her expression. Every single sketch I did while in Portland is scattered over the bed.

"West," she finally says, and there's laughter in her voice. "You're a stalker."

I burst into laughter. She turns to me, smiling, and I can't help but let my eyes drop to take her in smooth skin and gentle curves.

"Does that mean you're changing your mind?" I ask, returning my gaze to hers as I stalk toward her.

"I'm just glad my stalker turned out to be a hot lumberjack," she says, biting her lip to hide her smile. She slides her hands under my shirt, pushing it up and over my head.

"Finally dropped the older?" I ask, dropping my shirt on the floor at our feet.

"Hormones must make me forgetful," she shrugs.

"Harper, I wan-" I start.

"What is that?" she interrupts, grabbing my arm.

I smile as she examines Liam's work, no longer hidden by my long sleeves. Her mouth parts and she looks up at me with tears in her eyes.

"Liam did it this morning," I tell her, watching her closely.

She gently runs her finger over the wrapped design. The taller tree has rougher lines, darker edges, moodier shading. The slender tree is bathed in sunlight, sunbeams shining through, narrower branches. Beneath the surface, their roots are tangled together. Liam did some of his best work.

"West, I love it," she says, taking a shaky breath, hazel eyes finding mine. "I love you. I'm in love with you."

"Say it again," I say, tipping her chin up, looking into her hazel eyes, still bright with emotion.

"I'm in love with you," she says, bolding, clearly, and I slant my mouth over hers. "And I need you, right now."

"Harper," I whisper, still kissing her gently.

"I'm pregnant, not broken," she says, smiling against my lips at my gentleness. "Please take me, now."

With that, I quickly sweep my hand over the bed, scattering the pages to the floor. I lift her up and gently toss her onto the bed as she laughs. I'm on her as soon as I step out of my jeans, hovering above her, caging her in.

"Hi, Harper," I say, gazing down at her.

"Hi, West," she says, reaching up to run her fingers through my beard.

She pulls me down for a kiss, a sweet, gentle kiss.

"I love you," I whisper, deepening our kisses until they're greedy, frantic, and I can feel her writhing beneath me, arching toward me, wordlessly begging for more.

I unclasp her bra and drag her panties down her legs in record time, throwing my briefs on the floor with them just seconds later. I need her like nothing I've ever needed before.

"I love you," she whispers back as I push inside her.

No words have ever meant more, nothing has ever felt better.

When she's sprawled on my chest, her hand tracing my tattoos, the rest of her body sated and limp, I can hear a quiet sniffle. I roll us so we're face to face, pull her leg over mine, and rest my hand on her waist.

"Hi, West," she whispers, smiling through teary eyes.

"Hi, Harper," I whisper, reaching up to gently wipe a tear as it spills over.

"They're happy tears," she tells me.

"Are you sure?" I ask. I'm still gutted by the fact that she was hurt by my words. That she thought for even a second that I'd hesitate to start a family with her.

288

"You bought us a house. My favorite house. Even before you knew we were a family," she says, leaning forward to kiss me gently. "Definitely happy tears. And maybe a little hormonal-train-wreck tears."

"Your hormonal-train-wreck tears won't move me, Harper," I tell her, smiling as I remember that tree conversation on the beach. "I bought it because I realized that you're my home. And now, even more." I drop my hand to her waist and let my thumb rub her stomach.

If you would have told me five months ago that this would be my life, there's no way I would have believed it. I still can't.

"West?" Harper whispers, running her hand through my beard.

"Harper?" I reply, my eyes on hers.

"I love you."

Epilogue
Harper

"Megan?!" I say in disbelief, looking at the tall, dark-haired woman that just walked into the Mercantile.

"Harper?" She looks at me with wide eyes. "What are you doing here?"

"I live here now, what are *you* doing here?!" I reply, glancing between her and the even taller man that just walked in behind her. "Is this the lucky guy?"

"What? Oh, ew, no, this is my brother, Cooper. Coop, this is Harper, we met during my bachelorette in Austin," she says. "Coop's under contract on some land here, I just came along to get away from the lucky guy…who is only lucky because I didn't murder him."

"I might still murder him," Cooper says. "Hi, nice to meet you."

"You, too," I tell him with a smile. If Cooper is half as fun as Megan, I'll be happy to have him in town.

"Harper, I feel like I've met you before, but if you're from Texas, maybe not. If you live here now, I guess we will soon be neighbors." He gives me a searching look, like he doesn't believe I'm from Texas.

"Moved here last spring from Austin, not long after meeting your sister," I quickly explain. I turn to Megan. "So no murders? I have a tarp and shovel out back if needed, plus my best friend is a lawyer."

Megan snorts and holds up her bare left hand. "No murder, but also no husband. At least I got a fun bachelorette out of it though."

"That was fun, at least the part I crashed. Sorry about the asshole, though," I tell her, shaking my head. "I can't believe you're here. Don't you live in Missouri?"

"Kansas, it's a long story," she says, sounding a little defeated. "We're checking into a rental, a cute little garden house. Maybe we can hang out this weekend?"

"Oh, hey, I manage that rental! Jessie already did the final walk through and it's ready for y'all, so you're welcome to go by anytime," I tell her as the front door opens. I look over and give Liam a smile. "Our last community bonfire is tonight. I'm hosting, so come find me then! The info will be on a welcome card on the entry table at the cottage."

"That sounds fun. Coop, you can meet some more of your neighbors then," she says to her brother, who looks startled.

"I need to talk to him," I say, nodding toward Liam. "But Katie will get you at the register when you're ready. I'm excited to catch up tonight!"

I give Megan's arm a squeeze before I walk away.

"Hi, Harper," Liam says, giving me a smile. "How are you feeling? West said you had packing tape for us?"

"I haven't thrown up in hours, so I'm great," I tell him wryly. "The tape is in the back, can I make you a coffee first?"

I went to the doctor last week and she prescribed some anti-nausea medication but I'm still hesitant to take it. Jessie told me to try salt crackers before I get out of bed and it seems to help. Also, Zero loves the crumbs.

"No, thank you. I have enough nerves today, I don't need caffeine on top of it," he tells me with a small laugh. "I got these for you, they're supposed to help with nausea."

He hands me a small bag of ginger candy chews. For the last two weeks, Liam has been earning my trust. He's funny, thoughtful (see: ginger chews), very self-aware, and so many of his mannerisms remind me of Colt. We've slowly built a friendship and I'm cautiously optimistic that he will remain sober. He's definitely putting in the work every single day.

292

Today, he and West are helping Kelsey pack up Brian's truck. Tonight, he's coming to the bonfire. It will be the first time he sees Colt and I think all of us are a little nervous. Jessie is hoping that if things don't go well, the bonfire will be a good distraction for Colt.

"Hey, it's going to be great," I tell him. "Colt's an amazing kid, he's resilient. Jessie has been talking to him about this for days. Even if he has big emotions tonight, we'll all help him, and you, through it. One day at a time, right?"

"Thanks, Harper," Liam says. "I can't wait, but I'm also nervous about what this will do to my sobriety if he rejects me."

Like I said, he's very self-aware and he's also open about his fears. I wonder if that's part of AA. I know he goes to as many meetings as possible with Abe, his sober roommate.

"That's why you're staying with us tonight," I remind him.

Jessie and Colt are already moved into Mrs. G's house so Liam is spending the night in Colt's room. North House has a few more renters until we can close on it. Apparently the new key was just for show, it's not really ours yet. Luckily I'm a super patient person (said no one, ever, about me).

"It'll be okay," Liam says, blowing out a breath.

I smile to myself, remembering how many times I've said that to myself over the last few months.

"It will be," I tell him. And for once, I believe it.

***

"Hi, Tex-Harper," Brian says, giving me a side hug. "I got here early to take over hosting. No arguing. I'll light the fire in a few and get everything set up."

"Thanks, Brian, I appreciate it, I didn't get a nap this afternoon," I tell him. "Are you guys going to be okay tomorrow?"

"A new chapter," Brian says with a nod. "I'm so proud of her."

"She's amazing, I can't wait to visit her at school," I tell him, giving him another hug.

I give Sarah a hug and tell her thanks, then head for the waterline where West, Jessie, Grant, and Colt are splashing in the waves. I thought it'd be weird to have Grant here tonight, but he and Liam have struck up an unlikely friendship. It started because Liam wanted to apologize for being a massive, ragey, drunk asshole (his words) when Grant served him the divorce papers, and it's grown because Grant is the hardest person in the entire world to find a flaw with. Both Jessie and Grant maintain they're just friends, and Grant is amazing with Colt, so here we are.

"Hi, Harper," West says, wrapping an arm around my waist and pulling me in for a kiss.

"Hi, West," I say, smiling up at him like a fool.

"Hi, Almost Auntie Tex," Colt says, giving me a cold, wet hug. "Where's Zero?"

I see where I rank with him. Ouch. Although the "Almost Auntie" makes up for it.

"Hi, Almost Nephew Colt, she's with your dad and Miss Avery up at Uncle West's house, should I call them?" I ask, after getting a nod from Jessie.

"Do you think he knows how to make s'mores?" Colt asks, looking worried.

"If he doesn't, I'm sure we could teach him; we're pretty good at it," I tell him, ruffling his hair.

"Do you think he likes finding beach treasures?" Colt adds to his worries.

"I bet he does," West tells him reassuringly.

"Okay, he can come," Colt says. "As long as he brings Zero."

"I promise I won't let them forget her," I say, pulling my phone from my waistband.

We start to wander toward the creek, splashing in the waves, moving slowly enough that Avery and Liam will be able to catch up quickly. Zero races up to us within minutes, circling around our group, trying to herd us together. Avery and Liam wave as they walk our way and Colt drifts toward Jessie, taking her hand. He gives a small wave but stays at his mom's side.

While West, Jessie, and I seem to freeze, Grant strides toward Avery and Liam, his hands in his pockets, casual as can be. He takes his hand out of his pocket to shake Liam's hand and give Avery a side hug. They exchange greetings and then continue our way.

294

"Hi, Colt," Liam says as they approach. "I love your beach. You look really happy to live here, which makes me happy."

"Hi," Colt says softly, eyes down.

"Hi, Liam, thanks so much for bringing me the ginger chews earlier. I think they made me feel good enough to make a s'more later," I say, eyeing Colt.

"I love s'mores," Liam says enthusiastically. "But I always catch the marshmallow on fire. Maybe I need practice."

"Almost Auntie Tex taught me how to not burn them, she can teach you. I could maybe help," Colt says, giving a little half-shrug.

"That'd be great, but can we look for rocks and shells first? Grant told me you're really good at finding treasures," Liam says.

"Okay," Colt agrees.

Colt leads us down the beach, letting go of Jessie's hand but still keeping distance from Liam. I don't think Liam notices the distance though.

***

"Good job, just like that," Colt coaches Liam as they each roast a marshmallow.

"You're a great teacher, Colt, I hope my college teachers are as good as you," Kelsey says, licking sticky marshmallow goo from her fingers.

"Me too," Grant says. "If they're not, can you come teach?"

"I have to go to kindergarten!" Colt tells them. "I start in three days!"

"Me, too!" Kelsey and Grant say together.

"All three of you are going to have a great school year," Avery tells them as she gets graham crackers and chocolate ready for Liam and Colt. "School is the best."

"Nerd!" I cough, getting a laugh from Liam as he pulls his marshmallow away from the fire.

Colt swings his legs happily from the edge of my chair. He's nestled in my lap, I'm sure wiping marshmallows on my leggings. Zero lays in the sand between us and Liam, who beams every time Colt looks in his direction, which is fairly often. Jessie and West stand together across the fire, West's arm protectively around Jessie, chatting with Tom and Sarah.

"Hey Tex, thanks for letting me stay at your place tonight," Grant says from a couple chairs down. "She gets a cup and a half, right?"

"Yeah, her food is in the laundry room along with her bowl, you can just put her in West's house after you feed her. Thank you!" I'm relieved I don't have to walk up there and back, growing a baby is kicking my ass today.

"Can Zero sleep with me?!" Colt asks eagerly. "Mrs. G said someday she could have a sleepover!"

"Go check with her again," Jessie calls, stepping out from under West's arm.

Colt gleefully skips off, probably already knowing that there's no way Mrs. G turns him down. I stand and brush s'mores crumbs off my front.

"I'll make sure to get her for a walk in the morning," Jessie tells me, wrapping her arm around me. "Thank you, I think it's a good night for him to have her."

"What a night," I murmur, laying my head on her shoulder.

"No joke," Jessie says with a small laugh. "But a good night."

"She said yes!" Colt races back and throws himself at me.

"Zero is going to be so happy!" I tell him, picking him up and swinging him around. "Make sure she's a good girl and follows Mrs. G's rules though."

"Are you coming, too?" Colt asks Liam.

"I'm staying with Uncle West tonight," Liam reminds him.

"Maybe you can get special hot chocolate in the morning, it's really good," Colt suggests.

"I think that sounds like a great idea," Liam says, smiling at his son.

Don't cry, don't cry, don't cry. Stupid hormones.

"You okay?" West whispers, wrapping an arm around me and sneaking his hand under my hoodie to lightly grasp my waist.

"I'm just happy," I tell him.

"Do you need me to bring you anything from the house?" West asks. "Liam and I are going to call it a night. You deserve a night with Team Merc."

"If I wasn't so tired, I'd walk y'all home," I tell him.

"Stay, enjoy your night," West whispers, pulling me in for a kiss.

I sink back down into my chair and watch Colt lead Zero up the path, this time making sure to walk right next to Liam. Jessie, West, and Grant follow in their wake. Jessie turns back just before they're out of sight and shoots me a grin. What a freaking night.

"We did it, Team Merc, we crushed community events this summer," I tell Avery and Kelsey. "Kels, I'm so excited for you, I already can't wait for my visit in a few weeks."

"Aw, my pretend sisters are the best," Kelsey says, reaching for a roasting stick. "Damnit, we're almost out of marshmallows, I'll go get more from the store."

"No, you stay, I'll get them," Avery says, standing. "I could use a walk and it's your last night here."

Kelsey and I sit in silence for a few minutes, both lost in thought.

"I'm really thankful you moved here," Kelsey says suddenly.

"Me, too, Kels, me, too," I reply.

"Ooh! Annie!" she shrieks, bolting up from her chair and toward her friend.

Teenagers, almost as exhausting as five-year-olds and growing babies. I watch her run toward her friend and let the conversations from the rest of my community wash over me. Every once in a while there's a yell from the volleyball court, or raucous laughter from the group Tom migrated toward. What a way to wrap up summer.

"Harper, why are you sleeping in a chair by the fire?"

I open my eyes and Megan is standing in front of me, holding out a beer for me.

"Oh, hey guys," I say, sitting up. I tip my head toward Kelsey and Avery's now vacant chairs. "Have a seat!"

"Hi, Harper," Cooper says, stretching out in Avery's chair. I'm hit with how tall he is.

Megan waves the beer at me again.

"So, funny story," I say, shaking my head at her. "I'm kinda knocked up."

"Sorry, I swear I just heard you say you're pregnant," Megan says.

"That's awesome, congrats!" Cooper says, smiling at me.

"Yeah, long story short, we met in…March? Right? So, in May I dumped my live-in boyfriend, left Austin that night, and drove here. My best friend owns The Town Mercantile and offered me a job. She's a badass, you'll meet her in a few minutes, I'm sure. But short story even shorter, a hot lumberjack slash tattoo artist swept me off my feet and knocked me up."

"Wow, okay, well, congrats!" Megan laughs.

"So, how'd you guys end up here?" I ask curiously.

"I took a job, very last minute I should add, at Rock Beach Middle School," Cooper tells me. "I teach science."

"But why this town if you're from Kansas?"

"We came here the summer after I graduated high school, spent like a week here with our family, drove down 101, spent a week in San Francisco," Megan explains. "My brother really loved it and randomly decided to find a way to move here."

"I mean, same," I tell Cooper, laughing. "I understand that, one hundred percent."

"Just fell in love, couldn't stay away," Cooper says, shooting his sister a glance. "Someone showed me the old tsunami trail that summer, we hiked to the top, and I've wanted to build a house there ever since."

This story sounds familiar.

"*Someone* showed you, huh?" Megan asks with a smirk.

I think back to the few things Avery ever told me about ninth grade summer. But there's no way. No way.

"The old tsunami trail, you mean the one across the highway that's now a road?" I ask, testing my theory but not quite ready to sound like a crazy person.

"Yeah, best view ever," he says quietly.

Megan looks between the two of us, sensing something as well.

298

"It's amazing," I agree. "So you're building up there? Where are you staying in the meantime?"

"Working on figuring that out, might have to be Rock Beach but I'd love something here in Three Rocks," Cooper says, linking his hands behind his head as he leans back in his chair.

"Our short term rentals are slowing down for the season, maybe I can talk to Avery about long term for the winter," I say, trying to keep my voice casual as I watch him closely.

Megan's eyes widen and Cooper sits upright as soon as I say her name. I knew it.

"Hey, Aves, I think I just met your new neighbor," I say as she reappears across the bonfire.

Avery looks up and drops all three bags of marshmallows.

"Avery," Cooper breathes.

Afterword

I wrote a book. What's next? Well, I started writing about Zoe, hoping for a short story, using her as a writing exercise of sorts. It didn't work. My short story turned into a book, which became the second in the series. I didn't mean to, it just happened.

After that detour with Zoe, we're going back to Avery. With Avery, you'll see some closure with Harper's story; I'm sorry if that's driving you a little crazy right now. My bad. First time writer.

I'm so glad you gave a new author like me a chance. Thank you.

Love it? Hate it? Find me on Instagram and let me know! My favorite part about being an author? Connecting with readers. Seriously. Look me up.

Acknowledgement

Thank you to my husband for always knowing what I need, even when I don't. It's usually a cold brew.

Thank you to my reluctant editor and to my photographer. None of these characters are either of you. Please stop asking and go clean your room.

I also owe my hype girl, my husband's cousin, not only for her support, but for always knowing where lines are drawn.

To my Team Merc, thank you. For everything.

About the Author

Wesley Harper is an amateur author, semi-professional coffee drinker, and advanced overthinker. After spending thirty-nine-and-three-quarters years not writing books, she decided to write a book before her fortieth birthday.

When not making random goals and accidentally writing books, she enjoys working out in her garage gym, fostering puppies, and embarrassing her nearly adult offspring. And maybe sometimes running away to the Oregon Coast.

www.ingramcontent.com/pod-product-compliance
Lightning Source LLC
Chambersburg PA
CBHW010534100726
47903CB00011B/3000